套用‧替換 零失誤的 英文 寫作公式

全書MP3一次下載

9789864541560.zip

iOS系統請升級至iOS 13後再行下載，此為大型檔案，建議使用WIFI連線下載，
以免佔用流量，並確認連線狀況，以利下載順暢。

WRITING PATTERN DICTIONARY

本書

第 1 部分

按照寫作情況的主題來分類

涵蓋「開場白、本文鋪陳及結論」中，大約 200 種可運用的寫作情況。

500 多句可套用的句型公式

大量收錄寫作中，用來起承轉合的各種組織用詞，並附上使用時機的説明。

搭配句型來運用的例句

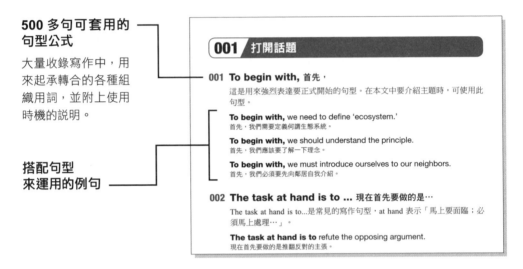

001 / 打開話題

001 To begin with, 首先，

這是用來強烈表達要正式開始的句型。在本文中要介紹主題時，可使用此句型。

To begin with, we need to define 'ecosystem.'
首先，我們需要定義何謂生態系統。

To begin with, we should understand the principle.
首先，我們應該要了解一下理念。

To begin with, we must introduce ourselves to our neighbors.
首先，我們必須要先向鄰居自我介紹。

002 The task at hand is to ... 現在首先要做的是…

The task at hand is to...是常見的寫作句型，at hand 表示「馬上要面臨；必須馬上處理…」。

The task at hand is to refute the opposing argument.
現在首先要做的是推翻反對的主張。

本書

第 2 部分

20 篇範例文章，讓你融會貫通寫作技巧

本書在後面第二部分會針對不同的作文題目，整理出 20 篇範例文章。

進入範例文章前，首先教你如何組織大綱架構，用幾個重點列出在**開場白、本文**發展及**結論**中要寫的內容。

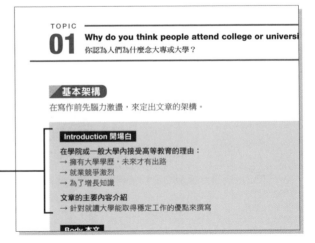

TOPIC
01 Why do you think people attend college or universi
你認為人們為什麼念大專或大學？

基本架構

在寫作前先腦力激盪，來定出文章的架構。

Introduction 開場白

在學院或一般大學內接受高等教育的理由：
→ 擁有大學學歷，未來才有出路
→ 就業競爭激烈
→ 為了增長知識

文章的主要內容介紹
→ 針對就讀大學能取得穩定工作的優點來撰寫

Body 本文

朗讀全文的 QR 碼音檔

完整的範例文章

利用前面第一部分學到的句型，來完成一篇完整的作文，並用顯眼的顏色標示其句型，讓你徹底搞懂一篇文章的脈絡及組織邏輯。

歸納出文章中用到的句型

歸納了範例文章中所用到的句型，並在每個句型後面附上第一部分「開場白、本文及結論」的句型編號，供你回到第一部分做前後對照與複習。

☞ 請見開場白句型 65

開場白句型 21

界 ☞ 請見開場白句

供讀者回到第一部分做前後對照的句型編號。

PART 01 開場白句型 Introduction Patterns 47

PART 02 本文句型 Body Patterns 91

PART
03　結論句型 Conclusion Patterns 225

第一部分

PART 01 開場白句型 Introduction Patterns 47

PART

02 本文句型 Body Patterns 91

contents 目錄

117 Again, 再次強調，

118 Above all, 綜觀以上各點，

119 At this point, 此時，

120 Most importantly, 最重要的是，

121 In the following example we will see ... 在以下的例子中，我們將會知道…

122 First(ly), 首先，

123 Second(ly), 其次，

124 In the second place, 其次，

125 Third(ly), 第三，

126 Lastly, 最後，

127 Finally, 終於，／最後，

128 And to conclude, 然後結論是，

129 Last, 最後，

130 Eventually, 終究，／最後，

131 Next, 接下來，

132 Then, 然後，

133 Now, here is the next step: 接著，下個步驟是：

134 It is difficult to believe that ... 很難相信…

135 Another ... 其他…／另一個…

136 Or, 或者，

137 Instead, 取而代之的是，／反之，

138 Another way of viewing this is as ... 用其他角度看這就像是…

139 Alternatively, 或者是，／兩者中擇一的，

140 One alternative is ... 其中一個選擇是…

304 In brief, 簡而言之，

contents 目錄

think are the best ways of reducing stress? Use specific details and examples to support your answer.

人們有許多方法逃離現代生活中的壓力和困難。有些人閱讀、有些人運動，另外有些人會在自己的花園裡忙東忙西。你認為減輕壓力最佳的方法有哪些？請運用具體的理由和例子來支持你的回答。 **364**

第一部分

PART I

Introduction Patterns

開場白句型

001 提出文章的主旨

1 The aim of this essay is to ... 這篇文章的目的是為了⋯

一般來說，在開頭部分很常用 aim 這個單字。在文章開頭部分要提出主旨時， The aim of this essay is to... 就是個適合的句型。

The aim of this essay is to explain how to drive a car.
這篇文章的目的是為了解釋如何開車。

The aim of this essay is to show why I deserve this award.
這篇文章的目的是為了說明為什麼我足以獲得這個獎項。

The aim of this essay is to instruct readers in chemical formulas.
這篇文章的目的是為了教讀者搞懂化學方程式。

2 The aim of this paper is to determine ...

這篇論文／報告的目的是要確定⋯

determine 表示「弄清楚，確定」，若要寫分析類的文章時，可在開場白用此句型，以預告這篇文章的目的。

The aim of this paper is to determine the length of kangaroos' pregnancies.
這份報告的目的是要確定袋鼠的孕期長度。

The aim of this paper is to determine the cause of the First World War.
這份報告的目的是要確定第一次世界大戰的緣由。

The aim of this paper is to determine the missing ingredient in my mother's pasta recipe.
這份報告的目的是要確定我母親的義大利麵食譜中缺少的食材。

3 The aim of this paper is to study ...

這篇論文／報告的目的是要研究⋯

是在論文或研究型報告等的開場白中常用的句型。

The aim of this paper is to study laboratory conditions in France.
這份報告的目的是要研究法國實驗室的條件。

The aim of this paper is to study common surgical procedures.
這份報告的目的是要研究常見的手術程序。

The aim of this paper is to study the work of Isaac Newton.
這份報告的目的是要研究艾薩克牛頓的成果。

4　The purpose of ... is to ...　…的目的是…

在一般的寫作時，也可用 The purpose of... 此句型來作為文章開頭，purpose 此單字為「目的」的意思。

The purpose of beekeeping **is to** collect honey.
養蜂的目的是採蜜。

The purpose of this argument **is to** prove that radium is dangerous.
此辯論的目的是證明輻射是危險的。

The purpose of my speech **is to** inform people about refugees.
我演講的目的是要讓人們知道關於難民的事。

5　I intend to analyze ...　我想要分析…

「intend to + 動詞原形」表示「想要做…」「打算做…」，是在論文或在一般文章寫作中明確揭示文章目的的句型。

I intend to analyze the history of evolution.
我想要分析進化史。

I intend to analyze the myth of Atlantis.
我想要分析亞特蘭蒂斯之謎。

I intend to analyze the influence of television on children.
我想要分析電視對孩童的影響。

6　In this paper I will ...　在這篇論文／報告中，我將…

想預告文章中將討論的內容，或提及撰寫此文章的目的時，可使用此句型。

In this paper I will explain the history of pi.
在此報告中，我將解釋圓周率的歷史。

In this paper I will demonstrate how to build a bicycle.
在此報告中，我將示範如何製造腳踏車。

In this paper I will argue that the U.S. should annex Mexico.
在此報告中，我將主張美國應合併墨西哥。

002 提出文章的主題

7 This paper will give an account of ...
這篇論文／報告將說明…

想點出論文或報告的主題或整體核心時，可使用此句型。動詞片語 give an account of... 是「說明、介紹～」的意思。

This paper will give an account of our experiment.
本文將說明我們的實驗。

This paper will give an account of Martin Luther King's teachings.
本文將說明馬丁路德金恩的教誨。

This paper will give an account of my chemical investigations.
本文將說明我的化學研究。

003 介紹文章的主要內容

8 This paper will focus on ...
這篇論文／報告的焦點將著重在…

可用在開場白的最後一句，以此帶出本文要討論的內容。接在此句型後面的內容為文章的核心重點。

This paper will focus on the extinction of the dinosaurs.
此報告將著重在恐龍滅絕。

This paper will focus on multiple aspects of the problem.
此報告將著重在此問題的多方角度。

This paper will focus on the causes of respiratory cancer.
此報告將著重於導致呼吸道癌的原因。

9 This paper will examine ... 這篇論文／報告將檢視…

一樣是用在開場白的最後一句，是帶出文章主旨的句型。

This paper will examine the role of mud in the formation of bird nests.
此報告將檢視泥巴在鳥巢結構中所扮演的角色。

This paper will examine Nazi literature and its uses.
此報告將檢視納粹文學及其用處。

This paper will examine the cost of prescription drugs.
此報告將檢視處方藥的成本。

10 This essay critically examines ...
本篇文章將以批判的方式檢視…

critically 表示「批判性地」，當想提出有別於一般認知的主張時，可在開場白時使用此句型來預告文章的走向。

This essay critically examines the U.S. welfare system.
這篇文章在批判美國的社會福利制度。

This essay critically examines the role of calcium in the body.
這篇文章在批判鈣在身體裡扮演的角色。

This essay critically examines the possibility of implementing the metric system in the U.S.
這篇文章在批判於美國執行公制量測系統的可能性。

11 This essay will discuss ... 這篇文章將討論…

discuss 表示「討論」，此句型一般來說較適合用在針對特定問題提出各種解決之道的文章開場白之中。

This essay will discuss comic books written by fans.
這篇文章將討論有關書迷們所創作的漫畫書。

This essay will discuss Denmark's unemployment rate.
這篇文章將討論丹麥的失業率。

This essay will discuss the visa requirements for children.
這篇文章將討論孩童辦簽證的條件。

12 This paper begins by ... 這篇論文／報告從…開始

想在開場白中先預告文章的目的，可使用此句型。或要寫一篇讀書心得或評論文章時，也可使用此句型。

This paper begins by discussing Tolstoy's early life.
這份報告從討論托爾斯泰的早年時期開始。

This paper begins by presenting the history of cancer research.
這份報告從呈現癌症研究的歷史開始。

This paper begins by outlining the steps of the experiment.
這份報告從概述實驗步驟開始。

13 The first section of this paper will examine ...

這篇論文／報告的第一部分將探討…

以論文或階段性探討主題的文章來說，在開頭先介紹文章架構，有助於讀者理解文章內容，用此句型的優點是，能清楚區分出段落，因為用到了「first section」這個單字，以明確預告第一部分將討論的內容。

The first section of this paper will examine cigarette use.
這份報告的第一部分將探討香菸的用途。

The first section of this paper will examine the invention of the tractor.
這份報告的第一部分將探討拖曳機的發明。

The first section of this paper will examine the modeling industry.
這份報告的第一部分將探討模特兒產業。

004 / 針對議題列出大綱

14 This paper seeks to address the following questions:

這篇論文／報告旨在解決以下議題：

進入文章本文之前，想先簡短預告文中探討內容的主軸或議題方向時，可使用此句型。此時，此句型的冒號（:）後面所提到的內容，將會在本文與結論部分被討論與解決。

This paper seeks to address the following questions: who can become a police officer, what the training is like, and how much officers are paid.
這份報告旨在解決以下議題：「誰能成為警察」、「訓練的狀況為何」，以及「警察的薪資待遇為何」。

This paper seeks to address the following questions: how honey is produced, how it is collected, and who or what is involved in each step.
這份報告旨在解決以下議題：「蜂蜜是如何產生的」、「如何採集」，以及「各階段中會有哪些人或物參與其中」。

This paper seeks to address the following questions: how television works, how radio works, and how we can use this technology to solve world problems.

這份報告旨在解決以下議題：「電視是如何運作的」、「無線電廣播是如何運作的」，以及「我們可以如何利用這項科技來解決世界的問題」。

15 The main questions addressed in this paper are:
這篇論文／報告所要解決的主要問題是：

是在進入本文前，先於開場白介紹本文將討論之主題的句型。當主題難以用一句話概括時，建議使用此句型。

The main questions addressed in this paper are: why do we sleep?, how did life begin?, and what is the next plague?
這份報告所要解決的主要問題是：「我們為何會睡覺？」、「生命是如何開始的呢？」，以及「接下來會流行什麼傳染病？」

The main questions addressed in this paper are: what is gravity?, how does the brain work?, and do ghosts exist?
這份報告所要解決的主要問題是：「重力是什麼？」、「大腦如何運作？」，以及「鬼魂是否存在？」

The main questions addressed in this paper are: is there life on other planets?, how many people have seen UFOs?, and what are UFOs?
這份報告所要解決的主要問題是：「是否有生命存在於其他星球？」、「有多少人看過飛碟？」以及「什麼是飛碟？」

16 This essay will deal with the following aspects of the question: 這篇文章將探討此問題的以下面相：

想寫較正式的開頭時，建議使用這個句型。如果寫的不是正式的文章，可將句型中的 essay 去掉，直接用 This will deal with...也無妨。

This essay will deal with the following aspects of the question: why it happened, and where.
這篇文章將探討此問題的以下面相：為何發生、以及在何處發生。

This essay will deal with the following aspects of the question: how Marie Curie discovered radium, and how she publicized her findings.
這篇文章將探討此問題的以下面相：瑪麗居禮如何發現輻射，以及她如何公開她的發現。

This essay will deal with the following aspects of the question: the size of the sample, and the method used to survey the participants.
這篇文章將探討此問題的以下面相：樣本的大小、以及用來調查參與者的方法。

17 **...is commonly defined as ...** …普遍被定義為（被視為）…

是最常用在開場白的經典句型之一，表示「…普遍被定義為（被視為）…」。若主題為複數，則 is 改為 are。

A shooting star **is commonly defined as** a meteor.
流星普遍被定義為一種隕石。

Yogurt **is commonly defined as** a healthy food.
優格普遍被定義為一種健康食品。

Happiness **is commonly defined as** a desirable state of mind.
快樂普遍被定義為一種滿足的心理狀態。

18 **The quality of ...** …的品質（本質）…

想以「…的品質／本質…」先下個定論，可使用這個句型。

The quality of the cake will depend on the quality of the ingredients.
蛋糕的品質取決於原料的品質。

The quality of the element that is most surprising is its luminosity.
這個元素最令人吃驚的性質是它的亮度。

The quality of Ben's that I most admire is his patience.
班最讓我佩服的特質是他的耐心。

19 **In this paper I argue that ...**
在這份報告中，我主張（認為）…

想要提出自己的主張時，可使用此句型。此句型主要是用在開場白的結尾部分。在開場白的前半段，先提出了對某議題的贊成或反對的主張，以引起讀者注意力之後，接著再用此句型來點明自己的立場。

In this paper I argue that all schools in the U.S. should be bilingual.
在這份報告中，我認為美國所有學校都應該使用兩種以上的語言。

In this paper I argue that global warming is a serious problem.
在這份報告中，我認為地球暖化是非常嚴重的問題。

In this paper I argue that the moon was formed when a comet crashed into earth.
在這份報告中，我認為月亮是彗星撞擊地球時形成的。

007 / 引用生活中的故事

20 We often hear that ... 我們常聽說…

想在開場白的一開始拋出跟主題相關的話題時，建議使用此句型。透過這個句型，可先預告讀者廣為流傳的事情或最近的熱門話題等。

We often hear that dogs are the smartest pet.
我們常聽說狗是最聰明的寵物。

We often hear that camels can store a lot of water in their bodies.
我們常聽說駱駝可以在身體裡儲存大量的水份。

We often hear that there are cockroaches in New York City.
我們常聽說紐約市裡有蟑螂。

21 It is often said that ... 人們常說…／常言道…

想在開場白中引用人們常說的話時，可使用此句型。

It is often said that you can't teach an old dog new tricks.
常言道，老狗玩不出新把戲。

It is often said that the best advice comes from our elders.
常言道，長輩總是能給出最好的建議。

It is often said that one shouldn't count his chickens before they are hatched.
常言道，別打如意算盤。

008 / 提及理解問題的重要性

22   It is crucial to understand ... 理解…是很重要的

進入本文之前，若需要先明確地說明問題的核心，或對可能混淆的意義提出正確的解釋時，可使用此句型。

It is crucial to understand the meaning of "handicapped."
理解「身障」的意義是很重要的。

It is crucial to understand the judge's decision.
理解法官的決定是很重要的。

It is crucial to understand the causes of slavery.
理解奴隸制度的緣由是很重要的。

009 / 提及一般的事實或狀況

23   Normally, 一般來說，

想說明一般情況時可使用此句型。

Normally, it is I who answer the door.
一般來說，都是我去應門。

Normally, it is difficult to teach a child to read.
一般來說，教小孩閱讀很困難。

Normally, it is easy to determine a criminal's motivation.
一般來說，判斷罪犯的動機是很容易的。

24   Naturally, 當然／自然而然地，

不僅口頭上很常使用這個句型，在寫作上也常派得上用場，是英美人士經常掛在嘴邊的句型，也是他們在書寫時常用的句型。

Naturally, the lion ate the zebra.
想當然爾，獅子吃了斑馬。

Naturally, he was able to solve the puzzle.
想當然爾，他有辦法解開了那道謎題。

Naturally, the control group responded favorably to the prompt.
想當然爾，對照組呈現了陽性反應。

25 **It is a well-known fact that ...** …是眾所皆知的事實

想表達「…是眾所皆知的事實」時，只要使用 It is a well-known fact，後面再接上 that 子句就行了。

It is a well-known fact that Mercury is closest to the sun.
水星最接近太陽是眾所皆知的事實。

It is a well-known fact that the sun will die someday.
太陽有一天會消逝是眾所皆知的事實。

It is a well-known fact that humans are social creatures.
人類是社會型動物是眾所皆知的事實。

26 **We live in a world in which ...** 我們活在一個…的世界

是在一般寫作中很常使用的句型，具修飾文章的效果。

We live in a world in which guns speak more loudly than voices.
我們活在一個槍聲比講話更有利的世界。

We live in a world in which singers make more money than teachers.
我們活在一個歌手賺錢賺得比老師多的世界。

We live in a world in which 20 million people die of starvation each year.
我們活在一個每年會有兩千萬人口死於飢餓的世界。

27 **The world offers us numerous examples of ...**
這世界上有許多…的例子

numerous 表示「許多」，語意等同於 a lot of 或 lots of，除了使用最常用的 a lot of 或 lots of，也可用 numerous 做替換。

The world offers us numerous examples of bad political decisions.
這世界上有許多政治決策糟糕的例子。

The world offers us numerous examples of good energy practices.
這世界上有許多善用能源的例子。

The world offers us numerous examples of sustainable farming.
這世界上有無數永續經營的農場。

010 / 提及問題值得關注的要點

28 **One of the most striking features of this problem is ...** 這問題中最值得關注的是⋯

先提出某個問題，再聚焦此問題中所要關注的某一個點時，可使用此句型。

One of the most striking features of this problem is its complexity.
這問題中最值得關注的是它的複雜性。

One of the most striking features of this problem is its apparent simplicity.
這問題中最值得關注的是其明顯的單純性。

One of the most striking features of this problem is its public interest.
這問題中最值得關注的是公眾利益。

011 / 說明問題的特性

29 **This issue is one that ...** 這個議題（是）⋯

在開場白的前半段提到某個熱門議題，並想說明此議題的特性時，可使用此句型。one 除了是「一（個）」的意思之外，在文章中其實更常當作不定代名詞使用。

This issue is one that everyone knows about.
這議題眾所皆知。

This issue is one that I am passionate about.
這議題是我非常熱衷的。

This issue is one that is close to my heart.
這議題非常貼近我的心。

012 / 提及一般的常識

30 It is common knowledge that ...

…是一般常識／是眾所皆知的事

想讓人回想起眾所皆知的觀念或想法時，可使用此句型。此句型（或語意相似的句型）最適合用在開場白的第一句。

It is common knowledge that golf is played by rich people.
高爾夫球是有錢人在打的，這是眾所皆知的事。

It is common knowledge that monkeys can learn human language.
猴子可以學習人類的語言，這是眾所皆知的事。

It is common knowledge that NcDonalds' food is unhealthy.
NcDonalds 的食物不健康，這是眾所皆知的事。

31 It is generally agreed today that ...

當前普遍認為（同意）…

在文章開頭用此句型，能夠呈現出你的寫作是以更多元的角度來探討文章主題的，主要是因為讓人感覺是以社會層面或學術面來陳述你的主題。

It is generally agreed today that obesity is a serious problem.
當前普遍認為肥胖是一個嚴重的問題。

It is generally agreed today that mankind has caused global warming.
當前普遍認為人類導致了全球暖化。

It is generally agreed today that the dinosaurs were killed by a comet.
當前普遍認為恐龍是被一顆彗星給滅絕的。

32 For the great majority of people, 對大部分的人來說，

the great majority of... 跟 most 同義，都表示「大多數、大部分」。此句型是用來提及一般人都認同某個共識的句型。

For the great majority of people, money equals success.
對大部分的人來說，金錢就是成功。

For the great majority of people, ice cream is delicious.
對大部分的人來說，冰淇淋非常美味。

For the great majority of people, suicide is a last resort.
對大部分的人來說，自殺是最後的手段。

013 / 提及相關決定

33 **In my decision-making,** 為了做出決定，

想在開場白中提及自己在做決定的過程中考量過某些情況時，可使用此句型。

In my decision-making, I try to weigh my options.
為了做出決定，我試著權衡我的選項。

In my decision-making, I try to be as fair as possible.
為了做出決定，我試著盡可能公平公正。

In my decision-making, I've found it helpful to write about my choices in a notebook.
為了做出決定，我發現把選項寫在筆記本裡很有幫助。

34 **Any important decision is ...**
任何（所有）重要的決定都是…

想在一開始就強調說明重要決定的定義時，可使用此句型。

Any important decision is difficult to make.
任何重要的決定都是很難的。

Any important decision is something to be proud of.
任何重要的決定都是值得驕傲的。

Any important decision is bound to take a long time.
任何重要的決定必定會需要很長的時間。

Part
1

開場白句型

013
提及相關決定／
014
對於事實的推論／
015
委婉表達主張

014 / 對於事實的推論

35 **They seem to believe that ...** 他們似乎相信…

用於某種不確定的情況時，可使用此句型。seem 表示「好像」、「似乎」，有推測的意味。

They seem to believe that controlling the economy is impossible.
他們似乎相信控制經濟是不可能的。

They seem to believe that cats can speak.
他們似乎相信貓會說話。

They seem to believe that Halloween is just for kids.
他們似乎相信萬聖節只是小孩子的節日。

36 **They may ...** 他們可能…

語意帶有不確定時，助動詞要用 may，而不用 They can... 或 They should... 這類的句型。

They may not come to the party.
他們可能不會來這個派對。

They may lie about their results.
他們可能會謊報他們的成績。

They may tell you one thing and do another.
他們可能會對你說一套做一套。

015 / 委婉表達主張

37 **Almost everyone ...** 幾乎所有人…

almost 表示「幾乎」，可在開場白中利用此句型委婉地表達自我的主張。若省略掉「almost」，語氣會過於肯定與果斷，而讓讀者產生難以接受的反感。

Almost everyone likes ice cream.
幾乎所有人都喜歡冰淇淋。

Almost everyone wants to learn something new.
幾乎所有人都想要學習新知。

Almost everyone believes that he or she is special.
幾乎所有人都相信自己是特別的。

38 **Some people ...** 某些人⋯

在文章開頭想表達「某些人認為⋯」或「某些人相信⋯」時，可使用
Some people think...、Some people believe... 這類句型。

Some people believe that God is a woman.
有些人相信上帝是一名女性。

Some people think the chicken came before the egg.
有些人認為先有雞才有蛋。

Some people argue that the U.S. moon landing was staged.
有些人主張美國登陸月球是演出來的。

39 **There are some people who ...** 有些人⋯

有 some 的句型非常適合用在開場白中，因為這個單字可避免自己在表達
個人意見時語氣過於主觀與強硬，而能更委婉或客觀地陳述問題或主張。

There are some people who refute the existence of ghosts.
有些人駁斥鬼魂的存在。

There are some people who still believe the earth is flat.
有些人仍相信地球是平的。

There are some people who believe the earth is only two thousand
years old.
有些人認為地球只存在兩千年而已。

40 **It is undeniable that ...** 不可否認（無庸置疑地），⋯

想在開場白中反駁對方意見、同時委婉地提出自己的主張時，可使用此句
型。

It is undeniable that the world needs good doctors.
不可否認，這個世界需要好醫生。

It is undeniable that poverty produces crime.
不可否認，貧窮引起犯罪。

It is undeniable that disease is a threat.
不可否認，疾病是個威脅。

41 It seems to me that ... 對我來說，…似乎…

想謹慎地陳述個人意見時，可使用此句型，that 後面接個人的意見。

It seems to me that smoking is bad.
對我來說，抽菸似乎是一件不好的事情。

It seems to me that there are some possible solutions.
對我來說，似乎有一些可行的解決方案。

It seems to me that typing should be taught in preschool.
對我來說，似乎在幼稚園就應該要教打字。

016 / 提到處理問題的方式

42 In approaching the issue, 在處理這個議題時，

要在開場白提出問題的解決方向與方式時，此句型能派得上用場，同時也是以個人角度定義問題、對讀者客觀陳述的表達方式之一。

In approaching the issue, we must consider every angle.
在處理這個議題時，我們必須考慮到每個面相。

In approaching the issue, one should be careful not to make hasty judgments.
在處理這個議題時，人必須謹慎不要做出倉促的判決。

In approaching the issue, we would do well to begin with the question of race.
在處理這個議題時，我們最好從種族的問題開始。

017 / 提出強烈主張

43 Everyone has to ... 每個人都應該要…

要提出強烈主張時，不論是在開場白、本文或結論，這都是十分常用的句型。請注意一下，everyone 是單數，所以要用單數的動詞「has to」。

Everyone has to brush their teeth.
每個人都應該要刷牙。

Everyone has to take care of their family.
每個人都應該要照料他們的家庭。

Everyone has to admit that pollution is dangerous.
每個人都必須承認污染很危險。

44 We must contemplate ... 我們必須深思…

contemplate 是「對…深思」的意思，是談到對某事要深思熟慮時適用的動詞。

We must contemplate the consequences of our actions.
我們必須深思行動後所帶來的後果。

We must contemplate the meaning of these findings.
我們必須深思這些調查結果的意義。

We must contemplate the ethics of his decision.
我們必須深思他的決定的道德標準。

018 / 陳述事實或問題

45 If we think about ... 如果我們想想（思考）…

是適合用在開場白中提出問題的句型。想讓讀者回想起對某件事的普遍看法，或是提出沒有想過的問題時，可使用此句型。

If we think about the meaning of life, we quickly become confused.
如果我們想想人生的意義，我們很快就會感到困惑。

If we think about the way that children learn, the strange-looking toy makes sense.
如果我們想想小孩學習的方式，這個看起來很奇怪的玩具就有其意義了。

If we think about birds making nests, we can understand our own desire to make our house a "home."
如果我們想想鳥類築巢，我們就可以理解我們會想將房子變成「家」的願望。

46 If you stop to consider ... 如果你稍微停下來思考一下…

想提出稍微回想一下就能馬上意識到問題的情況，或提出容易被忽略的問題時，可使用此句型。

If you stop to consider the ant, you will see that it is a very complex creature.
如果你研究一下螞蟻，你將會發現牠們是非常複雜的生物。

If you stop to consider the consequences, perhaps you won't cheat on Mary.
如果你思考一下後果，或許你就不會去欺騙瑪麗。

If you stop to consider the benefits of vitamins, you will realize how necessary they are.
如果你思考一下維他命的好處，你將會了解這些維他命的必要性。

47 **As you probably know,** 誠如各位所知，／大家可能都知道，

probably 表示「或許」、「大概」。想稍微提醒一下過去發生的某件事或某個事實時，可使用此句型。此句型的重點在於 probably 搭配 As you 使用，表示「大家可能都知道…」之意。

As you probably know, red has the longest wavelength.
誠如各位所知，紅色的波長最長。

As you probably know, Newton discovered the law of gravity.
誠如各位所知，牛頓發現了萬有引力定律。

As you probably know, there is much research left to be done.
誠如各位所知，還有許多研究尚待進行。

48 **As you may have noticed,** 各位也許已經察覺到，

想要提醒一下早已是眾所皆知的內容，或是想要喚起大家對某件事的記憶時，可使用此句型。或者，在文章中直接提及某個正熱烈被討論的新話題，例如「洗髮精會造成水汙染」，可能會有點唐突時，透過此句型可避免這種唐突感。

As you may have noticed, the earth is getting warmer.
各位也許已經察覺到，地球逐漸在暖化。

As you may have noticed, the elbow is a fragile joint.
各位也許已經察覺到，手肘是一個脆弱的關節。

As you may have noticed, apples are smaller this year.
各位也許已經察覺到，今年的蘋果比較小顆。

49 While ..., ... 儘管⋯，但⋯

while 是連接詞，具有「雖然」「儘管」之意。此句型可用來提起某個容易忽略的的情況。

While most men are honest, some are quick to deceive.
儘管大部分的男人都很誠實，但有些人卻說謊不眨眼。

While television is entertaining, it can limit a child's creativity.
電視雖然很有趣，卻會限制住孩子的創造力。

While the data in Figure 1 is important, we should pay more attention to Figure 2.
雖然圖表一的資料很重要，但我們應該多放點注意力在圖表二。

019 談到時下熱門話題

50 One of the most significant current discussions in ... is ... ⋯目前正在討論最重要的議題之一是⋯

一般來說，大部分讀者會對最近發生的時事或跟自身相關的事件產生關注。想撰寫時事類文章時，建議使用此句型。

One of the most significant current discussions in politics **is** health care reform.
政壇目前正在討論最重要的議題之一，是醫療保健的改革。

One of the most significant current discussions in medicine **is** the prevention of AIDS.
醫學界目前正在討論最重要的議題之一，是愛滋病的預防。

One of the most significant current discussions in science **is** the use of stem cells.
科學界目前正在討論最重要的議題之一，是幹細胞的運用。

51 In some business cultures, 在某些商業文化中，

此句型中的「business」可用其它單字取代，例如 school（學校）、novel（小說）等，屬於用途十分廣泛的句型。在開場白、本文中提出跟主題有關的例子時，可使用此句型。

In some business cultures, it is impolite to shake hands.
在某些商業文化中，握手是不禮貌的。

In some business cultures, it is necessary to work sixty hours per week.
在某些商業文化中，每個禮拜必須工作六十小時。

In some business cultures, it is appropriate to lie to make a good impression.
在某些商業文化中，為了有好印象而說謊是適當的。

52 In the past, 在過去，

進入本文之前，先在開場白提及主題的演繹史，是讓開場白內容變豐富的方法之一。就如同在描寫一位名人的全盛時期的文章之前，先提及他／她過往的遭遇，來突顯接下來會提到的全盛時期，可增添戲劇效果。

In the past, people cooked over log fires.
在過去，人們在柴火上烹煮。

In the past, there were no refrigerators.
過去並沒有冰箱。

In the past, scientists believed radium cured disease.
在過去，科學家相信鐳能治癒疾病。

53 At the outset, / At the outset of...,
在初期階段／在…的初期階段

想針對主題的淵源或其歷史變遷進行說明時，可在開場白中使用此句型。大多用於當目前的情況跟一開始的情況有所不同時，例如，撰寫「牛仔褲」的文章時，在開場白中可提到「牛仔褲在一開始是工人穿的褲子」。

At the outset, this solution seemed workable.
在初期階段，這個解決方法看似可行。

At the outset, I expressed my disapproval.
一開始，我就表示了反對。

At the outset of the experiment, the scientists were optimistic.
在這場實驗的初期階段，科學家很樂觀。

021 / 引起讀者興趣

54 Once in a great while, 有時候／偶爾／久久一次

想在開場白中用能引起讀者注意力的內容作開頭時，可使用此句型。

Once in a great while, Americans elect a good president.
有時候美國人會選出一名好總統。

Once in a great while, lightning strikes the same place twice.
有時候閃電會擊中同個地方兩次。

Once in a great while, there is a devastating tsunami.
有時候會出現毀滅性的海嘯。

022 / 直接或間接表達主題

55 I'm going to prove that ... 我要來證明⋯

是在文章裡提到個人主張時的句型。通常在開場白的前半段會先大範圍地描述主題，接著再慢慢縮小範圍，然後再使用這個句型來表達主題。

I'm going to prove that my opponents are wrong.
我要來證明我的對手都是錯的。

I'm going to prove that quality of sunlight affects people's moods.
我要來證明陽光的品質會影響人的心情。

I'm going to prove that depression is a chemical imbalance.
我要來證明抑鬱是化學性失衡。

Part
1

開場白句型

021
引起讀者興趣
／
022
直接或間接表達主題
／
023
下結論

56 I'd like to demonstrate ... 我想示範…

此句型跟上一個句型一樣，都是用來直接提及主題時的句型。would like to 表示「想要…」，demonstrate 則表示「示範」。

I'd like to demonstrate the physics of the wheel.
我想示範輪子的物理原理。

I'd like to demonstrate how to bake a cherry pie.
我想示範如何烤櫻桃派。

I'd like to demonstrate how to write an English sentence.
我想示範如何寫一句英文句子。

57 You may wonder why ... 各位可能會好奇為什麼…

是用來間接提及主題的句型。與其直接說「我要說…」，用「你們可能會想知道／好奇…」作為開頭的句子，更能勾起讀者的好奇心。

You may wonder why the sky is blue.
各位可能會好奇為什麼天是藍的。

You may wonder why Seattle is so cloudy.
各位可能會好奇為什麼西雅圖天氣陰陰的。

You may wonder why toilets are made out of porcelain.
各位可能會好奇為什麼馬桶是用瓷製的。

023 / 下結論

58 By many accounts, 許多依據顯示，／由於許多原因

想在開場白的段落下總結時，可使用此句型。account 的意思很多，用在文章中有「根據、理由」、「考慮事項」等語意。

By many accounts, Mozart was the best composer who ever lived.
許多依據顯示，莫札特是最優秀的作曲家。

By many accounts, Einstein was only half right.
許多依據顯示，愛因斯坦的言論只有一半是對的。

By many accounts, *Jaws* is a terrible movie.
許多依據顯示，大白鯊是部很爛的電影。

024 引用俗語或至理名言

59 There's a saying: 俗話說：

想引用俗語或名言時，可使用此句型。

There's a saying: "Too little, too late."
俗話說：「太少也太遲（為時已晚）」。

There's a saying: "Where there's smoke, there's fire."
俗話說：「有煙的地方就有火（無風不起浪）」。

There's a saying: "Give a man an inch, and he'll take five hundred."
俗話說：「得寸進尺」。

60 In the words of ..., …說：

想引用知名人士的名言或格言時，可使用此句型。

In the words of John Keats, "A thing of beauty is a joy forever."
約翰‧濟慈說：「美麗的事物是永恆的喜樂。」

In the words of Henry David Thoreau, "Sell your clothes and keep your thoughts."
亨利‧戴維‧梭羅說：「撤除物欲，留下思想。」

In the words of Gandhi, "You must be the change you want to see in the world."
甘地說：「你必須成為你想在世界看到的改變。」

025 舉例

61 If we take just one example ... 以…的例子而言

若單靠說明無法讓讀者充分理解，或容易造成讀者的混淆，此時想簡單舉個例子時，可使用此句型。

If we take just one example — the grizzly bear — we can see the damage that humans have done to forest habitats.
以灰熊的例子而言，人類破壞了森林棲息地。

If we take just one example — Roe vs. Wade — it is clear there is no clear right and wrong.
以羅訴韋德案的例子而言，顯然沒有明顯的對錯。

If we take just one example — the automobile — we can see that the gasoline engine is inefficient.
以汽車的例子而言，汽油引擎的效率很差。

026 / 陳述一般大眾錯誤的觀念

62 Most people consider ... 大部分的人認為…

是用來提出問題的句型。想指出大多數人普遍存在的錯誤認知時，可使用此句型。

Most people consider the earthworm a pest.
大部分的人認為蚯蚓是害蟲。

Most people consider writing to be a chore.
大部分的人認為寫作是乏味的事。

Most people consider George Washington the founding father of the U.S.
大部分的人認為喬治・華盛頓是美國開國元勳。

63 One of the misconceptions about ... is ...
對…錯誤的認知之一是…

打算寫批判性文章或分析類文章時，可用此句型指出常見的錯誤認知，同時進行批判或分析。

One of the misconceptions about cats **is** that they can see in the dark.
對貓錯誤的認知之一是以為牠們在黑暗中看得見。

One of the misconceptions about the earth **is** that it can heal itself.
對地球錯誤的認知之一是以為它有自己淨化的能力。

One of the misconceptions about orchids **is** that they are fragile.
對蘭花錯誤的認知之一是以為它們很脆弱。

64 The public in general tend to believe that ...
一般大眾傾向於相信（大部分人都相信）…

社會普遍的**觀念**也許在當時看似正確，但仔細思考之後會發現事實並非如此。想針對這種**觀念**進行批判時，可用此句型來指出社會大眾所抱持的看法是錯誤的。

The public in general tend to believe that roses are naturally red.
大部分人都相信玫瑰本來就是紅色的。

The public in general tend to believe that babies are cute.
大部分人都相信嬰兒很可愛。

The public in general tend to believe that early education is desirable.
大部分人都相信學前教育是有成效的。

027 文章主題的構成因素

65 There are many reasons why ... 基於許多原因，…

在陳述個人看法的文章中，有時會在開場白先簡短說明接下來在本文部分會談論到跟主題相關的構成因素，此時可利用此句型稍微提一下支持主題的理由。

There are many reasons why this is true.
基於許多原因，所以這就是事實。

There are many reasons why I believe this.
基於許多原因，所以我相信這個。

There are many reasons why nations fight each other.
基於許多原因，所以各國戰爭不斷。

66 Consider this: 想想看：

是個「直接點出問題，同時也強調此問題」的句型，冒號（:）後面接問題。

Consider this: his father was an alcoholic.
想想看：他的父親曾是酒鬼。

Consider this: subnuclear particles do not behave predictably.
想想看：次原子粒子不出所料毫無作用。

Consider this: there are billions of stars in the universe.
想想看：宇宙有數十億顆星星。

67 Most people don't know ... 大部分的人不知道…

想要提出有別於一般概念（如我們應該要阻止地球暖化）的嶄新觀點（如地球暖化只是一種意識形態）時，建議使用此句型。

Most people don't know that he was also a soldier.
大部分的人不知道他過去也是一名軍人。

Most people don't know what it's like to live in the jungle.
大部分的人不知道在叢林裡生活是什麼樣子。

Most people don't know how to drive a car with manual transmission.
大部分的人不知道如何用手動排檔開車。

68 You may not know ... 各位可能不知道…

想輕鬆帶過某個情況時，可用此句型。使用「may」這樣的助動詞可避免語氣太過於肯定或把話說死。

You may not know her very well.
各位可能不太認識她。

You may not know that her husband was killed in a car accident.
各位可能不清楚她的先生因車禍過世。

You may not know that carbon dioxide is poisoning the oceans.
各位可能不知道二氧化碳正在污染海洋。

69 **I question whether ...** 我懷疑…是否…／我對…感到質疑

question 表示「對…質疑」，此句型可委婉地提出質疑。相較於「我認為…不對」，用「我對…抱持懷疑」的語氣較為委婉。

I question whether the results are valid.
我對結果是否有效感到質疑。

I question whether her method was sound.
我對她的方法是否合理感到質疑。

I question whether he saw the rainbow or simply imagined it.
我懷疑他是真的看到了彩虹還是只是想像。

029 / 開啟話題

70 **Little is known about ...** 對…的了解不多／對…知道的不多

在正式進行說明之前，若認為一般人對接下來要討論的內容不太瞭解時，可用此句型點出主題。

Little is known about the universe.
對宇宙的了解不多。

Little is known about the origin of life.
對生命起源的了解不多。

Little is known about evolution.
對演化的了解不多。

71 **And what about ...** 那麼關於…，你怎麼看呢？

提完幾項意見或情況後，接著想再提出最想討論的內容時，可使用此句型。

And what about Mary's theory that home schooling is more effective?
那麼關於瑪麗的「在家自學將更有效果」這個理論，你怎麼看呢？

And what about the idea that intelligence is inherited?
那麼關於智商是遺傳的，你怎麼看呢？

And what about Mr. Lin's argument that video games are educational?
那麼關於 Lin 先生認為電玩遊戲都有教育性質，你怎麼看呢？

Part
1
開場白句型

029
開啟話題
／
030
提及複雜問題或特殊情況
／
031
目前無定論的主題

030　提及複雜問題或特殊情況

72　**It is a complicated question,**

（對…來說，）這是個複雜的問題，

提出問題後，可使用此句型來對該問題的複雜性表示認同。

It is a complicated question, but we must do our best to answer it.
這是個複雜的問題，但我們必須盡可能去解答。

It is a complicated question, and hard to answer.
這是個複雜的問題，而且也很難回答。

It is a complicated question for many.
對許多人來說，這是個複雜的問題。

73　**This situation is not unique;**　這種情況並不特殊；

某個問題雖然看似特殊，但因不斷發生以至於有點嚴重時，可使用此句型。此句型的後面請注意有分號，分號的後面接理由或例子。

This situation is not unique; many have experienced it before.
這個狀況並不特別，許多人都曾經經歷過。

This situation is not unique; in 1998, there was a much worse recession.
這個狀況並不特別，在 1998 年，經濟衰退更為嚴重。

This situation is not unique; as there have been droughts throughout history.
這個狀況並不特別，因為歷史上時常發生乾旱。

031　目前無定論的主題

74　**There is still no general agreement about ...**

目前對於…仍未有共識

針對想探討的主題因有各方說法，而無法提出定論時，可使用此句型。可用這類句型帶出自己接下來要提的主張或看法。

There is still no general agreement about the effect of artificial sweeteners on the body.
目前對於人工甜味劑對身體的影響仍未有共識。

There is still no general agreement about the ultimate fate of the earth.
目前對於地球最終的命運仍未有共識。

There is still no general agreement about who shot John F. Kennedy.
目前對於誰槍殺約翰・甘迺迪仍未有共識。

75 Today there has been little agreement on ...
至今對…仍意見紛紜

想以目前議論紛紛的問題作為主題時，可使用這類句型。

Today there has been little agreement on what causes AIDS.
至今對愛滋病的病因仍意見紛紜。

Today there has been little agreement on what happiness is.
至今，何謂快樂仍意見紛紜。

Today there has been little agreement on what makes one man smarter than another.
至今，是什麼讓一個人比另一個人聰明仍意見紛紜。

032 說明文章架構

76 The essay has been organized in the following way: 本篇文章的組織架構如下：

in the following way 表示「如下列方式」，想先向讀者說明文章的組織架構時，可使用此句型。

The essay has been organized in the following way: introduction, body, and conclusion.
本篇文章的組織架構如下：開場白、本文和結論。

The essay has been organized in the following way: causes, effects, and conclusions.
本篇文章的組織架構如下：起因、影響和結論。

The essay has been organized in the following way: materials, procedures, and outcomes.
本篇文章的組織架構如下：材料、步驟和結果。

77 This paper first gives a brief overview of ...
這份報告首先提供有關…的簡單概要

像是在論文或報告這類長篇文章，必須提到文章的組織架構時，可使用此句型。

This paper first gives a brief overview of prenatal care in China.
這份報告首先提供有關中國產前護理的簡單概要。

This paper first gives a brief overview of common prescription drugs.
這份報告首先提供有關一般處方藥的簡單概要。

This paper first gives a brief overview of women's traditional clothing in Nepal.
這份報告首先提供有關尼泊爾女性傳統服飾的簡單概要。

033　表達個人立場或自身經驗

78 In my opinion, 就我的觀點而言，／個人認為，

想直接表明個人主觀立場時，可使用此句型。在表達個人看法前，請用 In my opinion 作為開頭。

In my opinion, all men on this earth are created equal.
個人認為，地球上的所有人生而平等。

In my opinion, we have to decrease our use of fossil fuels.
個人認為，我們必須減少使用化石燃料。

In my opinion, all children should know two languages.
個人認為，所有孩童都應該要懂兩種語言。

79 I'd like to suggest that ... 我想建議…／我想提議…

用 would like to 可委婉表達個人的主張。想謹慎提出個人意見或想法時可使用此句型。

I'd like to suggest that all employees be required to attend the picnic.
我建議所有員工都應該參加野餐。

I'd like to suggest that all children be vaccinated.
我建議所有孩童都接種疫苗。

I'd like to suggest that this website be taken down.
我建議撤掉這個網站。

80 In my experience, 根據我的經驗，

一般來說，文章的支持論點較建議採用客觀事實，但如果想以主觀想法或感受作為論點的話，建議使用這類句型來陳述個人經驗。

In my experience, lawyers are always corrupt.
根據我的經驗，律師一直都很腐敗。

In my experience, writers seem to be lonely people.
根據我的經驗，作家似乎都是孤單的人。

In my experience of working in a laboratory, I learned very quickly that I am allergic to mice.
根據我在實驗室工作的經驗中，我很快就意識到我對老鼠過敏。

034 提出解決辦法

81 At the very least, ... should ... 至少應該要…

此句型若搭配 should 一起使用，可用來強調問題的嚴重性或喚醒警覺心，並提出解決辦法。

At the very least, you **should** brush your cat's teeth once a month.
你一個月至少應該要幫你的貓刷一次牙。

At the very least, we **should** reduce our soda consumption.
至少我們應該要減少消費碳酸飲料。

At the very least, you **should** limit your TV watching.
至少你應該要節制看電視的時間。

035 提出疑問

Part
1
開場白句型

034
提出解決辦法
／
035
提出疑問

82 **How can we be sure ...** 我們如何確信…？

想針對人們通常不會注意的問題，提出疑問時，可使用此句型。此時，疑問的答案會出現在本文的段落中。

How can we be sure that we are safe?
我們如何確信我們是安全的呢？

How can we be sure the findings are correct?
我們如何確信這個研究結果是正確的呢？

How can we be sure the students did not cheat?
我們如何確信學生們沒有作弊呢？

83 **What does this have to do with ...?**

這和…有什麼關聯呢？

have to do with... 表示「與…有關」，是常見的片語之一。在開場白想引起讀者的興趣而帶出與主題相關的話題時，可使用此句型。

What does this have to do with science?
這和科學有什麼關聯呢？

What does this have to do with history?
這和歷史有什麼關聯呢？

What does this have to do with the atomic bomb?
這和原子彈有什麼關聯呢？

84 **What if ...?** 如果…會怎麼樣呢？

針對既定觀念，若想再提出有別於以往認知的其它創新想法，或可激發想像力的問題時，可使用此句型。

What if the world was flat?
如果世界是平的，會怎麼樣呢？

What if there were no weekends?
如果沒有週末，會怎麼樣呢？

What if the internet had not been invented?
如果網路不曾被發明，會怎麼樣呢？

85 Could this be due to ... 這可能是因為⋯的關係嗎？

due to...是表示「因為⋯」的介系詞，後面要接名詞或動名詞。想分析原因時可使用此句型。

Could this be due to his weight?
這可能是因為他體重的關係嗎？

Could this be due to high levels of oxygen?
這可能是因為高濃度氧氣的關係嗎？

Could this be due to a temperature increase?
這可能是因為氣溫上升的關係嗎？

036 限定某情況來展開話題

86 In the case of ..., 關於⋯，

在開場白提出主題後，想從各種角度探討跟主題有關的內容時，可使用此句型。

In the case of education, I think that all children deserve equal opportunity.
關於教育，我認為所有的孩子都應該享有平等的機會。

In the case of basketball, I believe there should be only one referee.
關於籃球，我認為應該只需要一位裁判就可以了。

In the case of the waltz, dancers should be very graceful.
關於華爾滋，舞者應該都會很優雅。

87 Ideally, 理想的情況下，

ideal 表示「理想的」，想提及類似烏托邦這種接近完美但實際上不存在的情況時，可使用此句型。

Ideally, there would be world peace.
理想的情況下，應該會有世界和平。

Ideally, we would not need nuclear weapons.
理想的情況下，我們不需要核子武器。

Ideally, you should have a savings account in addition to a checking account.
理想的情況下，除了已經有了現金（支票）帳戶之外，你應該還要有一個儲蓄帳戶。

037 / 談到時下趨勢

88 These days, 最近，

想在文章中談論跟最近熱門趨勢相關的話題時，可在開場白使用這類句型。

These days, Mrs. Lee can barely walk.
最近，李太太幾乎不能走。

These days, everyone buys their groceries at the store.
最近每個人都在商店裡採購雜貨。

These days, you can't throw a plastic bottle away without feeling guilty.
最近，丟棄塑膠瓶讓人充滿罪惡感。

89 Nowadays, it is scarcely possible to ...
如今，幾乎不可能…

是談到幾乎沒有可能性的情況時所使用的句型。scarcely、hardly 表示「幾乎不…」，即使沒有搭配 not 或 never，也有否定意味。

Nowadays, it is scarcely possible to have a reasonable discussion.
如今，幾乎不可能有機會做理性討論。

Nowadays, it is scarcely possible to buy a house with a front porch.
如今，幾乎不可能買到有前廊的房子。

Nowadays, it is scarcely possible to find a real fur coat.
如今，幾乎不可能找到真皮大衣。

038 / 指出問題的主因

90 Yet we continue to ... 我們仍然繼續…

在開場白已充分說明了某情況的嚴重性之後，想強調此情況未改善且仍持續發生時，可使用此句型。

Yet we continue to pollute our environment at an alarming rate.
我們仍然繼續急速地污染我們的環境。

Yet we continue to watch television.
我們仍然繼續看電視。

Yet we continue to buy the product.
我們仍然繼續購買這個商品。

91   This is a cause for some confusion ...
這可能是造成混淆（誤解）的原因，

此句型主要是在質疑並指出研究中錯誤的部分。首先先提出某個人或一般社會大眾對某主題的看法，接著針對此看法提出質疑，此時可用此句型指出問題所在。

This is a cause for some confusion because babies typically can't read.
這可能是造成混淆的原因，因為寶寶們通常無法閱讀。

This is a cause for some confusion since Iowa is far from the ocean.
這可能是造成混亂的原因，因為愛荷華州離海洋很遠。

This is a cause for some confusion since Abraham Lincoln did not believe in slavery.
這可能是造成混亂的原因，因為亞伯拉罕・林肯不相信奴隸制度。

92   There's just one problem: 只有一個問題：

在談論某主題中忽然戲劇性地拋出一個問題，可使用此句型。

There's just one problem: we don't have enough trees.
這裡只有一個問題：我們沒有足夠的樹。

There's just one problem: humans can't survive on Mars.
這裡只有一個問題：人類無法在火星生存。

There's just one problem: the government has no money.
這裡只有一個問題：政府沒有經費。

039 / 強調議題的重要性

93 It is becoming increasingly difficult to ignore ...
愈來愈難以忽略…

要特別強調某議題的重要性或嚴重性時，常用此句型。

It is becoming increasingly difficult to ignore the air pollution.
愈來愈難以忽略空氣污染。

It is becoming increasingly difficult to ignore the hawks in the back yard.
愈來愈難以忽略後院的老鷹。

It is becoming increasingly difficult to ignore the African AIDS epidemic.
愈來愈難以忽略非洲愛滋病的擴散。

94 It is important to recognize ... 認識…非常重要

想在開場白引起讀者閱讀本文章的動機，可使用此句型。若無法引起讀者的興趣，文章寫再好也是枉然。此句型的功用在於強調議題的重要性，並吸引讀者繼續讀下去。

It is important to recognize the value of life.
認識生命價值是非常重要的。

It is important to recognize the symptoms of cancer.
認識癌症的症狀非常重要。

It is important to recognize the implications of the findings.
了解研究結果的意義非常重要。

040 / 用一句話簡述問題

95 The problem is (that) ... 問題是…

是用來簡述問題的句型，後面可接逗號，接著再提到問題，也可接 that 子句來連結問題的內容。

The problem is that Dr. Henderson cannot hear.
問題是韓德森博士聽不見。

The problem is, hats are difficult to make.
問題是製作帽子是很困難的。

The problem is, we are running out of oil.
問題是我們沒有油了。

96 **In any present society,** 現今社會中，

此句型中的 present（現在）可替換成 past（過去）、 future（未來）等，用途十分廣泛。

In any present society, people strive for peace.
現今社會中，人們都渴望和平。

In any present society, there are doctors.
現今社會中，到處都有醫生。

In any present society, there is strife.
現今社會中，處處有紛爭。

041 提及未來的發展

97 **The future direction of ... is ...** …的未來方向是…

是提及未來發展方向時會用到的句型。

The future direction of the program **is** in our hands.
這個節目的未來動向掌握在我們手上。

The future direction of the university **will be** decided by the president.
這間大學的未來方向會依照校長的決定來發展。

The future direction of the country **is** a matter of great importance.
這個國家的未來方向是非常重要的問題。

Part
1

開場白句型

041
提及未來的發展
／
042
第一次知道某事

042 / 第一次知道某事

98 I first became aware of ...

我第一次得知（意識到）…

become aware of... 是表示「得知／意識到…」的片語。想自然、輕鬆地介紹某話題時，可使用此句型。

I first became aware of the issue in high school.
我在高中的時候第一次意識到這個問題。

I first became aware of my mother's illness in 1999.
我在 1999 年的時候第一次得知媽媽的病。

I first became aware of global warming when I was watching TV.
我在看電視的時候第一次得知地球暖化。

99 A number of key issues arise from this statement ...

由此陳述引出許多關鍵性的問題，

在提到了某個問題的一段陳述之後，再利用此句型將該陳述與主題連結在一起。statement 表示「陳述、聲明」。

A number of key issues arise from this statement — most importantly, that of economic justice.
由此陳述引出許多關鍵性的問題，最重要的是關於經濟正義。

A number of key issues arise from this statement, which I will address one at a time.
由此陳述引出許多關鍵性的問題，我會一一說給各位聽。

A number of key issues arise from this statement, including the distrust of government.
由此陳述引出包含對政府不信任等許多重要的問題。

100 Recent developments in ... have heightened the need for ...

最近因為…的發展，對…有大量的需求

想表達在某地區或領域中，對於某人或事物的需求變多時，可用此句型。

Recent developments in medicine **have heightened the need for** doctors.
最近因為醫學的發展，對醫師有大量的需求。

Recent developments in Africa **have heightened the need for** translators.
最近因為非洲的發展，對翻譯人員有大量的需求。

Recent developments in the Middle East **have heightened the need for** peace talks.
最近因為中東的發展，和平會談的需求大幅增加了。

101 In recent years, there has been an increasing interest in ...

近年來，大眾對於…有相當高的興趣

在開場白使用此句型，有助於引起讀者對主題的注意力，非常適合放在文章的開頭。

In recent years, there has been an increasing interest in Henry Miller's political activities.
近年來，大眾對亨利‧米勒的政治活動有相當高的興趣。

In recent years, there has been an increasing interest in veterinary medicine.
近年來，大眾對獸醫學有相當高的興趣。

In recent years, there has been an increasing interest in plastic surgery.
近年來，大眾對整形手術有相當高的興趣。

Part
1
開場白句型

043
提及趨勢變化
／
044
談論新主題

102 Over the past century there has been a dramatic increase in ... 過去一個世紀以來，…急遽增加（成長）

dramatic 表示「急遽的」，此句型適合用在描述跟科技發展、政治、社會、文化風情等相關的文章中。

Over the past century there has been a dramatic increase in job opportunities.
過去一個世紀以來，工作機會急遽增加。

Over the past century there has been a dramatic increase in college enrollment.
過去一個世紀以來，大學入學率急遽增加。

Over the past century there has been a dramatic increase in divorce rates.
過去一個世紀以來，離婚率急遽增加。

103 The issue has grown in importance in light of ... 由於…增添了此議題的重要性

此句型可用來描述以前就存在，但最近因特定因素而被凸顯出來的議題。句型中的 in light of...後面接該特定因素。

The issue has grown in importance in light of recent developments.
由於最近的發展增添了此議題的重要性。

The issue has grown in importance in light of Mr. Lin's success.
由於林先生的成功增添了此議題的重要性。

The issue has grown in importance in light of technological advances.
由於技術的進步增添了此議題的重要性。

044 談論新主題

104 So far, there has been little discussion about ... 到目前為止，幾乎沒有對…的相關討論

當主題是至今沒有什麼人探討的陌生領域時，可使用此句型。

87

So far, there has been little discussion about the role of poetry in society.
到目前為止，幾乎沒有對詩在社會上所扮演角色的相關討論。

So far, there has been little discussion about immigration policies.
到目前為止，幾乎沒有對移民政策的相關討論。

So far, there has been little discussion about video games.
到目前為止，幾乎沒有對電玩遊戲的相關討論。

105 Far too little attention has been paid to ...
對…的關注太少了

當寫作主題是至今沒有什麼人探討的陌生領域時，可使用此句型，來說明自己寫此主題的原因。

Far too little attention has been paid to his fourth book.
他的第四本書受到的關注太少了。

Far too little attention has been paid to learning foreign languages.
學習外語受到的關注太少了。

Far too little attention has been paid to helping the homeless.
幫助無家可歸的人這件事受到的關注太少了。

106 It is a topic which is difficult to explore because ...
這是一個難以探討的主題，因為…

想撰寫陌生領域、艱澀主題的文章時，可使用此句型。

It is a topic which is difficult to explore because people are sensitive about it.
這是一個難以探討的主題，因為人們對此很敏感。

It is a topic which is difficult to explore because it is very complicated.
這是一個難以探討的主題，因為這相當的複雜。

It is a topic which is difficult to explore because it is often unclear.
這是一個難以探討的主題，因為常常不夠清楚。

045 反駁權威

107 Most ... want us to believe that ...

大多數的…要我們相信…

想反駁權威的看法時，可使用此句型。接著簡短說明兩邊完全不同的立場。

Most scientists **want us to believe that** global warming is real.
大多數的科學家要我們相信地球暖化是真的。

Most Republicans **want us to believe that** government intervention is always a mistake.
大多數的共和黨員要我們相信政府的介入一直都是個錯誤。

Most politicians **want us to believe that** they represent the people.
大多數的政治人物要我們相信他們代表了人民。

PART II

Body
Patterns
本文句型

001　打開話題

001 **To begin with,** 首先，

這是用來強烈表達要正式開始的句型。在本文中要介紹主題時，可使用此句型。

To begin with, we need to define 'ecosystem.'
首先，我們需要定義何謂生態系統。

To begin with, we should understand the principle.
首先，我們應該要了解一下理念。

To begin with, we must introduce ourselves to our neighbors.
首先，我們必須要先向鄰居自我介紹。

002 **The task at hand is to ...** 現在首先要做的是…

The task at hand is to...是常見的寫作句型，at hand 表示「馬上要面臨；必須馬上處理…」。

The task at hand is to refute the opposing argument.
現在首先要做的是推翻反對的主張。

The task at hand is to prove that werewolves exist.
現在首先要做的是證明狼人的存在。

The task at hand is to change people's attitudes.
現在首先要做的是改變人們的態度。

003 **We must first examine ...** 我們必須要先檢視…

要採階段性的陳述時，可利用此句型來介紹會先提及的內容，來帶出主題。

We must first examine the concept of justice.
我們必須先檢視正義的概念。

We must first examine the facts.
我們必須先檢視事實。

We must first examine the records.
我們必須先檢視紀錄。

004 Let us start by considering the facts about...
讓我們從思考…的真相開始

適用於在本文開頭的句型。

Let us start by considering the facts about skin cancer.
讓我們從皮膚癌的情況開始研究。

Let us start by considering the facts about the accident.
讓我們從事故的真相開始思考。

Let us start by considering the facts about electricity.
讓我們從電力的情況開始研究。

005 The first thing that needs to be said is that ...
必須說明的第一點是…／首先要說的是…

想正式開始進行討論時，可使用此句型，後面接續的內容通常是極為重要的議題。

The first thing that needs to be said is that I am not an impartial witness.
首先要說的是，我不是公正的證人。

The first thing that needs to be said is that this is the work of years of research.
首先要說的是，這是多年研究的成果。

The first thing that needs to be said is that this essay is not intended to shed light on every aspect of Mendel's life.
首先要說的是，本文並非旨在闡明孟德爾一生的所有面相。

006 The first aspect to point out is that ...
第一點要提出的是…

The first aspect to point out is that doctors now know that contagious diseases must be contained.
第一點要提出的是醫生現在知道必須控制傳染性疾病。

The first aspect to point out is that the scientific method was not used in this study.
第一點要提出的是科學方法在這個研究裡並未被採用。

The first aspect to point out is that there are more women in the workplace now.
第一點要提出的是更多女性投身職場。

007 In the first place, ... 首先，…

在進入本文前，可先使用此句型，來提及接下來要討論的議題。

In the first place, the book does not support the war.
首先，這本書不支持戰爭。

In the first place, ghosts do not exist.
首先，鬼魂是不存在的。

In the first place, theft is illegal.
首先，偷竊是違法的。

008 To start with, 首先，

可用於作為本文開頭部分的引言，做簡報時也會用到此句型。

To start with, the class was boring.
首先，課很無聊。

To start with, place your hands on your hips.
首先，將手放在臀部上。

To start with, students should buy their books.
首先，學生應該購買自己的書。

009 First of all, 首先，

要提及極為重要或需要被優先討論的話題時，可在前面使用此句型。通常在陳述自我主張的言論時，會在文章前面加上此句型，提到要先談論的主題。

First of all, we plan to describe this idea.
首先，我們計畫要說明這個構想。

First of all, we thank you for reading this.
首先，我們感謝你的閱讀。

First of all, we will present a new concept.
首先，我們將介紹新的概念。

010 First of all, let's try to understand ...
首先，讓我們先嘗試了解…

在本文的開頭，想針對極為重要或需要被優先討論的話題進行介紹，接著再切入正題時，可使用此句型。

First of all, let's try to understand the current system.
首先，我們來試著了解現在的體制。

First of all, let's try to understand the new concept.
首先，我們來試著了解新的概念。

First of all, let's try to understand the reason for the change.
首先，我們來試著了解改變的原因。

---

002 / 有條理地鋪陳

011 Logically, it follows that... 就邏輯而言，… 當然 …

想要有條理鋪陳文章時，可利用此句型來層層堆疊，以表達是因為前面的情況而造成某個結果。

Logically, it follows that fish do sleep.
就邏輯而言，魚當然會睡覺。

Logically, it follows that tomatoes are a fruit.
就邏輯而言，番茄當然算是一種水果。

Logically, it follows that toes evolved from fins.
就邏輯而言，腳趾當然是由鰭進化而成的。

012 This, in turn, 這反而…

是用來說明複雜關係的句型。舉例來說，「失業造成經濟萎縮，經濟萎縮又讓失業情況惡化。」這類情況就很適合用此句型來陳述。in turn 是「這反而…」「反過來」的意思。

This, in turn, caused unemployment.
這反而引起失業。

This, in turn, produced dissatisfaction.
這反而引起不滿。

This, in turn, made people less likely to shop at Wal-Mart.
這反而是讓人越來越不太可能去沃爾賣場購物了。

013 In the meantime, 在這段期間，

屬於簡單、常見的句型。主要是談到先前在某種情況下進展的事情時所用
的句型。

In the meantime, we should be satisfied with the current situation.
在這段期間，我們應該滿足於現狀。

In the meantime, we must drive carefully.
在這段期間，我們必須小心開車。

In the meantime, we should research the issue.
在這段期間，我們應該研究這個議題。

014 And so, ... 而且…

在描述過去的事件時，可利用此句型來提到該事件後續的發展。

And so, the process continues.
而且，這個過程持續進行。

And so, wars would not be won without engineers.
而且，在戰爭上沒有工程師是無法贏得勝利的。

And so, many people believe in life after death.
而且，許多人相信死後重生。

003 陳述事實

015 It is true that ... …是真的

此句型主要是用來陳述事實。除此之外，想要描述雖然彼此立場相異，但
也要接受或承認某個事實時，也可使用此句型。

It is true that newer computers are faster than old ones.
較新的電腦確實比舊的快。

It is true that Toyota is a successful company.
豐田確實是一間成功的公司。

It is true that Julia Child was six feet tall.
茱莉亞‧柴爾德確實有六呎高。

004 / 根據個人經驗

016 From my experience, I think (it is) ...
根據我的經驗，我認為…

以主觀經驗作為文章論點的依據時，可使用此句型來表述自身經驗，來讓內容更具可信度。

From my experience, I think it is important to handwrite letters to friends.
根據我的經驗，我認為親手寫信給朋友是很重要的。

From my experience, I think it is crucial we continue to teach handwriting.
根據我的經驗，我認為持續教導手寫是很重要的。

From my experience, I think it is stupid to pay baseball players so much money.
根據我的經驗，我認為支付大把鈔票給棒球選手是很愚蠢的。

017 I personally believe that ... 我個人相信…

想提及自身所相信的事或信念時，可使用此句型，that 後面接自己相信的內容。

I personally believe that poetry is dead.
我個人認為詩已死。

I personally believe that chicken is the most delicious meat.
我個人認為雞肉是最美味的肉類。

I personally believe that the judge was wrong to sentence John Rogers to death.
我個人認為法官判約翰‧羅傑死刑是錯誤的。

018 **My own point of view is that ...**
我的見解是⋯／我個人的觀點是，

是用來提及個人見解與想法的句型之一。

My own point of view is that Madonna is a bad singer.
我的見解是，瑪丹娜不是個會唱歌的歌手。

My own point of view is that movies are better than TV.
我的見解是，電影比電視好多了。

My own point of view is that Chaucer was actually a priest.
我的見解是，喬塞實際上曾經是一名神父。

019 **I suppose that ...** 我認為⋯

是想提出自己想法時的句型，類似「I think that」句型。

I suppose that any fear can be overcome.
我認為任何恐懼都可以被克服。

I suppose that television is the most popular form of entertainment.
我認為電視是最受歡迎的娛樂形式。

I suppose that ancient people worried about many of the same things that we do today.
我認為古代人煩惱的許多事情跟我們現在苦惱的事情是一樣的。

005 / 從某案例中引出結論

020 **This leads us to believe that ...** 這讓我們相信⋯

要用此句型時，前面會先提到某個讓人相信的案例的結論，此時 that 後面要接現在相信的內容。

This leads us to believe that there is much pressure to succeed.
這讓我們相信邁向成功前有很大的壓力。

This leads us to believe that more people are choosing to work from home.
這讓我們相信，愈來愈多人正選擇在家工作。

This leads us to believe that it is important to understand the background of an issue.
這讓我們相信，了解問題的背景很重要。

006 / 兩者相比較

021 This point can be made by comparing ...
藉由比較…可以推論出這一點

在本文部分可採用比較、舉例、論證等方式來豐富文章內容，而想藉由比較相似卻有些差異的論點來凸顯主題時，可利用此句型，後面要接比較的對象。

This point can be made by comparing the two studies.
這個論點是經過比較兩個研究後決定的。

This point can be made by comparing Susan's argument with Melissa's.
這個論點是經過比較蘇珊和梅麗莎兩人的理論後決定的。

This point can be made by comparing the Japanese data with the American data.
這個論點是經過比較日本和美國的數據後決定的。

022 Here I am presuming that ... 在此，我假設…

文章的筆者為了帶出自己設想好的結論，有時會先提出假設，在這種情況下可使用此句型來進行假設。

Here I am presuming that Einstein was correct.
在此我假設愛因斯坦是正確的。

Here I am presuming that the reader is familiar with Freud.
在此我假設讀者對佛洛依德都很熟悉。

Here I am presuming that the laws of gravity do not apply on alien planets.
在此我假設萬有引力不適用於外星球。

023 If... 如果／假如…

不論是在說話時或寫作時，想針對一個很熟悉的狀況做假設時，會使用此句型。

If classical music improves concentration, then it should be used in classrooms.
如果古典樂可以改善專注力，那就應該運用在教室裡。

If a child is interested in math, then he should be encouraged.
如果小孩子對數學有興趣，就應該鼓勵他。

If not for the discovery of penicillin, then many diseases would still be deadly.
如果沒有發現青黴素，那麼有許多疾病仍然會足以致命。

024 Assuming that ... , 假設…，…

此句型是用來假設 that 後面所接的內容為真，因此逗點之後的子句要支持前面 Assuming that 子句的假設內容。

Assuming that reading skills are important, elementary school teachers often assign book reports.
假設閱讀技巧很重要的狀況下，國小老師常會指派閱讀報告。

Assuming that consumers want to save money, many grocery stores send out coupons.
預設消費者想要省錢的狀況下，許多雜貨店都會發放折價券。

Assuming that vitamins maintain good health, many people take them daily.
假設維他命可以保持健康的狀況下，許多人每天都會服用。

025 If it is the case that ..., 如果…的話，

想針對某特定情況來討論時，可使用此句型。此句型在文章中主要是用來描述情況的可能性、應對方法或問題點等。

If it is the case that tornadoes can be predicted, then people can be warned in advance.
如果可以預測龍捲風，就可以提前警告民眾。

If it is the case that germs are transferred by shaking hands, then we should be sure to wash our hands regularly.
如果握手會傳染病菌，那我們應該要確保自己定期洗手。

If it is the case that the healthiest foods are often the most expensive, then people with low incomes may not be able to afford them.
如果最健康的食物經常都是最昂貴的，那低收入的人可能就無法負擔。

007 選擇某解決問題的理由

026 My reasons for taking this approach are ...
我採取這個方法（方式）的理由是…

雖然解決問題的方法相當多，但在文章中只能選擇某一種方法時，可使用此句型，來說明選擇該方法的理由。

My reasons for taking this approach are many.
許多理由讓我採取這個方式。

My reasons for taking this approach are complicated.
我採取這個方式的理由非常複雜。

My reasons for taking this approach are that it is more efficient and more logical.
我採取這個方式的理由是這更有效率而且更合邏輯。

008 概括而論

027 It is easy to generalize about ... 歸納…很簡單

逐一談到個別案例之後，想以其法則歸納前述內容時，可使用此句型。

It is easy to generalize about racial groups.
歸納出種族很簡單。

It is easy to generalize about other cultures.
歸納其他文化很簡單。

It is easy to generalize about people and things you do not know.
歸納人們和他們所不知道的事情很簡單。

028 Generally speaking, 一般而言，

想以大部分的案例為基礎來歸納出結論時，可使用此句型。

Generally speaking, the test was a success.
大體來説，測試是成功的。

Generally speaking, scientists learn from one another.
一般而言，科學家會相互學習。

Generally speaking, Nelson Mandela was a courageous man.
一般而言，尼爾森曼德拉是一個勇敢的人。

009 / 表達研究或案例中所透露的訊息

029 This implies that ... 這暗示⋯

imply 表示「暗示」「意指」，此句型可用來談論到研究或案例中所透露出的訊息。

This implies that service animals give handicapped people more freedom.
這意謂著服務性動物讓殘疾人士有更多自由。

This implies that many government programs lack adequate funding.
這意謂著許多政府計畫都缺乏足夠的資金。

This implies that there are many differences between reptiles and amphibians.
這意謂著爬蟲類和兩棲類動物間存有許多差異。

010 / 討論某議題的必要性

030 In order to properly understand ..., 為了正確理解⋯，

藉由原因與目的，來強調某件事被討論的必要性，或是表達自己的主張時，可用此句型。

In order to properly understand one another, we must learn to communicate.
為了正確理解彼此，我們必須學會交流。

In order to properly understand history, we look to a variety of sources.
為了正確理解歷史，我們尋找各種資源。

In order to properly understand the world, I am studying physics.
為了正確地了解世界，我正在學習物理學。

031 There has been much debate about ...
關於…曾有過許多爭論

提到相關的議題時可用的句型。此句型可用來強調文章主題需被討論的必要性，讓你更自然地表達自己的看法。

There has been much debate about whether Hollywood actors are overpaid.
關於好萊塢演員是否薪酬過高，一直有很多爭論。

There has been much debate about which video game is best.
關於哪種電動遊戲是最好的，一直有很多爭論。

There has been much debate about the city park.
關於那座城市公園的爭論很多。

011 / 異於常理的定論

032 Paradoxically, 反常地，／反常的是，

想描述實際結果與一般預期有落差時，可使用此句型。

Paradoxically, the killer was a woman!
反常地，兇手是一名女性。

Paradoxically, it never rains in Rainville.
反常地，蘭維爾從不下雨的。

Paradoxically, Mr. Kim does not like children.
反常地，金先生不喜歡小孩。

012 在原因或目的之後帶出結論

033 **That is why, in my opinion,** 這也是為什麼我認為…

先列舉出支持某主張的依據後,接著再用此句型來陳述個人意見。

That is why, in my opinion, the zoo should fix its fence.
這就是為什麼我認為,動物園應該要修好籬笆。

That is why, in my opinion, the cost of health care is too high.
這就是為什麼我認為,健康照護的成本太高。

That is why, in my opinion, every worker should take a vacation.
這就是為什麼我認為,每個員工應該要去休假。

034 **For this purpose,** 為此,

要說明達成某目的的手段時,可用此句型。先提及達成某目的,再利用此句型來說明自己的手段或主張。

For this purpose, I will summarize prior research.
為此,我將總結先前的研究。

For this purpose, I recommend black pepper.
為此,我推薦黑胡椒。

For this purpose, let us assume X = Y.
為此,我們來假設 X 等於 Y。

013 提及最好的要點

035 **And best of all,** 而最棒的是,

想對某件事給予肯定的評價,並提及其貢獻或意義時,可使用此句型。

And best of all is the fact that regular exercise fuels the mind and body.
而最棒的是,規律運動可以促進身心。

And best of all, the discovery of penicillin saved countless lives.
而最棒的是,青黴素的發現挽救了無數性命。

And best of all, the Renaissance ushered in a new era in art and architecture.
而最棒的是，文藝復興開啟了藝術與建築的新紀元。

014 / 為了要更明確表達而加以說明

036 ... , by which I mean ... …，我（在這裡）的意思是指…

寫文章難免會出現讓讀者陷入混淆、看不懂的內容，此時可在後面加上此句型，藉此解釋文意或重新定義。

... , by which I mean children.
…，我的意思是指小孩。

... , by which I mean the majority of people.
…，我的意思是指大多數人。

... , by which I mean that she was wrong.
…，我的意思是指她錯了。

037 ... , which seems to confirm the idea that ...
…，似乎再次確定了…的想法

此為關係代名詞的連續用法，用來針對前句內容進行附加說明。

... , which seems to confirm the idea that there is life on other planets.
…，似乎再次確定了其他星球有生命的想法。

... , which seems to confirm the idea that teachers are underpaid.
…，似乎再次確定了教師薪水低的想法。

... , which seems to confirm the idea that milk is good for you.
…，似乎再次確定了牛奶對你有好處的想法。

015 提及他人的意見

038 **Some people think that ...** 有些人認為…

此句型可用來提及他人的意見或看法。

Some people think that college sports should be eliminated.
有些人認為應該要取消辦理大學運動會。

Some people think that there should be a separation of church and state.
有些人認為應該要將教會與國家分開。

Some people think that healthy food tastes bad.
有些人認為營養的食物不好吃。

016 指出被忽略的問題點

039 **It would be negligent not to address ...**
若不提及…就會是個疏失

直接指出某問題被忽略時，可用此句型。

It would be negligent not to address the issue of homelessness.
若不提及無家可歸者的議題，就會是個疏失。

It would be negligent not to address her devotion to God.
若不提及她對神的奉獻，就會是個疏失。

It would be negligent not to address the role of the computer.
若不提及電腦的角色，就會是個疏失。

040 **And that doesn't take into account the fact that ...**
而這沒有考慮到…的事實

take ...into account 是表示「將…考慮進去」的片語，此句型可用來點出別人的主張或研究中的問題點。

And that doesn't take into account the fact that researchers often have personal biases.
而這並沒有考慮到研究人員時常會有個人偏見的事實。

And that doesn't take into account the fact that technology is changing every day.
而這並沒有考慮到技術每天都在改變的事實。

And that doesn't take into account the fact that illegal immigration is a controversial topic.
而這並沒有考慮到非法移民是個爭議的事實。

017 指出缺點

041 The downside is that ... 缺點是…

在比較利弊的情況下，要指出缺點時可使用此句型。

The downside is that cheese makes you fat.
缺點是起司蛋糕會讓你變胖。

The downside is that office work is boring.
缺點是在辦公室工作很無聊。

The downside is that divorce is increasing.
缺點是離婚率正在增加。

042 One of the most serious drawbacks of ... is that ...
…的最嚴重缺點之一是…

drawbacks 表示「缺點、弱點」。想提及其問題點很嚴重時，可使用此句型。

One of the most serious drawbacks of smoking cigarettes **is that** it causes lung cancer.
抽菸最嚴重的壞處之一是它會導致肺癌。

One of the most serious drawbacks of not attending college **is that** it limits one's career options.
不上大學最嚴重的缺點之一是，這樣限制了自己的職業選擇。

One of the most serious drawbacks of skydiving **is that** it is dangerous.
跳傘最嚴重的缺點之一就是危險。

018 / 說明研究目的

043 This study was developed in response to ...
本研究是為了…而發展的

此句型可用在開場白或本文的開頭,來說明研究目的。

This study was developed in response to a need for more accurate information.
這項研究是針對對於更準確資訊的需求而發展的。

This study was developed in response to the results of the previous study.
這項研究是針對先前研究的結果而發展的。

This study was developed in response to last year's investigation.
這項研究是針對去年的調查而發展的。

019 / 結果顯示

044 To this end, 為此,

在說明完所有理由之後,接著根據前述理由做出小結論時,可使用此句型。

To this end, she sold all her belongings.
為此,她賣掉所有財產。

To this end, the doctor washed his hands.
為此,這位醫生洗了手。

To this end, energy companies are building windmills all over the world.
為此,能源公司在全世界設置風車。

045 In as much as ..., 因為…,

此副詞子句可解釋為「因為…」,接表示原因的內容,以帶出文章的原因,後面再連接主句。主句是原因後的結果。

In as much as energy can never be destroyed, we will continue creating it.
因為能源是絕對不能被破壞的，因此我們將持續創造它。

In as much as history has yet to show a better type of government, capitalism seems to work.
在歷史上尚未出現更佳的政府典範前，資本主義似乎還算可行。

In as much as his powers allowed him, Superman defeated the monster.
在超人能力所及的狀況下，他抵禦了怪獸。

046 In response to ..., 針對⋯之後（做出的反應），

想說明人與人之間的互動反應，或是面對社會所產生的回應時，可使用此句型。

In response to an insult, the woman cried.
面對侮辱，這名女子哭了。

In response to pressure from the public, the mayor resigned.
面對來自社會大眾的壓力，市長辭職。

In response to the news report, they decided not to take a walk.
面對新聞報導，他們的反應是決定不要去散步。

047 Resulting from this ... is ... ⋯的結果顯示⋯

是用來銜接前面所討論的某某原因的句型，後面接續針對原因所得到的結論，此句型中的 this 意指前面所討論的原因。

Resulting from this study **is** the fact that people rely on public transportation.
這份研究結果顯示，人們依賴大眾運輸。

Resulting from this investigation **is** the fact that insomnia can be dangerous.
這份調查的結果顯示，失眠可能很危險。

Resulting from this study **is** the idea that animals' behavior is based mostly on instinct.
這份研究的結果顯示出，動物的行為主要來自於本能的這想法。

020 強調某現象與概念的真實性

048 In truth, 說實話，／事實上，

此句型可用來強調事實、真相，其語意跟 to tell the truth 相同。

In truth, we all make mistakes.
說實話，我們都會犯錯。

In truth, people will do anything to survive.
說實話，人們會為生存做任何事情。

In truth, more people carry credit cards than cash.
說實話，越來越多人攜帶信用卡勝過於帶現金。

021 提到某原因所導出的結論

049 Because of this, ... 因為（這個原因）

前面先提出某問題的原因，接著再用此句型來表達該原因所導致的結果，是用來連接原因與結果的因果句型，句中的 this 是表示前面提及的原因。

Because of this, many years of schooling are required to become a doctor.
因為這個原因，成為醫生需要多年的學校教育。

Because of this, engineers and architects work together on building projects.
因為這個原因，工程師和建築師要在建案上合作。

Because of this, it has been shown that smoking cigarettes can cause lung cancer.
因為這個原因，顯示吸菸會導致肺癌。

050 Thus, 因此，

此句型主要是用在本文或結論的中間，先針對前面提到的原因做出一個簡短的結論。

Thus, it can be proven that the number of children born with autism has increased.
因此，這可以證明天生有自閉症的孩童人數已經增加。

Thus, mystery has always surrounded the assassination of John F. Kennedy.
因此，約翰甘乃迪的暗殺事件一直是個謎團。

Thus, children who learn to read at an early age are more successful in school.
因此，很小的時候就學習閱讀的孩子們，在學校會比較優秀。

051 Hence, 因此，

在前面簡述原因之後，再利用此句型來陳述根據該原因所做出的決定，或產生的結論。

Hence, more and more people are using cellular phones.
因此，愈來愈多人使用手機。

Hence, President Lincoln is known as the Great Emancipator.
因此，林肯總統是眾所皆知偉大的解放者。

Hence, fewer trees are being used for the production of paper goods.
因此，很少樹木被用於製造紙製品。

052 For this reason, 因為這個原因，

在本文大多會提到論點的依據或支持的言論，此時可利用此句型來談針對這些依據所得到的結論。

For this reason, it is believed that electric cars are better for our environment.
因為這個原因，電動車被認為對我們的環境比較好。

For this reason, farmers use pesticides to keep their crops free of insects.
因為這個原因，農民使用農藥以避免農作物受到蟲害。

For this reason, life on earth depends on the sun.
因為這個原因，地球上的生命仰賴太陽。

022 提示會在之後的章節多做說明

053 I shall argue this point at greater length in ...
我將針對這點在…做更詳細的說明

在內容艱澀且長篇的文章中，為了讓讀者更容易理解，最好還是採用階段性的逐項說明。在還沒開始談到複雜的內容時，可使用此句型來預先說明。

I shall argue this point at greater length in the following pages.
我將在接下來幾頁中更詳細地說明這一點。

I shall argue this point at greater length in chapter five.
我將在第五章中更詳細地論述這一點。

I shall argue this point at greater length in Part Two.
我將在第二部分中更詳細地論述這一點。

023 提到令人感興趣的話題

054 Much more interesting ... 更有趣的是…

為了強調有趣的某個重點，而採用倒裝句的句型。be 動詞後面要接主詞。

Much more interesting is the love story between them.
更有趣的是他們之間的愛情故事。

Much more interesting is George's affair with his secretary.
更有趣的是喬治和他祕書之間的誹聞。

Much more interesting is the question of inspiration.
更有趣的是靈感的問題。

055 Of even greater appeal is... …更具吸引力

為了強調具有吸引力的某個重點，而採用倒裝句的句型。

Of even greater appeal is the democratic system.
民主制度更具吸引力。

Of even greater appeal is the artist's fifth painting.
這名畫家的第五張畫作更具吸引力。

Of even greater appeal is the theory of evolution.
演化論更具吸引力。

024 提出有見解的論點

056 ... makes a good point that ...
…說…是很有道理的／提出了一個很好的觀點：

想提出具歷史含義的論點，或從有啟發性的理論中導出箇中含義時，可使用此句型。

Adam Smith **made a good point that** no complaint is more common than that of a scarcity of money.
亞當‧史密斯說沒有比缺錢還常見的抱怨，是很有道理的。

Victor Hugo **made a good point that** opening more schools might equate to closing more prisons.
維克多‧雨果說，多設立幾間學校就可以多關閉幾間監獄，是很有道理的。

Benjamin Franklin **made a good point that** haste makes waste.
班傑明‧富蘭克林說急性子會造成浪費，是很有道理的。

025 提出確定的內容

057 To be sure, 確定的是，／可以肯定的是，

此副詞子句是用來強調文章整體內容的句型。

To be sure, the world is shrinking.
確定的是，世界正在蓬勃發展。

To be sure, we need to control immigration.
確定的是，我們必須管制移民。

To be sure, the coat was expensive, but he had to have it.
確定的是，雖然這件外套很貴，但是他當時還是得買下來。

058 **Undoubtedly,** 無疑地，

此副詞也是用來強調文章整體內容最為典型的句型。

Undoubtedly, the man is qualified for the job.
無疑的是，這名男子可以勝任這份工作。

Undoubtedly, this is the worst music I've ever heard.
無疑的是，這是我聽過最糟糕的音樂。

Undoubtedly, college is an important experience.
無疑的是，大學是很重要的經歷。

059 **Just as surely,** 同樣可以肯定的是，

此句型表示「同樣可以肯定的是，」之意，可用來強調或確認後面的內容。

Just as surely, the army invaded Poland.
同樣可以肯定的是，那支軍隊侵略了波蘭。

Just as surely as the sun rises, men and women fall in love.
就像太陽升起一樣確定，男人和女人必然會相愛。

Just as surely, the imported fish are a threat to the river.
同樣可以肯定的是，外來魚種對這條河流是種威脅。

026　針對不必要的狀況做陳述

060 **There is no need to ...** 不需要…

斷定某行為、狀況沒有必要性時，可使用此句型。

There is no need to worry.
沒有必要去擔心。

There is no need to discuss it.
沒有必要去討論這個。

There is no need to demolish the building.
沒有必要去拆除該建築物。

Part
2

本文句型

026
針對不必要的狀況做陳述
／
027
逐一說明各方面觀點

027 逐一說明各方面觀點

061 On the one hand, 一方面，

當某一情況沒有固定答案，而是可從多方面來逐項說明時，可使用此句型。

On the one hand, graduate school is long and expensive.
一方面，研究所耗時而且很花錢。

On the one hand, people need cars to get from place to place.
一方面，人們需要汽車來四處移動。

On the one hand, most people do not like paying taxes.
一方面，大多數人不喜歡納稅。

062 On the other hand, 另一方面，

當某情況可從多個層面來分析，已談完某一觀點，而想要轉換到其他觀點時，可使用此句型。

On the other hand, money is not the most important factor.
另一方面，金錢不是最重要的因素。

On the other hand, Islam and Christianity have much in common.
另一方面，伊斯蘭教和基督教有很多共同點。

On the other hand, soldiers returning home from war deserve
excellent medical care.
另一方面，從戰爭中退伍的軍人應該得到優質的醫療照護。

063 If, on the one hand, it can be said that ... , it can also be said that ... 一方面，如果說…，那麼也可以說…

on the one hand 表示「一方面」的意思。在無法立即定義而需要用多種角度去分析的情況下，用有些人認為是 A，有些人則認為是 B，像是這樣從不同立場來探討時可使用此句型。

If, on the one hand, it can be said that dogs make the best pets, **it can also be said that** cats are cleaner.
一方面，如果說狗是最好的寵物，那麼也可以說貓更乾淨。

If, on the one hand, it can be said that life begins at conception, **it can also be said that** life begins four months later.
一方面，如果説生命是從受孕開始的，那麼也可以説生命是在四個月後開始的。

If, on the one hand, it can be said that dancing is fun, **it can also be said that** it is embarrassing!
一方面，如果説跳舞很有趣，那麼也可以説跳舞令人感到尷尬。

064 The same is not true for ...
這對…來說不是事實／同樣的事在…就不適用

想先提出一個案例，接著再提出相反的論調時，可使用此句型。for 後面要接相反的論調。

The same is not true for the fifteenth century.
這對十五世紀來説不是事實。

The same is not true for honeybees.
這對蜜蜂來説不是事實。

The same is not true for winter.
這對冬天來説不是事實。

065 Perhaps I should also point out the fact that ...
或許我也應該要指出…的事實

point out 是表示「指出，點出」的片語，運用在指出問題的語句中。在指出了各種問題之後，想再謹慎地點出另一個問題時，可使用此句型。

Perhaps I should also point out the fact that Costa Rica has no army.
或許我也應該點出哥斯大黎加沒有軍隊這個事實。

Perhaps I should also point out the fact that Jesus was a carpenter.
或許我也應該點出耶穌曾是名木匠這個事實。

Perhaps I should also point out the fact that there are many Jewish people in New York City.
或許我也應該點出有很多猶太人在紐約市的事實。

066 **To look at this another way,**

從另一個角度看，／換一個角度看，

想從全方位的角度來分析一個現象時，可使用此句型。舉例來說，談到「增加福利預算」時，可提到與之相關的正反立場（即表示贊成增加預算與反對增加預算的兩方立場），於是就可分別從受益者、財政機構等立場來進行探討。

To look at this another way, we are the sons and daughters of very strong people.
換一個角度看，我們是強者的子女。

To look at this another way, there are many solutions to any problem.
換一個角度看，任何問題都有許多解決方式。

To look at this another way, study the map on page five.
從另一個方法來看，我們來研究第五頁上的地圖吧。

028 / 非陳述不可的論點

067 **I would even go so far as to say that ...**

我甚至會這麼說…

對於非陳述不可、非提到不可的論點，可以使用此句型。

I would even go so far as to say that the current economic slump will get worse before it gets better.
我甚至會這麼說，目前的經濟蕭條在恢復前可能會更惡化。

I would even go so far as to say that private cars should be outlawed in big cities.
我甚至會這麼說，大都市裡的私家客車都應該要被取締。

I would even go so far as to say that cigarette smokers are asking for health problems.
我甚至會這麼說，吸菸者會因為健康問題而自討苦吃。

029 列舉論點

068 The first argument suggests that ... 第一個論點意指…

在寫作過程中想列舉幾個論點時，可使用此句型。

The first argument suggests that the author was racist.
第一個論點意指這位作家是種族主義者。

The first argument suggests that the election was rigged.
第一個論點意指這次選舉被操控。

The first argument suggests that Harriet Tubman was a man.
第一個論點意指哈利特·塔布曼是一名男性。

069 While the second argument suggests that ...
反之，第二個論點意指…

在列舉第二個論點時，尤其是跟第一個論點持相反立場時，可使用此句型。while 為連接詞，語意帶有「然而、不過」之意。

While the second argument suggests that homosexuality is unnatural.
反之，第二個論點意指同性戀不合常理。

While the second argument suggests that the election was legal.
反之，第二個論點意指這次選舉是正當合法的。

While the second argument suggests that she was a former slave.
反之，第二個論點意指她以前是名奴隸。

070 In the second place, 第二是（其次），

跟 secondly 的使用時機相同，用來表達第二或次要論點時可使用此句型。

In the second place, maps are rarely accurate.
其次，地圖很少是準確的。

In the second place, most of the patients were Scottish.
其次，大部分患者都是蘇格蘭人。

In the second place, the company provides valuable equipment.
其次，這家公司提供高價的設備。

030 / 提出問題

071 **Many of us may ask ...** （我們之中）很多人也許會問…

在提出自己的論點之後，意識到自己的論點可能會被反駁，那麼此時就可用這句型，來剔除掉自己的論點可能會被質疑的可能性。

Many of us may ask, "What can I do to help fight AIDS?"
我們許多人可能會問：「我該怎麼做才能幫助對抗愛滋病？」

Many of us may ask what we can do to repair the forest.
我們許多人可能會問，我們該怎麼做才能修復森林。

Many of us may ask our senators about the bill.
我們許多人可能會向我們的參議員詢問關於該法案的問題。

031 / 提醒某項事實

072 **Nevertheless, one should accept that ...**
儘管如此，應該要接受…

nevertheless 是表示「儘管如此」「雖然」的副詞。用於表示不論先前的情況如何，現在應該要接受某事實。

Nevertheless, one should accept that time travel is impossible.
儘管如此，應該要接受穿越時空是不可能的事。

Nevertheless, one should accept that skiing is dangerous.
儘管如此，應該要接受滑雪是危險的這件事。

Nevertheless, one should accept that religion often causes war.
儘管如此，應該要接受宗教常常引起戰爭的事實。

073 **One must admit that ...** 必須要承認的（一點）是…

要提及一般人都會同意的論點時，可使用此句型。句中的 must 雖表示「必須」，但在此是有強調該論點是大家都同意的這個前提。

One must admit that he was a genius.
必須承認的是他是天才。

One must admit that she has a sense of humor.
必須承認的是她有幽默感。

One must admit that power corrupts people.
必須承認的是權力使人腐化。

074 One should always remember that ... 應該要永遠記住…

想要強調文章整體的某個要點來試圖說服他人時，可將想強調的重點放在此句型的 that 後面。通常會放在本文的最後來用此句型。

One should always remember that people are more alike than different.
應該要永遠記得，人們之間的相同之處遠比相異多。

One should always remember that people are basically good.
應該要永遠記得，人性本善。

One should always remember that safety is important.
應該要永遠記得安全很重要。

075 One should, however, not forget that ...
然而，不能忘記的是…

想要再次強調文章整體的某個要點時，可將想強調的重點放在此句型的 that 後面，通常會放在本文的最後來用此句型。

One should, however, not forget that children need guidance.
然而，不能忘記的是孩子們都需要被引導。

One should, however, not forget that mathematics is the language of science.
然而，不能忘記的是數學是科學的語言。

One should, however, not forget that ours is one of the best universities in the country.
然而，不能忘記的是我們是全國最好的大學之一。

032 / 提出建議或忠告

076 One should note here that ... 在此應該注意的是

想在文章中段再次強調重點內容，或在讀者可能會產生誤解的部分提出附加說明時，都可以使用此句型。

One should note here that the Berlin Wall was demolished in 1989.
在此應該注意的是，柏林圍牆在 1989 年拆除。

One should note here that Art Deco designs originated in the 1920s.
在此應該注意的是，裝飾藝術設計起源於 1920 年代。

One should note here that the sun is the center of our solar system.
在此應該注意的是，太陽是我們太陽系的中心。

077 We must distinguish carefully between ... and ...
我們必須要仔細地分辨…和…

想針對在本文開頭已談過的混淆用語或概念來建議讀者做分辨時，可使用此句型進行說明。

We must distinguish carefully between right **and** wrong.
我們必須仔細分辨對錯。

We must distinguish carefully between moral **and** immoral
activities.
我們必須仔細分辨道德與不道德活動。

We must distinguish carefully between what politicians say **and**
what they do.
我們必須仔細分辨政客的所言與所行。

078 But don't take my word for it;
可是不要只聽我講的；／但別直接採納我的想法；

雖然已提出自己的主張，但建議讀者以自身立場來思考時，可使用此句型。

But don't take my word for it; see for yourself.
可是不要只聽我講的，你親自去證實。

But don't take my word for it; do your own research.
可是不要只聽我講的，自己去探索吧。

But don't take my word for it; others have written on this topic as well.

可是不要只聽我講的，其他人也寫過這類主題。

079 We must take ... on its own terms.

我們必須以各自的情況（條件）來看待…

此句型主要是用來提醒讀者某個概念的明確意義，以避免產生混淆。在進行了多項的討論之後，經常會發生概念雜亂無章的情況，因此用這句型做提醒。

We must take the field of computer science **on its own terms**.

我們必須以其本身的情況來看待電腦科學這個領域。

We must take the theory of evolution **on its own terms**.

我們必須以其本身的情況來看待進化論。

We must take the problem **on its own terms**.

我們必須以其本身的情況來看待這問題。

---

033 / 點出欠缺之處

080 However, the study is limited in that ...

然而，這份研究受限於…

想針對先前別人做過、主題相同的其他研究來進行檢討，並提出此研究欠缺的部分時，可使用此句型。

However, the study is limited in that it does not describe the researcher's methodology.

然而，這份研究受限於未記載學者的研究方法。

However, the study is limited in that it cannot be applied in another environment.

然而，這份研究受限於無法應用於其他環境。

However, the study is limited in that its findings cannot be validated.

然而，這份研究受限於研究結果無法被證實。

034 強調客觀事實

081 Indeed, 的確,

indeed 表示「真的,的確」的意思,在這裡的用法是用來強調某件事實時。

Indeed, this is the case.
的確,這就是現在的狀況。

Indeed, she became a teacher.
的確,她成為了一名老師。

Indeed, atoms are the building blocks of life.
的確,原子是生命的組成要素。

082 In fact, 事實上,

想要謹慎地揭露某事實,或想針對剛提到的內容做補充說明時,可使用此句型。

In fact, mathematics is an important field.
事實上,數學是一門重要的領域。

In fact, the earth is getting cooler.
事實上,地球愈來愈冷。

In fact, light affects mood.
事實上,光會影響情緒。

083 In reality, 實際上,

當理論與現實不符時,可以先提及別人的主張或意見,再利用此句型講述在現實生活中的實際情況。

In reality, there is no such thing.
事實上,這種事情不存在。

In reality, the argument is weak.
事實上,這個論點很弱。

In reality, the hospital is understaffed and too small.
事實上,這間醫院員工不足而且太小。

084 In reality, it is found that ... 實際上發現⋯

想闡明理論與現實之間的相互關係（如理論與現實的差異）等時，可使用此句型。

In reality, it is found that this is not the case.
實際上發現目前並非如此。

In reality, it is found that prayer soothes the mind.
實際上發現祈禱可以平撫心靈。

In reality, it is found that some people are naturally smarter than others.
實際上發現某些人生來比其他人聰明。

085 The fact is that ... 事實是⋯

想以戲劇性的方式發表具衝擊性的事實時，常用此句型。

The fact is that no one informed me of the schedule change.
事實上是沒有人告訴我時間表的變更。

The fact is that you have two cakes, and I have none.
事實上是你有兩個蛋糕，而我一個也沒有。

The fact is that these children lied to their parents.
事實上是這些小孩對父母說謊。

035 / 回到先前的重點

086 To return to an earlier point, 回到先前的重點，

為了幫助讀者理解而做了詳細的補充說明後，可利用此句型再把話題拉回到主題重點。不論是寫文章或做簡報都很適合用此句型。

To return to an earlier point, dogs can be trained to do many things.
回到先前的重點，狗可以被訓練來做很多事情。

To return to an earlier point, the outcome of World War I led to the outbreak of World War II.
回到先前的重點，第一次世界大戰的結果導致了第二次世界大戰的爆發。

To return to an earlier point, the world's rainforests should be protected.
回到先前的重點，應該要保護世界上的熱帶雨林。

036 / 針對特定主題的想法

087 **As for ...,** 至於…，

對於某事物有特定想法，尤其是想表達個人想法時，可使用此句型。

As for me, I'd rather stay single.
至於我，我寧願保持單身。

As for coffee, Brazil produces the best.
至於咖啡，巴西產的最好。

As for Chicago, there are many good restaurants.
至於芝加哥，那裡有很多不錯的餐廳。

088 **As to ...,** 關於…，／說到…，

想從先前的一個話題轉到其他話題時，可使用此句型。as to 表示「與…有關」「關於…」。

As to law school, I'm not sure I want to go.
說到法學院，我不確定我是否想去。

As to swimwear, I prefer bikinis.
說到泳裝，我比較喜歡比基尼。

As to her children, Ms. Mason replied, "They are doing well."
說到她的小孩，梅森小姐說：「他們都很好。」

089 **With respect to ...,** 關於…，

與 As to... 的語意相同，想從先前的一個話題轉到其他話題時，可使用此句型。

With respect to French cooking, Julia Child was a master.
說到法式料理，茱莉亞・柴爾德是位大師級人物。

With respect to architecture, Wright was a pioneer.
說到建築，萊特是一名先驅。

With respect to dance, Fred Astaire is a legend.
說到舞蹈，弗瑞・亞斯德是個傳奇人物。

090 Regarding ..., 關於…，

語意同 about，是用來表達「關於…」的好用句型。不過 Regarding ... 這個句型是寫正式文章必用的句型。

Regarding diet, one should try to eat fresh fruits and vegetables.
關於節食，應該要試著吃新鮮的蔬菜和水果。

Regarding slavery, I think the U.S. was right to end it.
關於奴隸制度，我認為美國結束這個制度是正確的。

Regarding the production of toys, we should be more careful.
關於玩具製造，我們應該要更謹慎小心。

091 With regard to ..., 關於…，

想要針對主題做補充時，可使用此句型。語意與 regarding、with respect to、as to 類似。

With regard to the lunch break, no employee should leave the office before 11:30.
關於午休時間，任何職員都不得在 11 點半之前離開辦公室。

With regard to the issue of nuclear weapons, there is no right and wrong.
關於核武問題，沒有對與錯。

With regard to literature, the prize should be given to Annie.
關於文學，此獎項應該要頒發給安妮。

092 As far as ... is concerned, 就…而言，

此句型主要是用來表達，在限定條件之下某論點才會成立的情況。

As far as fashion **is concerned**, I am uninterested.
就時尚而言，我並不感興趣。

As far as cheese **is concerned**, Vermont makes the best.
就起司而言，佛蒙特州做的是最好的。

As far as mathematics **is concerned**, Dr. Jordan is a genius.
就數學而言，喬登博士是一位天才。

037 表達與前述內容語意相反

093 **And yet,** 然而

提到尚未解決的議題時，可使用此句型。yet 在此句型中是表示「然而」之意。

And yet, scientists do not agree on these issues.
然而，科學家們在這些議題上還沒有共識。

And yet, the cost of natural gas has risen in recent years.
然而，最近幾年的天然氣價格依舊上漲。

And yet, many students have no interest in studying economics.
然而，許多學生對念經濟學沒有興趣。

038 表達反對意見

094 **Although I sometimes ...,** 儘管有時候我…，

想避免強勢的口氣，而是以較委婉的語氣來表達個人反對的意見時，可使用此句型。sometimes 和 although 搭配可形成較委婉的語氣。

Although I sometimes shave my face, I prefer to have a heard.
儘管我有時候會刮鬍子，但我比較喜歡留鬍子。

Although I sometimes go to NcDonalds, I never go to Burger Kim.
儘管我有時候會去耐當勞，但我從不去漢堡金。

Although I sometimes write fiction, I usually write poetry.
儘管我有時候會寫小說，但我通常是寫詩居多。

095 **Nonetheless, many people believe that ...**
即使如此，許多人仍然認為…

即使存在著與自己的主張持相反意見的其他論點，但想先暫定某個結論時，可使用此句型。

Nonetheless, many people believe that it is important to make large amounts of money.
即使如此，許多人仍然認為賺大錢很重要。

Nonetheless, many people believe that bay leaves are poisonous.
即使如此，許多人仍然認為月桂葉有毒。

Nonetheless, many people believe that rock music is evil.
即使如此，很多人仍然認為搖滾樂是不好的。

096 Thus, although it is true that ...
因此，雖然…是事實，但…

雖然自己所下的結論存在著與事實不符的情況，但該事實對結論並不會造成太大影響時，可以使用此句型。也就是說，即使有這事實，但還是可以暫定這個結論。

Thus, although it is true that few people have swimming pools, many people know how to swim.
因此，雖然很少人家裡會有游泳池這件事是事實，但許多人都知道如何游泳。

Thus, although it is true that dogs are allowed in the park, they are not particularly welcomed.
因此，雖然狗被允許出現在公園中是事實，但他們卻不怎麼受歡迎。

Thus, although it is true that fish is a healthy food, I don't like it.
因此，雖然魚肉是健康的食物是事實，但我還是不喜歡。

097 Rather, 相反地，

要提出與先前陳述的內容持不同的見解時，可使用這個句型。Rather 放在句首修飾後面的內容。

Rather, the universe is expanding.
相反地，宇宙正在擴張。

Rather, he made the table out of oak.
相反地，他用橡木做了一張桌子。

Rather, the director gave the part to Susan.
相反地，導演給了蘇珊這個角色。

039 / 站在讀者的角度

098 **Of course, you can ...** 當然，你可以⋯

此句型大多出現在本文的後半段，想將先前已充分討論過的觀點，提供給讀者做選擇時，可使用此句型。

Of course, you can believe what you choose to.
當然，你可以相信自己的選擇。

Of course, you can form your own conclusion.
當然，你可以做出自己的結論。

Of course, you can decide for yourself.
當然，你可以為自己做決定。

040 / 補充說明

099 **Moreover,** 此外，／更甚者

用來對先前的內容多做說明的句型。也可用 In addition、Furthermore、Also 等來替換。

Moreover, I have tried to be kind.
此外，我還試著表示親切。

Moreover, no one should be forced to marry.
此外，誰都不應該被強迫結婚。

Moreover, a new roof can help you save money.
此外，新的屋頂可以幫你省錢。

100 **Furthermore,** 再者，

跟上一句型用於同樣的情況。

Furthermore, you will not be allowed to attend the ceremony.
再者，你將不能參加典禮。

Furthermore, we are responsible for our children's behavior.
再者，我們為我們小孩的行為負責。

Furthermore, I think it is important that a husband and a wife are best friends.
再者，我認為夫妻彼此是好朋友這點很重要。

101 Further, 更進一步（再者），

是用來做更進一步說明的句型。

Further, the waiter dropped the plates.
再者，服務生把盤子弄掉了。

Further, the teacher lied to his student.
再者，那名老師向該名學生說謊。

Further, the scientist failed to report his findings.
再者，科學家沒有報告他的發現。

102 What is more, 而且，

同樣為補充說明時，可使用的句型。more 後面所連接的內容有強調的效果。

What is more, the lawyer broke the law.
而且，這名律師違反了法律。

What is more, it won't solve the problem.
而且，這無法解決問題。

What is more, they have found several errors.
而且，他們發現了幾個錯誤。

103 As well as ..., 不僅是…，也…

此句型放在句子最前面，用來修飾後面的主要子句。主要是用在提到新的事實（逗點後面的主要子句），同時強調既有的內容時。

As well as an actor, Louie was a chef.
路易不僅是演員，也是一名主廚。

As well as doing research, Marie Curie painted.
瑪麗·居里不僅在做研究，也在畫畫。

As well as writing plays, Shakespeare was an actor.
莎士比亞不僅寫戲劇，同時也是一名演員。

104 **Not only ..., but (also)...** 不僅…，而且也…

語意及強調的效果與 as well as 相同。

Not only is he gorgeous, **but (also)** he is very nice.
他不僅帥，人也很好。

Not only does the restaurant serve beef, **but (also)** it serves fish.
這間餐廳不僅供應牛肉，也供應魚肉。

Not only is it cloudy, **but (also)** it's raining.
天氣不僅多雲，而且還在下雨。

105 **Besides,** 此外，

是提供新資訊時可使用的句型。此外，字尾沒有 s 的 Beside 是表示「在…旁邊」的介系詞，而 besides 則是表示「此外，而且」的副詞，兩者不要搞混。

Besides, the house was too small.
此外，這個房子太小了。

Besides, stem cells can cure cancer.
此外，幹細胞可以治療癌症。

Besides, she had already eaten lunch.
此外，她已經吃過午餐了。

106 **And that's not all-** 而且這還不是全部－

在前面提出各種想法或情況之後，想再補充說明時，可使用此句型。

And that's not all- he's a doctor, too!
而且這還不是全部─他也是一位醫生！

And that's not all- in 2004, the city banned dogs and cats.
而且這還不是全部─在 2004 年，這座城市禁止了貓和狗。

And that's not all- the hotel will do your laundry, too.
而且這還不是全部─這家飯店也會幫你洗衣服。

107 **Apart from that,** 除此之外，

想轉換話題或要做比較、對照時，可使用此句型。也可將句型中的 that 換成 this，變成 Apart from this，所想表達的意思相同。

Apart from that, the camera is easy to operate.
除此之外，這台相機操作容易。

Apart from that, the baby was healthy.
除此之外，嬰兒很健康。

Apart from that, the country's health system worked well.
除此之外，國家的醫療衛生制度運作良好。

108 **In addition,** 另外，

是用來做補充說明的句型，其含義跟「in addition to＋名詞」相同，都帶有「除此之外」的意思。

In addition, the children played games.
另外，孩子們還玩了遊戲。

In addition, the president speaks three languages.
另外，總統會講三國語言。

In addition, the policeman found bullets near the fence.
另外，警察在圍牆附近找到了子彈。

109 **In addition to this,** 除此之外，

主要用於補充說明前面提過的論點，此句型中的 to 是介系詞，後面要接名詞或動名詞。此外，句型中的 this 指的是前面討論過的內容。

In addition to this, parents should read to their children.
除此之外，父母應該念書給孩子聽。

In addition to this, the building will be used as a bus terminal.
除此之外，這棟建築物將會被用作公車總站。

In addition to this, the family will donate money to charity.
除此之外，這個家庭將捐錢給慈善團體。

110 **In addition to that,** 除此之外，

是一個跟前一句型 In addition to this 類似的句型，不過兩者還是有些微差異。In addition to this 是用在先前提出一項論述之後，緊接著又馬上再提出另一個論述時，兩個論述間的時間順序較近者用 this；反之，兩論點的時間相隔較久，先前提出一項論述之後，隔了一段時間才提出下一論述時，才用 that。

In addition to that, the magazine will print her life story.
除此之外，雜誌會發行她的人生故事。

In addition to that, the phone has a calculator.
除此之外，這電話還有計算機功能。

In addition to that, I was invited to speak at the event.
除此之外，我被邀去該活動做演講。

111 **Additionally,** 此外，

語意與 in addition、besides 相同。想補充新資訊時，可使用此句型。

Additionally, workers needed a day off.
此外，勞工需要一天休假。

Additionally, Homer wrote songs.
此外，荷馬也寫歌。

Additionally, he was a soldier.
此外，他曾是位軍人。

112 **Also,** 也／還

同樣是想補充新資訊時可使用的句型。Also 可放在句首，也常放在句尾或句中來做修飾。

Also, she was a talented musician.
她也曾是位才華洋溢的音樂家。

Also, the Brooklyn Zoo donated $500.
布魯克林動物園也捐了五百美金。

Also, the disease can be caused by poor nutrition.
此疾病也可能是因為營養不良所引起的。

113 Then, too, ... 那麼，同樣的，…

把 then 跟 too 這兩單字放在句子前連用，具有強調效果。

Then, too, people need water.
那麼，同樣的，人也需要水。

Then, too, the economy needs as much help as it can get.
那麼，同樣的，經濟狀況也需要獲得其所能得到的幫助。

Then, too, Mr. Peters is a nice man.
那麼，彼得斯先生也是位好人。

114 Yet another ... 然而，另一個…

Yet 表示「然而、但」。想補充提及與前述內容相反的新資訊時，可使用此句型。

Yet another conference was held in Berlin.
然而，在柏林又舉行了一場會議。

Yet another argument has been offered by Dr. Moody.
然而，穆迪博士又提出了另一個論點。

Yet another reason for the plane crash was the rainy weather.
然而，空難的另一個原因是雨天。

041 / 提出佐證

115 One argument in support of ... is that ...
支持…的一個論點是…

想提出跟自己的論點有關且支持此論點的根據時，可使用此句型。

One argument in support of stem cell research **is that** it might save lives.
支持幹細胞研究的一種說法是，它或許可以挽救生命。

One argument in support of outlawing tobacco **is that** it would cut down on the number of cases of lung cancer.
支持禁止菸草的一種論點是，它或許會減少肺癌的病例數。

One argument in support of buying a new telescope **is that** the university would attract more students.
支持購買新望遠鏡的一種因素是，大學或許能吸引更多的學生。

042 / 強調自己的主張

116 This point is often overlooked: 這點往往被忽略：

overlook 表示「忽視」的意思。想要強調自己的主張或提議時，大多會使用此句型。

This point is often overlooked: that men need more calories than women.
這點經常被忽略：男人比女人需要更多的卡路里。

This point is often overlooked: that pollution can be controlled.
這點經常被忽略：污染是可以被控制的。

This point is often overlooked: that baseball is an expensive sport to learn.
這點經常被忽視：學打棒球是個很花錢的運動。

117 Again, 再次強調，

想在文章中再次強調自己的主張或重要內容，需反覆提及時，可使用此句型來做強調。

Again, the next Olympics should be held in San Francisco.
再次強調，下一次的奧林匹克運動會應該會在舊金山舉辦。

Again, there is no pot of gold at the end of a rainbow.
再次強調，在彩虹的盡頭不會有一桶金。

Again, I assert that nurses should be paid more.
再次強調，我主張護士應該得到更多報酬。

118 **Above all,** 綜觀以上各點，

列舉完多項論點後，要在最後強調時，可使用這個句型。

Above all, we should exercise.
綜觀以上各點，我們應該要運動。

Above all, we should focus on Africa.
綜觀以上各點，我們應該把焦點放在非洲。

Above all, science should seek to help people.
綜觀以上各點，科學應該要去幫助人。

119 **At this point,** 此時，

在提出論據及做出結論的過程中，通常會用到一兩次這個句型。在做簡報時也常用此句型。

At this point, it is too late to start over.
此時，重新開始為時已晚。

At this point, we can proceed with our investigation.
此時，我們可以繼續進行調查。

At this point, scientists need to focus on environmental issues.
此時，科學家需要把焦點放在環境保護的問題上。

120 **Most importantly,** 最重要的是，

將此句型用在最重點的部分或想強調的部分前面，可讓讀者注意這部分。

Most importantly, it should be noted that not all snakes are venomous.
最重要的是，應該要注意並非所有蛇都有毒。

Most importantly, the ancient Egyptians believed in life after death.
最重要的是，古埃及人相信死後有來生。

Most importantly, most urban centers have a diverse population.
最重要的是，大多數市中心都聚集著非常多元的人口組成。

043 / 舉出立場相同的例子

121 In the following example we will see ...

在以下的例子中，我們將會知道…

想在文章中舉出立場相同的例子時，可使用此句型。

In the following example, we will see that this is true.
在以下的例子中，我們將會知道這是事實。

In the following example, we will see how the legal system works.
在以下的例子中，我們將會知道法律制度是如何運作。

In the following example, we will see the importance of workplace safety.
在以下的例子中，我們將會知道職場環境安全的重要性。

044 / 依序列舉

122 First(ly), 首先，

在列舉多項論點時，首先被提出來的論點可使用此句型。在一個段落一個主題的短篇文章中，此句型通常被用在第一段的開頭。

First(ly), she asked the university for money.
首先，她向大學要經費。

First(ly), let us assume the bear was a female.
首先，讓我們假設這隻熊是母的。

First(ly), let's examine the facts.
首先，讓我們檢視真相。

123 Second(ly), 其次，

在列舉多項論點時，第二個被提出來的論點可使用此句型。在一個段落一個主題的短篇文章中，此句型通常被用在第二段的開頭。

Second(ly), she set up her laboratory.
其次，她建立了自己的實驗室。

Second(ly), we will devise a thesis statement.
其次，我們要想出主題論述。

Second(ly), we should ask the zoo how the animal died.
其次，我們應該問問動物園說那隻動物是怎麼死的。

124 **In the second place,** 其次，

和 Second(ly) 相同，主要是提示即將進入第二個論點，或提及第二個要討論的項目時。

In the second place, if the army does not retreat, it will be destroyed.
其次，如果軍隊不撤退，將會被摧毀。

In the second place, Picasso was inspired by African dance.
其次，畢卡索是從非洲舞蹈中得到靈感的。

In the second place, maps are rarely accurate.
其次，地圖很少是準確的。

125 **Third(ly),** 第三，

在列舉多項論點時，第三個被提出來的論點可使用此句型。在一個段落一個主題的短篇文章中，此句型通常被用在第三段的開頭。

Third(ly), let us review the literature.
第三，讓我們來看看這篇文學作品。

Third(ly), we must disprove the argument.
第三，我們必須反證這個論點。

Third(ly), we will discuss the application of our findings.
第三，我們要針對我們發現結果的應用來做討論。

126 **Lastly,** 最後，

在列舉多項論點時，最後一個被提出來的論點可搭配此句型來使用。在短篇文章中，此句型通常被用在最後的段落中。

Lastly, Maple Street is wide enough to allow parking.
最後，楓樹街夠寬，能夠停車。

Lastly, the student did not follow instructions.
最後，學生並沒有依照指示。

Lastly, fruit contains vitamins.
最後，水果含有維他命。

127 Finally, 終於，／最後，

在寫短文時，此句型可用在本文最後一段的開始部分，下結論時也常用此句型。

Finally, we will offer suggestions for improvement.
最後，我們會針對改進部分提出建議。

Finally, we will present our argument.
最後，我們會提出我們的論點。

Finally, the man was taken to jail.
最後，這名男子被送進監獄。

128 And to conclude, 然後結論是，

此句型常用在文章最後一段的開頭。

And to conclude, I will make several recommendations.
然後結論是，我會提出幾個建議。

And to conclude, we will list our reseach methods.
然後結論是，我們要列舉研究方法。

And to conclude, we must recognize the difference between knowledge and information.
然後結論是，我們必須認清知識和資訊的差異。

129 Last, 最後，

此句型大多用於文章最後一段的引言部分或結論部分，提示文章進入收尾階段。

Last, I will list the books I read for this paper.
最後，我會列舉針對這份報告所讀過的書。

Last, eating vegetables gives you more energy.
最近，吃蔬菜會給各位更多能量。

Last, he is an excellent teacher.
最近，他是一位優秀的老師。

130 Eventually, 終究，/最後，

此句型可用來描述最後發生的事，或是提及事情的結果。

Eventually, she had the baby.
最後，她有了孩子。

Eventually, he opened his own bakery.
最後，他開了自己的麵包店。

Eventually, the university recognized the importance of their work.
最後，大學認可了他們研究的重要性。

131 Next, 接下來，

按照順序有條不紊地說明或指示，常用此句型。

Next, we will show you how to write a Chinese character.
接下來，我們將會向你示範如何寫漢字。

Next, we will prove that the formula is correct.
接下來，我們將會證明這個公式是正確的。

Next, the professor discussed Moby Dick.
接下來，教授將會討論《白鯨記》。

132 Then, 然後，

跟 Next 的使用時機相同。

Then, I will show you how to write an English sentence.
然後，我會向你示範如何寫英文句子。

Then, we will treat the subject of memory.
然後，我們會探討與記憶有關的主題。

Then, I will describe my plans for the future.
然後，我會描述一下我的未來計畫。

133 Now, here is the next step: 接著，下個步驟是：

想說明料理的步驟或下指令時，可使用此句型。

Now, here is the next step: place the potatoes in the oven.
接著，下個步驟是：將馬鈴薯放進烤箱。

Now, here is the next step: grade your students' papers.
接著，下個步驟是：為你的學生報告打成績。

Now, here is the next step: remove the tire from the car.
接著，下個步驟是：將輪胎從車子卸下。

045　敘述難以相信的事實

134　It is difficult to believe that ... 很難相信⋯

想描述一般很難讓人相信的事實時，可使用此句型。

It is difficult to believe that someday we might find life on another planet.
很難相信有一天我們可能會在另一個星球上找到生命。

It is difficult to believe that some people don't believe in the reality of global warming.
很難相信有些人不相信全球暖化的事實。

It is difficult to believe that there are animal species that we have not yet discovered.
很難相信仍有一些我們尚未發現的動物種類。

046　提出其他建議或對策

135　Another ... 其他⋯／另一個⋯

another 當作限定詞使用時，除了「另一個」之外，也有「其他」之意。在列舉多項內容時，除了使用 first、second、third 等序數之外，也可利用 one、another、the other 這類詞彙來表達。Another 後面接名詞，如 Another reason（其他的理由）、Another option（其他的選項）等。

Another option for dinner is to have a picnic.
晚餐的另一個選擇是去野餐。

Another way to solve this is to form a committee.
其他的解決辦法是組織一個委員會。

Another possible date for the wedding is June 11th.
其他可能的結婚日期是六月十一日。

136 Or, 或者，

可用在提出建議之後，再提供其他選擇時的句型。命令句中的 or 則有「不然，否則」之意。

Or, if the weather is good, we can have a picnic.
或者，如果天氣不錯，我們可以去野餐。

Or, alternatively, smoking could be completely banned.
或者，選擇完全禁菸。

Or, if there aren't enough resources, we can try solar power.
或者，如果沒有充份的資源，我們可以試試看太陽能。

137 Instead, 取而代之的是，／反之，

此句型主要用在提出替代方案時。雖然前面已提出對策，但該對策無法充分解決問題，便提出其他方案時，可使用此句型。

Instead, we should focus on treating the cause of the problem, not the symptoms.
反之，我們應該把焦點放在處理造成問題的原因，而非問題的表相。

Instead, many people prefer public transportation.
反之，許多人比較喜歡大眾交通工具。

Instead, some students choose to study abroad.
反之，有些學生選擇出國留學。

138 Another way of viewing this is as ...
用其他角度看這就像是…

想強調「抱持其他立場的人在看同一件事時，其理解的觀察角度也會不一樣」，這時可使用此句型來描述。

Another way of viewing this is as a complicated puzzle.
用其他角度看這就像是一個複雜的謎題。

Another way of viewing this is as a movie.
用其他角度看這就像是一部電影。

Another way of viewing this is as a child's game.
用其他角度看這就像是個孩子的遊戲。

139 **Alternatively,** 或者是，／兩者中擇一的，

想提出其他解決問題的方法，或其他看問題的角度時，可使用此句型。

Alternatively, mothers can carry their babies on their backs.
或者是，媽媽們可以把嬰兒揹在背後。

Alternatively, children can walk to school.
或者是，孩子們可以走路去上學。

Alternatively, we could start our own business.
或者是，我們可以展開自己的事業。

140 **One alternative is ...** 其中一個選擇是…

想從多個解決辦法中擇一提出來討論時，可使用此句型。此時，最先提出來的方案可搭配 one alternative 來使用，之後提出來的方案可搭配 another alternative。

One alternative is adoption.
其中一個選擇是領養。

One alternative is driving under the speed limit.
其中一個選擇是限速內行駛。

One alternative is solar power.
其中一個選擇是太陽能。

047 / 整合出結論

141 **Taken as a whole,** 整體而言，

是用來做整體判斷的句型。在透過比較、對照等方式來探討目標對象之後，接著再用此句型來進行整體的總結。

Taken as a whole, the school system is in trouble.
整體而言，學校體制是有問題的。

Taken as a whole, it seems likely that the industry will fail.
整體而言，這個產業看起來似乎會失敗。

Taken as a whole, the game is well designed.
整體而言，這個遊戲設計得很好。

048 提示自己的組織架構

142 The first part of the analysis will examine...
第一部分的分析將探討⋯

在寫分析式文章時，在開始要分析內容前可使用此句型，來向讀者做提示。在社會學或政策等相關的報告中也很常使用此句型。

The first part of the analysis will examine pregnancy.
第一部分的分析將會探討懷孕。

The first part of the analysis will examine radio.
第一部分的分析將會探討收音機。

The first part of the analysis will examine television.
第一部分的分析將會探討電視。

143 The second part of this analysis will consider ...
第二部分的分析將探討⋯

在寫分析式文章時，在進入第二部分的分析前，可使用此句型來向讀者做提示。

The second part of this analysis will consider the publishing industry.
第二部分的分析將探討出版業。

The second part of this analysis will consider Greek religion.
第二部分的分析將探討希臘的宗教。

The second part of this analysis will consider gambling.
第二部分的分析將探討賭博。

144 **The final level of the analysis consists of ...**
最後階段的分析包括…

同上一個句型，在進入最後一部分的分析前，可使用此句型來向讀者做提示。

The final level of the analysis consists of disproving the opposing argument.
最後階段的分析包括推翻反對意見。

The final level of the analysis consists of proving my thesis.
最後階段的分析包括驗證我的論點。

The final level of the analysis consists of refuting his data.
最後階段的分析包括推翻他所提出的資料。

049 / 轉換話題

145 **But when ...,** 但是當…時，

想將先前提到的論點，加上其他條件，並轉換成另一種情況時，可用此句型。but 是此類句型最常用的轉折連接詞。

But when we consider the victims, the issue becomes complex.
但是當我們考慮受害者時，這個問題就會變得複雜。

But when we examined our data, we realized we'd made a mistake.
但是當我們檢視資料時，我們發現我們犯錯了。

But when the car was tested, it fell apart.
但是當車子接受測試時，它解體了。

146 **Building off this idea,** 基於這個觀念，

想討論新的話題、延伸出新話題，或想讓話題流暢地繼續進行時，可使用這個句型。

Building off this idea, let's continue.
基於這個觀念，我們繼續。

Building off this idea, we can establish a working theory.
基於這個觀念，我們可以建立一個運作原理。

Building off this idea, we can go on to say that the nation was founded on religious ethics.
基於這個觀念，我們可以說這個國家是根據宗教倫理而建國的。

147 Meanwhile, 同時，

談了某個話題後，又再提及另一個話題時，可以使用此句型。

Meanwhile, the smoker's lungs have turned black.
同時，吸菸者的肺已經變成黑色了。

Meanwhile, the ship was sinking.
同時，這艘船在下沉。

Meanwhile, the university hired a new professor.
同時，這所大學聘請了一位新教授。

050 說明重要論點

148 Equally important is ...
同樣重要的是…／…也是同等的重要

要強調先前提到的某個論點也很重要時，可使用此句型。有時也會搭配逗號（,），將 Equally important 作為副詞使用。

Equally important is the fact that Henry was married.
亨利已經結婚的事實也一樣重要。

Equally important, the company fired its manager.
同樣重要的是，公司解雇了經理。

Equally important is her devotion to science.
她對科學的奉獻也是同等的重要。

149 It must also be noted that ... 也必須注意的是…

想針對重要的資訊多做說明或提醒時，可使用此句型。note 作為動詞時表示「注意、留心」。

It must also be noted that eyeglasses are expensive.
也必須注意的是，眼鏡很貴。

It must also be noted that Henry is an orphan.
也必須注意的是，亨利是一個孤兒。

It must also be noted that July is a popular month for tourism.
也必須注意的是，七月是旅遊旺季。

150 It must also be remembered that ... 也必須謹記的是⋯

想針對重要的資訊多做說明或提醒時，可使用此句型。

It must also be remembered that soda contains a lot of sugar.
也必須謹記的是，碳酸飲料含有許多糖分。

It must also be remembered that the southern U.S. has a warm climate.
也必須謹記的是，美國南部氣候溫暖。

It must also be remembered that many business are run by women.
也必須謹記的是，許多企業是由女性經營。

051 / 陳述有明確的目標

151 With this purpose in mind, 心中謹記著這個目標，

根據情況不同，此句型也可能解釋為「基於這個目的」。對於所描述的對象，其行為是有明確的目的或目標時，可使用此句型。

With this purpose in mind, Jenny moved to Boston.
珍妮心中謹記著這個目標，搬到了波士頓。

With this purpose in mind, Doris became a nurse.
朵麗絲心中謹記著這個目標，成為了一名護士。

With this purpose in mind, George Orwell wrote 1984.
喬治・歐威爾心中謹記著這個目標，寫了《1984》。

152 **Afterward,** 之後,

撰寫記述文或以敘述的方式談話時,常會用到此句型。

Afterward, the sailor returned to his ship.
之後,這名水手回到了他的船。

Afterward, the soldiers waved the flag.
之後,軍人們揮舞旗幟。

Afterward, the woman took a bath.
之後,這名女子洗了個澡。

153 **And then...** 然後…

撰寫記述文、產品使用說明,或要依序說明時,常會用到此句型。

And then, I changed my mind.
然後,我改變了心意。

And then, the waiter brought the food.
然後,服務生送來了食物。

And then, there's the issue of social class.
然後,有社會階層的議題。

154 **Before ...** 在…之前,

想在進行中的報告或文章中補充其他事實時,可使用此句型。

Before that, Ms. Todd was a schoolteacher.
在此之前,陶德小姐曾是位學校老師。

Before I continue, I'd like to add that my native language is German.
在我繼續之前,我想補充說明我的母語是德文。

Before we discuss Dr. Curie, we should mention her husband, Pierre.
在我們討論居禮夫人之前,我們應該談談她的丈夫,皮埃爾。

053 在本文中段做結論

155 **The upshot is that...** 結果是…

想在本文中提出某件事的結論時，可使用此句型。

The upshot is that the city will gain a beautiful bridge.
結果是這座城市將增加一座美麗的橋樑。

The upshot is that the war will end.
結果是戰爭即將結束。

The upshot is that Chicago will profit from increased tourism.
結果是芝加哥會因為增加的觀光客人數而從中獲益。

054 提及關於過去的事或最新消息

156 **Lately,** 最近，

late 表示「遲」，但 lately 是「最近、近來」之意。此外，還有一點要注意的是，使用這個句型時，後面接續的句子時態要用現在完成式、或現在完成進行式。

Lately, there has been an increase in the number of people getting married.
最近結婚的人數增加了。

Lately, the company has been trying to save money.
最近公司試著省錢。

Lately, there have been a lot of tornadoes.
最近有多起龍捲風。

055 表達目的

157 In an effort to ..., 為了（試著）⋯，

此句型是用來陳述某件事進行的目的性或動機。

In an effort to explain, I will begin with an illustration.
為了說明，我將從一張圖表開始。

In an effort to move forward, the researchers chose new participants.
為了向前推進，研究人員選擇了新的參與者。

In an effort to make myself clear, let me begin with a simple example.
為了說得更清楚，讓我從一個簡單的例子開始。

056 提到不遠的未來

158 Shortly ... 不久後⋯

short 表示「短的」，但副詞形的 shortly 卻表示「不久、馬上」之意。想描述在時間或順序上離現在不遠的情況，可使用此句型。

Shortly we will discover the truth.
不久後，我們將會發現真相。

Shortly Mr. King will receive the award.
不久後，金先生會得到這個獎項。

Shortly we will reveal our discovery.
不久後，我們將會揭示我們的發現。

159 Soon ... 很快地⋯

想提及在時間或順序上離現在很近，或馬上要發生的事時，可用此句型。

Soon the king will die.
國王很快就會過世的。

Soon there will be world peace.
很快就會世界和平。

Soon Hollywood will stop making stupid movies.
好萊塢很快就會停止製作這些愚蠢的電影。

057 / 針對問題做反思

160 **What I didn't know was that ...** 我所不知道的是…

要喚起對問題的覺醒，或對文章內容有所反思時，可用此句型。

What I didn't know was that my theory had already been proposed.
我所不知道的是，我的理論已經被提案出去了。

What I didn't know was that allergies can be developed later in life.
我所不知道的是，過敏可能會是後天形成的。

What I didn't know was that the Catholic Church was responsible for many deaths during the Spanish Inquisition.
我所不知道的是，天主教會應該要為許多在異端裁判所期間犧牲了的生命負責。

058 / 述說理由

161 **Since ...,** 既然（因為）…，

一般對 since 這個詞彙的概念都是「自從」之意，但事實上不管在口說或書寫方面，since 更常被用來表示「因為…」，即 because 之意。另外，接在 since 之後的結構為「主詞＋動詞」形態。

Since the bird flew away, we can't study it.
因為鳥飛走了，所以我們無法做研究。

Since we have ten cats, we have no mice.
因為我們有十隻貓，所以我們這裡不會有老鼠。

Since there was a full moon that night, she didn't need a flashlight.
因為那天晚上是滿月，所以她不需要手電筒。

162 **Owing to ...** 由於…

owning to... 為表示「因為／由於…」的句型。

Owing to my lack of information, I can't make an informed decision.
由於缺乏資訊，我無法做出明智的決定。

Owing to instinct, many animals migrate at the same time each year.
出自於本能，每年有許多動物在同一時間遷移。

Owing to a lack of funding, the program failed.
由於缺乏資金，該計畫失敗了。

163 Due to ..., 由於…的關係，

語意與之前提過的句型「owing to...、because of...、because＋主詞＋動詞」相同。

Due to this vaccine, polio is no longer a serious threat.
由於這種疫苗的關係，小兒麻痺症不再是一個嚴重的威脅。

Due to its lack of progress, the project was shut down.
由於缺乏進展的關係，該專案被停止。

Due to shorter days, leaves change color in the fall.
由於白天時間變短的關係，葉子在秋天會變色。

059 提及顛覆大眾觀念的論點

164 It may seem odd that ..., but...
也許會覺得奇怪的是…，但卻…

odd 是「奇怪的」的意思。在表示讓步的副詞子句，我們常會用「though」或「although」，但此句型也是表示相同語意的句型。

It may seem odd that women spend so much money on clothing, **but** it makes them happy.
也許會覺得奇怪的是，女性花這麼多錢在服飾上，但這卻讓她們感到快樂。

It may seem odd that he never shaves, **but** his religion requires it.
也許會覺得奇怪的是，他從不刮鬍子，但他信仰的宗教卻要求他要做（要刮鬍子）。

It may seem odd that Americans smile all the time, **but** they are just being polite.
也許會覺得奇怪的是，美國人總是面帶微笑，但他們只是想要表現禮貌。

060 說明種類或特徵

165 There are many different kinds of ...

…有很多不同的種類

是在文章中要做分類、分析時常見的句型。

There are many different kinds of employment.
有很多種職業。

There are many different kinds of solutions.
有很多種解決方法。

There are many different kinds of arguments.
有很多種論點。

166 Assuredly, there are certain ... 當然，有特定…

當要列出特定幾個能支持論點的事實、條件或特徵等時，可使用這類句型。用此句型有時可用來彰顯自己的立場。

Assuredly, there are certain valid points.
當然，有特定幾個有效的觀點。

Assuredly, there are certain rules we must follow.
當然，有特定幾個我們必須遵循的規則。

Assuredly, there are certain procedures scientists must perform.
當然，有特定幾個幾位科學家必須執行的程序。

061 喚起讀者的好奇心

167 Can it be that ... ? 會…嗎？

透過向讀者提問問題來喚起讀者的好奇心時，可使用此句型。

Can it be that some birds live to be over one hundred years old?
有些鳥會活超過一百年嗎？

Can it be that it's only been forty years since the U.S. moon landing?
自美國登陸月球至今真的只有四十年嗎？

Can it be that there are more cell phones in China than anywhere else?

比起其他地方，在中國會有更多人使用手機嗎？

062 / 提及類似的狀況或例子來做比較

168 Similarly, 同樣地，

和相似的事物做比較，或提出類似的案例時，可使用此句型。

Similarly, I support gay marriage.

同樣地，我支持同性婚姻。

Similarly, the Boyd building is made of brick.

同樣地，波依德大樓是用磚塊砌成的。

Similarly, restaurants require that customers wear shoes and shirts.

同樣地，餐廳都會要求顧客穿皮鞋和襯衫。

169 Correspondingly, 相同地，

與上一個句型 Similarly（同樣地）的使用時機相同。其動詞形態 correspond 是表示「符合、一致」。

Correspondingly, the length should decrease.

相同地，長度應該要縮短。

Correspondingly, the Jewish community was exciting.

相同地，猶太人的社會很有趣。

Correspondingly, the room was completely dark.

相同地，這個房間是完全暗的。

170 In the same way, 同樣地，

要做較複雜的說明時，可先舉出相似但較為簡單的例子，舉完簡單的例子之後，接著再用此句型說明要談論的主題。

In the same way, the government failed to stop the war.

同樣地，政府未能阻止戰爭。

In the same way, Shakespeare borrowed from other writers.

同樣地，莎士比亞從其他作家那借用了內容。

In the same way, cities are a human invention.
同樣地，城市是人類的發明。

171 Like ..., 就像…，

此句型是用來提到類似的案例時，作為介系詞用，表示「就像…」之意。

Like his wife, Bob disliked seafood.
就像他的妻子，鮑伯不喜歡海鮮。

Like most nurses, she worked too much.
就像大部分的護士，她工作過度。

Like all the international travelers, we were jet-lagged.
就像所有國際旅行者，我們都有時差。

172 Analogous to ..., 就跟…類似，／就相當於…，

analogous 是表示「類似的、相似的」的形容詞。想用相似的案例來說明時，可使用此句型，其用法與 similarly 相同。

Analogous to the seeds in a garden, knowledge must be planted and cultivated over time.
就相當於花園裡的種子，知識必須隨著時間進行來種植與培育。

Analogous to a gear in a machine, each employee is an integral part of a factory's assembly line.
就相當於機器中的齒輪，每個員工都是工廠裝配線上不可或缺的一部分。

Analogous to a computer, the human brain is capable of completing multiple processes simultaneously.
就相當於電腦，人腦可以同時完成多個程序。

063 做選擇

173 Rather than ..., 不是…，而是…

通常會用此句型來表達從數個對策中選出一個對策，屬於用途很廣的句型。

Rather than buy the apartment, Vera rented it.
維拉沒有買房子，而是租房子。

Rather than fix the problem, the government ignored it.
政府沒有解決問題，而是忽視它。

Rather than cut down trees, I propose we plant them.
我建議種植樹木，不是砍樹。

064 / 對照與比較

174 **By contrast,** 相較之下，

要進行兩相對照、比較時，可使用此句型。

By contrast, the population of the U.S. grew three percent.
相較之下，美國的人口增加了百分之三。

By contrast, Americans are getting shorter.
相較之下，美國人逐漸變矮。

By contrast, dogs cannot watch television.
相較之下，狗不會看電視。

175 **In contrast,** 相反地，

此句型的語意與 on the contrary 相同，都是用來指出相異兩點的句型。

In contrast, anthropologists study human society and culture.
相反地，人類學家則研究人類社會和文化。

In contrast, Martin Luther King, Jr. was a pacifist.
相反地，小馬丁・路德・金恩則是和平主義者。

In contrast, vegetarians do not eat meat.
相反地，素食者不吃肉。

176 **On the contrary,** 反而，

與 In contrast 相同，都是用來指出相異兩點的句型。

On the contrary, Sigmund Freud was widely-known in his own time.
相反地，佛洛伊德在他那個時代是眾所周知的人。

On the contrary, a glass of red wine every now and then is healthy.
相反地，偶爾喝一杯紅酒很健康。

On the contrary, many people are allergic to pollen.
相反地，許多人對花粉過敏。

177 Conversely, 相反地，／反過來，

這是在寫作時常會用到的重要句型。

Conversely, China is 5,000 years old.
相反地，中國已經有五千年了。

Conversely, how did Egypt view its past?
相反地，埃及是如何看待它的過去呢？

Conversely, I realized that being good at something is difficult.
相反地，我領悟到任何事情都要做到完美是很困難。

178 In comparison, 相較之下，

主要也是用來比較兩個對象時的句型，可用來比較相似性或相異性。

In comparison, the U.S. is huge.
相較之下，美國很大。

In comparison, the drug is useless.
相較之下，這個藥沒有用。

In comparison, domestic cars are cheaper.
相較之下，國產車比較便宜。

179 This is consistent with ... 這與…一致

想在可比較的對象之間做相互比較時，可使用此句型。

This is consistent with current theories.
這與當前的理論一致。

This is consistent with my argument.
這與我的論點一致。

This is consistent with expert opinion.
這與專家意見一致。

065 陳述意見分歧所帶來的結果

180 It is precisely these differences of opinion that ...
正是因為這些意見分歧…

提到因意見分歧而造成某結果時，可使用此句型。

It is precisely these differences of opinion that bring us together.
正是這些意見分歧使我們團結在一起。

It is precisely these differences of opinion that make this discussion so interesting.
正是這些意見分歧使這個討論變得如此有趣。

It is precisely these differences of opinion that have caused so much trouble over the past few years.
正是這些意見分歧在過去幾年中造成了這麼多麻煩。

066 點出矛盾論述

181 This contradicts the statement that ...
這與…的說法是矛盾的

想指出某個論點與現實或社會現象產生矛盾時，可使用此句型。

This contradicts the statement that history repeats itself.
這與歷史會重演的說法是矛盾的。

This contradicts the statement that patience is a virtue.
這與忍耐是美德的說法是矛盾的。

This contradicts the statement that truth is stronger than fiction.
這與事實比虛假強大的說法是矛盾的。

182 There exists a contradiction between... and
…和…間存在矛盾

想指出理論與現實不符，或是同一位學者的理論中有互相矛盾的地方時，都可使用此句型。

There exists a contradiction between what politicians say **and** what politicians do.
政客所說和所做間存在矛盾。

There exists a contradiction between the theory of evolution **and** the theory of divine creation.
進化論與神聖創造論間存在矛盾。

There exists a contradiction between the idea that most people believe marriage should be life-long **and** recent divorce rates.
在大多數人認為婚姻是終生大事的這個觀念和最近的離婚率之間存在矛盾。

067 / 強烈闡明一段論述

183 With this statement, 用這段話（聲明），

想對讀者強烈闡明一句話，或引用某格言時，可使用此句型。

With this statement, I must note that the tests were not conclusive.
我必須用這段話來指出測試不是結論。

With this statement, I will conclude my argument.
我將用這段話來總結我的論點。

With this statement, President Nixon resigned.
尼克森總統透過這段聲明辭職了。

068 / 陳述其他可能性

184 Another possibility is ... 另一個可能性是…

在分析某情況時，先點出造成此狀況最有可能的原因，再利用此句型提出另一種可能的原因。

Another possibility is that your computer has a virus.
另一個可能性是你的電腦有病毒。

Another possibility is that high prices are to blame.
另一個可能性是要歸咎於價格太高。

Another possibility is the construction of windmills.
另一個可能性是風車的建造。

185 There are other possible causes ...
還有其他可能的原因…

此句型大多用來揭開問題或現象的其他可能原因。

There are other possible causes for this phenomenon.
還有其他可能的原因，造成這個現象。

There are other possible causes of this accident.
還有其他可能導致此事故的原因。

There are other possible causes of death.
還有其他可能的死亡原因。

---

069 / 列舉不同的觀點

186 In view of this, 有鑒於此，

語意與 from this point of view 相同，此句型是用在根據某社會現象來做多種觀點的分析時。除此之外，此句型也可用來整理正反兩面的論點陳述。

In view of this, we are not in favor of the policy.
有鑑於此，我們不贊成這個政策。

In view of this, I propose the following.
有鑑於此，我提出下列建議。

In view of this, Michael took the job.
有鑑於此，麥可接受這份工作。

187 From that standpoint, 從這個觀點來看，

standpoint 表示「觀點、角度」之意，語意與 from that point of view 相同。

From that standpoint, Darwin's theory cannot be true.
從這個角度來看，達爾文的理論不會是對的。

From that standpoint, the failure of the test was a major setback.
從這個角度來看，這次測試失敗是很大的挫折。

From that standpoint, archeological excavations merely slow down construction projects.
從這個角度來看，考古發掘只會減慢建設工程的速度。

188 Considered from another perspective,

從另一個觀點思考的話，

此句型主要用在轉換觀點、換角度思考時，也可用來提出新的觀點。

Considered from another perspective, the problem is not intimidating.
從另一個觀點思考，這個問題並不那麼令人生畏。

Considered from another perspective, this investigation is unnecessary.
從另一個觀點思考，這個調查是不必要的。

Considered from another perspective, the argument takes a new form.
從另一個觀點思考，此論點採用一種新形式。

070 / 回到原主題

189 Turning now to the question of ..., 現在回到…的問題，

在寫文章或報告的過程中，為了要讓論點更加清楚明確，有時即使是與主題無直接關聯性的內容，也會提出來補充說明。在補充說明完之後，想再回到原本探討的主題時，可用此句型讓前後兩部分的討論很自然地銜接起來。

Turning now to the question of reform, we hope to suggest some good ideas.
現在回到改革問題，我們希望提出一些好的想法。

Turning now to the question of identity, I think that the crime was committed by Larry.
現在回到身分問題，我認為犯罪是拉里犯下的。

Turning now to the question of race, let me say that Rogers has missed the point.
現在回到種族問題，我想要說羅傑斯沒有抓到重點。

190 **With this in mind,** 有鑒於此，／請記住，

在某段討論結束後，並準備要進行到下一個論點之前，可利用此句型來重申目前此論點的重要性。

With this in mind, we can begin our investigation.
有鑒於此，我們可以開始著手偵查。

With this in mind, I will list the names of the authors.
有鑒於此，我將會列出作者們的姓名。

With this in mind, we recommend that the building be fixed.
有鑒於此，我們建議整修這棟建築物。

191 **Bearing this in mind,** 銘記這點，／請記住，／請留意，

想再次強調先前討論過的內容，接著再進入到下一個主題時，可使用此句型。

Bearing this in mind, please read the instructions carefully.
記住，請務必仔細閱讀說明。

Bearing this in mind, the study was corrupted from the start.
請留意，這項研究從一開始就遭到了篡改。

Bearing this in mind, both sides of the argument make sense.
請留意，此論點的正反兩方都有道理。

192 **Bearing in mind the previous points,**
將前面幾點銘記在心，

為了加深主題的印象，或是提醒讀者先記住前面討論過的論點，以進行下個階段的討論，可使用此句型。

Bearing in mind the previous points, let us continue.
將前面幾點銘記在心，好讓我們繼續討論下去。

Bearing in mind the previous points, let us press onwards.
將前面幾點銘記在心，好讓我們繼續進行下去。

Bearing in mind the previous points, we will attempt to solve the problem.

將前面幾點銘記在心，好讓我們嘗試解決此問題。

072 / 舉例

193 For example, 例如，／舉例來說，

此句型的語意與 for instance 等相同，是用來舉例的典型句型。

For example, I exercise five days a week.
例如，我一個禮拜運動五天。

For example, he wrote an English textbook.
例如，他寫了一本英文教科書。

For example, the manager of the company makes a million dollars a year.
例如，這間公司的經理每年賺一百萬美金。

194 For instance, 例如，／舉例來說，

語意與 for example 等相同，也是用來舉例說明時的句型。

For instance, the library is closed.
舉例來說，圖書館關閉了。

For instance, red wine can be good for you.
舉例來說，紅酒對你可能有益。

For instance, she does not obey traffic lights.
舉例來說，她沒有遵守交通號誌。

195 An example of this is...
這類（狀況的）例子是…，／…就是一個例子

也是用來舉例的句型之一，通常在使用此句型之前，前面都已先提過類似的案例了。

An example of this is the attendance policy.
出勤政策就是一個例子。

An example of this is Chinese New Year.
農曆新年就是一個例子。

163

An example of this is pizza.
披薩就是一個例子。

196 including... 包括…／包含…

想在主題討論之後舉出具體的例子時，可使用此句型。

I have taken many classes, **including** Japanese literature.
我選了許多課，包含日本文學。

They visited many countries, **including** South Korea.
他們造訪過許多國家，包含南韓。

He had three wives, **including** Marilyn Monroe.
他有過三任老婆，包含瑪麗蓮·夢露。

197 such as... 像是…

想在提出論點之前，先舉出具體的例子時，可使用此句型。

Loud noises, **such as** bells and alarms, hurt my ears.
像是鈴聲和鬧鐘之類大聲的噪音，會傷害我的耳朵。

Many foods, **such as** pizza and bacon, contain a lot of salt.
許多像是比薩和培根的食物，都含有許多鹽份。

Several computer games, **such as** Frogger, were invented in the 1980s.
幾款像是《青蛙過河》的電腦遊戲，都是在 1980 年代發明的。

073 / 用「特別是」強調特定事物

198 particularly... 特別是…／尤其…

語意與 in particular 相同，主要是想具體強調某內容時，可使用此句型。

Particularly, the park on 4th St. is poor.
特別是四號街的那座公園尤其簡陋。

Particularly, Harlem is a dangerous place to drive.
特別是在哈林區開車尤其危險。

Russia will be particularly hurt by global warming.
俄羅斯尤其會受到地球暖化的傷害。

199 **In particular,** 特別的是

想具體強調某部分內容時，可使用此句型。

In particular, students may not use calculators or cell phones during the exam.
特別的是，學生不可以在考試期間使用計算機或手機。

In particular, the company recommends that employees take longer lunch breaks.
特別的是，公司建議員工要有更長的中午休息時間。

In particular, they are very good at organizing events.
特別的是，他們很擅於辦活動。

200 **notably** 特別地／明顯地

副詞形的 notably，表示「顯著地、明顯地」的意思。

The relationship between the U.S. and China has **notably** improved.
美國和中國的關係有顯著改善。

Notably in the sciences, professors teach too much.
特別是在科學領域，教授們教導得太多了。

I am going to list five **notably** terrible video games.
我要列出五個特別糟糕的電玩遊戲。

201 **especially** 特別／尤其是

想具體舉出較為特殊的例子時，可使用此句型。

My parents watch a lot of TV, **especially** in the evenings.
我的父母很常看電視，尤其是在晚上時。

Brian is **especially** good at gardening.
布萊恩特別擅長於園藝。

Many workers die in accidents, **especially** in factories.
許多工人死於意外，特別是在工廠。

202 **Specifically,** 具體來說，／明確地說，

想特別強調或具體提及某內容時，可用此句型，能有效轉換氣氛。

Specifically, you should look for small, bright red strawberries.
明確地說，你應該要找體型小、顏色亮紅的草莓。

Specifically, I'm talking about workplace safety.
明確地說，我在討論的是職場環境安全。

Specifically, the loudest bird is the macaw.
明確地說，最吵鬧的鳥是金剛鸚鵡。

203 **More specifically,** 更具體地說，

一般想要更進一步做具體的討論時，可用此句型。另外，此句型用到 more，藉此暗示讀者接下來將進行更深一層的討論。

More specifically, students should take 19 credit hours.
更具體地說，學生應該要選十九個學分。

More specifically, I recommend that the city pay for a new bus.
更具體地說，我建議城市應支付新公車的費用。

More specifically, we need to drink more water and exercise more.
更具體地說，我們需要多喝水、多運動。

074 / 描述第一印象

204 **At first glance, it seemed ...** 乍看之下，似乎⋯

此句型可用來提及對某事物的第一印象。

At first glance, it seemed incomprehensible.
乍看之下，這似乎是無法理解的。

At first glance, it seemed like a simple problem.
乍看之下，這似乎是一個簡單的問題。

At first glance, it seemed as though the answer might never be found.
乍看之下，似乎永遠找不到答案。

075 / 描述大部分的情況

205 chiefly 主要

想描述並非百分之百確定，但大部分都是如此的情況時，可將此句型放在該情況句的前面或中間。

The paintings came **chiefly** from Belgium.
這些畫主要是來自比利時。

Bamboo is **chiefly** grown in China.
竹子主要生長在中國。

Chiefly I am concerned with nursing care.
我所關注的主要是看護。

206 mainly 大部分／主要

語意與 chiefly 相同。想描述大部分的情況時，可用此句型。

Mainly the classical radio station plays Mozart.
這台古典樂廣播電台主要都是播放莫札特的曲子。

Mainly the book is about trees of Illinois.
這本書主要是在講伊利諾州的樹木。

Mainly slaves were Christian.
大部分的奴隸都是基督徒。

207 mostly 大部分

語意與 chiefly、mainly 相同。想描述大部分的情況時，一樣也可用此句型。

Snakes are **mostly** harmless.
大部分的蛇都是無害的。

Christmas Day in Iowa, 1848, was **mostly** sunny.
1848 年愛荷華州的聖誕節大多都是有太陽的天氣。

The lawyer's statement is **mostly** true.
這位律師大部分的陳述都是正確的。

076 強調造成某結果的原因

208 **So that is why ...** 那正是為什麼⋯

此句型具有強調造成某結果的原因之效果。前面提及原因,接著用此句型接續該原因所造成的結果。

So that is why we should be less reliant on automobiles.
這正是為什麼我們應該減少對汽車依賴的原因。

So that is why Latin is a dead language.
這正是為什麼拉丁文是不復存在的語言。

So that is why I want to be a botanist.
這正是為什麼我想成為植物學家。

077 限定特定情況做說明

209 **In this situation,** 這種情況下,

此句型可用來限定某特別情況,並就此情況做說明。

In this situation, how should you act?
在這種狀況下,你應採取什麼行動?

In this situation, use the past tense.
在這種狀況下,要用過去式。

In this situation, the baby should be taken to the doctor.
在這種狀況下,應該要帶嬰兒去看醫生。

210 **In this case,** 在這情況下,

先提出某特定狀況,接著對此多做說明或分析論點時,可用此句型。this 也可以換成 that。

In this case, the president would meet with his/her staff.
在這情況下,總統可能會與幕僚會晤。

In this case, we need to stimulate domestic spending.
在這情況下,我們需要刺激國內消費。

In this case, ask the students to leave the classroom.
在這情況下，請學生都離開教室。

Part
2

本文句型

076
強調造成某結果的原因
／
077
限定特定情況做說明
／
078
提到相關的研究
／
079
以圖解說明

078 提到相關的研究

211 There is a great deal of research ... …的研究很多

想提到有很多支持自己主張的理論或依據時，可使用此句型。

There is a great deal of research behind us.
在我們之前有很多研究。

There is a great deal of research yet to be done.
有大量的研究有待完成。

There is a great deal of research to back up this theory.
有大量研究支持這一理論。

079 以圖解說明

212 As an illustration, 如圖所示，

論文中經常需要附上圖表、表格、插畫等資料，因為相較於文字敘述說明，運用圖表資料對論文會更有助益。此時，可使用此句型來進行說明。

As an illustration, I will describe a strategy you can use to make women like you.
如圖所示，我將會描述一種各位可以使用的策略，讓女生都喜歡您。

As an illustration, let's consider the following equation.
如圖所示，我們來思考一下以下方程式。

As an illustration, he dropped a leaf on the ground.
如圖所示，他掉了一片葉子到地上。

213 **To illustrate,** 為了要說明，／為了要用圖解說明，

此句型是用在為了幫助讀者理解而以圖解來說明時，可搭配使用的表達。

To illustrate, a bird may make a nest in an oak tree but not a maple tree.
用圖解來說明這點，小鳥可能會在橡樹上築巢，而不會選擇在楓樹上。

To illustrate this, I will include a graph.
為了說明這點，我將會提供一個圖表。

To illustrate, I will tell you a story.
為了說明這點，我將會跟你說一個故事。

080 闡述最能支持主張的理論

214 **... is best described as ...** 對於…最好的形容（描述）是…

此句型大多是用來導入最能支持自己主張的理論，後面要接該理論的詳細內容。

Religion **is best described as** a set of beliefs.
對於「宗教」最好的形容是「一套信仰」。

A theory **is best described as** an educated guess.
對於「理論」最好的描述是「有根據的猜測」。

Physics **is best described as** the study of matter, energy, motion, and force.
對於「物理學」最好的描述是「物質、能量、運動和力的研究」。

081 統整歸納

215 **In short,** 簡而言之，

在本文中想稍微做個簡短的結論時，可用此句型。除此之外，想將前面冗長的說明重新整理，用一句話來重新描述時，也可使用此句型。

In short, the meal was simple and wonderful.
簡而言之，這一餐簡單而美味。

In short, the book will help you get around London.
簡而言之，這本書將幫助你遊覽倫敦。

In short, the ability of a person to learn is related to his or her age.
簡而言之，一個人的學習能力與他或她的年齡有關。

216 **The point is,** 重點是…

想用一句話簡潔地概括先前列舉的幾個論點時，可使用此句型。做簡報時更常用到此句型。

The point is, public schools should teach students a second language.
重點是，公立學校應該要教學生第二個語言。

The point is, Charles Darwin's theory of evolution is only a theory.
重點是，達爾文的進化論只是一種理論。

The point is, each person is responsible for his or her own actions.
重點是，每個人都應當對自己的行為負責。

217 **That is (to say),** 也就是說，

想用更簡單或更直接的方式來重述前面提過的內容時，可使用此句型。

That is to say, many teachers are underpaid.
也就是說，許多老師的薪水都很低。

That is to say, alcohol can be an addictive substance.
也就是說，酒精可能會是一種成癮性物質。

That is to say, the life of a soldier can be difficult and lonely.
也就是說，士兵的生活可能很艱辛且孤獨。

082 陳述到目前為止的狀態

218 **So far,** 目前為此，

so far 表示「目前為止、至今」的意思。想提及到目前為止一直持續的事件、狀態或趨勢時，可使用此句型。

So far, everything is normal.
目前為止一切都正常。

So far, there are no problems.
目前為止沒有任何問題。

So far, the patient has not died.
目前為止，那位病患沒有失去生命。

083 強調內容的真實性

219 **Of course,** 當然

談到自己確定的資訊，並強調其真實性時可以使用此句型。

Of course, modern cell phones can do many things.
當然，現代的手機可以做許多事情。

Of course, the tree died after the storm.
當然，這棵樹在暴風雨過後就死亡了。

Of course, organic fruit is the best.
當然，有機的水果是最好的。

220 **Truly,** 確實，／真的，

此句型中的 Truly 可以換成 Really 或 Indeed 等，有強調後句內容整體真實
性的效果。

Truly, we must be concerned.
我們確實必須關注。

Truly, I cannot explain it.
我確實無法解釋此事。

Truly, it is a tragedy.
這確實是一場悲劇。

221 **Really,** 真的，

really 放在句首可用來強調整句話，是語意與 indeed 相似的常用句型。

Really, the man was a spy.
這名男子過去真的是一個間諜。

Really, the painting was done by a child.

這幅畫真的是出自一名小孩之手。

Really, the doctor had given poison to his patient.
這名醫生真的給了他的病患毒藥。

084 引用至理名言

222 Consider the following quotation:

細想以下所言：／請見以下語錄：

想直接引用知名人物的格言時，可使用此句型。

Consider the following quotation: "Humanity is acquiring all the right technology for all the wrong reasons."
請見以下語錄：「人類因為錯誤而獲得正確的技術。」

Consider the following quotation: "Men have become the tools of their tools."
請見以下語錄：「人類已經成為他們工具的工具。」

Consider the following quotation: "Technology has to be invented or adopted."
請見以下語錄：「技術必須被發明或被採用。」

085 表示讓步的內容

223 Nonetheless, 儘管如此，

我們在閱讀英文文章的過程中，會發現內容中常會出現像是 Nevertheless、Nonetheless 等的詞彙，都是表示「雖然如此」的副詞。當遇到與自己的主張、意見相反的內容，但仍想先暫定結論時，可使用此句型。

Nonetheless, he asked her to marry him.
儘管如此，他還是向她求婚了。

Nonetheless, business is slowly improving.
儘管如此，生意正在逐步改善。

Nonetheless, we cannot stop trying.
儘管如此，我們不能停止嘗試。

224 Despite ..., 儘管…,

也是表示「雖然如此」「儘管」的句型之一，類似句型為「notwithstanding」「in spite of」等。請注意到，Despite 句型後面接名詞，且一般會放在句首。

Despite Jack's many years of experience, he is still not qualified for the position.
儘管傑克擁有多年經驗，但仍沒有資格擔任該職位。

Despite twenty years of searching, I have never found a four-leaf clover.
儘管我找了二十年，我從未發現過四葉草。

Despite her broken leg, she won the race.
儘管腿部骨折，她仍贏得了那場賽跑。

225 Despite that, 儘管如此,

使用時機跟 Despite 相同，不過此句型中的 that 指的是這句之前提到的內容。

Despite that, I plan to study philosophy.
儘管如此，我仍計畫念哲學。

Despite that, the story of Oedipus lives on.
儘管如此，伊底帕斯的故事仍然持續傳唱。

Despite that, industrial waste has continued to build.
儘管如此，工業廢棄物仍持續增加。

226 Notwithstanding..., 儘管…,／縱使…,

是與「In spite of」或「Despite」語意相同的句型。

Notwithstanding her beauty, she lived a life of poverty.
儘管擁有美貌，她仍過著貧窮的日子。

Notwithstanding the actor's charm, he is rarely cast in movies.
儘管擁有演員魅力，他卻很少在電影中演出。

Notwithstanding his name, the man was elected president.
儘管是他的名字，這位男子仍被選為總統。

227 Even so, 即便如此，／即使是這樣，

這裡的 so 意指先前討論過的內容，因此此句型有「即使之前討論過的內容都是事實」的意思。

Even so, many children are not vaccinated.
即便如此，許多兒童仍未接種疫苗。

Even so, the research continues.
即使是這樣，研究仍持續進行。

Even so, women have few rights in some cultures.
即使是這樣，在某些文化中女性僅有很少的權利。

228 Even though ..., 即使⋯

跟 although、though 一樣都是表示「讓步」的連接詞，後面要接完整句子。

Even though the study has been completed, a further examination of its implications is needed.
即使研究已經完成，也必須對其影響進行進一步檢查。

Even though college can be expensive, many students enroll every year.
即使大學的費用可能很高，每年仍有許多學生註冊。

Even though it is illegal, drug trafficking continues.
即使是非法的，仍持續有毒品販運。

229 For all that, 儘管如此，

此句型的使用時機與 Even so 一樣，that 意指先前所有的討論內容。

For all that, the cure is years away.
儘管如此，能治療的方法／藥物也要數年後才會問世。

For all that, additional research is needed.
儘管如此，仍需要進行更多研究。

For all that, experts were unable to reach a conclusion.
儘管如此，專家們仍無法得出結論。

230 In spite of ..., 儘管…，

語意與 despite 相同，of 是介系詞，所以後面要接名詞或動名詞。

In spite of my reluctance, I will describe my personal and professional biases.
儘管不情願，我將會說明我個人且專業的意見。

In spite of the overwhelming evidence, some people refuse to believe in the Holocaust.
儘管有壓倒性的證據，但仍有一些人拒絕相信納粹大屠殺。

In spite of dwindling funds, the project must be carried forward.
儘管資金縮減，這個企劃務必要持續進行。

231 However, 然而，

however 是副詞，可擺在句首或句中來表示「然而、不過」之意。

However, it should be noted that this is an unofficial report.
然而，應該要注意的是，這是一份非正式的報告書。

However, researchers remain optimistic that the cure isn't far away.
然而，研究學者仍對治療藥物即將問世表示樂觀。

However, it has been proven that water is an excellent conductor of electricity.
然而，水已經被證實是極佳的導電體。

232 Though ..., 雖然…

Though 表示「儘管／雖然…，但…」，是具有讓步意味的連接詞。包含 though 的句子為從屬子句，though 後面接的主句內容則是主要想表達的內容。

Though it is illegal, smuggling persists.
雖然是違法的，但走私仍然存在。

Though a bit confused, the basic idea is clear.
雖然有點混亂，但基本思路很明確。

Though rock climbing is dangerous, many people find it fun.
雖然攀岩很危險，但許多人卻覺得很有趣。

086 / 從吸引人目光的觀點來思考

233 It is tempting to characterize ... as ...

將（某性格、特色）描繪成…，是挺吸引人目光的

當一個問題可從多種角度來觀察的情況下，想從一個吸引人目光的角度來進行探討時，可使用此句型。

It is tempting to characterize Adolf Hitler **as** evil incarnate.
將阿道夫・希特勒描繪成邪惡的化身，是挺吸引人目光的。

It is tempting to characterize history **as** a set of useless facts.
將歷史描述為一連串無用的事實，是挺吸引人目光的。

It is tempting to characterize the results of this study **as** redundant and unenlightening.
將這項研究的結果描述為多餘且毫無啟發性，是挺吸引人目光的。

087 / 堅持自己的立場

234 Even if ... is true, 即使…是事實，

在文章中提及自己的觀點時，通常也會同時提到反對自己觀點的其他立場，但仍堅持自己的主張，此時可使用此句型，帶有「雖然…是事實，但（自己的觀點）」。

Even if it **is true** that he has cancer, it does not mean that he will die.
即使他罹患癌症是事實，但這也不意味著他會死。

Even if the story **is true**, we are in no danger.
即使這個報導是真的，但我們並不處於危險中。

Even if the rumor **is tru**e, I will continue to be his friend.
即使這謠言是真的，但我還是會繼續當他是朋友。

235 Although ... may have a good point,
即使⋯有很好的見解（看法），

語意跟上一個句型 Even if ... is true 類似，都用於堅持自己主張的情況，即雖然承認其他看法也很合理，但仍堅持自己與其他看法相反的意見。

Although my doctor **may have a good point** about exercise, I don't have time to jog every day.
雖然我的醫生對運動可能有很好的見解，但我沒有時間每天去慢跑。

Although the car salesman **may have a good point**, I can't afford to buy a car.
雖然那位汽車銷售員可能有很好的見解，但我買不起一輛車。

Although Professor Harris **may have a good point**, Dr. Peter's argument is stronger.
雖然哈里斯教授可能有很好的見解，但彼得教授的論點更強而有力。

236 All the same, it is possible that ... 同樣地，⋯可能⋯

All the same 在語意上帶有「雖然有考量到其他方面也一樣」的意思。一般在寫議論文時，會提到反對自己觀點的其他看法，並加以反駁，而此句型往往是用來表達「雖然有考量到對方的看法，但⋯」。

All the same, it is possible that life on other planets exists somewhere in the universe.
同樣地，宇宙的某個地方可能會有生命存在於其他行星上。

All the same, it is possible that further experiments will disprove my theory.
同樣地，進一步的實驗有可能會推翻我的理論。

All the same, it is possible that there is another explanation for the statues on Easter Island.
同樣地，復活節島上的雕像可能還有其他解釋方式。

237 Although it may be true that ..., 儘管⋯也許是事實，

雖然接受與自己主張對立的其他看法，但仍堅持自己的主張時，可使用此句型。

Although it may be true that my conclusion is only a theory, in time I will be able to prove it.
儘管我的結論可能只是理論，但我有辦法立刻證明。

178

Although it may be true that two snowflakes are alike, this cannot be proven for certain.
儘管確實可能會有兩片一樣的雪花，但這無法被證實。

Although it may be true that solar energy can be used in more ways than it is currently, it can't replace traditional forms of energy entirely.
儘管比起現在，太陽能在未來確實可以被利用在更多元的方式，但它不能完全取代傳統的能源形態。

238 While this may be true, 雖然這也許是事實，但…

是議論文中常用的句型。主要是在針對某主題，在整合正反兩方立場的看法之下提出自我主張時，會用到此句型。在這種情況下，通常會從各個不同的立場中找出折衷的共通點，來表達自己的主張。

While this may be true, researchers still don't believe that a high-fat diet is healthy.
雖然這也許是事實，但研究人員仍不相信高脂飲食對健康有益。

While this may be true for some people, it is not true for all.
雖然這對某些人來說也許是事實，但並不代表對所有人都是如此。

While this may be true, little has changed.
雖然這也許是事實，但幾乎沒有什麼改變。

088 提到有趣的內容

239 It is interesting, though, that ... 然而，有趣的是…

想從一連串的事實中指出有趣的部分時，可使用此句型。

It is interesting, though, that Van Gogh didn't sell many of his paintings while he was alive.
然而，有趣的是梵谷在生前並沒有賣掉自己很多的畫作。

It is interesting, though, that bamboo is one of the fastest growing plants.
然而，有趣的是竹子是生長最快的植物之一。

It is interesting, though, that this theory has not been discredited.
然而，有趣的是這個理論並未被懷疑過。

089 明確指出事實

240 It is clear that ... 顯然…／很明顯地，

想陳述觀察到的事實時可使用此句型。句型中的 clear 也可替換成 obvious 或 evident，語意不變。

It is clear that she knows what she is talking about.
很明顯地，她知道自己在說什麼。

It is clear that he has studied the problem for many years.
他顯然已經研究這個問題很多年了。

It is clear that farming has changed in the past hundred years.
顯然在過去幾百年以來，農業發生了改變。

241 It is obvious that ... 顯然…

此句型的語意與 It is clear that... 相同，通常是用來描述多數人都接受的事實。

It is obvious that boys and girls behave differently.
男孩和女孩的行為顯然不同。

It is obvious that sharks cannot live in fresh water.
鯊魚顯然無法在淡水中生活。

It is obvious that human beings need food and water to survive.
人類顯然需要食物和水才能生存。

242 It is evident that ... 顯然…

此句型的語意與 It is clear that 相同，通常也是用來描述多數人都接受或認可的事實。

It is evident that military force has been used by many nations throughout history.
顯然歷史上有許多國家都使用軍事力量。

It is evident that children need to be reminded to brush their teeth.
顯然必須提醒孩童刷牙。

It is evident that television has replaced radio as a means of mass communication. 顯然電視已經取代了收音機，成為大眾傳播的方式。

243 So far, it is clear that ... 目前為止，⋯很明顯地⋯

想陳述目前為止所觀察到的事實時，可使用此句型。句型中的 clear 就算替換成 obvious 或 evident，語意仍不變。

So far, it is clear that the polar ice caps are melting.
目前為止，南北極冰層很明顯地正在融化。

So far, it is clear that we need to find alternate forms of energy.
目前為止，我們很明顯地需要發現替代能源。

So far, it is clear that genetics play a large part in cancer studies.
目前為止，遺傳學很明顯地在癌症研究中擔任很重要的一角。

244 Doubtless, 毫無疑問，

此句型的語意與 surely, of course 相同，可用來提及確定的資訊。

Doubtless, the test was a success.
毫無疑問，這項測試成功了。

Doubtless, the Vikings were avid sailors.
毫無疑問，維京人是狂熱的水手。

Doubtless, historians rely on archeological evidence.
毫無疑問，歷史學家仰賴考古證據。

245 One cannot deny that ... 人們無法否認⋯

想提出確信的觀察，或一般大眾會毫不猶豫接受的內容時，可使用此句型。

One cannot deny that creation stories exist in many cultures.
人們無法否認許多文化中都存有創世故事。

One cannot deny that women are denied equal rights in some countries.
人們無法否認某些國家中的婦女是被剝奪平等權利的。

One cannot deny that the purpose of medical science is to help mankind.
人們無法否認醫學的目的是幫助人類。

090 / 指出偶發事件

246 **Rarely is it the case that ...** …是鮮少發生的情況

是提到某現象的發生機率極低時可使用的句型。當 rarely 出現在句首時，表示這是將主詞及動詞倒裝的倒裝句。rarely 或 hardly 具有否定意味。

Rarely is it the case that a wild animal will attack a person without a good reason.
野生動物毫無理由地攻擊人是鮮少發生的情形。

Rarely is it the case that a woman dies during childbirth these days.
女性在生產時死亡的情形最近鮮少發生。

Rarely is it the case that a new animal species is discovered.
發現新動物品種的情形鮮少發生。

091 / 再次強調

247 **As is obvious from the previous discussion,**
從前面的討論中可以明顯看出…

想再次強調先前討論中顯而易見的重點，或是要比較多項論點時，可使用此句型。

As is obvious from the previous discussion, people can live in harmony with nature.
從前面的討論中可以明顯看出，人們可以與自然和諧相處。

As is obvious from the previous discussion, farming is no longer a leading occupation.
從前面的討論中可以明顯看出，農業不再是主要職業。

As is obvious from the previous discussion, military action was a last resort.
從前面的討論中可以明顯看出，軍事行動曾是不得已的選擇。

248 **As previously demonstrated,** 如前所述，

想藉由重提之前證明過的內容來提醒讀者時，可使用此句型。

As previously demonstrated, the universe is infinite in size.
如前所述，宇宙是無限的。

As previously demonstrated, electrons are the fastest things on earth.
如前所述，電子是地球上最快的事物。

As previously demonstrated, no amount of testing can prove this theory.
如前所述，沒有大量測試可以證明這一理論。

092 / 給予建議並強調其重要性

249 **It is necessary to ...** … 是必要的

此句型可用來提及必要性，優點是能簡潔明瞭地傳達主張或看法。

It is necessary to read poetry.
讀詩是必要的。

It is necessary to reduce the sale of weapons.
減少武器銷售是必要的。

It is necessary to value life.
珍惜生命是必要的。

250 **It is important to ...** …是重要的

使用時機跟 It is necessary to 相同，都可用來提及必要性。

It is important to feed your cat every morning.
每天早上餵貓是很重要的事。

It is important to read this before you begin.
在你開始之前，請務必閱讀這個。

It is important for a doctor **to** be ethical.
對醫生來說，遵守道德規範很重要。

251 It is useful to ... …是有用的

想提出有效且合理的對策，或想委婉地表達自己的主張時，經常使用此句型。

It is useful to note that consumers prefer fresh foods.
注意消費者比較喜歡新鮮的食物是很有用的。

It is useful to keep accurate notes.
精確記錄很有用。

It is useful to speak more than one language.
會說一種以上的語言很有用。

093 兩者擇其一的狀況

252 Either ..., or ... 不是…，就是…／要嘛…，要嘛…

either 跟 or 常同時一起出現，適用於描述二者擇一的情況。當只有兩個選項，因而必須從兩者中擇一的情況時，或者是只有一個選項，但如果不執行此選項就會導致不好的結果時，都可使用此句型來表達，以強調主張的必要性。

Either the workday is shortened, **or** I am quitting.
不是工作時間縮短，就是我辭職。

Either we fix global warming **or** live with the consequences.
我們要嘛解決全球暖化，要嘛就是要承擔後果。

Either the city must build a new swimming pool **or** else fix the old one.
這個城市要嘛建一個新的游泳池，要嘛就是把舊的游泳池修復。

094 在提出案例後闡述其目的

253 This is to point out that ... 這是為了指出…

前面已先提出了跟主張有關的案例或其他理論後，接著再利用此句型來闡述其主題或目的。

184

This is to point out that young children are often more susceptible to airborne illnesses.
這是為了要指出幼童通常更容易感染透過空氣傳播的疾病。

This is to point out that my theory can only be proven by scientific experimentation.
這是為了要指出我的理論只能透過科學實驗來證明。

This is to point out that two people can have different understandings of the same subject.
這是為了要指出兩個人對同一個主題會有不同的理解。

254 **This is to highlight ...** 這是為了強調…

此句型的使用時機與前一個句型「This is to point out that ...」相同，主要是用來強調其目的或主題。

This is to highlight the fact that healthcare can be very expensive.
這是為了要強調醫療保健可能會是個很花錢的事實。

This is to highlight the similarities between native cultures.
這是為了要強調本土文化之間的相似性。

This is to highlight the importance of Frank Lloyd Wright's career as an American architect.
這是為了要強調法蘭克‧洛依萊特身為一位美國建築師此職業生涯的重要性。

255 **This is to emphasize that ...** 這是為了強調…

與前面學過的 point out、highlight 用法相同，都是用來強調其目的或主題。

This is to emphasize that Charles Darwin's theory of evolution is reasonable.
這是為了強調達爾文的進化論是合理的。

This is to emphasize that people from different cultures can live together in peace.
這是為了強調來自不同文化的人可以和平共處。

This is to emphasize that climate change will have a negative impact on our environment.
這是為了強調氣候變遷將會對我們的環境產生負面影響。

095 點出論點的核心重點

256 **My point will be that ...** 我的重點是⋯

在開場白或本文的開頭部分,想針對主旨進行重點說明時,可使用此句型。

My point will be that the workday is too long.
我的重點是,工作時間太長。

My point will be that there are many ways to look at history.
我的重點是,有很多檢視歷史的方法。

My point will be that science is advancing too quickly.
我的重點是,科學進步地太快了。

257 **The key aspect of this argument is that ...**
這個論點的重點是⋯

前面已先提到跟論點有關的理論或研究案例,接著想列出論點的核心重點時,可使用此句型。

The key aspect of this argument is that men and women respond differently in various situations.
這個論點的重點在於男性和女性在許多狀況下會有不同的反應。

The key aspect of this argument is that stress can cause people to lose sleep.
這個論點的重點在於壓力會導致人們失眠。

The key aspect of this argument is that the sale of organic produce is on the rise.
這個論點的重點在於有機產品的銷售正在上升。

258 **The most crucial point made so far is that ...**
目前為止最關鍵的一點是⋯

此句型主要是用在本文的中段,來強調論點。

The most crucial point made so far is that history does not repeat itself.
目前為止最關鍵的一點是歷史不會重演。

The most crucial point made so far is that classical music reduces students' stress levels.
目前為止最關鍵的一點是古典樂會降低學生的壓力。

The most crucial point made so far is that slavery was not the only cause of the American Civil War.
目前為止最關鍵的一點是奴隸制並非美國內戰的唯一原因。

096 / 談到兩者皆非的情況

259 Neither A nor B 既不是 A 也不是 B

是跟 nor 搭配使用帶有否定意味的句型，表示兩者皆非的情況。

Neither I **nor** my sister agrees with the changes.
我和我的妹妹都不同意這些改變。

Neither Chicago **nor** Los Angeles has free parking.
芝加哥和洛杉磯都沒有免費停車場。

Neither Madame Curie **nor** her husband, Pierre, was wealthy.
居里夫人和她的丈夫皮埃爾都不富有。

097 / 指出案例的重點含義

260 This suggests that ... 這意味著…

從案例中整理出重點、擷取出其含義，或是透過實例說明時，大多會使用此句型。

This suggests that certain fish contain high levels of mercury.
這意味著某些魚類含有高量的汞。

This suggests that there are many differences between plant and animal cells.
這意味著動植物的細胞之間存有許多差異。

This suggests that a bicycle can be a reliable form of transportation in a large city.
這意味著腳踏車可以在大城市中成為一種可靠的交通工具。

261 It follows that ... 由此可見⋯

想透過類似的案例來做說明，或針對可套用同一原理或狀況的案例來做說明時，可使用此句型。

It follows that children learn from their parents.
由此可見，孩子們會向父母學習。

It follows that senior citizens need better healthcare.
由此可見，銀髮族需要更好的醫療保健。

It follows that more cities should have recycling centers.
由此可見，更多城市應該要有資源回收中心。

098 / 委婉地表達意見

262 Sometimes 有時候

在表達自己的想法時，即使自己對此想法十分有把握，但為了要讓表達更加婉轉，而非太過肯定，此時可以加上 Sometimes，以降低對方提出反駁的可能性。除此之外，利用這類句型來讓自己的論點聽起來有點曖昧、模稜兩可，也是避免需要清楚標明出處的方法之一。

Sometimes it is not popular to do what's right.
有時候做對的事情並不見得受歡迎。

Sometimes the world is a scary place.
有時候這個世界是個恐怖的地方。

Sometimes we dream in color.
有時候我們會做彩色的夢。

263 It could be said that ... 可以（這麼）說⋯

想委婉表達自己的主張或他人的意見時，可使用此句型。

It could be said that the disappearance of dinosaurs is a mystery.
恐龍滅絕可說是一起神祕事件。

It could be said that computers and the Internet will soon replace television.
可以這麼說，電腦和網路即將替代電視。

It could be said that Charles Dickens is the greatest English author of all time.

查爾斯‧狄更斯可說是有史以來最偉大的英國作家。

264 **It might be said that** … 或許可以（這麼）說…

此句型的語意與上一個句型 It could be said that 類似，都可用來委婉表達自己的主張或他人的意見。

It might be said that spending money on new clothes is wasteful.

或許可以這麼說，花錢買新衣服可說是種浪費。

It might be said that pet owners are generally happy people.

或許可以這麼說，寵物的主人一般都是快樂的人。

It might be said that the advent of air conditioning has changed the American landscape.

或許可以這麼說，空調的出現改變了美國的景觀。

265 **It seems that ...** 似乎是…／看起來…

此句型可用來委婉表達自己的想法。雖然 that 後面所接的內容本身就足以表達自己的想法，但用此句型來委婉表達，既可降低對方提出反駁的可能性，而且也是避免需要清楚說明出處的方法之一。用來表達個人觀點時，此句型和 I think that... 類似。

It seems that fertilized crops grow more quickly than non-fertilized crops.

有施肥的作物似乎長得比沒施肥的作物快。

It seems that some dog breeds are smarter than others.

有些犬種似乎比其他聰明。

It seems that our oceans are being overfished.

看起來我們的海洋正被過度捕撈。

266 **It appears that ...** 顯然…

此句型的語意與上一個句型 It seems that 類似，都可用來委婉表達自己的意見。用來表達個人觀點時，此句型和 I think that... 類似。

It appears that the ancient Romans understood the benefits of supplying their cities with clean water.

顯然，古羅馬人了解供給城市乾淨水源的好處。

It appears that most libraries have digitized their catalogs.
顯然，大多數的圖書館都已經將館藏數位化。

It appears that voting is an important part of democracy.
顯然，投票是民主很重要的一環。

267 I believe that ... 我相信…

想提出自己十分有把握的內容或主張時，可使用此句型。無論是在開場白、本文或結論部分，都很常使用此句型。

I believe that violence is wrong.
我相信暴力是錯誤的。

I believe that we can reduce the speed of global warming.
我相信我們可以降低全球暖化的速度。

I believe that children should be taught the benefits of physical fitness.
我相信應該要教導孩子身體適應能力的益處。

099 提出一般的觀念

268 It is generally thought that ... 一般認為…

想提出人們通常會相信的觀念或學術界公認的理論時，可使用此句型。

It is generally thought that gingivitis is the main cause of tooth decay.
一般認為牙齦炎是導致蛀牙的主因。

It is generally thought that ancient people navigated by the stars.
一般認為古人是根據星辰來航行。

It is generally thought that Napoleon was short.
一般認為拿破崙很矮小。

269 It is considered that ... 普遍認為…

此句型的使用時機與上一個句型 It is generally thought that 相同，都可用來提出人們通常會相信的觀念或學術界公認的理論。

It is considered that Cleopatra committed suicide.
普遍認為埃及豔后是自殺而亡的。

It is considered that blue jeans are a worldwide fashion.
普遍認為牛仔褲是全球的流行時尚。

It is considered that researchers should be aware of their own biases.
普遍認為研究人員應該要意識到自己的偏見。

270 Many people believe that ... 許多人相信…

一樣是想提出人們通常會相信的觀念或學術界公認的理論時，可使用此句型。

Many people believe that violence cannot solve the world's problems.
許多人相信暴力無法解決這個世界的問題。

Many people believe that doctors earn a lot of money.
許多人相信醫生賺很多錢。

Many people believe that Elvis Presley is still alive.
許多人相信貓王仍活著。

100 提出研究結果

271 It has been found that ... 研究發現…／人們發現

想提出是經過研究證實所得到的結果，或被證實過的事實時，可使用此句型。

It has been found that red wine contains vitamins.
研究發現紅酒含有許多維他命。

It has been found that many people suffer from depression.
調查結果發現有許多人深受憂鬱症之苦。

It has been found that coffee contains caffeine.
研究發現咖啡含有咖啡因。

272 Research has shown that ... 研究顯示⋯

此句型的使用時機與上一個句型 It has been found that 相同，想提出是經過研究證實所得到的結果，也可使用此句型。

Research has shown that mosquitoes can carry disease.
研究顯示蚊子能傳播疾病。

Research has shown that homeownership has increased in recent years. 研究顯示房屋自有率在近幾年有增加的趨勢。

Research has shown that eating chocolate has certain health benefits. 研究顯示吃巧克力有一定的健康益處。

101 / 提出證據

273 The most compelling evidence of this is that ...
最有說服力的證據是⋯

當提到了某問題或現象之後，接著再提出針對此問題或現象最強而有力的證據時，可使用此句型。

The most compelling evidence of this is that every culture has had its own unique traditions.
最有說服力的證據是，每個文化都有自己獨特的傳統。

The most compelling evidence of this is that since the widespread use of the polio vaccine, very few cases have been reported.
最有說服力的證據是，在小兒麻痺疫苗被廣泛使用之後，被通報的病例就很少了。

The most compelling evidence of this is that people all over the world are still fighting for civil rights.
最有說服力的證據是，世界上許多人仍在為公民權奮戰。

274 Further evidence for ... is that ...
針對⋯更進一步的證據是⋯

前面已提出了有力證據，想再提出其他證據時，可使用此句型。

Further evidence for this argument **is that** the first Europeans to travel to the New World carried diseases to which native people had no immunity.

針對這個論點更進一步的證據是，第一批到新世界的歐洲人帶來了當地原住民沒有免疫力的疾病。

Further evidence for this conclusion **is that** slavery was not abolished in the United States until the nineteenth century.
針對這個結論更進一步的證據是，美國直到十九世紀才廢除奴隸制。

Further evidence for my argument **is that** scientists are still learning new things about human DNA.
針對我這個論點更進一步的證據是，科學家仍在學習關於人類 DNA 的新知。

275 And to prove it, here is ... 為了證明這點，這是…

前面已提出了個人的主張，想提出證據來支持該主張時，可使用此句型。

And to prove it, here is my argument.
為了證明此事，這是我的論點。

And to prove it, here is the evidence that has been given by many scientists.
為了證明此事，這是許多科學家提供的證據。

And to prove it, here is a list of facts that cannot be disputed.
為了證明此事，這張表是不容爭辯的一連串事實。

276 This is most clearly seen in ...
這在…中最為明顯／這在…上看得最清楚

想提出最有力的或十分確定的證據時，可使用此句型。in 後面大多會接相關案例或書名等。

This is most clearly seen in the case of Pavlov's dog.
這在巴夫洛夫的狗身上最為明顯。

This is most clearly seen in Daniel Defoe's *Robinson Crusoe*.
這在丹尼爾狄佛的《魯濱遜漂流記》中最為明顯。

This is most clearly seen in the number of AIDS victims in Africa.
這從非洲愛滋病受害者的人數中最能明確知道。

277 This is also evident in ... 這在⋯也很明顯

前面已先提出證據之後，接著想再提出其他證據時，可使用此句型。in 是介系詞，所以後面要接名詞或動名詞。

This is also evident in Jane Austen's narrative style.
這在珍奧斯丁的敘事風格中也很明顯。

This is also evident in the amount of destruction caused by Hurricane Katrina.
卡翠娜颶風造成的損害金額也很可觀。

This is also evident in the fact that high school sports can bring communities together.
高中體育可以讓社區團結在一起的事實也很明顯。

102 / 轉換立場

278 Suppose you are ... 假設你⋯

想以假設某前提或轉換其他立場的方式來鋪陳，可使用此句型。

Suppose you are a scientist.
假設你是一名科學家。

Suppose you are a student from a poor community.
假設你是一個來自窮困社區的學生。

Suppose you are a Roman citizen living in Pompeii in 79 AD.
假設你是一名住在西元 79 年的龐貝城羅馬市民。

279 But what if you could ... ? 但如果你能⋯？

此句型通常用在本文前半段部分，藉此提出問題或轉換立場。

But what if you could control the animal's behavior?
但如果你能控制動物的行為呢？

But what if you could look at this problem from another perspective?
但如果你能從一個角度來看這個問題呢？

But what if you could ignore the directive?
但如果你能忽略這個命令呢？

103 點出值得討論的問題

280 An important aspect of the problem is ...
這個問題其中一個重要的面向是…

當要指出容易忽略的問題核心或重要部分時，可用此句型。

An important aspect of the problem is our reliance on foreign oil.
這個問題其中一個重要的面向是我們對國外石油的依賴。

An important aspect of the problem is the fact that some public schools do not receive adequate funding.
這個問題其中一個重要的面向是有些公立學校拿不到充裕資金的事實。

An important aspect of the problem is that prescription medication can be expensive.
這個問題其中一個重要的面向是處方藥可能很貴。

281 It is worth stating at this point that ...
在這個論點上值得一提的是…

此句型大多用在本文前半段部分，要提及某項值得討論的議題時，或在本文中段部分要轉換話題時。

It is worth stating at this point that forest fires are often naturally occurring.
在這個論點上值得一提的是，森林大火往往是自然發生的。

It is worth stating at this point that Christmas has become an increasingly secular holiday.
在這個論點上值得一提的是，聖誕節已逐漸成為世俗的節日。

It is worth stating at this point that I do not agree with the current theory.
在這個論點上值得一提的是，我不同意現今的學說。

282 It is worth noting that ... 值得注意的是…

跟上一個句型 It is worth stating at this point that 類似，大多用在本文前半段部分，要提及值得討論的問題時，或是在本文中段部分要轉換話題時。

It is worth noting that a child generally learns a new language more quickly than an adult.
值得注意的是，一般來說兒童學習新語言的速度比成人快。

It is worth noting that animals that are extinct can never be brought back to life.
值得注意的是，絕種的動物不太可能再復活。

It is worth noting that computer education is now taught in most public schools.
值得注意的是，大多數的公立學校現在都在教導電腦。

104 探討案例的一體兩面

283 On the one hand, ... ; on the other hand, ...
一方面⋯，但另一方面⋯

當情況是可以從兩個方面來分析，想先從其中一個方面來探討，接著再從另一個方面來探討時，可使用此句型。

On the one hand, I'm glad Burt is home again**; on the other hand,** it means I have to cook more.
一方面，我很高興伯特又回來了；但另一方面，這表示我得煮多一點。

On the one hand, having a pet is fun**; on the other hand,** it is a big responsibility.
一方面，養寵物很有趣；但另一方面，這是一項重責大任。

On the one hand, I like to make money**; on the other hand**, it takes too much time.
一方面，我喜歡賺錢；但另一方面，這會花太多時間。

105 引用專家的說法

284 Experts believe that ... 專家相信⋯

想間接引用專家學者們的意見或專業見解來提高文章可信度時，可使用此句型。

Experts believe that sharks have existed for millions of years.
專家相信鯊魚已經存在數百萬年。

Experts believe that global warming is the result of human activity.
專家相信地球暖化是人類活動的結果。

Experts believe that obesity leads to heart disease.
專家相信肥胖會誘發心臟病。

285 Experts say that ... 專家表示…

跟上一個句型 Experts believe that 一樣，當想間接引用專家學者們的意見或專業見解來提高文章可信度時，可使用此句型。

Experts say that the human brain is composed of 75% water.
專家表示人腦的組成有 75% 是水。

Experts say that 1 out of every 100 people is color-blind.
專家表示每一百個人之中有一人是色盲。

Experts say that dinosaurs lived more than 65 million years ago.
專家表示恐龍生活在六千五百萬年前。

286 Experts suggest that ... 專家建議…

跟前面兩個句型一樣，都是用來間接引用專家學者們的意見或專業見解。

Experts suggest that teeth should be brushed twice a day.
專家建議一天應該要刷兩次牙。

Experts suggest that we need to end our dependence on oil.
專家建議我們需要終止對石油的依賴。

Experts suggest that the organization should act quickly.
專家建議該組織應該要迅速展開行動。

287 Experts are convinced that ... 專家確信…

是間接引用專家學者們確信內容的句型。請注意此句型是用被動形態（be 動詞+P.P.），即 be convinced that...句型。

Experts are convinced that mosquitoes are attracted to the color blue.
專家確信，蚊子會被藍色吸引。

Experts are convinced that there is a hole in the ozone layer.
專家確信，臭氧層破了一個洞。

Experts are convinced that calcium builds strong bones.
專家確信，鈣可以增強骨骼。

288 Experts point out that ... 專家指出…

此句型主要是用來間接引用專家學者們所指出的某段內容。動詞 point out 表示「指出」之意。

Experts point out that the habitat of the polar bear is shrinking.
專家指出，北極熊的棲息地正在縮小。

Experts point out that more and more children are born with autism.
專家指出，愈來愈多小孩天生有自閉症。

Experts point out that sharks cannot swim backwards.
專家指出，鯊魚不會倒退游泳。

289 Experts emphasize that ... 專家強調…

此句型主要是用來提到專家學者們所強調的論點。emphasize 與之前提到的 point out 都有「強調…」的意味。

Experts emphasize that vaccines save lives.
專家強調疫苗拯救許多性命。

Experts emphasize that children can recognize patterns very early on.
專家強調兒童在很小的時候就能辨認出行為模式。

Experts emphasize that illegal hunting is reducing the number of wild African elephants.
專家強調非法狩獵正導致野生非洲象的數量減少。

290 According to some experts, 根據一些專家的說法，

是英文寫作時很常用到的句型之一。according to 是「根據…」的意思，主要是用來引用對方所說的話時。

According to some experts, it is possible to genetically engineer our children.
根據一些專家的說法，利用基因工程打造我們的孩子是有可能的。

According to some experts, cockroaches have been around for millions of years.
根據一些專家的說法，蟑螂已經存在數百萬年了。

According to some experts, there will always be war somewhere in the world.
根據一些專家的說法，世界上的某些地方總是會有戰爭。

106 / 具體說明

291 Take, for example, ... 以…為例，／舉例來說，…

在陳述某個概念或想法的過程中，想舉一個例子來具體說明的話，可使用此句型來銜接前後文。

Take, for example, the United Nations.
以聯合國為例。

Take, for example, the work of Leonardo da Vinci.
以李奧納多‧達文西的作品為例。

Take, for example, the fact that newspaper subscriptions have decreased.
舉例來說，報紙的訂閱數已經下滑。

292 To illustrate this point, 為了說明這一點，

此句型是用在想提出詳細、具體的例子來幫助讀者理解時，可搭配使用的表達。

To illustrate this point, I have conducted an informal survey of married college students.
為了說明這一點，我對已婚的大學生做了非正式的調查。

To illustrate this point, I will research the rate of automobile sales from year to year.
為了說明這一點，我將研究每年的汽車銷售率。

To illustrate this point, I have included a table of my results.
為了說明這一點，我附上了我的成績表格。

293 **To offer one example,** 舉一個例子，

想舉例子來說明時，可使用此句型，其語意與 Take one example 相同。

To offer one example, Columbus discovered the New World by mistake.
舉一個例子，哥倫布誤打誤撞發現了新大陸。

To offer one example, the gangster Al Capone was arrested for income tax evasion.
舉一個例子，黑幫艾爾卡彭因逃漏稅而被捕。

To offer one example, researchers must validate their findings.
舉一個例子，研究者必須驗證他們的發現。

107 提到歷史事件或社會現況

294 **Given the history of ...** 有鑑於⋯的歷史

寫文章時，若可以針對特定對象的相關歷史背景來進行探討，能讓文章內容更豐富。可先使用此句型提到該特定對象，後面再進行歷史背景的討論。

Given the history of conflict in the Middle East, it is not a popular vacation spot.
有鑑於中東世界的衝突歷史，這裡並不是熱門的度假勝地。

Given the history of violence in urban ghettos, many people fear those areas.
有鑑於城市貧民窟的暴力歷史，許多人對那些地區感到恐懼。

Given the history of assistance given by the Red Cross, it is not surprising that the group is often the first to help out in a crisis.
有鑑於紅十字會提供援助的歷史，就不會意外他們經常是第一個在危機中提供協助的組織。

295 **Until recently ...** 直到最近，

此句型可用來說明最近才產生的現象，非常適合用來說明急遽變化的社會現象。

Until recently there were more home phones than cell phones.
直到最近，家用電話仍比手機多。

Until recently all cars ran on gasoline alone.
直到最近，所有的汽車都還是靠汽油來行駛。

Until recently bald eagles were an endangered species.
直到最近，禿鷹仍是一種瀕臨滅絕的物種。

296 Over the course of the 20th century,
在過去的 20 世紀期間，

寫文章時經常會回顧跟主題有關的歷史變遷，此時大多會以世紀來分類描述。

Over the course of the 20th century, many technological advances were made.
在過去的 20 世紀期間，有許多技術進步。

Over the course of the 20th century, populations became more mobile.
在過去的 20 世紀期間，人口的流動變得更加頻繁。

Over the course of the 20th century, literacy rates rose.
在過去的 20 世紀期間，識字率上升了。

297 Nowadays we don't ... 現在我們不…

想說明急遽變化的社會現象時，經常使用此句型。

Nowadays we don't discriminate between genders.
如今，我們不再有性別歧視。

Nowadays we don't rely upon newspapers as primary information sources.
如今，我們不再仰賴報紙作為主要消息來源。

Nowadays we don't believe in a policy of isolationism.
如今，我們不相信孤立主義政策。

298 Still, 儘管如此，／依然…／仍然…

想提出尚未解決的問題，或是想提出不受時代變遷的影響，仍具合理性的主張時，可使用此句型。

Still, he is the best teacher I've ever had.
儘管如此，他還是我遇過最好的老師。

Still, there's no substitute for a professional symphony orchestra.
專業的交響樂團依然是無可替代的。

Still, it is hard to say how another researcher might have reacted.
儘管如此，另一位研究者可能會有什麼反應，這很難說。

299 **By this time,** 到這個時候，／此時，…

此句型可廣泛運用在敘述式的寫作中，或主題是跟新的社會變遷相關的文章中。

By this time, the study will be complete.
這個時候，研究將完成。

By this time, the German army occupied Poland.
這個時候，德軍佔領了波蘭。

By this time, Alexander the Great was already dead.
這個時候，亞歷山大大帝已經駕崩。

108 提到理所當然的事

300 **Needless to say,** 不用說，

語意與 not to mention 相同。對於先前別人提到的想法或觀察表示支持的立場時，可使用此句型。

Needless to say, major universities benefit from the work of their graduate students.
不用說，各大學可以從他們的畢業生身上獲得利益。

Needless to say, most people like to save money.
不用說，大多數人都喜歡存錢。

Needless to say, many children prefer sweets to vegetables.
不用說，許多孩子喜歡甜食更勝於蔬菜。

301 **Regardless of whether ...,** 不論是否…，

whether 大多用在二者擇一的情況。當出現兩種情況，且這兩種情況不論是哪一種，都不會影響到其論點時，可使用此句型。

Regardless of whether or not all his theories are correct, the man was still a great thinker.

不論他的所有理論是否正確，這男子仍是個傑出的思想家。

Regardless of whether one agrees with another's religion, one should always be respectful.

無論一個人是否同意另一個宗教，他／她都應該要保持尊重。

Regardless of whether we will ever find a cure for cancer, we should keep trying.

無論我們是否會找到治癒癌症的方法，都應該繼續嘗試。

302 **Not to mention the fact that ...** 不用說，

Not to mention 擺在句首時表示「不用說」，語意與 No need to mention 相同。此句型主要用在因某件事理所當然而毋須多說的情況，或是談到本來就會接受的事時。

Not to mention the fact that Mr. Jobs is rich.
不用說，賈伯斯先生很有錢。

Not to mention the fact that murder is a crime.
不用說，謀殺是犯罪行為。

Not to mention the fact that diamonds are expensive.
不用說，鑽石很昂貴。

109 / 簡而言之

303 **To put it (more) simply,** 簡而言之，

對於複雜的內容，想以簡單的方式來做說明，以幫助讀者理解時，可使用此句型。

To put it (more) simply, he loved her.
簡而言之，他愛過她。

To put it (more) simply, I don't have an answer.
簡而言之，我沒有答案。

To put it (more) simply, there is no such thing as evil.
簡而言之，沒有邪惡這種東西。

304 In brief, 簡而言之，

想針對前面討論過的內容用一句話做說明時，可使用此句型。

In brief, we must consider all possible side effects before proceeding with this research.
簡而言之，在進行這項研究之前，我們必須考慮所有可能的副作用。

In brief, Zeus was considered to be the king of the gods in Greek mythology.
簡而言之，宙斯曾被認為是希臘神話中的眾神之王。

In brief, hospitals must be kept as clean as possible.
簡而言之，醫院必須盡可能保持乾淨。

110 說明原因

305 Another reason why ... is that ...
為什麼…的另一個原因是因為…

當前面已經舉出某個原因，接著想再舉出另一個原因來支撐論點時，可使用此句型。

Another reason why I agree with Darwin's theory **is that** it is supported by parts of the fossil record.
我同意達爾文理論的另一個原因是，有部分化石紀錄支持他的理論。

Another reason why there are more homeless people in California **is that** the area has a temperate climate.
在加州有更多無家可歸的人的另一個原因是，該地區氣候溫和。

Another reason why scientists publish their findings **is that** others may benefit from them.
科學家們發表他們的發現的另一個原因是，其他人可以從中受益。

306 The second reason for ... is ... …的第二個原因是…

此句型可用來提出第二個原因，for 後面先接結果，be 動詞後面再接理由。

The second reason for the South's secession from the Union was the issue of states' rights.
南方脫離聯邦的第二個原因是州的權利問題。

The second reason for learning to play an instrument is that it is relaxing.
學樂器的第二個原因是，它能讓人放鬆。

The second reason for studying medicine is that it can help people.
研讀醫科的第二個原因是，它可以幫助人。

111 / 假設狀況

307 What would happen if ...? 如果⋯會怎樣？

想提出問題或假設某情況時，可以使用此句型。雖然這樣的假設可能很極端，但提出這樣的假設能針對主題做討論。

What would happen if there was another world war?
如果再發生一次世界大戰會怎樣？

What would happen if education was only for an elite few?
如果教育只為了少數精英會怎樣？

What would happen if all the world's governments were democratic?
如果世界各國政府都民主化，會怎樣？

308 Imagine what it would be like if ...
想像一下如果⋯那會是什麼樣子

此句型的使用時機同上一個句型 What would happen if，可用來提出問題或假設某些狀況。

Imagine what it would be like if Columbus had not found the New World in 1492.
想像一下如果哥倫布在 1492 年沒有找到新世界，那會是什麼樣子。

Imagine what it would be like if everyone spoke the same language.
想像一下如果每個人都說相同的語言，那會是什麼樣子。

Imagine what it would be like if there was no electricity.
想像一下如果沒有電，那會是什麼樣子。

112 / 提及贊成者與反對者的立場

309 Those in favour of ... 那些贊成…的人

在表明自己的立場與提到主題之前，有時會先談到對該主題抱持贊成意見的人的立場，此時可利用此句型。

Those in favour of tax cuts for the wealthy are almost always wealthy themselves.
那些贊成富人減稅的人，自己往往也是富有的人。

Those in favour of the individuals' right to own firearms are often hunters.
那些贊成武器持有權的人通常是獵人。

Those in favour of women's right to vote were called suffragists.
那些贊成婦女投票權的人，曾被稱為女性參政主義者。

310 Those opposed to ... 那些反對…的人

此句型的語意與前面提到的 Those in favour of 相反，主要是用來談到對主題或問題抱持反對立場的那些人。

Those opposed to the war are called pacifists.
那些反對戰爭的人被稱為和平主義者。

Those opposed to this petition should be sure to vote.
反對這項請願的人一定要去投票。

Those opposed to government policies have the right to speak out.
那些反對政府政策的人，有表達自己意見的權力。

113 / 用「如下所示」來列舉或舉出範例

311 ... is as follows: ... …如下所示…

此句型後面大多會是直接引用的內容，或者是將內容品項一個一個列舉出來。is 可替換成 goes 或隨主詞替換成 are。

The song goes **as follows:** row, row, row your boat.
這首歌如下：划，划，划小船。

The saying is **as follows:** when it rains, it pours.
俗話說：禍不單行。

The ingredients are **as follows:** milk, butter, sugar, flour.
成分如下：牛奶、奶油、糖、麵粉。

312 **... as in the following examples** 如以下範例所示

是在使用說明書中，尤其是產品組裝等這類說明中常見的句型。

Cite your references, **as in the following examples.**
如以下範例所示，引用你的參考資料。

You must insert a comma, **as in the following examples.**
你必須如以下範例所示插入一個逗號。

The apostrophe is used to make a noun possessive, **as in the following examples.**
如以下範例所示，撇號是用來表示名詞的所有格。

114 / 換句話說

313 **In other words,** 換句話說，

想補充說明或換個方式再做說明時，可使用此句型。除此之外，想舉例時也可使用此句型。

In other words, scientists working with toxic chemicals need to be careful.
換句話說，從事有毒化學物質研究的科學家必須小心。

In other words, we must keep asking questions if we want to progress.
換句話說，如果我們要有所進展，就必須不斷提出問題。

In other words, I want to be a doctor because I want to help people.
換句話說，我想成為一名醫生是因為我想幫助別人。

314 **To put it another way,** 換個方式說，

想改變說明的方式，尤其是想以稍微簡潔的方式來重新說明前面提到的論點時，可使用這類句型。

To put it another way, more vacation time reduced employees' stress levels.
換個方式說，更多的休假時間減輕了員工的壓力指數。

To put it another way, high-speed trains have made commuting between cities easy.
換個方式說，高速火車使城市之間的通勤變得便利。

To put it another way, more effort should be made to interest young people in science.
換個方式說，應該要多花點心力讓年輕人對科學感興趣。

115 / 提及具公信力的研究結果

315 **(The UN) has published an interesting survey ...** （聯合國）公佈了⋯的有趣調查

想在本文中提出具公信力的研究結果作為依據時，可使用此句型。句型中的 The UN 可替換成其他機構、學者或機關名稱。

The UN has published an interesting survey that supports my argument.
聯合國公布了一項有趣的調查可以支持我的論點。

The UN has published an interesting survey that contradicts the previous study.
聯合國公布了一項與先前研究相牴觸的有趣調查。

The UN has published an interesting survey relating to emergency response to diseases.
聯合國公布了一項針對疾病之緊急應變措施相關的有趣調查。

316 ... presents a useful concept …提出了一個有用的概念

此句型可用來說明學者或機關等所提出的研究成果，此句型之後再接針對研究結果的詳細說明。

The scientist **presents a useful concept.**
科學家提出了一個有用的概念。

This article **presents a useful concept.**
這篇文章提出了一個有用的概念。

Dr. Forester **presents a useful concept.**
佛斯特博士提出了一個有用的概念。

116 / 重述要點

317 As noted before, 如前所述，

反覆提及核心重點能達到強調的效果，此時可藉此句型來強調重點。

As noted before, frogs are amphibians.
如前所述，青蛙是兩棲動物。

As noted before, blindness is not hereditary.
如前所述，失明沒有遺傳性。

As noted before, milk contains high amounts of calcium.
如前所述，牛奶中含有高量的鈣。

318 As already mentioned, 如先前所提到的，

在本文中想再次提及核心重點時，可使用此句型。

As already mentioned, whole wheat is important in a balanced diet.
如先前所提到的，全麥在均衡飲食中很重要。

As already mentioned, studies have shown that the influenza virus mutate into various forms.
如先前所提到的，研究發現流行性感冒病毒會突變成多樣化的形態。

As already mentioned, teachers should be good listeners.
如先前所提到的，教師們應該要當個好的聆聽者。

319 **I agree that ...** 我同意⋯

自己對於提出的某個問題，想明確表明贊成的立場時，可使用此句型。

I agree that cigarettes should be taxed.
我同意應該對香菸課稅。

I agree that gambling should be illegal.
我同意賭博應該是非法的。

I agree that Plato was the greatest philosopher of all time.
我同意柏拉圖是有史以來最偉大的哲學家。

320 **I admit that ...** 我承認⋯

即使立場跟自己的不同，但還是認同對方的說法的情況下，可使用此句型來表達。

I admit that healthy food does not always taste good.
我承認健康食品通常都不好吃。

I admit that government-run healthcare has its drawbacks.
我承認，政府運作的醫療保健有其缺點。

I admit that the early American economy was dependent on large cash crops.
我承認美國早期的經濟仰賴大量的經濟作物。

321 **I totally agree that ...** 我完全同意⋯

對於提出的某個問題是屬於贊成的那一方，而想明確表明贊成的立場時，可使用此句型。totally 也可替換成 fully。

I totally agree that the results of this research were compromised.
我完全同意這項研究結果是折衷的辦法。

I totally agree that vitamins are no substitute for a healthy diet.
我完全同意維他命不能替代健康飲食。

I totally agree that pigs are as intelligent as dogs.
我完全同意豬和狗一樣聰明。

322 I disagree with ... 我不同意⋯

想明確表達反對意見時，可以用此句型。

I disagree with the leading scholars.
我不同意那些主事的學者們。

I disagree with most literary critics.
我不同意大部分的文學評論家。

I disagree with the idea that there could be life on Mars.
我不同意火星上可能有生命的想法。

323 I don't agree with the statement that ...
我不同意⋯的說法

想明確且簡潔有力地表達自己的反對立場時，可使用此句型。

I don't agree with the statement that all cities should have public libraries.
我不同意所有城市都應設有公共圖書館的說法。

I don't agree with the statement that Napoleon was a tyrant.
我不同意拿破崙是暴君的說法。

I don't agree with the statement that Shakespeare was a genius.
我不同意莎士比亞是個天才的說法。

324 However, I disagree with ... because I think ...
然而，我不同意⋯，因為我認為⋯

前面先提到與自己立場相反的論述，接著可用此句型來談論自己的立場，並提出自己反駁的意見與理由。

However, I disagree with this theory **because I think** it lacks support.
然而，我不同意這個理論，因為我認為它缺乏證據。

However, I disagree with my classmates **because I think** they have been misled.
然而，我不同意我的同學們，因為我認為他們一直被誤導。

However, I disagree with the validity of public opinion **because I think** it is controlled by the media.
然而，我不同意輿論的正確性，因為我認為是被媒體控制了。

118 提及一樣重要的事

325 At the same time, 同時，

是撰寫記敘文時常派得上用場的句型，主要是用在敘述同時發生的事情時。

At the same time, teachers need to be good listeners.
教師必須同時也是好的聆聽者。

At the same time, I do not see the need for additional research.
同時，我認為沒有必要進行其他研究。

At the same time, I will attempt to explain the origins of my theory.
同時，我會試圖說明我的理論由來。

326 But at the same time, 但同時，

主要是用來談論某事件或現象之其他值得被納進來討論的樣貌時。

But at the same time, unemployment rates can't be ignored.
但同時，失業率也不容忽視。

But at the same time, recycling our garbage requires energy as well.
但同時，回收我們的垃圾也需要能源。

But at the same time, laws can be changed.
但同時，法律可以被改變。

119 強調問題的嚴重性

327 Otherwise, 否則，

是適合用來提出警告的句型。前一句先提到主張，接著用此句型來提及若不按照該主張去執行的話會產生的問題。

Otherwise, the project would come to an end.
否則，這個專案將會結束。

Otherwise, rehabilitation would not be possible.
否則將無法康復。

Otherwise, patients might avoid treatment.
否則，患者可能會逃避治療。

328 Make no mistake about it, 毫無疑問地，／的確，

想藉著強調問題的嚴重性，來喚起讀者們的警覺心時，可使用此句型。

Make no mistake about it, radium is dangerous.
毫無疑問地，鐳很危險。

Make no mistake about it, universities need funding.
毫無疑問地，大學需要資金。

Make no mistake about it, science is important.
毫無疑問地，科學很重要。

120 / 從不同角度切入

329 Another way of looking at this question is to ...
看待這個問題的另一種方式是，

前面先用了其中一種觀點之後，接著改用其他觀點來分析，想以多種角度來分析問題時，可使用此句型。

Another way of looking at this question is to put yourself in the victim's position.
看待這個問題的另一種方式是，讓自己處於受害者的立場。

Another way of looking at this question is to look at it as a scientist might.
看待這個問題的另一種方式是，以科學家的能力去看待。

Another way of looking at this question is to examine the possibilities.
看待這個問題的另一種方式是研究其可能性。

330 Look at it this way: 這麼說吧：／如此看來：

想提出看待問題的不同角度或設定某立場時，可使用此句型。

Look at it this way: beauty is in the eye of the beholder.
這麼說吧：情人眼中出西施。

Look at it this way: if you don't try, you will never succeed.
這麼說吧：如果不嘗試，將永遠不會成功。

Look at it this way: civil disobedience is a peaceful form of protest.
這麼說吧：公民不服從是一種和平的抗議。

331 One should, nevertheless, consider the problem from another angle — ...

然而，人們應該從其他角度思考這個問題－…

前面已先從某個角度充分分析過問題後，接著想再從另一種角度來討論時，可使用此句型。

One should, nevertheless, consider the problem from another angle — perhaps the perspective of the victims.
然而，人們應該從其他角度思考這個問題—也許從受害者的角度來看。

One should, nevertheless, consider the problem from another angle — the researchers' perspective.
然而，人們應該從其他角度思考這個問題—從研究人員的角度來看。

One should, nevertheless, consider the problem from another angle — the economic viewpoint.
然而，人們應該從其他角度思考這個問題—從經濟的角度。

121 引起對問題的關注

332 We could go further and ask ourselves whether ...
我們可以更進一步自問是否…

此句型可用來讓讀者們思考對問題本身的認知。此句型比較常用在本文的開頭部分以引起讀者的注意力，偶爾也會用在本文後半段來一邊進行收尾，一邊請讀者們回想對問題本身的認知。

We could go further and ask ourselves whether men think differently than women do.
我們可以更進一步自問，男人想的是否與女人想的不同。

We could go further and ask ourselves whether there is life on other planets.
我們可以更進一步自問，其他星球上是否有生命。

We could go further and ask ourselves whether there should be a national poet.
我們可以更進一步自問，是否應該要有一位民族詩人。

333 It is interesting to note that... 值得關注的是⋯

此句型大多用來提出問題，句中的 interesting 表示「令人關注的」，而非「有趣的」。

It is interesting to note that many public schools do not receive adequate funding.
值得關注的是，許多公立學校沒有得到足夠的資金。

It is interesting to note that polluted water harms our environment.
值得關注的是，污水危害我們的環境。

It is interesting to note that women are often believed to be better communicators.
值得關注的是，女性時常被認為是更好的溝通者。

334 What's worse is that ... 更糟的是⋯

想採漸進式方式提出更嚴重的狀況或問題時，可使用此句型。

What's worse is that the cost of housing is rising every day.
更糟的是，房價每天都在上漲。

What's worse is that he was never credited for his work.
更糟的是，他之前從未在工作中得到認可。

What's worse is that the survey was never completed.
更糟的是，這份調查之前從未完成。

335 The real problem, however, is that ...
然而，真正的問題是⋯

想採漸進式方式提出狀況或問題時，像是從簡單的問題談到複雜的問題，或從較不重要的問題談到重要的問題，這樣依重要性或依複雜度循序漸進提出問題時，都可使用此句型。

The real problem, however, is that our experiment failed.
然而，真正的問題是我們的實驗失敗了。

The real problem, however, is that teachers need more training.
然而，真正的問題是教師需要更多的培訓。

The real problem, however, is that the researchers were unprepared.
然而，真正的問題是研究者沒有做好準備。

336 However, the problem is that ...　然而，問題是⋯

在進行了一段討論之後，接著想提出問題時，可使用此句型。

However, the problem is that unemployment rates continue to rise.
然而，問題是失業率持續增加。

However, the problem is that no discussion will change the current situation.
然而，問題是任何討論都無法改變現在的情況。

However, the problem is that the two parties cannot agree.
然而，問題是這兩個政黨的意見沒有一致。

337 It would be unfair not to mention the fact that ...
沒提到⋯是不公平的

前面已先提出足以說服讀者的論點之後，接著想再進一步提出另一個狀況或問題時，可使用此句型。

It would be unfair not to mention the fact that he is retired.
沒提到他退休的事實是不公平的。

It would be unfair not to mention the fact that he tried his best.
沒提到他已盡全力的事實是不公平的。

It would be unfair not to mention the fact that the team was missing five players.
沒提到這支隊伍已失去五名隊員的事實是不公平的。

338 We cannot ignore the fact that ...
我們不能忽視⋯的事實

想強烈提出某狀況或問題，或想進一步強調該狀況或問題時，可使用此句型。

We cannot ignore the fact that he murdered his wife.
我們不能忽視他謀殺自己妻子的事實。

We cannot ignore the fact that children are suffering.
我們不能忽視孩童正在受苦的事實。

We cannot ignore the fact that our climate is changing.
我們不能忽視氣候正在改變的事實。

122 提到相關論點

339 It would also be interesting to see ...
看到…也會是挺有趣的

想在本文部分的末段或結論部分提出可進一步做的研究時，可使用此句型。

It would also be interesting to see the infrastructure of the organization.
看到這個組織的基礎設施，也會是挺有趣的。

It would also be interesting to see the participants' reactions.
看到參與者的反應，也會是挺有趣的。

It would also be interesting to see the difference between the two studies.
看到這兩項研究之間的差異，也會是挺有趣的。

340 Equally relevant to the issue is the question of ...
與此議題同樣有關的是…的問題

想在本文部分的末段或結論部分，同時提到相關的狀況或問題，或是想更進一步提出研究題材時，可使用此句型。

Equally relevant to the issue is the question of timing.
與此議題同樣有關的是時機的問題。

Equally relevant to the issue is the question of funding the project.
與此議題同樣有關的是資助該計畫的問題。

Equally relevant to the issue is the question of how the study will be carried out.
與此議題同樣有關的是此研究將如何進行的問題。

341 Another relevant point is that ... 另一個相關的點是…

想讓提出來的問題受到更多關注，可用列舉其他相關的案例的方式來突顯其重要性，此時可使用此句型。

Another relevant point is that many political parties receive corporate funding.
另一個相關的點是，許多政黨得到企業資助。

Another relevant point is that the cost of education is rising every year.
另一個相關的點是，教育成本每年都在上升。

Another relevant point is that interreligious dialogue fosters understanding between cultures.
另一個相關的點是，不同宗教的對話可以促進對文化之間的理解。

123 / 帶出結論

342 As a result, 因此，

要帶出先前討論內容的結論時，可用此句型。

As a result, more and more people are recycling.
因此，越來越多的人在做資源回收。

As a result, crime rates have gone down.
因此，犯罪率下降了。

As a result, nurses are always in need.
因此，對於護士的需求一直都有。

343 So then, 所以，

此句型的語意與 Thus 相同。在提出充分的理由後，想作出結論時，可使用此句型。

So then, bee stings can be deadly.
所以，蜜蜂的叮咬可能會致命。

So then, plants need water as well as sunlight.
所以，植物需要水和陽光。

So then, freshwater fish cannot live in the ocean.
所以，淡水魚不能生活在海洋中。

344 This highlights the fact that ... 這凸顯了⋯的事實

想帶出先前引用的理論（或看法）的重點時，可用此句型。

This highlights the fact that healthcare can be expensive.
這凸顯了醫療保健可能很昂貴的事實。

This highlights the fact that progress is being made every day.
這凸顯了進步是每天一點一滴累積的事實。

This highlights the fact that the architecture of Mies Van der Rohe was very influential.
這凸顯了路德維希·密斯·凡德羅的建築非常有影響力的事實。

345 It can be seen that ... 可以看出⋯

想在討論了某案例、現象之後提出自己的看法或結論時，可使用此句型。後面所接的內容可以是主觀看法，也可以是客觀的見解。

It can be seen that illegal drugs are a problem in many countries.
可以看出，非法藥物在許多國家中都是問題。

It can be seen that trees can live for hundreds of years.
可以看出，樹木可以生存數百年。

It can be seen that many people are afraid of heights.
可以看出，很多人都怕高。

124 / 針對分歧的看法做總結

346 At any rate, 無論如何，／總之，

雖然各家看法眾說紛紜，但仍得下個結論時，可使用此句型。

At any rate, scientists cannot confirm the existence of life on other planets.
無論如何，科學家無法確定其他行星上是否有生命存在。

At any rate, it is important to understand other peoples' viewpoints.
無論如何，了解其他人的觀點很重要。

Part
2
本文句型

123
帶出結論
／
124
針對分歧的看法做總結

At any rate, less women die during childbirth now than in years past.
無論如何，現在死於分娩期間的婦女人數比過去幾年還要少。

125 談到一般社會現象

347 We can see that ... 我們可以知道…

此句型可用來提及普遍的社會現象。對於讀者們都已經知道的事實，透過此句型再次提及，有凸顯客觀性的效果。

We can see that more and more people are learning a second language.
我們可以知道愈來愈多人正在學習第二語言。

We can see that this medication is not working.
我們可以知道這種藥物無效。

We can see that violence solves nothing.
我們可以知道暴力無法解決任何問題。

126 提及證明過的事實來引起關注

348 As it turns out, 事實證明，

想透過提及證明過的事實，來讓讀者關注此事實時，可使用此句型。

As it turns out, it is good for children to be exposed to some illnesses.
事實證明，讓孩童接觸一些疾病是有益的。

As it turns out, we have enough tables and chairs for the meeting.
事實證明，我們有足夠的桌椅來供會議使用。

As it turns out, Mr. Clark is the most qualified person for the job.
事實證明，克拉克先生是最適合該職位的人。

349 In effect, 事實上，

談到實際發生的事實時可用此句型。in effect 有「實際上，事實上」的意味。

In effect, the aim of this study is to test the toxicity of certain chemicals.
實際上，這項研究的目的是測試某些化學品的毒性。

In effect, physical exercise is good for the mind and body.
實際上，體能運動對身心都有益。

In effect, the Queen of England is only a figurehead.
實際上，英格蘭女王只是個象徵性的人物。

350 In all actuality, 事實上，

語意與 actually 相同，大多是用在說明某件被證實的現象的情況下。

In all actuality, wolves prefer to keep away from people.
事實上，狼偏好遠離人類。

In all actuality, music can help children concentrate.
事實上，音樂可以幫助孩子集中精神。

In all actuality, television can be educational.
事實上，電視可以有教育作用。

351 Perhaps it is worth acknowledging here that ...
或許在這裡值得被承認的是⋯／或許在這裡值得被注意的是⋯

想補充說明值得思考的事實時，可使用此句型。

Perhaps it is worth acknowledging here that doctors do make mistakes.
或許在這裡得承認的一點是，醫生也會犯錯。

Perhaps it is worth acknowledging here that this evidence is over forty years old.
或許在這裡得承認的一點是，這個證據已經超過四十年了。

Perhaps it is worth acknowledging here that we may never know the answers to some of these questions.
或許在這裡得承認的一點是，我們可能永遠都不知道這些問題中某些問題的答案。

127 / 提及顯而易見的現象

352 It is noticeable that ... 顯而易見的是…

想點出事件或狀態中自己所觀察到特別顯眼的現象時，可使用此句型。

It is noticeable that celebrities drive nice cars.
顯而易見的是，名人都開不錯的車。

It is noticeable that women are attracted to men with skills.
顯而易見的是，女人會被有能力的男人吸引。

It is noticeable that men are attracted to good cooking.
顯而易見的是，男人會被出色的廚藝吸引。

128 / 提及參考資料來源

353 The answers to this question can be found in ...
這個問題的答案可以在…找到

想指出能解決某問題的某個理論或案例的出處時，可使用句型，後面大多接續著作的名稱。

The answers to this question can be found in the Bible.
這個問題的答案可以在聖經裡找到。

The answers to this question can be found in my research.
這個問題的答案可以從我的研究裡找到。

The answers to this question can be found in any basic science textbook.
這個問題的答案可以在任何一本基礎的科學教科書中找到。

129 描述自己一般的習慣

354 I usually... 我通常⋯

usually 表示「通常」，此句型大多用在舉例時或表達想法，來描述自己的一般習慣。

I usually ask my parents before buying a car.
我通常在買車前會詢問我的父母。

I usually ask my professor for help.
我通常會向我的教授尋求協助。

I usually ask Mrs. Lee for advice.
我通常會向李太太尋求建議。

130 用學者們的想法，來支撐自己的論點

355 Scholars disagree on ... 學者對⋯持不同意見

想提出依據來支持主張時，沒有比引用學者們的研究成果還要更好的方式了。想提及跟自己抱持相同意見的眾多學者的想法時，可以使用此句型，以表示學者們都不認同自己也正反對的想法。

Scholars disagree on many things.
學者在許多事情上都不認同。

Scholars disagree on the uses of hydrogen.
學者不認同氫的使用。

Scholars disagree on the issue of civil rights.
學者不認同公民權的問題。

PART III

Conclusion Patterns
結論句型

001 以一句話下結論

001 **Therefore,** 因此，

是做總結時最好用的句型，可帶給讀者一種將先前提過的所有論點用一句話來做結的感覺。

Therefore, we must proceed with our investigations.
因此，我們必須開始著手進行調查。

Therefore, we still have much to learn.
因此，我們還有很多需要學習的。

Therefore, our information is inconclusive.
因此，我們的資訊沒有定論。

002 **So,** 所以，

此句型的使用時機與 Therefore 相似，都能用來做總結。Therefore 比較適用於較正式的場合，而 so 則較常用於輕鬆或口語的場合。

So, the evidence indicates that the universe is much larger than previously imagined.
所以，證據指出宇宙比之前想像的更龐大。

So, these studies will continue.
所以，這些研究將持續下去。

So, it is likely that such questions will continue to arise.
所以，看起來這樣的問題會持續出現。

003 **After all,** 結果，／畢竟，

在文章最後要下結論時，可使用此句型。此外，也可用此句型來指出最重要的問題點。

After all, marijuana is legal in some countries.
畢竟大麻在某些國家是合法的。

After all, he was only sixteen.
畢竟他只有十六歲。

After all, no one was hurt.
結果沒有人受傷。

004 **My conclusion is that ...** 我的結論是…

是直接點出結論的句型。當結論十分明確、清楚,且需要特別強調這個結論時,可使用此句型。

My conclusion is that science is not infallible.
我的結論是,科學並不是絕對正確的。

My conclusion is that spirituality is as essential to life as food and water.
我的結論是,身心性靈就如同食物和水一樣,對生命而言都是不可或缺的。

My conclusion is that cosmetics should not be tested on animals.
我的結論是,不應該在動物身上測試化妝品。

005 **In conclusion,** 總之,/結論是,

同 My conclusion is that,是可直接點出結論的句型,尤其常用在提出對策或方案的情況下。

In conclusion, this university needs to recruit a larger number of graduate students in order to make this program cost-effective.
總之,為了讓這個計畫具有成本效益,該大學需要招到更多的研究生。

In conclusion, variations in room temperature do not help patients suffering from migraine headaches.
總之,室溫溫差的變化對深受偏頭痛所苦的患者並沒有幫助。

In conclusion, children who are taught that reading is fun will be avid readers for the rest of their lives.
總之,被教導閱讀這件事很有趣的孩子,在他們往後的人生都會成為熱愛閱讀的人。

006 **To conclude,** 總而言之,/結論是,

也是適合作為下總結的句型,但後面接的內容最好能包含到開場白與本文提到的主旨。

To conclude, the battle for civil rights is still being fought in many places and will not end until all human beings are treated equally.
結論是,爭取公民權利的鬥爭在許多地方仍在進行,要直到所有人類都受到平等對待之後,這場鬥爭才會結束。

To conclude, public television stations can be important educational tools.
總而言之,公共的電視台可以成為重要的教育工具。

To conclude, archeology can reveal the histories of everyday people that are not often mentioned in traditional sources.
總而言之，考古學可以揭露傳統資料中不常提及的人類日常生活史。

007 The bottom line is that ... 最後的結論是⋯

bottom 表示「底部」的意思，在這裡 bottom line 指的是不斷挖掘到最後所得到的結果，也就是「結論」的意思。不管在朋友之間的日常對話，還是在公司做簡報時，都很常用到此句型。

The bottom line is that we need to find new sources of energy.
最後的結論是，我們需要找到新的能源。

The bottom line is that education is important.
最後的結論是，教育很重要。

The bottom line is that communication can solve disputes.
最後的結論是，溝通可以解決糾紛。

008 The consequence is that ... 結果是⋯

consequence 表示「結果，後果」，可用來點出某件事經一番思考與推論後，所得到的結論。

The consequence is that most photography nowadays is digital.
結果是現今大多數的照片都是數位化。

The consequence is that new technologies are created every day.
結果是每天都會產生新技術。

The consequence is that the Internet has replaced newspapers in many ways.
結果是，網際網路以許多方式取代了報紙。

002 統整前述論點

009 On the whole, 整體來說，

將之前提到的幾個案例重新整理，並做出總結時，可使用此句型。

On the whole, people have been brewing beer for thousands of years.
整體來說，人們已經釀造啤酒數千年了。

On the whole, *The Twelfth Night* is one of Shakespeare's best works.
整體來說,《第十二夜》是莎士比亞最好的作品之一。

On the whole, sailors in ancient times relied partly on luck.
整體來說,古代的水手有部分是依靠運氣。

010 Altogether, 總而言之,

想將本文部分討論過的內容,綜合性地整理出大方向時,可使用此句型。

Altogether, the evidence is inconclusive.
總而言之,這個證據不具決定性。

Altogether, this study proves that the new medication is effective.
總而言之,這項研究證明了這種新藥是有效的。

Altogether, it is clear that we are still years away from any real progress.
總而言之,很清楚的是,我們距離真正的進步還有很長的路要走。

011 All things considered, 考量一切根據,

即 When all things are considered, 的意思。想透過前面提過的幾項根據總結出結論時,可使用此句型。

All things considered, Bram Stoker is remembered for his novel, *Dracula*.
考量一切根據,布拉姆·斯托克因為他的小說《吸血鬼》被人們記住。

All things considered, veterinary medicine is a complex course of study.
考量一切根據,獸醫學是一門學起來很複雜的學科。

All things considered, the year 1968 was a year of revolutions.
考量一切根據,1968 年是革命的一年。

012 Taking everything into account,
考慮到所有因素,結論是…

想將前面討論到的議題,拿來作全盤的思考時,可透過此句型來表達。

Taking everything into account, military service can benefit many young people.
考慮到所有因素,兵役可以造福許多年輕人。

Taking everything into account, skydiving is dangerous.
考慮到所有因素，跳傘是危險的。

Taking everything into account, Sir Isaac Newton was surely a genius.
考慮到所有因素，艾薩克牛頓無疑是一位天才。

013 **All this points to the conclusion that ...**

整體得到的結論是…

想將先前鋪陳的內容自然地銜接到結論，並點出重點時，可使用此句型。

All this points to the conclusion that racism is not as prevalent today as it once was.
整體得到的結論是，如今種族主義不像從前那樣普遍。

All this points to the conclusion that the whale population is increasing.
整體得到的結論是，鯨魚的數量在增加。

All this points to the conclusion that stricter laws are needed.
整體得到的結論是，需要更嚴格的法律。

003 提出其他可能的結論

014 **Or, if you prefer,** 或者如果你願意，

想在結論部分提起其他可能性，或提出其他意見時，可使用此句型。

Or, if you prefer, we can think about it from the government's viewpoint.
或者如果你願意，我們可以從政府的觀點來思考。

Or, if you prefer, the problem can be approached from another angle.
或者如果你願意，這個問題可以用其他角度看待。

Or, if you prefer, the issue can be thought of as a question of ethics.
或者如果你願意，此議題可視為道德問題。

004 / 在結論部分的開頭下總結

015 To summarize, 總結來說,

最常用在結論部分的開頭。是在本文部分提出根據後,於結論部分重新整理並做總結可用的句型。

To summarize, physical fitness programs are an important part of school curricula.
總結來說,體育健身計畫是學校課程中的重要部分。

To summarize, a bee sting is only deadly to a person who is allergic to it.
總結來說,蜂螫只會使對蜂螫過敏的人致命。

To summarize, volunteer work can create well-rounded citizens.
總結來說,志工工作可以培育全面性的公民。

016 To sum up, 總結來說,

所有類型的文章在需要下結論時,都可在結論部分的開頭用此句型。

To sum up, human cloning would not be possible without years of genetic research.
總結來說,如果沒有多年的基因研究,就不可能會有複製人。

To sum up, natural disasters can't be avoided, but they can often be predicted.
總結來說,自然災害是無法避免的,但往往可以被預測。

To sum up, many ships have been lost at sea over the years.
總結來說,多年來有許多船隻在海上消失。

017 To sum up briefly, 簡單扼要地說,

此句型常用來重新整理前述內容,並用一句話簡短給予總結。

To sum up briefly, we will need more funds for the project.
簡單扼要地說,為了這項計畫我們需要更多資金。

To sum up briefly, this investment has been a catastrophe.
簡單扼要地說,這項投資是一場災難。

To sum up briefly, ad campaigns have helped reduce the amount of litter on our highways.
簡單扼要地說，廣告活動有助於減少高速公路上的廢棄物。

018 **In summary,** 總之，

是寫文章下結論時最常使用的句型，在冗長的說明之後，用此句型將內容簡略地濃縮成一句話。

In summary, the first Europeans to travel to the New World saw it as an earthly paradise.
總之，最早到新世界的歐洲人將其視為人間天堂。

In summary, there is no time like the present to begin our investigations.
總之，要開始著手我們的調查，沒有比現在更適合的時間點了。

In summary, there is truth behind many old legends.
總之，許多古老的傳說背後都有其真相。

---

005 透過本文的論點導出結論或啟示

019 **From these arguments one can conclude that ...**
從這些論點可以得出…的結論

想透過本文部分所提出的案例或論點來導出結論時，可使用此句型。使用「one」這個詞來表達「一般人」，能讓陳述內容達到更客觀的效果。

From these arguments one can conclude that bats use sonar to navigate in the dark.
從這些論點可以得出，蝙蝠使用聲納在黑暗中飛行的結論。

From these arguments one can conclude that pesticides are sometimes needed to grow healthy crops.
從這些論點可以得出，為了種植健康的作物，有時需要殺蟲劑的結論。

From these arguments one can conclude that not enough is being done to save the rainforests.
從這些論點可以得出，為保護熱帶雨林所做的工作還不夠的結論。

020 Accordingly, 因此，

accordingly 主要是用來整理本文部分中提到的根據，進而導出結論的句型。

Accordingly, our results were inaccurate.
因此，我們的結果不準確。

Accordingly, the sea lion population has remained stable.
因此，海獅的數量維持穩定。

Accordingly, parents should teach their children to be responsible.
因此，父母應該教導子女要有責任感。

021 What all this means is that ... 這一切意味著…

此句型主要是用來針對本文部分中提出來的所有案例與資訊，以進行整體的分析。從前面提到的多項例子中，總結出一個共通點或主旨時，也可用此句型。也可用 All of this would indicate that ...來表示。

What all this means is that the earth is constantly changing.
這一切意味著地球正不斷地在變化。

What all this means is that we can expect more hot days as time goes on.
這一切意味著隨著時間的流逝，我們預計會有更多炎熱的日子。

What all this means is that education is important.
這一切意味著教育很重要。

022 Thus we can ... 因此我們可以…

將本文部分提到的例子拿來總結或點出一個結論時，可使用此句型。

Thus we can say that the poem is a haiku.
因此，我們可以說這首詩是俳句。

Thus we can argue that television is indeed harmful to children.
因此，我們可以主張電視真的對孩童有傷害。

Thus we can help our students more effectively learn English grammar.
因此，我們可以幫助我們的學生更有效率地學習英文文法。

023 **Thus we can see that ...** 因此我們可以知道…

同樣是將本文部分討論到的例子拿來導出一個結論或點出一個重點時，可使用此句型。

Thus we can see that 1066 AD was a pivotal year.
因此，我們可以知道西元 1066 年是關鍵的一年。

Thus we can see that alcohol can damage the liver.
因此，我們可以知道酒精會損害肝臟。

Thus we can see that the role of women differed from culture to culture.
因此，我們可以知道女性的角色在各文化中有所不同。

024 **The arguments I have presented suggest that ...**
我所提出的論點意味著…

想透過本文中討論過的內容來帶出啟示時，可用此句型。

The arguments I have presented suggest that dolphins are very intelligent.
我提出的論點意謂著，海豚非常聰明。

The arguments I have presented suggest that birds evolved from dinosaurs.
我提出的論點意謂著，鳥類是從恐龍進化而來的。

The arguments I have presented suggest that Stonehenge is an ancient calendar.
我提出的論點意謂著，巨石陣是古代的日曆。

006 / 表達「整體來說」的結論

025 **In general what this means is that ...**
整體來說，這代表…

此句型主要是將先前討論過的內容用一句話來簡述一遍，好讓讀者充分理解。this 表示先前討論的內容。

In general what this means is that we will need to try again.
整體來說，這代表著我們將需要再次嘗試。

In general what this means is that my hypothesis was incorrect.
整體來說，這代表著我的假設是錯誤的。

In general what this means is that depression is treatable.
整體來說，這代表著憂鬱症是可以治療的。

026 In general what this suggests is that ...
整體來說，這意味著…

同上一個句型，此句型也是將先前討論過的內容用一句話來簡述其重點，

In general what this suggests is that our research is going nowhere.
整體來說，這意味著我們的研究不會有什麼成果。

In general what this suggests is that music can be therapeutic.
整體來說，這意味著音樂有療癒作用。

In general what this suggests is that bones can become brittle with age.
整體來說，這意味著骨骼會隨著年齡的增長而變得脆弱。

027 In general what this indicates is that ...
整體來說，這暗示著…

同前面兩句型，此句型主要是針對前面提到的根據或證據，來進行統整，簡述出其重點。句中的 indicate 具有「指出，暗示」之意。

In general what this indicates is that a major change in policy is needed.
整體來說，這暗示著需要對政策進行重大改革。

In general what this indicates is that whole wheat is an important part of a balanced diet.
整體來說，這暗示著全麥是均衡飲食很重要的一部分。

In general what this indicates is that most people do not drink enough water.
整體來說，這暗示著大多數人沒有喝足夠的水。

007 堅持自己的主張

028 For my part, I must argue ... 對我來說，我必須主張…

有時在結論部分，有必要反覆提及文章整體的論點，此時可利用此句型，藉此強調文章的目的與相關的重點。

For my part, I must argue against this theory.
對我來說，我必須反對這個理論。

For my part, I must argue that our laws need better enforcement.
對我來說，我必須表明我們的法律需要加強落實。

For my part, I must argue against my colleague's position.
對我來說，我必須反對我那位同事的立場。

029 Though ..., I think ... 儘管…，但我認為…

議論文的本文部分常會有主張正反不同立場的情況，此時可在結論部分使用此句型，藉此表達在某程度上肯定對方的立場，但仍堅持自己主張之意。

Though I may be wrong, **I think** that this theory is unfounded.
儘管我可能是錯的，但我認為這個理論沒有根據。

Though gold is beautiful, **I think** that its softness is a disadvantage.
儘管黃金很美，但我認為它的柔軟度是個缺點。

Though money is useful, **I think** it can't buy happiness.
儘管錢很有用，但我認為它買不到幸福。

030 Although ... it is not ... 雖然…，但不…

同上個句型 Though ..., I think，同樣是表達在某程度上肯定對方的立場，但仍堅持自己主張之意。

Although the research has just begun, **it is not** far from being concluded.
雖然研究才剛開始，但結論並不遙遠。

Although skin cancer can be deadly, **it is not** always so.
雖然皮膚癌可能會致命，但並非絕對如此。

Although modern technology makes life easier, **it is not** really a necessity.
雖然現代科技使生活更便利，但並非必需品。

031 While I can ..., I prefer ... 雖然我能…，但我偏好…

遇到像是「比較喜歡搭巴士還是捷運」這類需從兩者擇一的主題時，在結論部分可使用此句型，來表達自己的偏好。

While I can understand this argument, **I prefer** to make my own.
雖然我能理解這個論點，但我更偏好提出我自己的主張。

While I can appreciate modern art, **I prefer** traditional religious art.
雖然我能欣賞現代藝術，但我更偏好傳統宗教藝術。

While I can do research for other people, **I prefer** to do it for myself.
雖然我能替其他人做研究，但我更偏好為自己做。

032 But, as for me, it's ... 但這對我來說…

針對前面討論的議題想表明自己的立場時，可使用此句型。

But, as for me, it's not so easy.
但這對我來說一點也不簡單。

But, as for me, it's a challenging problem.
但這對我來說，這是一個有挑戰性的問題。

But, as for me, it's clearly a misunderstanding.
但這對我來說，這明顯是個誤解。

008 強調論點的重要性

033 For now, 現在，／目前，

用「目前」「現在」這類詞，可用來強調論點的急迫性、重要性，像是正在發生一樣。

For now, it is clear that communication skills are important.
此時，顯然溝通技巧很重要。

For now, we should take things one step at a time.
現在，我們應該一步一步來謹慎地處理事情。

For now, we must remember that time is limited.
現在，我們必須記住時間是有限的。

009 假設特定狀況

034 If this is to happen, 如果發生這種情況，

想在結論部分針對可能會發生的情況提出替代方案或解決對策時，非常適合用此句型。

If this is to happen, doctors must make an effort to communicate effectively with their patients.
如果發生這種情況，醫生必須努力與患者進行有效溝通。

If this is to happen, we must continue our research.
如果發生這種情況，我們必須繼續我們的研究。

If this is to happen, we will need cooperation from our government.
如果發生這種情況，我們將需要來自政府的配合。

035 Under these conditions, 在這些情況（條件）下，

此句型可用在簡報或正式的文章中。想針對前面提到過的特定情況或問題作假設時，可使用此句型。

Under these conditions, it is not surprising that the polar ice caps are melting.
在這些情況下，極地冰帽融化也就不令人意外了。

Under these conditions, we must be sure to act carefully.
在這些情況下，我們務必要謹慎行事。

Under these conditions, the Russian Revolution began.
在這些情況下，俄國革命開始了。

036 Granted that ... 即使⋯

這裡 granted 的語意與 if、although、though 相同。也是針對某特定情況做推測時可使用的句型。

Granted that change is difficult, it is often necessary.
即使改變很困難，但它往往是必要的。

Granted that it may be a work of fiction, a book can still be educational.
即使這可能是虛構的作品，但一本書仍可以是具有教育意義的。

Granted that I am a student, my research is important to the university.
即使我是學生，但我的研究對大學很重要。

010 / 推斷未來的事

037 Perhaps people cannot ... 或許人們不能⋯

此句型主要是用來推測某極端狀況無法達到的情形。

Perhaps people cannot change.
或許人們無法改變。

Perhaps people cannot understand their doctors.
或許人們無法理解他們的醫生。

Perhaps people cannot control their own destinies.
或許人們無法控制自己的命運。

038 Sooner or later, 遲早，

sooner or later 表示「遲早、早晚有一天」的意思。主要是用來推測跟未來有關的事物時。

Sooner or later, the question will arise.
問題遲早會出現。

Sooner or later, we will have to decide.
我們遲早得做出決定。

Sooner or later, cars will fly.
車子遲早會飛起來。

039 More consideration needs to be given to ...
針對⋯需要多加思量／研究

當要針對某重要議題在未來的發展上做討論時，大多會用到此句型來描述。

More consideration needs to be given to the importance of a good diet.
對於健康飲食的重要性需要多加思量。

More consideration needs to be given to alternate theories.
針對替代理論，需要多加研究。

More consideration needs to be given to this research.
針對這項研究，需要多加思量。

040 **In the future,** 在未來，

有時會在結論部分提到跟議題有關的未來發展，此時可利用此句型。

In the future, we need to be more careful.
在未來，我們需要更小心。

In the future, overseas travel will be even faster.
在未來，海外旅遊將會更快速。

In the future, today's mysteries will become clear.
在未來，今日的謎題將會真相大白。

011 強調所確信的內容

041 **I definitely prefer to ...** 我當然偏好選擇…

在句中加上 definitely 的話，能讓語意更確定、讓表達更加肯定。

I definitely prefer to work alone.
我當然偏好選擇一個人工作。

I definitely prefer to study philosophy.
我當然偏好選擇研究哲學。

I definitely prefer to read fiction rather than nonfiction.
比起非虛構作品，我當然偏好選擇讀小説。

042 **I'm sure that ...** 我確信…

sure 表示「確定」「確信」的意思，此句型中的 that 可以省略，that 後面
接自己確信的資訊。

I'm sure that I am correct.
我確定我是正確的。

I'm sure that things will improve.
我確定事情將會好轉。

I'm sure that this research will be of great scientific value.
我確定這研究將帶來很大的科學價值。

043 I am convinced that ... 我確信⋯

是用來表示對自己的內容或主張很確信時的句型。

I am convinced that democracy is the only viable form of government.
我確信民主是唯一可行的政府型態。

I am convinced that children learn more quickly than adults.
我確信，孩子學習速度比成人更快。

I am convinced that prehistoric fish still live in our oceans.
我確信史前時代的魚類仍然生活在我們的海洋中。

012 點出原因與結果

044 with the result that ... 結果是⋯／因此⋯

前面先提到原因，接著再用 with the result that 來銜接導致該原因的結果。

Prices continued to rise, **with the result that** the people became poor.
價格繼續上漲，因此人民變得貧窮。

Betty's parents worked full-time, **with the result that** Betty was a lonely child.
貝蒂的父母全職工作，因此貝蒂是個孤獨的孩子。

The U.S. signed the agreement, **with the result that** international trade began.
美國簽署該份協議，因此展開國際貿易。

045 This leads us to believe that ... 這讓我們相信⋯

前面提出某件讓人相信的事件緣由，接著用此句型，此時 that 後面接讓人相信的結果。

This leads us to believe that obesity contributes to health problems.
這讓我們相信肥胖會導致健康問題。

This leads us to believe that many young people are interested in politics.
這讓我們相信許多年輕人對政治感興趣。

This leads us to believe that the world's population will continue to rise.
這讓我們相信世界人口將持續增加。

046 **On that account,** 由於這緣故，

是寫作時會用到的句型，主要用來表示「由於這緣故」，以陳述因前面提及的內容而導致後來的結果。

On that account, the experiment was a failure.
由於這緣故，這項實驗失敗了。

On that account, children are our future.
由於這緣故，孩子是我們的未來。

On that account, I have decided to study psychology.
由於這緣故，我決定研讀心理學。

047 **For this reason,** 為此，

以議論文來說，在開場白部分會先針對論點進行討論，並藉此引起讀者對問題的關注，在本文部分提出該論點的理由與依據，最後在結論部分則會將本文所討論的內容統整成一個重點，此時可用此句型來提及因本文中所推論到的理由與依據而導致某結果或結論。

For this reason, I will succeed.
為此，我將會成功。

For this reason, Julius Caesar was killed.
為此，凱薩大帝被殺了。

For this reason, governments make laws.
為此，政府便制定法律。

048 **For all these reasons,** 由於這些原因，

同上個句型，想提及因本文中所討論到的理由與依據而導致某結果或結論時，可使用此句型。

For all these reasons, we must proceed.
由於這些原因，我們必須繼續。

For all these reasons, radium is deadly.
由於這些原因，鐳是致命的。

For all these reasons, I believe that testing drugs on animals is wrong.
由於這些原因，我認為對動物進行藥物測試是不對的。

013 依序提出結果

049 Subsequently, 而後，／隨後，

當要按照順序或邏輯來陳述時，可使用此句型。

Subsequently, alcohol was outlawed in the United States for a long time.
而後，酒精在美國禁止了好長一段時間。

Subsequently, scientists often look for patterns in nature.
而後，科學家經常尋找自然界的模式。

Subsequently, the results of the study were disregarded.
而後，這項研究結果被忽視。

050 In this way, 如此一來，

在陳述事件所導致的結果時，可使用此句型。

In this way, we can see the progress we have made.
如此一來，我們可以看到我們達到的進步。

In this way, the American Revolution began.
如此一來，美國獨立戰爭開始了。

In this way, scientists can meet their goals.
如此一來，科學家就可以實現他們的目標。

051 In view of these facts, it is quite likely that ...
有鑑於這些事實，…很有可能…

在本文部分提到各種意見或事實之後，想根據這些事實在結論部分做出總結時，可使用此句型。

In view of these facts, it is quite likely that we will succeed.
有鑑於這些事實，我們很有可能會成功。

In view of these facts, it is quite likely that the fossil record is incomplete.
有鑑於這些事實，化石紀錄很可能是不完整的。

In view of these facts, it is quite likely that the population will continue to grow.
有鑑於這些事實，人口很有可能會繼續增加。

052 It is clear from these observations that ...
從這些觀察中可以清楚得知…

前面已先提到充分的依據之後，想根據這些依據來表達自己的觀察，並做總結時，可使用此句型。

It is clear from these observations that music can help children fall asleep.
從這些觀察中可以清楚得知，音樂可以幫助孩子入睡。

It is clear from these observations that we all have different tastes in art.
從這些觀察結果可以清楚得知，我們每個人在藝術上都有不同的品味。

It is clear from these observations that science fiction is more popular than ever.
從這些觀察結果可以清楚得知，科幻小說大受歡迎的程度是前所未有的。

053 It is clear from the above that ...

從以上內容可以清楚得知…

前面已先提到充分的依據之後，想根據這些依據統整出一個重點或結論時，可使用此句型，有強調自己立場的效果。不過，當證據不夠充足時，就不適合使用這個句型了。

It is clear from the above that not everyone is in agreement.
從以上內容可以清楚得知，並非所有人都同意。

It is clear from the above that tradition is important in many cultures.
從以上內容可以清楚得知，傳統在許多文化中都很重要。

It is clear from the above that transition from one career to another can be difficult.
從以上內容可以清楚得知，轉職可能會很困難。

054 In order that ..., 為了…，

此句型的語意與 In order to 相同，都是用來表達目的的句型。不過，使用 In order that... 時，請記得後面要接有主詞與動詞的完整句子

In order that products sell, many companies use marketing devices.
為了銷售產品，許多公司使用行銷策略。

In order that the results of this study are used, they must be published.
為了讓本研究的結果被採用，這些結果必須被公佈。

In order that children learn to behave, they must be disciplined by their parents.
為了讓孩子學習行為舉止，父母必須管教他們。

015　喚起讀者的共鳴

055 **And now you can ...** 而現在你可以…

是常用於結論部分的句型。在本文部分已充分提出案例和依據後，可利用此句型在結論部分來取得讀者的共鳴。

And now you can see for yourself.
而現在你可以自己領會。

And now you can travel from coast to coast with ease.
而現在你可以輕鬆地旅遊全國。

And now you can understand why we need to find new sources of energy.
而現在你可以理解為什麼我們需要找到新的能源。

016　重複已陳述過的內容

056 **As was previously stated,** 如前所述，

結論部分的內容，很常是將開場白與本文部分的內容濃縮整理成一段內容，以劃下句點。在濃縮整理的過程中，可利用此句型重覆提及想強調的內容。

As was previously stated, humans have 32 permanent teeth.
如前所述，人類有 32 顆恆牙。

As was previously stated, Alaska became a state in 1959.
如前所述，阿拉斯加於 1959 年升格為州。

As was previously stated, Latin-based languages often have much in common.
如前所述，以拉丁文為基礎的幾個語言通常有很多共同點。

057 As I have said, 如我之前所說，

想在結論部分簡述或強調在本文中提出的案例時，可使用此句型。此時，可以直接引用本文中使用到的句子。

As I have said, teaching is a skill.
如我之前所説，教學是一門技術。

As I have said, life cannot exist in a vacuum.
如我之前所説，生命無法在真空狀態生存。

As I have said, Thomas Edison did not really invent the light bulb.
如我之前所説，湯瑪士愛迪生並沒有真的發明燈泡。

058 As you can see, 如你所見，

有時會在結論部分再度強調在本文中已根據某些證據充分討論過的內容，利用此句型可讓論點更顯客觀。

As you can see, gorillas are quite intelligent.
如你所見，大猩猩非常聰明。

As you can see, many people take their health for granted.
如你所見，許多人視健康為理所當然。

As you can see, some people learn more quickly than others.
如你所見，有些人學得比其他人更快。

059 In retrospect it is clear that ... 回想起來，顯然⋯

想在結論部分重新整理一下在本文中提到的重點或結論時，可使用此句型。

In retrospect it is clear that mistakes were made.
回想起來，顯然錯誤已經造成。

In retrospect it is clear that our research was incomplete.
回想起來，顯然我們的研究沒有完成。

In retrospect it is clear that most wars are not worth the loss of so many lives.
回想起來，顯然大部分的戰爭不值得失去那麼多生命。

060 **Over and above,** 除此之外，

此句型可用來補充說明，類似的句型為「in addition」。

Over and above, the program is doing well.
除此之外，這個計畫做得很好。

Over and above, I believe that I have accomplished my goals.
除此之外，我相信我已經實現了我的目標。

Over and above, teachers are of major importance in most children's lives.
除此之外，老師對於大部分孩童的生命是非常重要的。

061 **But that's not all;** 但這還不是全部

想提供補充資訊，或探討更深層的問題時，可使用此句型。請留意此句型後面是用分號。

But that's not all; destruction of the world's rainforests also destroys many animal populations.
但這還不是全部，世界熱帶雨林的破壞也消滅了許多動物族群。

But that's not all; Copernicus also theorized that the earth turns on its axis.
但這還不是全部，哥白尼還提出地球自轉的理論。

But that's not all; listening to music can also be a form of stress release.
但這還不是全部，聽音樂也可以是釋放壓力的一種形式。

062 **And in addition to that,** 除此之外，

已下了某個結論之後，想再多補充時，可使用此句型 And in addition to that。

And in addition to that, infant mortality rates have decreased.
除此之外，嬰兒死亡率也有下降。

And in addition to that, we must act quickly if we are to succeed.
除此之外，如果我們要成功的話就必須迅速採取行動。

And in addition to that, the World Health Organization was created.
除此之外，還創建了世界衛生組織。

Part
3

結論句型

017
補充說明
／
018
提及無法確定的結果
／
019
提及更重要的觀念

018 / 提及無法確定的結果

063 We cannot be sure ... 我們無法確定⋯

想在結論部分提到議題有尚未確定的部分，並藉此暗示有必要針對此不確定性多做研究或討論時，可使用此句型。

We cannot be sure how the public will react to this news.
我們無法確定大眾對這則新聞會有何反應。

We cannot be sure of the results of this survey.
我們無法確定這項調查結果。

We cannot be sure that the sample has been contaminated.
我們無法確定樣品已被污染。

019 / 提及更重要的觀念

064 And remember, 請記住，

想在結論部分強烈提醒讀者某重要內容時，可使用此句型。

And remember, cheaters never prosper.
記住，騙子永遠不會飛黃騰達。

And remember, honesty is the best policy.
請記住，誠實是上策。

And remember, a contaminated sample must be thrown out.
請記住，必須將被污染的樣品扔掉。

065 More important than that is ... 比這更重要的是⋯

想強調更重要的訊息時可使用的句型。

More important than that is the fact that new laws are being passed every day.
比這更重要的事實是，每天都有新的法律通過。

More important than that is the success record of this company.
比這更重要的是，這間公司的成功記錄。

More important than that is the comfort that religion brings to millions of people.
比這更重要的是，宗教帶給數百萬的人們慰藉。

066 One thing's for sure: 有一點可以肯定的是：

此句型可用來強調自己的論點或想強調的訊息。分號(:)後面接想強調的內容。

One thing's for sure: the world needs doctors.
有一點可以肯定的是：這個世界需要醫生。

One thing's for sure: education destroys ignorance.
有一點可以肯定的是：教育破除無知。

One thing's for sure: technology will continue to improve.
有一點可以肯定的是：科技會不斷進步。

067 But the most important factor is that ...
但最重要的因素是…

是用來強調所有訊息中最重要的訊息時可用的句型。可依情況省略句中的but。

But the most important factor is that no two fingerprints are alike.
但最重要的因素是，沒有兩個指紋是相同的。

But the most important factor is that prisons are necessary.
但最重要的因素是，監獄是必要的。

But the most important factor is that diabetics must test their blood sugar.
但最重要的因素是，糖尿病病患必須檢測他們的血糖。

Part
3
結論句型

020
提及常被忽略的問題
／
021
下最終結論

020 提及常被忽略的問題

068 These problems pale in comparison with ...
這些問題與⋯相比顯得遜色

想指出某問題時常被人忽略，因為與其他議題相比，此問題稍顯遜色，以凸顯此問題應該要被探討時，可用此句型。

These problems pale in comparison with those of our ancestors.
這些問題與祖先的問題相比，顯得遜色。

These problems pale in comparison with those of previous years.
這些問題與前幾年的問題相比，顯得無足輕重。

These problems pale in comparison with the ones we can expect in the future.
這些問題與我們在未來能預期的問題相比，顯得無足輕重。

021 下最終結論

069 Consequently, 結果，／因此，

在列舉了造成某現象的幾個因素之後，接著想描述這些因素會造成何種結果時，可使用此句型。

Consequently, people live longer today than they did 100 years ago.
結果，今天的人們比 100 年前的人更長壽。

Consequently, every community should have a supply of fresh water.
因此，每個地區都該供應有乾淨的水源。

Consequently, many farmers live in isolated areas.
因此，許多農民生活在偏遠地區。

070 At last, 最後，

語意與 Finally 相同，主要是用在本文最後一段的開頭，或是用在結論部分。

At last, the end is in sight.
終於，終點就在眼前。

At last, this technology has been perfected.
最後，這項技術已經完善。

At last, we recognize the mistakes we have made in the past.
最後，我們承認我們過去所犯的錯誤。

071 Ultimately, 終究，／最終，

大多是用來表達做出最終結論，或提出最終的替代方案時。

Ultimately, the choice is ours.
選擇權終究是我們的。

Ultimately, every living thing dies.
所有生物終究會死去。

Ultimately, we will have to find a way to produce less waste.
我們最終得找到一個減少廢棄物產生的方法。

072 In the end, 最後，

此句型是用來做出最終結論，或是推測未來的發展。

In the end, nuclear war became a reality.
最後核戰真的發生了。

In the end, every battle leaves behind innocent victims.
最後，每次的鬥爭總是會留下無辜的犧牲者。

In the end, the prisoners were released.
最後囚犯被釋放。

073 When all is said and done, 說到最後，／畢竟，

想預測最終結局或未來發展時，可使用此句型。

When all is said and done, there will always be more questions than answers.
說到最後，疑問總是會產生得比答案還多。

When all is said and done, the project will be a success.
說到最後，這個專案將會成功。

When all is said and done, civilization marches on.
說到最後，文明會繼續前進。

074 **In the final analysis,** 在最後的分析中，

此句型的語意與 in the end 相似，是用來陳述透過分析與討論之後得到了某結論。

In the final analysis, errors were found.
在最後的分析中，錯誤被找到了。

In the final analysis, we might find our answers.
在最後的分析中，我們也許會找到答案。

In the final analysis, scientists were able to corroborate their earlier assumptions.
在最後的分析中，科學家能夠證實他們早期的假設。

022 / 提出解決方案

075 **There is much to be done ...**
（在…前），要做的事還很多

想陳述跟主題相關的替代方案或對策，或是想提出警訊時，可使用此句型。

There is much to be done before we have exhausted all possibilities.
在我們用盡所有可能性之前，還有很多事情要做。

There is much to be done in the field of genetic engineering.
在基因工程領域還有許多工作要做。

There is much to be done before our studies are complete.
在我們的研究完成之前，還有很多事情要做。

076 **If we can imagine ...** 如果我們能想像…

針對目前討論的議題，想在結論部分提出值得思考的替代方案或解決辦法時，可使用此句型。

If we can imagine it, we can build it.
如果我們能想像得到，我們就可以打造它。

If we can imagine the possibilities, we will succeed.
如果我們能想像到可能性，那麼我們將會成功。

If we can imagine the difficulties of the past, those of the present will seem less daunting.
如果我們能想像過去的困難度，那麼現在的困難似乎就不那麼艱鉅了。

077 Perhaps it is time to ... 或許是時候⋯

想在結論部分提出替代方案或解決對策時，可使用此句型。透過此句型能更自然地喚起讀者們的警覺心。

Perhaps it is time to reexamine our motives.
或許是時候重新檢視我們的動機。

Perhaps it is time to look back on past research.
或許是時候回顧過去的研究。

Perhaps it is time to bring in additional researchers.
或許是時候增加更多研究員。

078 It is time for us to ... 是時候讓我們⋯

同上個句型，想在結論部分提出替代方案或解決對策時，可使用此句型。

It is time for us to take a look back.
是時候讓我們回顧一下。

It is time for us to count our blessings.
是時候讓我們正面思考了。

It is time for us to move forward with this research.
是時候讓我們推動這項研究了。

079 It might be useful to ... ⋯可能會有用

想提出自己認為可行的替代方案或解決對策時，可使用此句型。

It might be useful to consider a new career.
去想想新的職業可能會有用。

It might be useful to reexamine our past research.
重新檢驗我們過去的研究可能會很有用。

It might be useful to take another look at Edgar Allen Poe's *The Black Cat*.
再看看埃德加・愛倫坡的《黑貓》可能會有幫助。

080 **We might start by ... -ing** 我們或許可以先從…開始

想針對特定問題討論其解決的線索，或是想提出可行的替代方案或解決對策時，可使用此句型。

We might start by conserv**ing** energy in our homes.
我們或許可以先從節省自己的家庭能源開始。

We might start by tak**ing** small samples from different areas.
我們或許可以先從不同地區抽取小樣本開始。

We might start by mak**ing** new use of existing buildings rather than constructing new ones.
我們或許可以先利用現有建築物，而不是建造新建築物。

081 **It is also easier to ...** 也會…更容易

有時在寫文章時，會需要在結論部分提出相比較之後的對策或方案，此時可用這類句型。

It is also easier to keep quiet than to speak out.
保持沉默也會比說出來容易。

It is also easier to follow orders than to question them.
遵循指令也會比質疑這些指令容易。

It is also easier to find a good job if you are well trained.
如果你有受到良好訓練，也會比較容易找到好工作。

082 **Is it possible that ... ?** 有沒有可能…？

在結論部分拋出一個假設性的問題，能有效針對問題建立起討論空間，以導出針對問題的解決方案。

Is it possible that we were wrong?
有沒有可能我們其實是錯的？

Is it possible that the test results were inconclusive?
有沒有可能測試結果並不具決定性？

Is it possible that members from different political parties can agree?
有沒有可能讓來自不同政黨的黨員都同意？

023 提出更好的方案

083 **Better yet,** 更理想的是，／不但如此，

想提出建議或更好的選擇時，可使用此句型。

Better yet, let's assume the whole world participates.
更理想的是，我們來假設全世界都會參與其中。

Better yet, let's assume 100% improvement.
更理想的是，我們來假設會有 100％的改善。

Better yet, the Internet can be used in classrooms as an educational tool.
更理想的是，網路可以在教室裡當成一種教育工具來使用。

024 向讀者提出請求或建議

084 **I ask you to ...** 我請你（去做…）

在文章進行到收尾階段時，可透過向讀者提出訴求的方式來做結。

I ask you to give this a try.
我請你們試試看。

I ask you to keep an open mind.
我請你們保持開闊的心胸。

I ask you to read carefully.
我請你們仔細閱讀。

085 **We should not be surprised that ...**
我們不應該對…感到驚訝

此句型帶有「…一點也不意外」、「…是司空見慣的事」的語意。主要是間接請讀者接受某件事實。

We should not be surprised that influenza can be deadly.
流行性感冒可能會致命，這點並不令人意外。

We should not be surprised that people are slow to change.
人類對改變是遲鈍的，這點並不令人意外。

We should not be surprised that people are living longer today than they were one hundred years ago.
人們現在能活得比一百年前的人更為長壽，這點並不令人意外。

086 **We have to accept that ...** 我們必須接受…

在表達自己意見或說服他人的文章中，可利用此句型來陳述自己的論點。有直接向讀者取得認同的語氣。

We have to accept that patience is a virtue.
我們必須接受，忍耐是種美德。

We have to accept that experience is the best teacher.
我們必須接受，經驗是最好的老師。

We have to accept that science will never provide all the answers to life's questions.
我們必須接受，科學無法為生活中的問題提供所有答案。

087 **If you are making ...** 如果你要…，那就…

想向對方提出建議或條件時，可使用此句型。

If you are making an argument, begin with your thesis.
如果你要論證，就從你的論文開始。

If you are making a birdhouse, you need wood.
如果你要做一個鳥屋，你需要木頭。

If you are making a point, try using facts.
如果你要表明一種看法，試著用一些事實。

025 提及相關問題以引起注意

088 You may be wondering ... 你也許會想知道⋯

此句型適合用在結論部分提及相關問題,也適合用於開場白部分,以引起讀者的關心。

You may be wondering why the earth revolves around the sun.
你可能會想知道為什麼地球繞太陽旋轉。

You may be wondering what we can learn from fossils.
你可能會想知道我們可以從化石中學到什麼。

You may be wondering how photosynthesis works.
你可能會想知道光合作用如何進行。

026 針對對策的未來發展做思考

089 So you'll be glad to know that ... 因此你會很高興知道⋯

結論部分大多會針對某議題在未來的發展上做討論,可利用此句型來描述正面的結果或展望。

So you'll be glad to know that the experiment was a success.
因此,你會很高興知道實驗成功了。

So you'll be glad to know that the answer is now clear.
因此,你會很高興知道答案已經很清楚了。

So you'll be glad to know that we have finally found a cure.
因此,你會很高興得知我們終於找到了治療方法。

090 Today we must ask whether ... 今天我們必須問⋯是否⋯

想在結論部分提及某項研究、政策或決定的未來發展或結果時,可使用此句型。

Today we must ask whether or not we choose to fight.
今天,我們必須問自己是否要選擇戰鬥。

Today we must ask whether our government's new policies are for the greater good.
今天，我們必須問政府的新政策是否能帶來更大益處。

Today we must ask whether this research will have any practical applications.
今天，我們必須問這項研究是否會有實際應用。

027 / 用前面的討論來做出推論

091 The foregoing statement proves that ...
前述內容證明…

在結論部分想總結或再次提到本文部分的討論內容時，可使用此句型。

The foregoing statement proves that our air is polluted.
前述內容證明我們的空氣被污染了。

The foregoing statement proves that my theory is correct.
前述內容證明了我的理論是正確的。

The foregoing statement proves that men and women react differently in emergencies.
前述內容證明了男人和女人在緊急情況下的反應不同。

028 / 總結出樂觀或悲觀的結論

092 There is no single reason that ...　毫無理由…

大部分的結論都是一邊提及跟主題有關的未來發展，一邊進行收尾，此時可利用此句型來提出較為悲觀的結論，或是較為樂觀的結論，此句型依情況不同，會有不同的用法。

There is no single reason that we can't succeed.
沒有我們無法成功的理由。

There is no single reason that a person needs more than one car.
一個人需要超過一台車，這挺沒道理的。

There is no single reason that some children are afraid of the dark.
有些孩童沒有理由會怕黑。

029 / 以長期觀點來陳述

093 In the long run, 長期來說,

一般想在結論提出問題的解決對策時,可按照短期觀點、長期觀點來分別進行陳述。若想以長期觀點來提出解決對策時,可使用此句型。

In the long run, a good education is priceless.
長期來說,優良的教育是無價的。

In the long run, history remembers victories.
長期來說,歷史會記得勝利。

In the long run, communism was not successful in the Soviet Union.
長期來說,共產主義在蘇維埃聯盟並未成功。

030 / 從先前討論的例子中總結出一個重點

094 Briefly, we can say that ... 簡而言之,我們可以說…

想將前面討論的內容做出簡短的結論,並從之前的例子中導出箇中含義時,可使用此句型。也可以用 Briefly, it can be said that ... 來表達相同語意。

Briefly, we can say that the results of these studies are contradictory.
簡而言之,我們可以說這些研究的結果是矛盾的。

Briefly, we can say that the current method leaves much room for improvement.
簡而言之,可以說當前的這個方法還有很多改進的空間。

Briefly, we can say that Thomas Aquinas is one of the best known theologians.
簡而言之,我們可以說湯瑪斯‧阿奎那這位人物是最著名的神學家之一。

095 **All in all,** 總而言之，

想從本文部分討論過的所有例子中所考量到因素中，總結出一個重點時，可使用此句型。

All in all, Napoleon was a skilled leader.
總而言之，拿破崙是一個熟稔的領導者。

All in all, our current state of affairs is only temporary.
總而言之，我們目前的狀況只是暫時的。

All in all, this chemical engineering program is very successful.
總而言之，這個化學工程計畫非常成功。

096 **To put it differently,** 換句話說，

想用更簡單的話來解說，或簡述複雜的情況時，可使用此句型。

To put it differently, magnetic forces have been understood for a long time.
換句話說，磁力已經被理解很長一段時間了。

To put it differently, this idea does not make sense in light of our recent discoveries.
換句話說，有鑑於我們最近的發現，這個想法不合裡。

To put it differently, authority must be obeyed.
換句話說，必須服從權威。

031 舉出具體例子

097 **... namely ...** 即⋯／也就是⋯

想針對前述內容，以具體的例子來稍微附加說明時，可使用此句型，好讓讀者更清楚你的論點。

She discovered two elements, **namely** radium and polonium.
她發現了兩種元素，也就是鐳和鉕。

My favorite hotel — **namely,** the Holiday Inn — was very clean.
我最喜歡的飯店，也就是假日飯店，非常乾淨。

Many students were late, **namely** Mary, Chris, Tom, and Pat.
許多學生遲到了，分別是瑪麗、克里斯、湯姆和帕特。

032 / 用一句話提出警告

098 A word of caution: 請注意：

caution 表示「警告，小心」。此句型中使用了冒號(:)，而冒號的主要功用是用來「列舉」，此句型可用來列舉要警告的內容。

A word of caution: do not give money to strangers.
這句話提醒你：不要把錢交給陌生人。

A word of caution: be careful to use power tools.
這句話提醒你：使用電動工具要小心。

A word of caution: if you plant onions too soon, they will die.
這句話提醒你：如果你太早種植洋蔥，它們會死。

033 / 強調特定事物

099 It is just as ... 這正是…／這就跟…一樣

為強調的句型，在這裡 just 是「正是」、「就是」的意思。It is just as 後面接「主詞＋動詞」。

It is just as she wanted it.
這正是她所想要的。

It is just as I have described.
這正是我所描述的。

It is just as it seems.
這就跟看起來的一樣。

Part
3
結論句型

032
用一句話提出警告
／
033
強調特定事物

第二部分

Exercise
練習題

練習題 1

❶ _____ prove that bats are mammals.

文章的目的是為了證明為何蝙蝠是哺乳類。

❷ _____, Shakespeare was a genius.

就我的觀點而言（個人認為），我認為莎士比亞是一名天才。

❸ _____ today that mankind has caused global warming.

當前普遍認為人類導致了全球暖化。

❹ _____ the meaning of life, we quickly become confused.

如果我們思考人生的意義，我們很快就會感到困惑。

❺ _____ multiple aspects of the problem.

本文將著重在此問題的多方角度。

❻ _____ global warming is a serious problem.

在這份報告中，我認為地球暖化是非常嚴重的問題。

❼ _____ the best advice comes from our elders.

常言道，長者總是能給出最好的建議。

❽ _____ humans are social creatures.

人類是社會型動物是眾所皆知的事情。

❾ _____ Seattle is so cloudy.

你可能會好奇為什麼西雅圖雲很多。

❿ _____, red has the longest wavelength.

如你可能已經注意到的，紅色的波長最長。

📖Answer 解答

❶The aim of this essay is to ❷In my opinion, ❸It is generally agreed ❹If we think about ❺This paper will focus on ❻In this paper I argue that ❼It is often said that ❽It is a well-known fact that ❾You may wonder why ❿As you probably know

⑪ _____: "Where there's smoke, there's fire."

俗話說：「有煙的地方就有火（無風不起浪）」。

⑫ _____ writing to be a chore.

大部分的人認為寫作是乏味的事。

⑬ _____ cats is that they can see in the dark.

對貓的錯誤認知之一是以為牠們在黑暗中看得見。

⑭ _____ discussing Tolstoy's early life.

這份報告從討論托爾斯泰的童年時期開始。

⑮ _____ why this is true.

有很多原因說明這是事實。

⑯ Scholars _____ many things.

學者在許多事情上都不認同。

⑰ _____ I am passionate about.

這議題是我非常有熱忱的。

⑱ _____ disease is a threat.

不可否認，疾病是一個威脅。

⑲ _____, we are running out of oil.

問題是我們沒有油了。

⑳ _____ global warming when I was watching TV.

我在看電視的時候第一次得知地球暖化。

📖 **Answer 解答**

⑪ There's a saying ⑫ Most people consider ⑬ One of the misconceptions about ⑭ This paper begins by ⑮ There are many reasons ⑯ disagree on ⑰ This issue is one that ⑱ It is undeniable that ⑲ The problem is ⑳ I first became aware of

❶ _____ the cake will depend on the quality of the ingredients.

蛋糕的品質取決於原料的品質。

❷ _____ humans should be responsible for global warming.

我們常聽説，人類應該要為地球暖化負責。

❸ _____ you can't teach an old dog new tricks.

常言道，老狗玩不出新把戲。

❹ _____, the scientists disagree about how effective the treatment will be.

想當然爾，科學家們當然不會認同那個療法的效果。

❺ _____ golf is played by rich people.

高爾夫球是有錢人在打的，這是眾所皆知的事。

❻ _____, I try to weigh my options.

為了做出決定，我試著權衡我的選項。

❼ _____ difficult to make.

任何重要的決定都是很難的。

❽ _____ controlling the economy is impossible.

他們似乎相信控制經濟是不可能的。

❾ _____ uses a cellular phone.

幾乎所有人都用手機。

❿ _____ refute the existence of ghosts.

有些人拒絕承認鬼魂的存在。

📖 Answer 解答

❶The quality of ❷We often hear that ❸It is often said that ❹Naturally ❺It is common knowledge that ❻In my decision-making ❼Any important decision is ❽They seem to believe that ❾Almost everyone ❿There are some people who

⑪ _____ poverty produces crime.

不可否認的是，貧窮引起犯罪。

⑫ _____, one should be careful not to make hasty judgments.

在處理這個議題時，人必須小心不要做出倉促的判決。

⑬ _____ the ethics of his decision.

我們必須深思他這個決定的道德標準。

⑭ _____ the way that children learn, the strange-looking toy makes sense.

如果我們想想小孩學習的方式，這個看起來很奇怪的玩具就合理了。

⑮ _____ the ant, you will see that it is a very complex creature.

如果你稍微停下來研究一下螞蟻，你將會發現牠們是非常複雜的生物。

⑯ _____, there is much research left to be done.

誠如各位所知，還有許多研究尚待進行。

⑰ _____, the earth is getting warmer.

各位也許已經察覺到，地球逐漸在暖化。

⑱ _____ television is entertaining, it can limit a child's creativity.

電視雖然很有趣，卻會限制住孩子的創造力。

⑲ _____ science is the use of stem cells.

科學界目前正在討論最重要的議題之一，是幹細胞的運用。

⑳ Once _____, there is a devastating tsunami.

有時候會出現毀滅性的海嘯。

📖 Answer 解答

⑪ It is undeniable that ⑫ In approaching the issue ⑬ We must contemplate ⑭ If we think about
⑮ If you stop to consider ⑯ As you probably know, ⑰ As you may have noticed ⑱ While ⑲ One
of the most significant current discussions in ⑳ in a great while

269

練習題 3

❶ _____ the concept of justice.

我們必須先檢視正義的概念。

❷ _____ about the accident.

讓我們從事故的真相開始思考。

❸ _____ this essay is not intended to shed light on every aspect of Mendel's life.

首先必須要說的是，本文並非旨在闡明孟德爾一生的所有面相。

❹ _____, we will present a new concept.

首先，我們將介紹新的概念。

❺ _____ toes evolved from fins.

就邏輯而言，腳趾當然是由鰭進化而成的。

❻ _____, made people less likely to shop at Wal-Mart.

這反而是讓人越來越不太可能去沃爾賣場購物了。

❼ _____, we should research the issue.

在這段期間，我們應該研究這個議題。

❽ _____ her success was that she had very good parents.

然而，另一個她成功的原因是，她有一對非常優秀的父母。

❾ _____ crucial we continue to teach handwriting.

從我的經驗，我認為持續教導手寫是很重要的。

❿ _____ chicken is the most delicious meat.

我個人認為雞肉是最美味的肉類。

📖 **Answer 解答**

❶ We must first examine **❷** Let us start by considering the facts **❸** The first thing that needs to be said is that **❹** First of all **❺** Logically, it follows that **❻** This, in turn **❼** In the meantime **❽** Yet another reason for **❾** From my experience, I think it is **❿** I personally believe that

⑪ _____ Chaucer was actually a priest.

我的見解是，喬塞實際上曾經是一名神父。

⑫ If it _____ tornadoes can be predicted, then people can be warned in advance.

如果可以預測龍捲風，就可以提前警告民眾。

⑬ _____ history, we look to a variety of sources.

為了正確理解歷史，我們尋找各種資源。

⑭ _____, it never rains in Rainville.

反常地，蘭維爾從不下雨的。

⑮ _____, the cost of health care is too high.

這就是為什麼我認為，健康照護的成本太高。

⑯ _____, the Renaissance ushered in a new era in art and architecture.

而最棒的是，文藝復興開啟了藝術與建築的新紀元。

⑰ _____ in the following pages.

我將在接下來幾頁中更詳細地說明這一點。

⑱ _____ is the love story between them.

更有趣的是他們之間的愛情故事。

⑲ _____ that Costa Rica has no army.

或許我也應該點出哥斯大黎加沒有軍隊這個事實。

⑳ _____, we are the sons and daughters of very strong people.

換一個角度看，我們是強者的子女。

目 **Answer 解答**
⑪My own point of view is that ⑫is the case that ⑬In order to properly understand
⑭Paradoxically ⑮That is why, in my opinion ⑯And best of all ⑰I shall argue this point at
greater length ⑱Much more interesting ⑲Perhaps I should also point out the fact ⑳To look at
this another way

271

練習題 4

❶ _____, it should be noted that this is an unofficial report.

然而，應該要注意的是，這是一份非正式的報告書。

❷ _____ it is illegal, smuggling persists.

雖然這是違法的，但走私仍然存在。

❸ _____ the story _____, we are in no danger.

即使這個報導是真的，但我們並不處於危險中。

❹ _____ Professor Harris _____, Dr. Peter's argument is stronger.

雖然哈里斯教授可能有很好的觀點，但彼得教授的論點更強。

❺ All _____ that there is another explanation for the statues on Easter Island.

同樣地，復活節島上的雕像可能還有其他解釋方法。

❻ _____, that this theory has not been discredited.

然而，有趣的是這個理論並未被懷疑過。

❼ _____ that genetics play a large part in cancer studies.

目前為止，遺傳學很明顯地在癌症研究中擔任很重要的一角。

❽ _____, historians rely on archeological evidence.

毫無疑問，歷史學家仰賴考古證據。

❾ _____ that a wild animal will attack a person without a good reason.

野生動物毫無理由地攻擊人是鮮少發生的情形。

❿ _____, military action was a last resort.

從前面的討論中可以明顯看出，軍事行動曾是不得已的選擇。

📑 **Answer 解答**

❶ However **❷** Though **❸** Even if, is true **❹** Although, may have a good point **❺** the same, it is possible **❻** It is interesting, though **❼** So far, it is clear **❽** Doubtless **❾** Rarely is it the case **❿** As is obvious from the previous discussion

⑪ _____ that private cars should be outlawed in big cities.

我甚至會這麼說，大都市裡的私家客車都應該要被取締。

⑫ _____ that the election was rigged.

第一個論點意指這次選舉被操控。

⑬ _____ that the election was legal.

反之，第二個論點意指這次選舉是正當合法的。

⑭ _____ what we can do to repair the forest.

我們許多人可能會問，我們該怎麼做才能修復森林。

⑮ _____ that skiing is dangerous.

儘管如此，應該要接受滑雪是危險的事。

⑯ _____ that safety is important.

應該要永遠記得安全很重要。

⑰ _____ ; others have written on this topic as well.

可是不要只聽我講的，其他人也寫過這類題目。

⑱ _____ that some people are naturally smarter than others.

實際上發現，某些人生來比其他人聰明。

⑲ _____ , the world's rainforests should be protected.

回到先前的重點，應該要保護世界上的熱帶雨林。

⑳ _____ mathematics _____ , Dr. Jordan is a genius.

就數學而言，喬登博士是一位天才。

273

練習題 5

❶ _____ **that** it does not describe the researcher's methodology.

然而，這份研究受限於未記載學者的研究方法。

❷ _____ **that** few people have swimming pools, many people **know how to swim.**

因此，雖然很少人家裡會有游泳池這件事是事實，但許多人都知道如何游泳。

❸ _____, the waiter dropped the plates.

再者，服務生掉了盤子。

❹ _____ - she's a pilot, too!

而且這還不是全部—她也是一位飛機駕駛員！

❺ _____ **this,** the building will be used as a bus terminal.

除此之外，這棟建築物將會被用作公車總站。

❻ _____, **too,** the economy needs as much help as it can get.

那麼，同樣的，經濟狀況也需要獲得其所能得到的幫助。

❼ _____ **of** buying a new telescope **is that** the university **would attract more students.**

支持購買新望遠鏡的一種論點是，那間大學或許能吸引更多的學生。

❽ _____: that baseball is an expensive sport to learn.

這點經常被忽視：學打棒球是個很花錢的運動。

❾ _____ **all,** science should seek to help people.

綜觀以上各點，科學應該要去幫助人。

❿ _____ **see** the importance of workplace safety.

在下述案例中，我們將會知道職場環境安全的重要性。

📖 **Answer 解答**
❶ However, the study is limited in ❷ Thus, although it is true ❸ Further ❹ And that's not all ❺ In addition to ❻ Then ❼ One argument in support ❽ This point is often overlooked ❾ Above ❿ In the following example, we will

⑪ _____, we must recognize the difference between knowledge and information.

然後結論是，我們必須區分知識和資訊的差異。

⑫ _____, the university recognized the importance of our work.

最後，那間大學認可了我們研究的重要性。

⑬ Now, _____: remove the tire from the car.

接著，下個步驟是：將輪胎從車子卸下。

⑭ _____ that there are animal species that we have not yet discovered.

很難相信仍有一些我們尚未發現的動物種類。

⑮ _____, we should focus on treating the cause of the problem, not the symptoms.

反之，我們應該把焦點放在處理造成問題的原因，而非問題的表相。

⑯ _____ is as a movie.

用其他角度看這就像是一部電影。

⑰ _____, mothers can carry their babies on their backs.

或者是，媽媽們可以把嬰兒揹在背後。

⑱ Taken _____, the school system is in trouble.

整體而言，此學校體制是有問題的。

⑲ _____ marriage.

第一部分的分析將會探討婚姻。

⑳ _____ that July is a popular month for tourism.

也必須注意的是，七月是旅遊旺季。

■ Answer 解答

⑪ And to conclude　⑫ Eventually　⑬ here is the next step　⑭ It is difficult to believe　⑮ Instead　⑯ Another way of viewing this　⑰ Alternatively　⑱ as a whole　⑲ The first part of the analysis will examine　⑳ It must also be noted

練習題 6

① _____ , marijuana is legal in some countries.

畢竟大麻在某些國家是合法的。

② _____ that science is not infallible.

我的結論是，科學並不是絕對正確的。

③ _____ that most photography nowadays is digital.

結果是現今大多數的照片都是數位化。

④ _____ briefly, we will need more funds for the project.

簡單扼要地說，為了這項計畫我們需要更多資金。

⑤ _____ that pesticides are sometimes needed to grow
healthy crops.

從這些論點可以得出，為了種植健康的作物，有時需要殺蟲劑的結論。

⑥ _____ that birds evolved from dinosaurs.

我提出的論點意謂著，鳥類是從恐龍進化而來的。

⑦ _____ that music can be therapeutic.

整體來說，這意味著音樂有療癒作用。

⑧ _____ against my colleague's position.

至於我，我必須反對我那位同事的立場。

⑨ _____ money is useful, _____ it can't
buy happiness.

儘管錢很有用，但我認為它買不到幸福。

⑩ _____ do research for other people, _____
to do it for myself.

雖然我能替其他人做研究，但我更偏好為自己做。

📖 **Answer 解答**

❶ After all ❷ My conclusion is ❸ The consequence is ❹ To sum up ❺ From these arguments one
can conclude ❻ The arguments I have presented suggest ❼ In general what this suggests is
❽ For my part, I must argue ❾ Though, I think ❿ While I can, I prefer

⑪ _____ understand their doctors.

或許人們無法理解他們的醫生。

⑫ _____, cars will fly.

車子遲早會飛。

⑬ _____ to the importance of a good diet.

對於健康飲食的重要性需要多加思量。

⑭ _____ to read fiction rather than nonfiction.

比起非虛構作品，我當然偏好選擇小說。

⑮ _____ that prehistoric fish still live in our oceans.

我確信史前時代的魚類仍然生活在我們的海洋中。

⑯ _____ that many young people are interested in politics.

這讓我們相信許多年輕人對政治感興趣。

⑰ On _____, I have decided to study psychology.

由於這緣故，我決定研讀心理學。

⑱ _____ that music can help children fall asleep.

從這些觀察中可以清楚得知，音樂可以幫助孩子入睡。

⑲ _____, Van Gogh was not a successful artist during his lifetime.

如前所述，梵谷在他一生中並不是一個成功的藝術家。

⑳ _____ that most wars are not worth the loss of so many lives.

回想起來，顯然大部分的戰爭不值得失去那麼多生命。

📄 Answer 解答

⑪ Perhaps people cannot ⑫ Sooner or later ⑬ More consideration needs to be given ⑭ I definitely prefer ⑮ I am convinced ⑯ This leads us to believe ⑰ that account ⑱ It is clear from these observations ⑲ As was previously stated ⑳ In retrospect it is clear

277

第三部分

主題文章
範例

01 Why do you think people attend college or university?

你認為人們為什麼念大學？

基本架構

在寫作前先腦力激盪，來定出文章的架構。

Introduction 開場白

在一般大學內接受高等教育的理由：
→ 擁有大學學歷，未來才有出路
→ 就業競爭激烈
→ 為了增長知識

文章的主要內容介紹
→ 針對就讀大學能取得穩定工作的優點來撰寫

Body 本文

提及大學學歷在職場上的重要性
→ 沒有大學學歷很難找到工作

許多上了年紀的人重返大學
→ 很難憑藉年資獲得升遷
→ 為了爭取更好的工作機會

沒有大學學歷很難賺取維持生活的最低薪資
→ 沒有念到大學的人，所從事的行業薪資好像會比較低

但並非所有人都能負擔得起就讀大學的花費
→ 並非所有人都需藉由大學學歷來獲得幸福人生
→ 對某些人來說，從事一般的服務業能獲得滿足感。

Conclusion 結論

對於想要獲得升遷機會的人來說，大學學歷是必需的
→ 經濟上不寬裕的人可利用政府的就學貸款或獎學金。
→ 最好的薪資待遇與就業機會僅提供給擁有學位的人

文章範例

本書前面所學到的部分句型，會在以下文章範例中出現。

Introduction 開場白

[1]**There are many reasons why** a person chooses to pursue higher education at college or university. [2]**It is often said that** the key to a successful future is a college degree. [3]**We live in a world in which** the competition for jobs gets tougher every year. [4]**There are some people who** attend college to expand their knowledge. They may enjoy the intellectual discussions and a chance to improve themselves. [5]**For the great majority of people,** though, college is a gateway to a stable and fulfilling career. [6]**This paper will focus on** the benefits of attending college to achieving a long-term career.

Body 本文

[7]**First of all, let's try to understand** why it's important to have a college degree in the working world. [8]**In the first place,** it is difficult in today's world to get a job without one. Many of us may ask, "doesn't experience and loyalty count anymore?" [9]**Indeed,** it does, but [10]**the fact is that** a college degree is now at the top of the list of requirements for most jobs.

[11]**That is why, in my opinion,** many older people are going back to college. [12]**At this point,** the number of years they have worked is not enough to get them a promotion. [13]**And that's not all** — they often have to compete for high level positions with people much less experienced. [14]**Of course,** these younger, less experienced people have college degrees. [15]**Additionally,** the more advanced degree a person holds, the higher level he/she can reach in the work place. [16]**In view of this,** we are seeing more people return to school to get their Master's or Doctoral degrees in order to compete for better jobs.

[17]**The point is,** without a college degree in today's working world, it is difficult to make a living wage. [18]**Chiefly** jobs open to a non-degreed applicant are often in the service industry (food server, bus driver, newspaper delivery). [19]**Doubtless,** these jobs are important, but for the career-minded person with a large family, they will not be sufficient for long. [20]**Rarely is it the case that** a

food server can support a family of five on his/her wages alone. ²¹As a result, the current economy ²²sometimes requires that people to return to college.

²³**Perhaps it is worth acknowledging here that** not everyone can afford to attend college. ²⁴**I agree that** a college degree is a person's best chance for a successful career today. ²⁵**However, I disagree with** the idea that everyone needs a college degree in order to have a happy life, **because I think** not everyone can succeed in higher education. ²⁶**I admit that** for some, work in the service industry can be fulfilling. ²⁷**Not to mention the fact that** society needs people to fulfill these roles.

Conclusion 結論

²⁸**On the whole,** for the person seeking a career with promotion opportunities, a college degree is a necessity. ²⁹**Perhaps people cannot** afford to attend college early in their lives, but there are government loans and scholarships available to them. ³⁰**As was previously stated,** college is not for everyone. ³¹**The arguments I have presented suggest that** the best wages and opportunities are available to a degreed person. ³²**To conclude,** ³³**I am convinced that** most people attend college for these purposes.

詞彙

pursue 追求 | **college** 大專學院、大學 | **degree** 學位 | **competition** 競爭
expand 擴展 | **long-term** 長期的 | **gateway** 途徑、方法 | **stable** 穩定的
fulfilling 實現個人抱負的 | **loyalty** 忠誠 | **count** 有重要意義 | **requirement** 必要條件
compete 競爭 | **work place** 工作場所 | **living wage** 生活給付 | **applicant** 應徵者
career-minded 重視事業的 | **sufficient** 足夠的 | **loan** 貸款 | **scholarship** 獎學金
available 可得到的；開放給…

句型

以下來複習文章範例中出現的精選句型。☞ 後面的數字對應本書前面的句型。

開場白部分出現的句型

1 **There are many reasons why ...** 基於許多原因，⋯ ☞ 請見開場白句型 65

2 **It is often said that ...** 人們常說⋯；常言道⋯ ☞ 請見開場白句型 21

3 **We live in a world in which ...** 我們生活在一個⋯的世界 ☞ 請見開場白句型 26

4 **There are some people who ...** 有些人⋯ ☞ 請見開場白句型 39

5 **For the great majority of people,** 對大部分的人來說，⋯ ☞ 請見開場白句型 32

6 **This paper will focus on ...** 這這篇論文的焦點將著重在⋯ ☞ 請見開場白句型 8

本文部分出現的句型

7 **First of all, let's try to understand ...** 首先，讓我們先嘗試了解⋯ ☞ 請見本文句型 10

8 **In the first place,** 首先，☞ 請見本文句型 7

9 **Indeed,** 的確，☞ 請見本文句型 81

10 **The fact is that ...** 事實上，☞ 請見本文句型 85

11 **That is why, in my opinion,** 這也是為什麼我認為⋯ ☞ 請見本文句型 33

12 **At this point,** 此時，☞ 請見本文句型 119

13 **And that's not all-** 而且這還不是全部－ ☞ 請見本文句型 106

14 **Of course,** 當然，☞ 請見本文句型 219

15 **Additionally,** 此外，☞ 請見本文句型 111

16 **In view of this,** 有鑑於此⋯ ☞ 請見本文句型 186

17 **The point is,** 重點是⋯ ☞ 請見本文句型 216

18 **Chiefly** 主要⋯ ☞ 請見本文句型 205

19 **Doubtless,** 毫無疑問，☞ 請見本文句型 244

20 **Rarely is it the case that ...** ⋯是鮮少發生的情況 ☞ 請見本文句型 246

21 **As a result,** 因此，☞ 請見本文句型 342

22 **Sometimes** 有時 ☞ 請見本文句型 262

23 **Perhaps it is worth acknowledging here that ...**
    或許在這裡值得被注意的是⋯ ☞ 請見本文句型 353

24 **I agree that ...** 我同意⋯ ☞ 請見本文句型 319

25 **However, I disagree with ... because I think ...**
    然而我不同意⋯，因為我認為⋯ ☞ 請見本文句型 324

26 **I admit that ...** 我承認⋯ ☞ 請見本文句型 320

27 **Not to mention the fact that ...** 不用說⋯ ☞ 請見本文句型 302

28 **On the whole,** 整體來說， ☞ 請見結論句型 9

29 **Perhaps people cannot ...** 或許人們不能… ☞ 請見結論句型 37

30 **As was previously stated,** 如前所述， ☞ 請見結論句型 56

31 **The arguments I have presented suggest that ...**
我所提出的論點意味著… ☞ 請見結論句型 24

32 **To conclude,** 結論是， ☞ 請見結論句型 6

33 **I am convinced that ...** 我確信… ☞ 請見結論句型 43

範例中文翻譯

請試著練習將以下加粗的中文，翻成英文看看。

開場白

　　有許多原因讓一個人選擇在大專或大學追求更高的教育程度。**大家常說**，一個有成就的未來關鍵就在於大學學位。我們**生活在一個**求職競爭一年比一年激烈的**世界裡，有些人**進入大學是為了擴展他們的知識廣度，他們可以享受知性的討論，並有機會提昇自己。然而，**對絕大多數的人而言**，大學是一個可以獲得一個穩定且實現個人理想職業的途徑。**這篇文章將著重在**為了達到長期職涯目標而進入大學就讀的優點。

本文

　　首先，讓我們試著了解為什麼擁有大學學位在職場上是重要的。**第一**，在現今的世界，沒有大學學位而想獲得一份工作會是很困難的，許多人可能會問，「經驗和忠誠度不再重要了嗎？」**確實**，那很重要，**但事實上**大學學位現在已經位居大多數工作的首要必備條件。

　　這也是為什麼我認為許多年長的人會回到大學裡。**就這點而言**，他們工作的年資不足以讓他們獲得升遷。**不僅如此**，他們經常需要與經驗遠不如他們的人競爭更高的職位。**當然**，這些年輕、經驗較少的人擁有大學學位。**此外**，學位的等級愈高，他/她在職場中能達到的階級愈高。**有鑑於此**，我們看到愈來愈多人回到學校去取得碩士或博士學位，目的是競爭更好的工作。

　　重點是，在今日的職場，沒有大學學位是很難賺取生活費的，**大部分**開放給不具備大學學位應徵者的工作經常是服務業（餐飲服務員、公車司機、送報員）。這些工作**無疑**很重要，但是對於有個大家庭、重視事業的人來說，這些工作就長遠來看將會不足。僅單獨靠糧食供應者就能撫養一家五口**的狀況十分少見**。**因此**，有時候經濟狀況會迫使

人們回到大學。

也許在這裡值得注意的是，並非每個人都能負擔進入大學就讀。我同意大學學位在今日是一個人擁有成功事業的最佳機會，**然而我不同意**為了擁有一段快樂的生活，每個人都需要有大學學位的觀念，**因為我認為**不是每個人都可以在更高的教育中獲得成功。我承認，對某些人而言，在服務業工作就能實現個人抱負。**更別說**社會需要有人來執行這些角色的工作。

結論

總體而言，對於尋找一個有升遷機會職業的人而言，大學學位是必要的。**也許人們無法**在他們年輕時負擔進入大學就讀，但是他們可以取得政府貸款以及獎學金。**就像先前所說的**，大學不是為每一個人開設，**我所提出的論點意味著**最好的薪資和機會都是開放給擁有大學學位的人。**結論是**，我相信大多數的人為了這些目的進入大學就讀。

02 A large factory is being built near my community. What are the advantages and disadvantages?

我居住的地區附近正在蓋一座大工廠,這件事情的優點和缺點為何?

基本架構

在寫作前先腦力激盪,來定出文章的架構。

Introduction 開場白

· 工業是城市的原動力
也有反對大廠到城市內設廠的地區
→ 雖然會為城市帶來更多工作機會與稅金,但相反地也會有汙染

提出文章的主旨
→ 探討在一個地區內設廠的優缺點

Body 本文

· 支持蓋工廠的理由
→ 工廠是世界自動化的一部分
→ 工廠促進了所在地區的經濟發展

· 工廠為小型城市帶來工作機會
→ 工廠提供的工作機會大多不要求大學學位
→ 聘僱一般勞動者,為市民創造工作機會
→ 透過創造新的工作機會,來吸引更多人來此地

· 擔心環境汙染的反對聲浪
→ 所有工廠皆會排放廢棄物,但種類不同
→ 許多工廠表示將做好環境保護

Conclusion 結論

· 在一個地區設廠各有利弊
→ 雖然有環境汙染的疑慮,但大致上對該地區是有益的
→ 對於未來持續存在的工廠,應鼓勵這些工廠遵守環保法規

 **文章範例**

本書前面所學到的部分句型，會在以下文章範例中出現。

Introduction 開場白

¹**It is often said that** industry is the life blood of a city. ²**It is a well-known fact that** cities with many businesses also have many parks and public services. ³**You may wonder why**, then, some communities object to large factories being built. ⁴**While** factories bring jobs and taxes into a city, they can often be a source of pollution. ⁵**The purpose of** this essay **is to** examine the advantages and disadvantages of having a factory inside the community.

Body 本文

⁶**The first thing that needs to be said is that** factories will continue to be built. ⁷**We cannot ignore the fact that** we live in an automated world, and factories are a part of it. ⁸**Given the history of** automation since the industrial revolution, we now depend on factories for most of our products and many of our jobs. ⁹**Until recently** factories have been viewed largely as positive additions to our communities. ¹⁰**Experts emphasize that** without factories producing military supplies during WWII, we would not have come out of the Great Depression. ¹¹**To put it simply,** factories have a history of stimulating the economy in communities where they are placed.

¹²**Of even greater appeal is** the fact that factories bring jobs to town. ¹³**In fact,** for some cities, a factory can be the primary employer. ¹⁴**Equally important is** the fact that factory jobs often do not require a college degree. ¹⁵**Instead,** they mostly employ unskilled workers, creating jobs for many citizens. ¹⁶**Assuredly, there are certain** management positions to be filled, but the great majority of jobs are open to the average person. ¹⁷**It might be said that** a factory can create opportunities where they did not exist before. ¹⁸**That is,** a town with hundreds of factory jobs will attract more people to live and work there.

¹⁹**Those opposed to** the presence of factories are often worried about pollution. ²⁰**Some people think that** all factories are a source of pollution. ²¹It

is easy to generalize about this issue, yet some factories are worse than others. All factories produce waste. But ²²**one must admit that** a meat processing factory creates a different type of waste than a vegetable cannery. ²³**We must distinguish carefully between** factories that follow regulations **and** those that don't, too. ²⁴**In reality, it is found that** many factories are now environmentally sound. ²⁵**Furthermore,** several use solar and wind power, and more are recycling their waste.

Conclusion 結論

²⁶**In conclusion,** factories can bring both good and bad things to a community. ²⁷**Granted that** not all factories obey pollution regulations, ²⁸**the consequence is that** factories which do obey them are often as unwelcome as those that don't. ²⁹**Sooner or later,** the majority will have to adopt better practices. ³⁰**We have to accept that** automated production continues to supply most of today's work force. ³¹**While I can** understand the concerns about pollution, **I prefer** to think that factories are mostly good for communities. ³²**In the end,** they will be around well into the future, ³³**so,** we must encourage them to adopt cleaner practices.

詞彙

life blood 生命泉源 | **public service** 公共設施 | **object to ...** 反對… | **pollution** 污染 | **automated** 機械自動化的 | **revolution** 革命 | **view** 視（為）| **addition** 附屬物 | **military supplies** 軍事補給品 | **come out of ...** 走出… | **Great Depression** 經濟大蕭條 | **stimulate** 刺激 | **unskilled** 未特別受訓的 | **create** 創造 | **presence** 存在 | **cannery** 罐頭工廠 | **regulation** 規則 | **sound** 健全 | **solar** 太陽能 | **obey** 遵守 | **adopt** 採用 | **practice** 作法

句型

以下來複習文章範例中出現的精選句型。☞ 後面的數字對應本書前面的句型。

開場白部分出現的句型

1 **It is often said that ...** 人們常說…／常言道… ☞ **請見開場白句型 21**

2 **It is a well-known fact that ...** 是眾所皆知的事情 ☞ **請見開場白句型 25**

3 **You may wonder why ...** 各位可能會好奇為什麼… ☞ **請見開場白句型 57**

4 **While..., ...** 儘管…，但… ☞ **請見開場白句型 49**

5 **The purpose of ... is to ...** …的目的是… ☞ **請見開場白句型 4**

本文部分出現的句型

6 **The first thing that needs to be said is that ...** 首先要說的是… ☞ **請見本文句型 5**

7 **We cannot ignore the fact that ...** 我們不能忽視…的事實 ☞ **請見本文句型 338**

8 **Given the history of ...** 有鑑於…的歷史 ☞ **請見本文句型 292**

9 **Until recently ...** 直到最近， ☞ **請見本文句型 293**

10 **Experts emphasize that ...** 專家強調… ☞ **請見本文句型 287**

11 **To put it (more) simply,** 簡而言之， ☞ **請見本文句型 303**

12 **Of even greater appeal is...** …更具吸引力 ☞ **請見本文句型 55**

13 **In fact,** 事實上， ☞ **請見本文句型 82**

14 **Equally important is ...** 同樣重要的是… ☞ **請見本文句型 148**

15 **Instead,** 取而代之的是，／反之， ☞ **請見本文句型 137**

16 **Assuredly, there are certain ...** 當然，有特定… ☞ **請見本文句型 166**

17 **It might be said that ...** 或許可以（這麼）說… ☞ **請見本文句型 264**

18 **That is,** 也就是， ☞ **請見本文句型 217**

19 **Those opposed to ...** 那些反對…的人 ☞ **請見本文句型 310**

20 **Some people think that ...** 有些人認為… ☞ **請見本文句型 38**

21 **It is easy to generalize about ...** 歸納…很簡單 ☞ **請見本文句型 27**

22 **One must admit that ...** 必須要承認的（一點）是… ☞ **請見本文句型 73**

23 **We must distinguish carefully between ...and ...**
我們必須要仔細地分辨…和… ☞ **請見本文句型 76**

24 **In reality, it is found that ...** 實際上發現… ☞ **請見本文句型 84**

25 **Furthermore,** 再者， ☞ **請見本文句型 100**

結論部分出現的句型

26 **In conclusion,** 總之，／結論是， ☞ **請見結論句型 5**

範例中文翻譯

請試著練習將以下加粗的中文，翻成英文看看。

開場白

　　常言道，工業是一個城市的生命泉源。眾所皆知的是，城市中有許多企業、也有許多公園和公共設施。那麼，**你可能會想知道為什麼**有些地區反對興建大型工廠。雖然工廠會為一個城市帶來工作機會和稅收，但也往往可能是污染源。本篇文章的**目的在於**檢視地區內設立工廠的優點和缺點。

本文

　　必須說明的第一件事是，工廠會持續興建。**我們不能忽視**我們居住在一個自動化世界的事實，而工廠是其中的一部分。**考量到**工業革命開始的機械自動化**歷史**，現在我們大部分的產品和許多工作機會都仰賴工廠。**直到最近**，工廠已經被廣泛地視為在我們的社區中有建設性的附屬物。**專家強調**，二次世界大戰期間，如果沒有工廠供應軍事補給品，我們就無法走出經濟大蕭條。**簡單來說**，工廠過去曾經刺激他們所在地區的經濟。

　　更具吸引力的是，工廠會為城鎮帶來工作機會。**事實上**，對某些城市而言，工廠可能是主要的雇主。**同樣重要的是**，工廠的工作經常不要求具備大學學位。他們大部分反而雇用未曾受過特別訓練的勞工，創造工作機會給許多居民。**確實**會有些管理職缺需要填補，但是絕大多數的工作機會都是開放給一般民眾的。**也許可以這麼說**，工廠可以創造出以前不存在的機會。**也就是**，有數百個工作機會的城鎮會吸引更多人來此居住和工作。

　　那些**反對**工廠存在的人們經常是擔心污染。**有些人認為**，所有工廠都是污染來源。**要歸納**這議題**很容易**，有些工廠比其他工廠還要糟糕。所有工廠都會製造廢棄物，但**我們必須承認**，肉品加工工廠製造的廢棄物類型和蔬菜罐頭工廠所製造的並不一樣。**我們也必須謹慎地區別**那些遵守規則以**及**未遵守規則的工廠。**實際上，人們發現**現在許多工

廠都是對環境無害的。**此外**，有些工廠採用太陽能以及風力發電，而且更多工廠回收利用他們的廢棄物。

結論

　　總之，工廠可以為一個地區同時帶來好處和壞處。**就算**並非所有工廠都遵守污染規定，結果是那些遵守規定的工廠經常和那些不遵守規定的工廠一樣不受歡迎。大多數的工廠**遲早**必須採取更好的運作方式。**我們必須接受**自動化的生產持續提供今日大部分的勞動力。**雖然我能**了解對污染的憂慮，**但是我寧**可認為工廠對一個地區大多還是有益的。**最後**，工廠將仍舊會出現在我們四周，直到未來。**所以**，我們必須鼓勵他們採用更乾淨的作法。

03 Parents are the best teachers.

父母就是最好的老師。

基本架構

在寫作前先腦力激盪，來定出文章的架構。

Introduction 開場白

· 簡述「教導」一詞的含義與「老師」的型態
→ 老師與學生之間的認同感與和諧最為重要
→ 對孩子來說最重要的人是父母

提及文章的主旨
父母是我們第一位也是最棒的老師

Body 本文

· 新生兒從誕生那一刻起就會對父母的聲音和肢體接觸有反應
→ 從出生的那一刻起，對彼此互動的感性特質留有深刻印象
→ 從出生時就受到保護和關愛的孩子，會比同齡者在各方面表現優異

· 孩子們即使到學校上課，但仍需要父母的教導
→ 父母是孩子們道德標準的典範

· 父母可指導孩子寫作業
→ 能幫助孩子提升解決問題的能力
→ 協助孩子們建立良好人際關係

· 父母的教導不侷限於年幼時期
→ 青少年雖然看似常會無視父母的關心，但還是會默默將這份關心放在心裡

· 不是所有父母都會對孩子帶來正面影響
→ 什麼樣的父母就會培養出什麼樣的孩子

Conclusion 結論

· 父母是最棒的老師
→ 父母與子女之間的聯繫是靠著互相學習與關愛
→ 父母的教導會左右孩子未來的發展

 **文章範例**

本書前面所學到的部分句型，會在以下文章範例中出現。

Introduction 開場白

"Teach" [1]**is commonly defined as** "to impart knowledge or skill." Teachers can take many forms including professors, clergymen, world leaders, and perhaps most important, our parents. [2]**There's a saying:** "What the teacher is, is more important than what he teaches." [3]**If we think about** its meaning, the identity and integrity of the teacher to the pupil is of the greatest importance. [4]**It seems to me that** no one holds more importance to a child than his/her parents. [5]**In this paper I argue that** parents are our first and perhaps best teachers.

Body 本文

[6]**To begin with,** a newborn baby responds to its parent's voice and touch from the moment of birth. [7]**I personally believe that** learning about the world in which we live begins as early as the day we are born. [8]**Here I am presuming that** while the baby may not remember these early events, the emotional quality of these interactions will leave a lasting impression. [9]**Undoubtedly,** an infant who feels safe and loved from the start will have an advantage. [10]**I would even go so far as to say that** he/she may surpass his/her peers in life in terms of achievement. [11]**The fact is that** infants who are encouraged emotionally from an early age tend to thrive in childhood.

[12]**With regard to** childhood, parents have much to teach their children, even when they attend school. [13]**Indeed,** a child receives his/her moral compass from his/her parents. [14]**Of course, you can** argue that school teachers will reinforce his/her understanding of right and wrong. [15]**And yet,** it is the parent's model the child will most likely follow.

[16]**It must also be noted that** through homework, a parent helps to shape a child's abilities in problem solving. [17]**In the same way,** parents guide their children in friendships. [18]**For example,** if two children are having an argument, a parent can suggest ways to compromise.

¹⁹It is tempting to characterize parental teaching **as** something that occurs only in early childhood. **²⁰On the one hand,** the early years are when children learn the most. **²¹On the other hand,** these children grow to be teenagers and then adults. **²²Research has shown that** although teenagers often appear to ignore their parents, they still value their advice. **²³To offer one example,** a report by the Carnegie Council on Adolescent Development states teens want more attention and guidance from parents.

²⁴Regardless of whether a parent's instruction is welcomed by a child or teenager, they will receive that influence. **²⁵Needless to say,** not all parental influence is positive. **²⁶However,** in most cases, a strong, intelligent parent will raise a strong, intelligent child.

Conclusion 結論

²⁷All this points to the conclusion that parents, givers-of-life, are the first and best teachers of children. **²⁸All things considered,** they have the most influence over their child's intellectual, physical and emotional development. **²⁹After all,** the parent-child bond is one of reciprocal learning and love. **³⁰The bottom line is that** even in cases where parents and children are at odds, the child has already learned a great deal from his/her mother and father. **³¹My conclusion is that** these lessons are fundamental to the person that child will become in life. **³²Accordingly,** this makes his/her parents his/her greatest teachers.

詞彙

impart 傳授 | **clergyman** 牧師 | **identity** 身分，個性 | **integrity** 正直 | **pupil** 學生，學徒 | **respond to ...** 對⋯有反應 | **interaction** 互動 | **lasting** 持久的 | **infant** 嬰兒 | **surpass** 超越 | **peer** 同儕 | **in terms of ...** 就⋯方面而言 | **thrive** 成長茁壯 | **moral compass** 道德感 | **reinforce** 加強 | **shape** 塑造 | **compromise** 和解 | **guidance** 指導 | **instruction** 教育 | **parental** 父母的 | **bond** 聯繫 | **reciprocal** 互相的 | **be at odds** 不一致 | **fundamental** 根本的，十分重要的

句型

以下來複習文章範例中出現的精選句型。☞ 後面的數字對應本書前面的句型。

開場白部分出現的句型

1 **...is commonly defined as ...** …普遍被定義為（被視為）… ☞ 請見開場白句型 17

2 **There's a saying:** 俗話說： ☞ 請見開場白句型 59

3 **If we think about ...** 如果我們思考… ☞ 請見開場白句型 45

4 **It seems to me that ...** 對我來說，…似乎… ☞ 請見開場白句型 41

5 **In this paper I argue that ...** 在這份報告中，我主張（認為）… ☞ 請見開場白句型 19

本文部分出現的句型

6 **To begin with,** 首先， ☞ 請見本文句型 1

7 **I personally believe that ...** 我個人相信… ☞ 請見本文句型 17

8 **Here I am presuming that ...** 在此，我假設… ☞ 請見本文句型 22

9 **Undoubtedly,** 無疑地， ☞ 請見本文句型 58

10 **I would even go so far as to say that...** 我甚至會這麼說… ☞ 請見本文句型 67

11 **The fact is that ...** 事實是… ☞ 請見本文句型 85

12 **With regard to ...,** 關於…， ☞ 請見本文句型 91

13 **Indeed,** 確實，／的確， ☞ 請見本文句型 81

14 **Of course, you can ...** 當然，你可以… ☞ 請見本文句型 98

15 **And yet,** 然而， ☞ 請見本文句型 93

16 **It must also be noted that ...** 也必須注意的是… ☞ 請見本文句型 149

17 **In the same way,** 同樣地， ☞ 請見本文句型 170

18 **For example,** 例如，／舉例來說， ☞ 請見本文句型 193

19 **It is tempting to characterize ... as ...**
將（某性格、特色）描繪成…，是挺吸引人目光的 ☞ 請見本文句型 233

20 **On the one hand,** 一方面， ☞ 請見本文句型 61

21 **On the other hand,** 另一方面， ☞ 請見本文句型 62

22 **Research has shown that ...** 研究顯示… ☞ 請見本文句型 272

23 **To offer one example,** 舉一個例子， ☞ 請見本文句型 291

24 **Regardless of whether ...,** 不論是否…， ☞ 請見本文句型 301

25 **Needless to say,** 不用說， ☞ 請見本文句型 300

26 **However,** 然而， ☞ 請見本文句型 231

27 All this points to the conclusion that ... 整體得到的結論是… ☞ 請見結論句型 13

28 All things considered, 考量一切根據, ☞ 請見結論句型 11

29 After all, 結果, ／畢竟, ☞ 請見結論句型 85

30 The bottom line is that ... 最後的結論是… ☞ 請見結論句型 30

31 My conclusion is that ... 我的結論是… ☞ 請見結論句型 4

32 Accordingly, 因此, ☞ 請見結論句型 20

範例中文翻譯

請試著練習將以下加粗的中文,翻成英文看看。

開場白

　　「教導」**普遍被定義為**「傳授知識或技術」。老師有許多種類型,包括:教授、牧師、全世界的領導人,以及可能是最重要的:我們的父母。**有一句話是這麼說的:「老師是什麼樣的人,比他教什麼更來得重要。」如果我們思考**它的涵意,老師的個性和正直對於學生而言就是最重要的事。**我認為**,對孩子來說,沒有人比他們的父母更重要。**這篇文章中,我主張**父母是我們的第一個、也可能是最好的老師。

本文

　　首先,新生兒從出生的那一刻起就對父母的聲音和觸摸有反應。**我個人相信**,早在我們出生的那一天,我們對生活在這個世界的學習和認識就開始了。**在此我假設**,雖然嬰兒可能不記得這些早期事件,但這些互動的情感特性將留下持久的印象。**無疑地**,一個從一開始就感到安全而且被愛的嬰兒會得到好處。**我甚至會這麼說**,就成就而言,他／她可能會超越同儕。**事實是**,年幼時期就在情感上受到鼓勵的嬰兒,在童年時期的表現會傾向卓越。

　　關於童年,父母有許多事情要教導他們的孩子,甚至是在他們已經進入學校就讀的時期。**確實**,孩子會從父母得到他／她們的道德觀。**當然,你可以**主張學校老師會加強他／她們對正確和錯誤的理解力;**然而**,孩子最可能遵循的典範是父母。

　　同時必須注意的是,透過家庭作業,父母可協助塑造孩子解決問題的能力。**同樣地**,父母可引導孩子認識友誼。**例如**,如果兩個孩子有爭執,父母可以建議和解的方法。

　　將父母的教育**描述為**那只是童年初期才需要的東西,這樣的說法**是挺引人注目的**。**一方面**,童年早期是孩子最大量學習的時候;**另一方面**,這些孩子長大變成青少年,然

後成年。**研究顯示**，雖然青少年經常表現出忽略他們的父母，但他們仍重視父母的忠告。**舉一個例子**，卡內基青少年發展委員會表示，青少年希望從父母得到更多注意和指導。

　　無論父母的教育**是否**被兒童或青少年接受，他們都會受到影響。**更不用說**，並非所有父母的影響都是正面的，**然而**，在大多數的例子裡，堅強、有智慧的父母會教育出堅強、有智慧的孩子。

結論

　　整體得到的結論是，父母，也就是賦予生命的人，是孩子第一個、也是最好的老師。**從全方面考量**，他們對孩子的智力、身體、情感上的發展有最大的影響。**畢竟**，親子之間的聯繫是一種互相的學習與愛。**最後的結論是**，即使是在父母與孩子有差異的案例中，孩子也已經從他／她的父母親身上學習到很多。**我的結論是**，這些學習對於孩子在人生中即將成為哪種人是非常重要的。**因此**，光是這一點，就足以讓他／她們的父母成為他／她最偉大的老師。

04 Not everything that is learned is contained in books.
並非所有知識都在書本中。

基本架構

在寫作前先腦力激盪，來定出文章的架構。

Introduction 開場白

現在的世界非常重視教育
提及文章目的
探討除了書本以外的學習方法

介紹文章的主要內容
討論運用於教育的各類型學習工具與技術，並探討這些技術與工具如何取代書籍。

Body 本文

針對電腦技術被引進教室的角度來進行探討
→ 自 1980 年代後期起，個人電腦的使用開始普遍化

全球資訊網為我們蒐集資訊的方式帶來急遽變化
→ 圖書館採用電子型態的資源
→ 可取得以往只能在書中找到的政府紀錄、歷史文件、公車時間表…等資訊

指出網路並非永遠是可靠的資訊來源
以最受歡迎的資訊來源-維基百科上亦有錯誤資訊來作為例子

還有另一種技術發達而形成的新教育型態-遠距教學
→ 學習者可透過遠距教學學習到國外的課程

Conclusion 結論

書籍仍是很好的學習工具，但未來的社會需要更多的資訊
→ 最後，教室內的新的技術將取代書籍。

文章範例

本書前面所學到的部分句型，會在以下文章範例中出現。

Introduction 開場白

[1]We live in a world in which education is highly valued. [2]It is undeniable that books have historically played a large part in our ability to learn. [3]The aim of this essay is to explore the ways we learn about the world outside of books. [4]One of the most significant current discussions in education is the role technology can play in our learning. [5]We must contemplate our growing use of the Internet and other forms of telecommunication as learning aids. [6]This essay will discuss the various forms of technology used in education and how they threaten to replace the use of books as learning tools.

Body 本文

[7]We must first examine the point at which computer technology entered the classroom. Since the late 1980's, use of the personal computer has become widespread. [8]Truly, the World Wide Web revolutionized our access to information. [9]More specifically, entire libraries are now at our fingertips in electronic form. [10]In addition to this, we can now access government records, historical documents, literature, bus schedules — all information previously found only in books. [11]It is difficult to believe that we once had to spend hours at the public library to find the information we needed, yet it's true. [12]Nowadays we don't have to leave our homes if we want to look up the capital of New Zealand or a recipe for vegetable soup.

[13]Make no mistake about it, the Internet is not always a reliable source of information. [14]It would be unfair not to mention the fact that Wikipedia, the most popular Internet information source, has been criticized for inaccuracies. [15]An important aspect of the problem is that anyone can post information to a Wikipedia entry. [16]For instance, someone might post an incorrect year of an historical battle. [17]Either someone else discovers the error, or the incorrect information continues to be presented as fact. [18]It appears that the Internet, while a powerful educational tool, is not without its weaknesses.

[19]**Yet another** growing form of educational technology is long-distance learning. [20]**One cannot deny that** visiting a foreign country is a great learning experience. [21]**But what if you could** bring that country into your classroom on a television screen? [22]**To put it another way,** we now are capable of connecting a classroom in Brussels to a classroom in Buenos Aires.

Conclusion 結論

[23]**What all this means is that** books are still useful to us, but becoming a thing of the past. [24]**For my part, I must argue** that books still have value. [25]**I definitely prefer to** hold a book in my lap than to read from a brightly lit computer screen. [26]**In the future,** however, we will likely download more information than we will hold in our hands. [27]**Although** we welcome this new technology in the classroom, **it is not** without some sadness that we must say goodbye to the book.

詞彙

play a part 扮演一個角色 | **explore** 探究 | **telecommunication** 電子通訊 |
threaten 威脅 | **widespread** 廣泛的 | **revolutionize** 徹底改變 | **entire** 整體的 |
at one's fingertips 唾手可得的 | **look up** 查詢 | **reliable** 可靠的 | **criticize** 批評 |
inaccuracy 不正確 | **post** 張貼 | **entry** 詞條 | **battle** 戰爭 | **weakness** 缺點 |
long-distance 遠距離 | **connect** 連接 | **lap** 膝上 | **lit** 照亮的 | **sadness** 感傷、悲傷

句型

以下來複習文章範例中出現的精選句型。☞ 後面的數字對應本書前面的句型。

開場白部分出現的句型

1 **We live in a world in which ...** 我們活在一個⋯的世界 ☞ 請見開場白句型 26

2 **It is undeniable that ...** 不可否認（無庸置疑地），⋯ ☞ 請見開場白句型 40

3 **The aim of this essay is to ...** 這文章的目的是為了⋯ ☞ 請見開場白句型 1

4 **One of the most significant current discussions in ... is**
⋯目前正在討論最重要的議題之一是⋯ ☞ 請見開場白句型 50

5 **We must contemplate ...** 我們必須深思⋯ ☞ 請見開場白句型 44

6 **This essay will discuss ...** 這篇文章將討論⋯ ☞ 請見開場白句型 11

本文部分出現的句型

7 **We must first examine ...** 我們必須要先檢視⋯ ☞ 請見本文句型 3

8 **Truly,** 確實，／真的，☞ 請見本文句型 220

9 **More specifically,** 更具體地說，☞ 請見本文句型 203

10 **In addition to this,** 除此之外，☞ 請見本文句型 109

11 **It is difficult to believe that ...** 很難相信⋯ ☞ 請見本文句型 134

12 **Nowadays we don't ...** 現在我們不⋯ ☞ 請見本文句型 297

13 **Make no mistake about it,** 毫無疑問地，／的確，☞ 請見本文句型 328

14 **It would be unfair not to mention the fact that ...**
沒提到⋯是不公平的 ☞ 請見本文句型 337

15 **An important aspect of the problem is ...**
這個問題其中一個重要的面向是⋯ ☞ 請見本文句型 280

16 **For instance,** 例如，／舉例來說，☞ 請見本文句型 194

17 **Either ..., or ...** 不是⋯，就是⋯／要嘛⋯，要嘛⋯ ☞ 請見本文句型 252

18 **It appears that ...** 顯然⋯ ☞ 請見本文句型 266

19 **Yet another ...** 然而，另一個⋯ ☞ 請見本文句型 114

20 **One cannot deny that ...** 人們無法否認⋯ ☞ 請見本文句型 245

21 **But what if you could ...?** 但如果你能⋯？ ☞ 請見本文句型 279

22 **To put it another way,** 換個方式說，☞ 請見本文句型 314

結論部分出現的句型

23 **What all this means is that ...** 這一切意味著⋯ ☞ 請見結論句型 21

24 **For my part, I must argue ...** 對我來說，我必須主張⋯ ☞ 請見結論句型 28

範例中文翻譯

請試著練習將以下加粗的中文，翻成英文看看。

開場白

　　我們生活在一個極為重視教育**的世界。不可否認的，**書本在歷史上對我們學習的能力扮演重要的角色。**本篇文章的目的是**要探究除了書籍之外作為我們學習認識這個世界的方法。**關於**教育，**目前正在討論最重要的議題之一是**就是科技在我們的學習中所扮演的角色。**我們必須仔細思考**我們對於網際網路日益增加的使用量，以及作為學習輔助工具的其他電子通訊形式。**本篇文章將會討論：**使用於教育的各種科技型態，以及他們如何威脅並取代書籍作為學習工具的使用。

本文

　　我們必須先檢視電腦科技進入教室的意義何在。個人電腦的使用自 1980 年代晚期已經變得很廣泛。**的確，**全球資訊網路徹底改變了我們取得資訊的方式。**更具體地說，**整個圖書館現在以數位形式存在於我們唾手可得之處。**除此之外，**我們現在可以取得政府記錄、歷史文件、文學、公車時刻表等所有以前只能在書上找到的資訊。**很難相信**我們曾經必須花上好幾個小時待在公共圖書館，尋找我們所需要的資訊，但這是真的。**現今，**如果我們想要查詢紐西蘭的首都、或是蔬菜湯的食譜，**我們不需要離開家。

　　的確，網際網路並非永遠是資訊的可靠來源。**不提起這件事實的話就不公平，**維基百科是最熱門的網際網路資訊來源，但它就曾被批評內容不正確。**這個問題其中一個重要的面向就是，**任何人都可以張貼訊息到維基百科的詞條。**例如，**某個人可能張貼了某個歷史戰爭的錯誤年份，**若非另一個人發現這個錯誤，否則**這個錯誤的資訊將持續被當作事實呈現。**顯然，**網際網路雖然是一個強大的教育工具，但並非沒有缺點。

　　另一種正在逐漸成形的教育科技是遠距教學。**人們不能否認的是，**拜訪外國是一個很棒的學習經驗，**但如果你可以**把那個國家搬到教室裡的電視螢幕上呢？**換句話說，**我們現在能夠將布魯塞爾的教室與在布宜諾斯艾利斯的教室做連線。

結論

　　這一切意味著書本仍對我們有用處，但是它正在變成一個過時的東西。**對我來說，**

我必須主張書本仍有其價值。**我當然寧可選擇**拿一本書放在膝上，勝過拿一台光亮的電腦螢幕閱讀。然而**在未來**，我們下載的資訊將可能比拿在手上的還更多。**雖然**我們欣然接受這個教室裡的新科技，**但**對於我們必須揮別書籍這件事來説，**並非**不會感到感傷。

05 What are the qualities of a good neighbor?

好鄰居的特質有哪些？

基本架構

在寫作前先腦力激盪，來定出文章的架構。

Introduction 開場白

好鄰居被當作一種祝福
→ 鄰居是在需要時伸出援手的人，但也可能會妨礙私生活。
→ 引用 Arthur Baer 說過的話：「好鄰居是會在籬笆後面對你微笑，且不會攀過籬笆越界的人」

Body 本文

提及好鄰居的特徵
→ 在你外出時會幫你看家的人

缺點：雖然也有無私淡泊的鄰居，但最好拜託值得信任的鄰居
→ 遇到小事時會伸出援手幫忙，或看到家中寵物在外面亂跑時會打電話通知

提及壞鄰居的特徵
→ 只考慮到自己
→ 遇到小事時不會像好鄰居一樣伸出援手，反而有很大的可能性會出聲抱怨

要牢牢記住我們每個人都應該成為好鄰居
→ 努力不要對別人造成困擾

提到很多鄰居會成為一輩子的朋友
→ 和諧共處是最棒的鄰里環境

Conclusion 結論

大部分的鄰居都是好鄰居
→ 我們不僅重視自己的私生活，也重視跟其它人的關係
→ 好鄰居源自於互相理解與尊重

 **文章範例**

本書前面所學到的部分句型，會在以下文章範例中出現。

Introduction 開場白

[1]**Most people consider** a good neighbor to be a blessing. [2]**In my experience,** there is a fine line sometimes between what makes a good neighbor and what makes a bad one. [3]**Ideally,** a neighbor is someone who will help when needed, but not interfere in your private life. [4]**What if**, however, your neighbor stops by to visit every day? [5]**By many accounts,** some neighbors think this is only friendly. [6]**In the words of** Arthur Baer, "A good neighbor is a fellow who smiles at you over the back fence, but doesn't climb over it."

Body 本文

[7]**My own point of view is that** a good neighbor is someone who will watch your home while you are away. [8]**The downside** of this **is that** some neighbors may like to snoop through your home while you are gone. [9]**For this reason,** it is important to ask a neighbor you trust. [10]**In truth,** most neighbors will respect your privacy, because they may need you to return the favor one day. [11]**To this end,** a good neighbor will also lend a hand when you have a small project, or call when your pet is loose in the neighborhood. [12]**There is no need to** pay the neighbor for his/her help. It is an understood kindness.

[13]**The same is not true for** the bad neighbor. [14]**The first aspect to point out is that** the bad neighbor generally thinks only of himself/herself. [15]**With respect to** the small project, the bad neighbor is likely to complain about the noise or mess you are making. [16]**Just as surely,** he/she will call to complain about your loose pet. [17]**Moreover,** he/she may not call you at all, but call the police directly with his/her complaints! [18]**One should note here that** we all have to be good neighbors. [19]**This implies that** we should try to minimize our noise, mess, and loose pets to keep from being a nuisance. [20]**Many of us may ask,** "Don't I have the right to live as I choose?" [21]**Again,** we do have rights as property owners, but [22]**in an effort to** live peacefully with our

neighbors, we must exercise respect.

[23]It is worth noting that many neighbors become lifelong friends. Sometimes their children grow up together, and sometimes whole families socialize. **[24]I believe that** this is the best neighborly situation. **[25]In spite of** our differences as neighbors, we can make the best of living near one another. I usually give new neighbor relationships a full year to develop before deciding whether they are "good" or "bad."

Conclusion 結論

[26]On the whole, most neighbors are good neighbors. **[27]In general what this suggests is that** we all value our privacy while also valuing connection with others. **[28]We cannot be sure** that our next new neighbor will be a good one. **[29]But the most important factor is that** we extend our "best" neighbor hand to them upon meeting. **[30]Therefore,** we start with understanding and respect, from which good neighbors can grow.

詞彙

blessing 福氣 | **interfere** 妨礙 | **fellow** 人，伙伴 | **fence** 圍籬 | **be away** 離家 | **snoop** 窺探 | **return** 回報 | **the favor** 恩惠 | **lend a hand** 伸出援手 | **loose** 不受束縛的、不受控制的 | **understood** 被理解的 | **kindness** 好意、善意 | **noise** 噪音 | **mess** 髒亂 | **minimize** 減少到最低、降到最低 | **nuisance** 麻煩 | **property owner** 財產擁有者 | **exercise** 行使、執行 | **lifelong** 一輩子的 | **socialize** 參與社交活動 | **neighborly** 和睦的、鄰居的 | **a full year** 一整年 | **hand** 幫助

句型

以下來複習文章範例中出現的精選句型。☞ 後面的數字對應本書前面的句型。

開場白部分出現的句型

1 **Most people consider ...** 大部分的人認為… ☞ 請見開場白句型 62

2 **In my experience,** 根據我的經驗，☞ 請見開場白句型 80

3 **Ideally,** 理想的情況下，☞ 請見開場白句型 87

4 **What if ...?** 如果…會怎麼樣呢？☞ 請見開場白句型 84

5 **By many accounts,** 許多依據顯示，／由於許多原因 ☞ 請見開場白句型 58

6 **In the words of ...,** …說：☞ 請見開場白句型 60

本文部分出現的句型

7 **My own point of view is that ...** 我的見解是…／我個人的觀點是，☞ 請見本文句型 18

8 **The downside is that ...** 缺點是… ☞ 請見本文句型 41

9 **For this reason,** 因為這個原因，☞ 請見本文句型 52

10 **In truth,** 說實話，／事實上，☞ 請見本文句型 48

11 **To this end,** 為此，☞ 請見本文句型 44

12 **There is no need to ...** 不需要… ☞ 請見本文句型 60

13 **The same is not true for ...**
這對…來說不是事實／同樣的事在…就不適用 ☞ 請見本文句型 64

14 **The first aspect to point out is that ...** 第一點要提出的是… ☞ 請見本文句型 6

15 **With respect to ...,** 關於…，☞ 請見本文句型 89

16 **Just as surely,** 同樣可以肯定的是，☞ 請見本文句型 59

17 **Moreover,** 此外，／更甚者 ☞ 請見本文句型 99

18 **One should note here that ...** 在此應該注意的是… ☞ 請見本文句型 76

19 **This implies that ...** 這暗示… ☞ 請見本文句型 29

20 **Many of us may ask ...** （我們之中）很多人也許會問… ☞ 請見本文句型 71

21 **Again,** 再次強調，☞ 請見本文句型 117

22 **In an effort to ...,** 為了（試著）…，☞ 請見本文句型 157

23 **It is worth noting that ...** 值得注意的是… ☞ 請見本文句型 282

24 **I believe that ...** 我相信… ☞ 請見本文句型 267

25 **In spite of ...,** 儘管…，☞ 請見本文句型 230

結論部分出現的句型

26 **On the whole,** 整體來說，☞ 請見結論句型 9

27 **In general what this suggests is that ...** 整體來說，這意味著⋯ ☞ 請見結論句型 26

28 **We cannot be sure ...** 我們無法確定⋯ ☞ 請見結論句型 63

29 **But the most important factor is that ...** 但最重要的因素是⋯ ☞ 請見結論句型 67

30 **Therefore,** 因此， ☞ 請見結論句型 1

範例中文翻譯

請試著練習將以下加粗的中文，翻成英文看看。

開場白

　　大部分的人都**認為**擁有好鄰居是一種福氣。**根據我的經驗**，好鄰居與壞鄰居之間的差別有時候很細微。**理想的狀況是**，鄰居是有需要時會幫助你、但不會妨礙你私人生活的人。然而，**假如**你的鄰居每天路過你家來拜訪你呢？**由於許多原因**，有些鄰居認為這只是表示友善。用亞瑟·拜爾**的話來說**：「一個好鄰居，就是會在圍籬另一頭對你微笑，但不會跨過來的人。」

本文

　　我個人的觀點是，一個好鄰居就是當你外出時會為你看家的人，這件事情的**缺點在於**，有些鄰居可能喜歡在你不在家時窺探你的家。**因為這個原因**，請一個你信任的鄰居幫忙是很重要的。**事實上**，大部分的鄰居都會尊重你的隱私，因為有一天他們可能需要你回報這個恩情。**為此**，一個好的鄰居也會在你必須居家修繕時伸出援手，或是當你的寵物在鄰近地區遊盪時打電話給你。**不需要**為鄰居的幫忙而付錢給他／她，這是一種難以言喻的善意。

　　同樣的事在壞鄰居身上**就不適用了**。**第一點要提出的是**，壞鄰居通常只想到他／她自己。**關於**居家修繕，壞鄰居可能會對你製造的噪音或髒亂提出抱怨。**同樣可以肯定的是**，他／她會打電話給你，抱怨你的寵物在外遊盪，**甚至**他／她可能根本不會打電話給你，反而直接打電話給警察提出他／她的抱怨！**在此應該注意的是**，我們都必須成為好鄰居，**這意味著**我們應該試著使噪音、髒亂降到最低，並且盡可能減少放任寵物亂跑以避免造成麻煩，**我們之中有很多人會問**，「難道我沒有權力選擇我的生活方式嗎？」**再次重申**，身為財產擁有者，我們確實有權力，但**為了盡力**與我們的鄰居和平生活，我們必須展現尊重。

　　值得注意的是，許多鄰居會變成一輩子的朋友。有時候他們的孩子一起長大，有時彼此全家參與社交活動。**我相信**這是鄰居和睦相處的最佳狀態，**儘管**我們身為鄰居有怎麼樣的差異，都能充分發揮互為鄰居的生活方式。通常在決定他們是「好」或「壞」之

前，我會給鄰居一整年的時間來發展彼此的關係。

結論

　　整體來說，大多數的鄰居都是好鄰居。**這一般意味著**，我們都重視彼此的隱私，同時也重視與其他人的關係。**我們無法確定**我們的下一個鄰居是否為好鄰居，**但是最重要的事情**是在遇見他們的那一刻，我們向他們伸出我們「最佳鄰居」之手。**因此**，我們從諒解和尊重這兩點開始，發展良好的鄰居關係。

06 What are some important qualities of a good boss/supervisor?

一位好老闆／好主管具備哪些重要特質？

基本架構

在寫作前先腦力激盪，來定出文章的架構。

Introduction 開場白

針對完美的上司是否存在這一點提出質疑
→ 讓工作氣氛愉快的上司擁有特定的個人素質

提及文章主題
→ 針對好上司的幾種素質進行説明

Body 本文

是什麼讓職員們產生工作動力
→ 上司尊重職員的話，職員就會為了讓這種上司滿意而努力工作

指出沒有完美之人
→ 表現得畢恭畢敬的職員可能很懶惰
→ 但根據員工成就感的相關研究顯示，可獲得尊重的工作環境是最具生產力且成功的職場環境

以身作則是最好的領導者
→ 好的主管會和員工保持密切的聯繫，了解自身的影響力，增強責任感。

好上司也知道讓工作變有趣的方法
→ 規劃慶生會、公司郊遊、社交聚會的時間
→ 透過這些活動對員工們表示同感且展現個人關心，讓上司變得「親民」

要重新投入工作時，應恢復作為上司的權威
→ 維持明確的職場關係對上司跟職員都是很重要的一件事

Conclusion 結論

再次強調前面提到的好上司素質
→ 希望能有最好的工作環境

本書前面所學到的部分句型，會在以下文章範例中出現。

Introduction 開場白

¹I question whether anyone is the perfect boss. ²One of the misconceptions about the working world is that the "perfect" job with the "perfect" boss actually exists somewhere. First of all, no human being is perfect. However, ³it is generally agreed today that certain personal qualities in a supervisor can make any job a more pleasant one. ⁴This paper will give an account of some of these qualities. ⁵I'd like to demonstrate why they are effective in supervising a working staff.

Body 本文

⁶The task at hand is to recognize what motivates employees to do their best work. ⁷From my experience, I think it is most important that the boss treat employees respectfully. ⁸As far as the employee is concerned, a boss who gives respect will quickly earn respect. ⁹Logically, it follows that a respectful employee will work hard to please his/her respectful supervisor. ¹⁰Perhaps I should also point out the fact that again, no person is perfect. ¹¹Thus, a respectful employee could also be lazy, and may disprove this theory. ¹²There is a great deal of research being done on employee performance, however. ¹³So far, it is clear that respectful work environments are the most productive and successful.

¹⁴Turning now to the question of the boss' personality, ¹⁵many people believe that a supervisor who leads by example is the best kind of boss. ¹⁶It seems that a boss who is punctual, hard working, and a team player encourages these qualities in his/her employees. ¹⁷Conversely, a boss who is always late, talkative, and isolates himself/ herself will encourage these behaviors in his/her staff. ¹⁸With this in mind, the smart boss will recognize his/her responsibility to his/her own work while remembering his/ her influence over the employees.

¹⁹Although it may be true that a good boss knows how to motivate his/

her employees, he/she also knows how to make their work enjoyable. **[20]It has been found that** the boss who makes time for birthday parties, retreats, and off-work socializing is more accepted by his/her staff as one of them. **[21]It could be said that** these activities "humanize" the boss, when he/she can show empathy and a personal interest in his/her workers. He/She is **[22]neither** boss **nor** employee in these social situations, and he/she can enjoy the company of his/her employees without being an authority figure. **[23]Still,** when it is time to return to work, he/she must be able to reclaim that authority in order to get the job done. **[24]In other words,** he/she is still the boss when the birthday party is over. It is important to the boss and the employees that even when relaxed in the off-work hours, this working relationship remains clear.

Conclusion 結論

   [25]In conclusion, a good boss is someone who respects his/her employees, leads by example, and isn't afraid to have fun once in a while. **[26]Under these conditions,** we can hope for the best possible work environment. **[27]I'm sure that** there are exceptions to this, **[28]but, as for me, it's** proven an effective management strategy time and again. **[29]One thing's for sure:** a boss without these qualities will struggle as an authority figure and have trouble keeping his/her employees.

詞彙

supervisor 上司 ∣ **effective** 有效的 ∣ **motivate** 激發 ∣ **respectfully** 尊敬地 ∣ **earn** 贏得 ∣
disprove 駁斥 ∣ **performance** 績效 ∣ **productive** 有生產力的 ∣ **personality** 人格特質 ∣
punctual 準時的、守時的 ∣ **talkative** 喜歡說話的 ∣ **isolate** 孤立 ∣
retreat 公司舉辦的員工休閒或度假活動 ∣ **off-work** 下班後 ∣ **socializing** 社交 ∣
humanize 變得有人性化 ∣ **empathy** 同理心、同情心 ∣ **authority figure** 權威角色 ∣
reclaim 要求收回、重新恢復 ∣ **once in awhile** 偶爾 ∣ **exception** 例外 ∣
time and again 屢次 ∣ **struggle** 掙扎

句型

以下來複習文章範例中出現的精選句型。☞ 後面的數字對應本書前面的句型。

開場白部分出現的句型

1 I question whether ... 我懷疑…是否…／我對…感到質疑 ☞ **請見開場白句型 69**

2 One of the misconceptions about ... is ...
對…錯誤的認知之一是… ☞ **請見開場白句型 63**

3 It is generally agreed today that ... 當前普遍認為（同意）… ☞ **請見開場白句型 31**

4 This paper will give an account of ... 這篇論文／報告將說明… ☞ **請見開場白句型 7**

5 I'd like to demonstrate ... 我想示範… ☞ **請見開場白句型 56**

本文部分出現的句型

6 The task at hand is to ... 現在首先要做的是… ☞ **請見本文句型 2**

7 From my experience, I think (it is) ... 根據我的經驗，我認為… ☞ **請見本文句型 16**

8 As far as ... is concerned, 就…而言， ☞ **請見本文句型 92**

9 Logically, it follows that... 就邏輯而言，…當然… ☞ **請見本文句型 11**

10 Perhaps I should also point out the fact that ...
或許我也應該要指出…的事實 ☞ **請見本文句型 65**

11 Thus, 因此， ☞ **請見本文句型 50**

12 There is a great deal of research ... …的研究很多 ☞ **請見本文句型 211**

13 So far, it is clear that ... 目前為止，…很明顯地… ☞ **請見本文句型 243**

14 Turning now to the question of ..., 現在回到…的問題， ☞ **請見本文句型 189**

15 Many people believe that ... 許多人相信… ☞ **請見本文句型 270**

16 It seems that ... 似乎是…／看起來… ☞ **請見本文句型 265**

17 Conversely, 相反地，／反過來， ☞ **請見本文句型 177**

18 With this in mind, 有鑒於此，／請記住， ☞ **請見本文句型 190**

19 Although it may be true that ..., 儘管…也許是事實， ☞ **請見本文句型 237**

20 It has been found that ... 研究發現…／人們發現… ☞ **請見本文句型 271**

21 It could be said that ... 可以（這麼）說… ☞ **請見本文句型 263**

22 Neither A nor B 既不是 A 也不是 B ☞ **請見本文句型 259**

23 Still, 儘管如此，／依然…／仍然… ☞ **請見本文句型 298**

24 In other words, 換句話說， ☞ **請見本文句型 313**

結論部分出現的句型

25 In conclusion, 總而言之， ☞ **請見結論句型 5**

範例中文翻譯

請試著練習將以下加粗的中文，翻成英文看看。

開場白

　　我懷疑是否有人可以成為一位完美的上司。對於職場錯誤的認知之一，是在某個地方會有「完美」上司的「完美」工作。首先，沒有人是完美的。然而，**當前人們普遍認為**，一個主管的某些人格特質，可以讓任何工作變得更令人愉悅。**本篇文章將說明**一些特質。**我想說明**這些特質為什麼在管理工作人員上是有效的。

本文

　　現在首先要做的任務就是，要辨別出什麼能夠激發員工，以達到最佳的工作成果。**從我的經驗看來**，我認為最重要的就是上司以尊重的態度看待員工。**就員工而言**，尊重員工的上司能很快地贏得尊重。**用邏輯來推論**，當然是尊重人的員工會為尊重人的上司努力付出，來獲得上司的滿意。**或許我也應該再次點出這個事實**：沒有人是完美的。**因此**，一位尊重他人的員工也可能懶散，也可能證明這個理論是不正確的。然而，**針對員工工作績效有許多研究，到目前為止，很明顯的是**，尊重他人的工作環境是最富成效，也是最成功的。

　　現在回到上司人格特質的問題，許多人相信以自身榜樣來領導的主管是最好的上司。似乎嚴正守時、勤奮工作、能團隊合作的主管會在他／她的員工身上激發出這些特質。**相反地**，一個總是遲到、多嘴、自我孤立的上司也會助長他／她的員工這些行為。**有鑑於此**，聰明的上司會認清他／她自身工作該負起的責任，同時牢記他／她對員工的影響。

　　雖然好上司可能真的懂得如何激發他／她的員工，但他／她也知道如何讓他們的工作更有樂趣。**人們發現**那些肯花時間辦理生日派對、員工度假活動、以及下班後社交活動的上司，會更被他／她的職員接納成為他們的一員。**我們可以這麼說**，當他／她可以對他／她的員工展現同理心以及個人興趣時，這些活動讓上司「人性化」。在這些社交場合中，他／她**既不是**上司**也不是**員工，而且他可以享受員工們的陪伴，而非扮演一個權威角色。**儘管如此**，當是時候返回工作崗位，他／她必須能夠重新取回權威以便完成

工作。**換言之**，生日派對結束後，他／她仍然是上司，就連下班放鬆的時候，工作關係仍然是清楚的。這點對上司和員工而言非常重要。

結論

　　總而言之，一位好上司是尊重他／她員工的人、以榜樣來領導、而且不在意偶爾可以開心一下。**在這些條件之下**，我們可以期待最佳可能的工作環境。**我確信**有例外，**但是對我而言**，**這**已經再再證明是有效的管理策略。**有一點可以肯定的是**：不具備這些特質的上司，作為一個權威角色會非常吃力，而且在管理他／她的員工時會有困難。

07 Is it better for children to grow up in the countryside than in a big city?

讓孩子在鄉下長大，是否比在大城市長大來得好？

基本架構

在寫作前先腦力激盪，來定出文章的架構。

Introduction 開場白

據說鄉下小孩比城市小孩更健康
→ 但也要考量到學習機會、接觸美術或運動的機會，或者生長在各種文化環境下等城鄉差距問題
→ 關於鄉下環境比城市更好的說法未取得共識

介紹文章主要內容
以批判角度來探討城市與鄉下的優缺點

Body 本文

指出鄉下跟城市一樣都有缺點
→ 鄉下孩子們因為缺乏接觸各種文化的經驗，在社交方面處於劣勢
→ 只了解自身文化的孩子，一旦脫離該文化就可能出現適應不良的情況
→ 可能會因為害怕或抗拒跟自己不一樣的人，而排斥接觸更廣闊的社會

接下來要指出鄉下學校的缺點
→ 相較於城市學校，書籍跟設備可能較為老舊，提供給學生的課程也較為不足

城市學校不僅提供比較多課程，書籍、設備跟教室也比較新
→ 沒辦法像鄉下孩子一樣擁有向大自然學習的機會

Conclusion 結論

鄉下與城市都各自有優缺點
→ 城市更忙碌且更競爭，但亦擁有更多機會
→ 在鄉下從大自然中學習是非常重要的
→ 孩子們可藉由接觸多樣化的學習環境來達到最佳學習效果

本書前面所學到的部分句型，會在以下文章範例中出現。

Introduction 開場白

¹**We often hear that** children who grow up in the countryside are healthier than children raised in a big city. ²**Could this be due to** the pollution, noise, and crowded conditions that exist in a big city? And, ³**how can we be sure** that these factors are the most important considerations for a child's environment? ⁴**It is a complicated question** involving many things besides these, including opportunities for learning, access to arts and athletics, and exposure to diverse cultures. ⁵**There is still no general agreement about** whether clean country air and quiet living is better for a child than all the things a city has to offer. ⁶**This essay critically examines** the pros and cons of country vs. city living for today's children.

Body 本文

⁷**If, on the one hand, it can be said that** cities produce noise, air and crowded conditions that are unhealthy, **it can also be said that** country living has its own drawbacks. ⁸**In as much as** many country children grow up without experiencing people of other cultures, they are at a social disadvantage in the larger world. ⁹**This point is often overlooked:** a child who knows only his/her own culture may have trouble adapting if he/she should leave that culture one day. ¹⁰**Not only** will that child confront people of many races, colors and religions, **but** he/she will **also** have to expand his/her attitudes and acceptance of these differences. ¹¹**Even though** for most people, this is a positive experience, the child raised to accept only his/her own kind may be afraid or intolerant of people different from him/her and reject the larger world.

¹²**To look at this another way**, country schools often do not have the same advantages as city schools. ¹³**That is,** their books and equipment may be outdated and they often have fewer programs for students. ¹⁴**It may seem odd that** not all public schools have the same resources, **but** the size of the

school and community determine their funding levels.

¹⁵In contrast, city schools often have numerous programs. **¹⁶Correspondingly,** their equipment, books and classrooms are often newer, too. **¹⁷While this may be true,** a city child may have to compete with more students for a spot on the basketball team or a part in the school play. **¹⁸Then, too,** the city child may not have the opportunity to learn from nature like the country child. **¹⁹Further,** a city child may not know animals living in the wild, forests or mountains as a country child would. **²⁰From that standpoint,** the country child is at an advantage. **²¹Specifically,** he/she may understand nature's processes better from having watched them, **²²such as** a chick hatching from an egg. **²³In that case, ²⁴it is useful to** grow up in a quiet environment where such miracles occur. **²⁵Imagine what it would be like if a** chick tried to hatch in a busy city intersection!

Conclusion 結論

²⁶Experts point out that there are advantages and disadvantages to both childhood environments. **²⁷As noted before,** the city may be busier and more competitive, but it also has more opportunities. It is just as important, though, for our children to learn from nature, which **²⁸experts say that** most children in today's world are missing. **²⁹What's worse is that** our natural habitats are disappearing. **³⁰At any rate,** our children will be best served by being exposed to many different learning environments.

詞彙

countryside 鄉下、農村 | **crowded** 擁擠的 | **consideration** 考量、考慮 | **athletics** 運動 | **diverse** 多元的 | **pros and cons** 優缺點 | **drawback** 缺點、短處 | **disadvantage** 不利之處 | **confront** 經歷、遭遇 | **race** 種族 | **religion** 宗教 | **attitude** 態度 | **acceptance** 接受度 | **intolerant** 無法忍受 | **reject** 拒絕 | **equipment** 設備 | **outdated** 老舊的、過時的 | **funding** 基金、獲得資金 | **numerous** 許多的 | **spot** 職位 | **hatch** 孵化 | **intersection** 十字路口 | **competitive** 競爭的 | **miss** 遺漏、錯失 | **habitat** 棲息地 | **disappear** 消失

句型

以下來複習文章範例中出現的精選句型。☞ 後面的數字對應本書前面的句型。

開場白部分出現的句型

1　**We often hear that ...** 我們常聽說… ☞ **請見開場白句型 20**

2　**Could this be due to ...** 這可能是因為…的關係嗎？ ☞ **請見開場白句型 85**

3　**How can we be sure ...** 我們如何確信…？ ☞ **請見開場白句型 82**

4　**It is a complicated question**（對…來說，）這是個複雜的問題 ☞ **請見開場白句型 72**

5　**There is still no general agreement about ...**
　　目前對於…仍未有共識 ☞ **請見開場白句型 74**

6　**This essay critically examines ...** 本篇文章將以批判的方式檢視… ☞ **請見開場白句型 10**

本文部分出現的句型

7　**If, on the one hand, it can be said that ..., it can also be said that ...**
　　一方面，如果說…，那麼也可以說… ☞ **請見本文句型 63**

8　**In as much as ...,** 因為…， ☞ **請見本文句型 45**

9　**This point is often overlooked:** 這點往往被忽略： ☞ **請見本文句型 116**

10　**Not only ..., but (also)...** 不只…，而且… ☞ **請見本文句型 104**

11　**Even though ...,** 即使…， ☞ **請見本文句型 228**

12　**To look at this another way,** 從另一個角度看，／換一個角度看， ☞ **請見本文句型 66**

13　**That is (to say),** 也就是說， ☞ **請見本文句型 217**

14　**It may seem odd that ..., but ...** 也許會覺得奇怪的是…，但卻… ☞ **請見本文句型 164**

15　**In contrast,** 相反地， ☞ **請見本文句型 175**

16　**Correspondingly,** 相同地， ☞ **請見本文句型 169**

17　**While this may be true,** 雖然這也許是事實，但… ☞ **請見本文句型 238**

18　**Then, too, ...** 那麼，同樣的，… ☞ **請見本文句型 113**

19　**Further,** 更進一步（再者）， ☞ **請見本文句型 101**

20　**From that standpoint,** 從這個觀點來看， ☞ **請見本文句型 187**

21　**Specifically,** 具體來說，／明確地說， ☞ **請見本文句型 202**

22　**such as...** 像是… ☞ **請見本文句型 197**

23　**In this(that) case,** 在這情況下， ☞ **請見本文句型 210**

24　**It is useful to ...** …是有用的 ☞ **請見本文句型 251**

25　**Imagine what it would be like if ...** 想像一下如果…那會是什麼樣子 ☞ **請見本文句型 308**

26 **Experts point out that ...** 專家指出… ☞ **請見本文句型 288**

27 **As noted before,** 如前所述， ☞ **請見本文句型 317**

28 **Experts say that ...** 專家表示… ☞ **請見本文句型 285**

29 **What's worse is that ...** 更糟的是… ☞ **請見本文句型 334**

30 **At any rate,** 無論如何，／總之， ☞ **請見本文句型 346**

範例中文翻譯

請試著練習將以下加粗的中文，翻成英文看看。

開場白

　　我們常聽說在鄉下長大的孩子比在大城市養大的孩子還健康，**這可能是因為**大城市裡存在污染、噪音和擁擠的環境**嗎**？再者，**我們如何確定**這些因素是孩子生活環境中最重要的考量？**這是一個複雜的問題**，牽涉到的事情除了這些外，還包括學習機會、接觸藝術和運動的機會、接觸多元文化。對孩子而言，乾淨的鄉間空氣以及安靜的生活是否比城市可以提供的所有事物都更好？**目前關於這點仍沒有普遍共識。本篇文章將以批判的方式檢視**鄉村和城市生活對今日的孩子們的優點與缺點。

本文

　　如果，我們**一方面說**城市製造不健康的噪音、空氣以及擁擠的環境，**那麼也可以說**鄉村生活有其缺點。**由於**鄉村孩童的成長過程中沒有遇過其他文化的人，他們在更廣大的世界中就處於社交不利的地位。**這一點經常被忽略：**只認識自己文化的孩子，如果有一天要離開這個文化，可能在適應上會有問題。這個孩子**不僅**會遇到許多種族、膚色和宗教的人，**而且**他／她也必須發展自己面對這些差異的態度和接受度。**即使**對大多數的人而言，這是正面的經驗，但是對從小到大只接觸過與自己文化相同的孩子來說，他們可能會對與自己不同的人感到害怕或無法忍受，並且拒絕更廣大的世界。

　　從另一個角度來看，鄉下學校經常沒有城市學校的優點。**也就是說**，他們的書籍和設備可能都很老舊，而且鄉下學校給學生的教育計畫通常比較少。**也許會覺得奇怪的是**，並非所有公立學校都擁有相同的資源，**但是**學校以及社區的規模會決定他們獲得資金的等級。

　　相反地，城市的學校經常有許多教學方案。**同樣地**，通常他們的設備、書籍和教室也比較新。**雖然這也許是事實**，一個城市孩童可能必須與更多學生競爭籃球隊裡的一個位置、或是學校表演裡的一個角色。**那麼，同樣地**，城市孩童可能沒有機會像鄉村孩童

那樣從大自然中學習。**再者**，城市孩童可能無法像鄉村孩童那樣認識生活在野外、森林或山中的動物。**從這個觀點看來**，鄉村孩童是處於有利位置的。具體來說，他／她可能從觀察中更了解大自然的生產過程，**像是**母雞孵蛋。**在這情況下**，在一個這樣會有奇蹟發生的寧靜環境中長大，**是件有益的事情**。**想像一下**，一隻雞在繁忙都市的十字路口孵蛋**會是什麼樣子**。

結論

　　專家指出，兩種童年環境都有其優缺點。**正如先前所述**，城市可能比較繁忙且更具競爭性，但它也有比較多的機會。雖然對我們的孩子而言，從大自然學習是相同重要的事情，但**專家們也指出**：這是現今大多數孩童缺乏的部分。**更糟的是**，我們的自然棲息地正在消失。**無論如何**，讓我們的孩童受到許多來自不同環境的學習會是最好的。

08 Is it a good idea for teenagers to have jobs while they are still students?

讓青少年半工半讀是好事嗎？

基本架構

在寫作前先腦力激盪，來定出文章的架構。

Introduction 開場白

提及哪些行業普遍雇用青少年
→ 餐廳、戲院…等各種場所經常雇用青少年
→ 青少年的工作是邁向成人的重要階段

說明文章結構
→ 簡述青少年的求職理由，並提出支持其的論據

Body 本文

・**一般而言，青少年都是為了支付娛樂開銷才去工作**
→ 除此之外，青少年還有許多想工作的理由
→ 即使如此，還是不確定他們去工作這件事是好事還是壞事

・**部分專家認為：青少年應專注課業**
→ 工作會影響他們的成績

・**大部分雇主認為：青少年也需要體驗社會生活的時間**
→ 對未成年的工作時間有制定相關法律

・**贊成青少年去工作的人認為：視其為成長的機會**
→ 青少年在工作的過程中，能被賦予更多責任感，將來可能成為領導階級
→ 有機會獲得更多獎學金

・**以另一種角度來思考高中生打工這件事**
→ 對青少年的挑戰
→ 讓他們知道沒有大學學位的話，能從事哪些工作
→ 幫助他們決定是否要讀大學

Conclusion 結論

・**高中生工作有可能妨礙讀書，但也是成長的重要階段**
概述前面提到過的高中生打工的優點
→ 基於前述所有理由，支持青少年擁有工作經驗

 **文章範例**

本書前面所學到的部分句型，會在以下文章範例中出現。

Introduction 開場白

¹In some business cultures, it is common to hire teenagers. **²As you may have noticed,** many restaurants employ teenagers as waiters, and movie theaters hire them to sell tickets and popcorn. **³If you stop to consider** all the places you've seen teenagers working, you would be surprised at how many are employed. **⁴In my opinion,** teenage jobs are an important step toward becoming an adult. **⁵This paper first gives a brief overview of** why teenagers seek jobs, followed by my reasons for supporting this.

Body 本文

⁶Generally speaking, most teenagers want to work so they can afford to have fun. **⁷Nonetheless, many people believe that** some teens are saving money for college or learning a trade. **⁸Another possibility is** that he/she may be saving his/her money for his/her first car or a trip to Europe. **⁹It is obvious that** there are many reasons for teenagers to want to work. **¹⁰Even if** this **is true,** is it a good idea?

¹¹According to some experts, teens should focus on their studies in high school to improve their college entry scores. **¹²Take, for example,** the high school student who works every night of the week and neglects his/her homework. **¹³We cannot ignore the fact that** his/her grades will suffer for it.

¹⁴In all actuality, most employers recognize that teenagers need **¹⁵not only** time for studies**, but** for socializing, too. **¹⁶It is worth stating at this point that** there are also laws limiting the number of hours a minor child can work.

¹⁷Those in favour of teen employment, such as myself, see it as an opportunity for growth. **¹⁸This is most clearly seen in** teens who are given increasing responsibilities on the job. **¹⁹It is generally thought that** these teens are our future leaders. **²⁰Another reason why** teens benefit from high school jobs **is that** more scholarships are available to them. **²¹Particularly,**

they may qualify for an employee scholarship, or [22]**owing to** their work history, may be seen as a good risk by a scholarship committee.

[23]**Another way of viewing this is as** a challenge to the teen. [24]**Or,** the high school job can show the teenager the kind of work available to him/her without a college degree. [25]**With this purpose in mind,** it may help him/her make a decision about whether to go to university. [26]**Assuming that** most high school jobs are hard work for low pay, he/she will quickly realize the benefits of a college degree.

Conclusion 結論

[27]**Though** a high school job can be disruptive to a teen's study habits, **I think** it is an important stage in his/her development. [28]**It is clear from the above that** there are many benefits to having a high school job. [29]**To summarize,** a job can give the teenager self-confidence, experience, scholarship opportunities and a view of the real world. [30]**When all is said and done,** it is an investment in the teen's future. [31]**For all these reasons,** I support the idea of a high school job experience.

詞彙

learn a trade 學習一項技能 | **entry** 進入 | **neglect** 忽略 | **grade** 成績 | **minor** 年幼的 | **qualify** 具備條件、取得資格 | **good risk** 好的冒險 | **disruptive** 分裂的 | **self-confidence** 自信

句型

以下來複習文章範例中出現的精選句型。☞ 後面的數字對應本書前面的句型。

開場白部分出現的句型

1 **In some business cultures,** 在某些商業文化中，☞ 請見開場白句型 51

2 **As you may have noticed,** 各位也許已經察覺到，☞ 請見開場白句型 48

3 **If you stop to consider...** 如果你思考一下⋯ ☞ 請見開場白句型 46

4 **In my opinion,** 就我的觀點而言，／個人認為，☞ 請見開場白句型 78

5 **This paper first gives a brief overview of ...**
這份報告首先提供有關⋯的簡單概要 ☞ 請見開場白句型 77

本文部分出現的句型

6 **Generally speaking,** 一般而言，☞ 請見本文句型 28

7 **Nonetheless, many people believe that ...**
即使如此，許多人仍然認為⋯ ☞ 請見本文句型 95

8 **Another possibility is...** 另一個可能性是⋯ ☞ 請見本文句型 184

9 **It is obvious that ...** 顯然⋯ ☞ 請見本文句型 241

10 **Even if ... is true,** 即使⋯是事實，☞ 請見本文句型 234

11 **According to some experts,** 根據一些專家的說法，☞ 請見本文句型 290

12 **Take, for example, ...** 以⋯為例，／舉例來說，☞ 請見本文句型 291

13 **We cannot ignore the fact that ...** 我們不能忽視⋯的事實 ☞ 請見本文句型 338

14 **In all actuality,** 事實上，☞ 請見本文句型 350

15 **Not only ..., but (also)...** 不只⋯，而且⋯ ☞ 請見本文句型 104

16 **It is worth stating at this point that ...**
在這個論點上值得一提的是⋯ ☞ 請見本文句型 281

17 **Those in favour of ...** 那些贊成⋯的人 ☞ 請見本文句型 309

18 **This is most clearly seen in ...**
這在⋯中最為明顯／這在⋯上看得最清楚 ☞ 請見本文句型 276

19 **It is generally thought that ...** 一般認為⋯ ☞ 請見本文句型 268

20 **Another reason why ... is that ...** 為什麼⋯的另一個原因是因為⋯ ☞ 請見本文句型 305

21 **particularly...** 特別是⋯／尤其⋯ ☞ 請見本文句型 198

22 **Owing to ...** 由於⋯ ☞ 請見本文句型 162

23 **Another way of viewing this is as ...** 用其他角度看這就像是⋯ ☞ 請見本文句型 138

24 **Or,** 或者，☞ 請見本文句型 136

25 **With this purpose in mind,** 心中謹記著這個目標，☞ 請見本文句型 151

結論部分出現的句型

範例中文翻譯

請試著練習將以下加粗的中文，翻成英文看看。

開場白

　　在某些商場文化中，雇用青少年是很普遍的。**各位可能已經注意到，**許多餐廳雇用青少年來當服務生，電影院雇用青少年販賣電影票和爆米花。**如果你停下腳步來思考一下，**在你見過青少年工作的所有場合，你會驚訝有許多青少年在受僱。**就我的觀點而言，**青少年的工作是邁向成人的重要步驟。**本篇文章首先提出一個簡略概要：**青少年為什麼要找工作，接著是我支持這個論點的理由。

本文

　　一般來說，大多數的青少年想要工作，這樣才能負擔娛樂支出。**儘管如此，許多人仍認為，**有些青少年是為了大學存錢或學習一項技能。**另一種可能是，**他／她正為了他／她的第一輛車、或是到歐洲旅行而存錢。**很顯然地，**青少年去工作有許多原因。**就算**這是真的，這是好事嗎？

　　根據有些專家的說法，青少年應該專注於他們的高中學業，以提升他們得以進入大學的成績。**以此為例，**每個周間晚上都工作的青少年會疏忽他們的成績。**我們不能忽略這個事實，**也就是他／她的成績會因此受到影響。

　　事實上，大多數的雇主認同青少年**不僅**需要時間學習，**而且也**需要時間參與社交生活。**在這個論點上值得一提的是，**法律也限制未成年孩童工作的時數。

　　贊成青少年就業**的人，**例如我自己，是將它視為成長的機會。**這在**那些工作上被賦予愈來愈多責任的青少年身**上看得最清楚，**這些青少年**普遍被認為**是我們未來的領導者。青少年之所以可以從高中打工中獲益**的另一個理由是：**他們可以獲得更多獎學金，**特別是**他們可能會得到員工獎學金，或是因為他們的工作經歷，而被獎學金委員會視為

是一個不錯的嘗試。

　　另一個看待這件事情的角度，是把它當作是青少年的挑戰。**或者，**在高中找到的工作可以讓青少年清楚，在沒有大學學位的狀況下，可以找到什麼樣的工作。**心中謹記著這件事，**工作可以幫助他／她決定是否要進入大學就讀。**假設**大多數的人在高中時找到低薪的辛苦工作，他很快就會了解大學學位的好處。

結論

　　雖然高中時找的工作可能會分掉一些青少年的學習習慣，**但我認為**那是他／她成長過程中的一個重要階段。**從以上內容可以清楚得知，**高中時期去工作是有許多好處的。**總結來說，**工作可以給予青少年自信、經驗、申請到獎學金的機會，以及看到真實的世界。**畢竟，**那對青少年來說是未來的投資。**基於這所有的理由，**我支持高中有工作經驗的這個想法。

09 People should sometimes do things that they do not enjoy doing.

人們有時應該要做他們不喜歡做的事。

基本架構

在寫作前先腦力激盪,來定出文章的架構。

Introduction 開場白

· 人們有時必須做自己不喜歡的事
針對問題做簡單的描述
→ 針對自己不喜歡做的事提出幾點好處

Body 本文

· 朋友與家人可能會向你提議來做你不喜歡做的事
→ 跟朋友或家人一起參與某活動,有時是值得的
→ 雖然有時會有危險,但我們必須按照自己的邏輯接受各種活動
→ 對我們所愛的人喜歡的事物持開放態度

· 用過去不好的經驗來判斷,並不妥當
→ 任何體驗都值得再次嘗試

· 挑戰自我很重要
→ 雖然是不喜歡的活動,但試著嘗試看看,可能會因此改觀
→ 還可以鼓勵自己嘗試新事物

· 人們相信這個社會不允許人們做自己不喜歡做的事情
→ 可能面臨無政府狀態
→ 每個人的行為舉止都可能會影響到整個社會

Conclusion 結論

· 做自己不喜歡的事,有時能獲得最大利益
→ 我們有時需要走出舒適圈來挑戰自我
→ 不僅是為自己,也要為所愛之人與社會的幸福做出貢獻

本書前面所學到的部分句型，會在以下文章範例中出現。

Introduction 開場白

¹Once in a great while, people should do something they do not enjoy. **²You may wonder why** this is important. **³Normally,** it is against our nature to choose activities that do not appeal to us. **⁴This essay will deal with the following aspects of the question:** Why should we push ourselves to do things we do not enjoy? **⁵I'd like to suggest that** there are several benefits.

Body 本文

⁶First, our friends and family may ask us to join them in an activity we don't enjoy. **⁷If** joining them prevents hurting their feelings, it is **⁸sometimes** worthwhile to go along with them. **⁹I suppose that** there are cases when the suggested activity is too dangerous to consider. **¹⁰We must take** each activity **on its own terms, ¹¹however,** and be open to some of the things our loved ones enjoy.

¹²Second, it might not be fair to judge a past bad experience as unenjoyable. **¹³If it is the case that** the one time you went swimming the water was too cold, this time, it might be warm and pleasant. **¹⁴One should always remember that** every experience is worth a second try. **¹⁵But don't take my word for it;** go out and see for yourself!

¹⁶Third, it is important to continue to challenge ourselves. **¹⁷One of the most serious drawbacks of** avoiding unenjoyable experiences **is that** we begin to close ourselves to new experiences. **¹⁸While the second argument** in this essay **suggests that** another try at an unenjoyable activity could change your mind. It can also encourage you to try new things. **¹⁹An example of this is** a person who gives the opera a second chance and finds he/she actually enjoys it might be more willing to attend a ballet.

²⁰Lastly, ²¹experts say that we are becoming a society in which people believe they should not have to do things which they do not enjoy. **²²This**

suggests that people today are objecting to rules and laws in the workplace, schools, and the community. [23]**It follows that** if this trend continues, we could face anarchy. [24]**Though** we are likely a long way from living in a lawless state, [25]**this is to point out that** our individual actions can affect entire communities. [26]**What would happen,** [27]**for example,** if we all stopped obeying traffic lights and paying taxes?

Conclusion 結論

[28]**From these arguments one can conclude that** it is in our best interest to do some things that we do not enjoy from time to time. But this doesn't mean we need to walk through fire or jump out of airplanes. [29]**In general what this means is that** we need to continue to challenge ourselves in ways that are not always comfortable. [30]**If we can imagine** the benefits of doing so, perhaps these activities will not be so unenjoyable. [31]**In this way,** we will contribute to our own well being and also the well being of our loved ones and communities.

詞彙

push oneself 強迫自己 | **worthwhile to ...** 值得去做… | **go along with** 和…一起 |
anarchy 無政府狀態 | **lawless** 沒有法治的 | **contribute** 貢獻

句型

以下來複習文章範例中出現的精選句型。☞後面的數字對應本書前面的句型。

開場白部分出現的句型

1　**Once in a great while,** 有時候／偶爾／久久一次 ☞ 請見開場白句型 54

2　**You may wonder why ...** 各位可能會好奇為什麼… ☞ 請見開場白句型 57

3　**Normally,** 一般來說， ☞ 請見開場白句型 23

4　**This essay will deal with the following aspects of the question :**
這篇文章將探討此問題的以下面相： ☞ 請見開場白句型 16

5　**I'd like to suggest that ...** 我想建議…／我想提議… ☞ 請見開場白句型 79

本文部分出現的句型

6　**First(ly),** 首先， ☞ 請見本文句型 122

7　**If...** 如果／假如… ☞ 請見本文句型 23

8　**Sometimes** 有時候 ☞ 請見本文句型 262

9　**I suppose that ...** 我認為… ☞ 請見本文句型 19

10　**We must take ... on its own terms.**
我們必須以各自的情況（條件）來看待… ☞ 請見本文句型 79

11　**However,** 然而， ☞ 請見本文句型 231

12　**Second(ly),** 其次， ☞ 請見本文句型 123

13　**If it is the case that ...,** 如果…的話， ☞ 請見本文句型 25

14　**One should always remember that ...** 應該要永遠記住… ☞ 請見本文句型 74

15　**But don't take my word for it;**
可是不要只聽我講的；／但別直接採納我的想法； ☞ 請見本文句型 78

16　**Third(ly),** 第三， ☞ 請見本文句型 125

17　**One of the most serious drawbacks of ... is that ...**
…的最嚴重缺點之一是… ☞ 請見本文句型 42

18　**While the second argument suggests that ...**
反之，第二個論點意指… ☞ 請見本文句型 69

19　**An example of this is...** 這類（狀況的）例子是…，／…就是一個例子 ☞ 請見本文句型 195

20　**Lastly,** 最後， ☞ 請見本文句型 126

21　**Experts say that ...** 專家表示… ☞ 請見本文句型 285

22　**This suggests that ...** 這意味著… ☞ 請見本文句型 260

23　**It follows that ...** 由此可見… ☞ 請見本文句型 261

24　**Though ...,** 雖然…， ☞ 請見本文句型 232

範例中文翻譯

請試著練習將以下加粗的中文，翻成英文看看。

開場白

　　人們**偶爾**應該做一些自己不喜歡的事情。**你可能會好奇為什麼**這很重要。**一般來說**，選擇對於我們沒有吸引力的活動，這是違反天性的。**這篇文章將探討此問題的以下面相**：為什麼我們要逼自己去做自己不喜歡的事情？**我想提出**幾個好處。

本文

　　首先，我們的朋友和家人可能會要求我們加入自己不喜歡的活動。**如果**加入他們可以避免傷害他們的感情，那**有時候**是值得加入他們的。**我認為**在有些狀況可能是他們建議的活動過於危險，讓你不去考慮。**但是，我們必須以其各自的狀況**去看待每個活動，並對我們所愛的人喜歡的某些事物持開放態度。

　　其次，用一個過去的不好經驗來判斷這樣的經驗就是令人不悅，這可能不太公平。**如果**有一次你去游泳的時候覺得水太冷，那麼這一次應該會溫暖宜人。**大家應該永遠要記得**，每一次經歷都值得再次嘗試。**但別直接採納我的想法**，去自己觀察吧！

　　第三，繼續挑戰自我是很重要的。避免產生令人不愉快經驗**的最嚴重的缺點之一**，就是我們開始對新的體驗變得封閉。本篇文章**的第二個論點指出**，再次嘗試一項令人不愉快的活動可能會改變你的想法，還可以鼓勵你嘗試新事物。**舉個這類情況的例子**：一個給歌劇第二次機會、並發現他／她其實喜歡歌劇的人，可能更願意觀賞芭蕾舞演出。

　　最後，專家說，我們正在成為這樣的一個社會：人們相信自己不應該做自己不喜歡做的事情。**這意味著**現今的人們會在工作場所、學校和社區中反對規則和法律。**由此可**

見，如果這種趨勢繼續下去，我們可能會面臨無政府狀態。**儘管**我們離一個無法無天的狀態還很遠，但**這主要是為了點出**我們的個人行為可能會影響到整個社會。**例如，**如果我們都不再遵守交通號誌、也不再納稅，**可能會發生什麼事？**

結論

從這些論點**我們可以推斷出一個結論，**偶爾做一些我們不時享受的事情，其實會符合我們的最大利益。但這並不意味著我們需要穿越火場或跳出飛機。**整體來說，這意味著**我們需要繼續以並非很舒服的方式挑戰自己。**如果我們能想像**這樣做的好處，也許這些活動就不會那麼令人不愉快。**如此一來，**我們將為自己、以及我們所愛的人和社會的福利做出貢獻。

10 What should a person moving to your city know about it; likes and dislikes.

對於要搬到你所居住的城市的人,他們應該要知道什麼?包含喜歡的事和討厭的事。

基本架構

在寫作前先腦力激盪,來定出文章的架構。

Introduction 開場白

· 每個人一生都應該要去愛荷華城旅行
→ 過去一個世紀以來,愛荷華城的大學和城鎮受到越來越多矚目

介紹文章主旨
→ 愛荷華城所應提供的許多東西,以及作為居住地的缺點

Body 本文

· 指出錯誤的認知:有人認為愛荷華城是單調乏味的農村地區
→ 愛荷華大學是美國最好的大學之一
→ 2009 年被聯合國教科文組織命名為「文化之都」

· 談談愛荷華城的「第一」
→ 是愛荷華州的第一個首都
→ 愛荷華大學為第一間接納男學生跟女學生的公立大學

· 提及愛荷華城令人愉快的特性
→ 當地居民熱情待人,大多是互相照顧的好鄰居
→ 是犯罪率低,屬於相對安全的地區

· 愛荷華城最大的缺點
→ 嚴寒的冬季天氣

· 消費水準高於大部分的中部城市
→ 較多人擁有博士學位且為高薪階層,所以生活水平與物價也較高

Conclusion 結論

· 若有經濟能力且能耐得住嚴寒,愛荷華城是理想的居住地
→ 安全且地方居民總是熱情款待,當地人具有新穎而具前瞻性的想法
→ 務必親自去愛荷華城走走

文章範例

本書前面所學到的部分句型，會在以下文章範例中出現。

Introduction 開場白

¹**Everyone has to** make a trip to Iowa City, Iowa in their lifetime. ²**You may not know** that it is the home of the University of Iowa. ³**Over the past century there has been a dramatic increase in** the attention our University and town have received. ⁴**I first became aware of** its uniqueness only recently. ⁵**This paper begins by** exploring the many things Iowa City has to offer and some of its drawbacks as a place to live.

Body 本文

⁶**On the one hand,** people tend to think of Iowa as flat farm country. Although it is farm country, it is hardly flat. ⁷**Taken as a whole,** Iowa is often mislabeled. ⁸**There exists a contradiction between** what most people believe Iowa to be like **and** how it actually is. ⁹**In particular,** Iowa City is home to one of the best universities in the country. ¹⁰**As it turns out,** the university's world-class writing programs earned Iowa City the title of "UNESCO City of Literature" in 2009. ¹¹**This highlights the fact that** Iowa is not just a state of farmers, but home to writers and intellectuals.

¹²**It would be negligent not to address** Iowa City's "firsts." It was the first capital city of Iowa. The University of Iowa is ¹³**especially** known for being the first public university to admit men and women on an equal basis. ¹⁴**What I didn't know was that** it is also the first public university to officially recognize a gay student organization on campus.

¹⁵**Another** pleasant quality of Iowa City is its people. Besides being warm and welcoming, most are great neighbors who look out for one another. ¹⁶**In addition,** Iowa City is a relatively safe community with a low crime rate.

¹⁷**As to** the drawbacks of living in Iowa City, winter weather tops the list. ¹⁸**By contrast,** the warmth of Iowa's people is matched by the chill of its winters. ¹⁹**To illustrate,** some winters bring ice and blizzards with

temperatures well below zero. An Iowa winter **[20]is best described as** "six months of cold and snow!"

[21]It is necessary to point out that Iowa City has a higher cost of living than most Midwestern cities. **[22]But at the same time,** it also has a higher population of people with doctoral degrees. **[23]It can be seen that** with more high wage earners, the standard and cost of living will be higher. **[24]The real problem, however, is that** not everyone can afford to own a home in Iowa City.

Conclusion 結論

[25]Thus we can see that Iowa City is a desirable place to live, as long as you can afford it and tolerate the winters. **[26]Is it possible that** any city is without drawbacks? I doubt it. **[27]I definitely prefer to** live in a place where I feel safe and welcome and where new, forward-thinking ideas are generated. **[28]For all these reasons,** I like living here. **[29]I ask you to** visit one day and see for yourself all Iowa City has to offer.

詞彙

make a trip 旅遊 | **in one's lifetime** 某人的一生中 | **uniqueness** 獨特之處 | **flat** 單調的 |
mislabel …貼錯標籤 | **be home to ...** …的家鄉 | **world-class** 世界級的 |
intellectual 知識分子 | **first** 第一名、優等 | **on an equal basis** 以平等的基礎 |
organization 組織 | **look out for ...** 替…注意，照顧… | **relatively** 相當 |
crime rate 犯罪率 | **top the list** 列為首位 | **warmth** 熱情 | **chill** 寒冷 | **blizzard** 暴風雪 |
standard of living 生活水準 | **forward-thinking** 前瞻的 | **generate** 生產、產出

句型

以下來複習文章範例中出現的精選句型。☞ 後面的數字對應本書前面的句型。

開場白部分出現的句型

1 **Everyone has to ...** 每個人都應該要… ☞ **請見開場白句型 43**
2 **You may not know ...** 各位可能不知道… ☞ **請見開場白句型 68**
3 **Over the past century there has been a dramatic increase in ...**
   過去一個世紀以來，…急遽增加（成長） ☞ **請見開場白句型 102**
4 **I first became aware of ...** 我第一次得知（意識到）… ☞ **請見開場白句型 98**
5 **This paper begins by ...** 這篇論文／報告從…開始 ☞ **請見開場白句型 12**

本文部分出現的句型

6 **On the one hand,** 一方面， ☞ **請見本文句型 61**
7 **Taken as a whole,** 整體而言， ☞ **請見本文句型 141**
8 **There exists a contradiction between ... and ...** 和…間存在矛盾 ☞ **請見本文句型 182**
9 **In particular,** 特別的是 ☞ **請見本文句型 199**
10 **As it turns out,** 事實證明， ☞ **請見本文句型 348**
11 **This highlights the fact that ...** 這凸顯了…的事實 ☞ **請見本文句型 344**
12 **It would be negligent not to address ...** 若不提及…就會是個疏失 ☞ **請見本文句型 39**
13 **especially** 特別／尤其是 ☞ **請見本文句型 201**
14 **What I didn't know was that ...** 我所不知道的是… ☞ **請見本文句型 160**
15 **Another ...** 其他… ☞ **請見本文句型 135**
16 **In addition,** 另外， ☞ **請見本文句型 108**
17 **As to ...,** 關於…，／說到…， ☞ **請見本文句型 88**
18 **By contrast,** 相較之下， ☞ **請見本文句型 174**
19 **To illustrate,** 為了要說明，／為了要用圖解說明， ☞ **請見本文句型 213**
20 **... is best described as ...** 對於…最好的形容（描述）是… ☞ **請見本文句型 214**
21 **It is necessary to ...** …是必要的 ☞ **請見本文句型 249**
22 **But at the same time,** 但同時， ☞ **請見本文句型 326**
23 **It can be seen that ...** 可以看出… ☞ **請見本文句型 345**
24 **The real problem, however, is that ...** 然而，真正的問題是… ☞ **請見本文句型 335**

結論部分出現的句型

25 **Thus we can see that ...** 因此我們可以知道… ☞ **請見結論句型 23**
26 **Is it possible that ... ?** 有沒有可能…？ ☞ **請見結論句型 82**

27 **I definitely prefer to ...** 我當然偏好選擇… ☞ 請見結論句型 41
28 **For all these reasons,** 由於這些原因， ☞ 請見結論句型 48
29 **I ask you to ...** 我請你（去做…） ☞ 請見結論句型 84

範例中文翻譯

請試著練習將以下加粗的中文，翻成英文看看。

開場白

　　每個人一生**都應該要**去愛荷華州的愛荷華市旅行一次。**你可能不知道**，這是愛荷華大學的所在地。**從過去一個世紀以來**，我們的大學和城鎮所受到的關注**急劇增加**。**我最近才初次意識到**它的獨特之處。**本文將從**愛荷華市提供的許多事物，以及其作為居住地的一些缺點**開始談起**。

本文

　　一方面來說，人們容易將愛荷華視為單調的農業城市。雖然是農業城市，但它一點也不單調。**總體而言**，愛荷華市經常被貼錯標籤。大多數人認為愛荷華市的模樣與實際情況**之間存在著矛盾**。**尤其是**，愛荷華市是全國最好大學之一的家鄉。**事實證明**，該大學的世界級寫作課程讓愛荷華市在 2009 年獲得了「聯合國教科文組織文學之都」的稱號。**這凸顯了一個事實**，即愛荷華州不僅是一個農業城市，還是作家和知識分子的故鄉。

　　如果不提及愛荷華市的「第一」，**那就太疏忽大意了**。它是愛荷華州的第一個首都，愛荷華大學**特別是**以第一所允許男女以平等地位就讀的公立大學而聞名。**我原先所不知道的是**，它也是第一所正式認定校園內同性戀學生組織的公立大學。

　　愛荷華市的**另一個**令人喜愛的特質就是它的人民。大多數人除了熱情好客之外，都是會互相照顧的好鄰居。**此外**，愛荷華市是一個相對安全的地區，犯罪率低。

　　至於在愛荷華市生活的缺點，冬季天氣會居首位。**相較之下**，愛荷華市居民的熱情恰好與寒冷的冬天相映成趣。**進一步說明**，某些冬天帶來的結冰和暴風雪氣候，讓溫度降到零下好幾度。**對**愛荷華的冬天**最好的**形容是「六個月的寒冷和冰雪」！

　　有必要指出的是，愛荷華市的生活支出比大多數中西部城市更高。**但是與此同時**，擁有博士學位的人也比較高。**可以看出**，隨著更多的高薪階層，生活水準和生活支出將會更高。**然而**，**真正的問題是**，並非每個人都負擔得起在愛荷華市的房價。

結論

　　因此我們可以發現，只要你負擔得起並且可以忍受冬天，愛荷華市是理想的居住地。**有沒有可能**是有哪個城市是完全沒有缺點的？我對此感到懷疑。**我當然偏好選擇**生活在一個我感到安全和受到歡迎的地方，一個孕育新穎、具有前瞻性想法的地方。**由於這些原因**，我喜歡住在這裡。**我想請你**找一天去當地走走，並親眼看看愛荷華市所能提供的一切。

11

Do you agree or disagree that progress is always good? Use specific reasons and examples to support your answer.

對於「進步往往都是件好事」這一點，你是贊同還是反對？請運用具體的理由和例子來支持你的回答。

基本架構

在寫作前先腦力激盪，來定出文章的架構。

Introduction 開場白

· 近來科學、技術、商業和國際貿易的發展帶來了進步，需要對此做周密的探討
→ 「進步」是否代表正向發展這點，還有待商榷

說明文章結構
→ 舉出幾個失敗的發展，並提出防止該情況發生的策略

Body 本文

· 針對個人電腦的使用來探討
→ 個人電腦為 20 世紀的通訊帶來了急遽變化
→ 引用比爾蓋茲說過的話：個人電腦不僅只有益處

· 鮮少有人討論電腦會產生出的廢棄物，以及該廢棄物對環境的影響

· 個人電腦對我們安全造成的威脅
→ 個資被盜用事件相當頻繁
→ 駭客對國安的威脅
→ 學者們不認同個人電腦的優點遠勝於其所帶來的威脅

· 針對個人電腦的風險提出解決問題的方法
→ 需要找出環境保護的方法
→ 在找到防止駭客的辦法之前，敏感個資不宜上傳到網路上

Conclusion 結論

· 個人電腦所引發的問題並未受到廣大的注目
→ 我們未來仍會廣泛使用個人電腦
→ 附帶的好處

本書前面所學到的部分句型，會在以下文章範例中出現。

Introduction 開場白

[1]Recent developments in science, technology, business, and international trade have heightened the need for a closer look at how progress affects our society. [2]One of the most striking features of this problem is that "progress" is a positive word, yet progress does not always have a positive impact on us. [3]A number of key issues arise from this statement. [4]It is crucial to understand that [5]sometimes, we move ahead with new ideas that improve our lives today, only to later learn they have caused irreparable damage. [6]The essay has been organized in the following way: I will first look at an example of progress gone wrong, and then suggest strategies for preventing this in the future.

Body 本文

[7]The first part of my analysis will examine the rising use of personal computers over the last 30 years. [8]It is considered that the personal computer revolutionized communications in the 20th century. [9]Mainly it has improved our ability to record, store, and transmit information over the Internet. [10]Consider the following quotation by Bill Gates: "It's not just that the personal computer has come along as a great tool. The whole pace of business is moving faster. Globalization is forcing companies to do things in new ways." [11]With this statement, Gates claims only positive things coming from the personal computer. [12]Considered from another perspective, Gates has also made a huge fortune developing and improving upon the personal computer. His formula for business [13]is as follows: create a product that requires regular updates, and then sell the updates. As a business model, it [14]presents a useful concept: create a need in order to fill that need and make a profit.

[15]And what about all that outdated hardware and software, the piles of computer instruction books, CDs and floppy disks? [16]So far, there has been little discussion about the massive waste some computers produce, or its impact on the environment.

[17]**The second reason for** questioning whether personal computers are entirely positive **is** their threat to our security. [18]**Further evidence for** this **is that** identity theft is on the rise, and hacker threats to national security, such as nuclear defense systems have already been discovered. Scholars disagree on whether the benefits outweigh the risks when it comes to personal computers. [19]**They seem to believe that** this form of technology holds too much promise to be contained.

[20]**In approaching the issue,** we first need to find environmentally friendly ways of updating our systems, such as replacing small parts rather than whole systems. [21]**It would also be interesting to see** better regulation of the industry in terms of the frequency of these required updates. [22]**Equally relevant to the issue is** the question of security. [23]**Today there has been little agreement on** what can be done to prevent hackers from accessing private information. [24]**It is precisely these differences of opinion that** should concern us. [25]**Little is known about** how to detect or stop them, and until we can, sensitive information should be kept off line.

Conclusion 結論

[26]**These problems pale in comparison with** global poverty, destruction of the rainforests, and human disease. [27]**In view of these facts, it is quite likely that** the problems generated by personal computers will not receive as much attention. [28]**In general what this indicates is that** in all likelihood, we will continue to expand on our use of them in the future. [29]**Over and above,** they do have their advantages. [30]**If we can imagine** advantages to their use, though, we should also be able to imagine advantages to using them wisely.

詞彙

have an impact on ... 對⋯有衝擊、對⋯有影響 | **move ahead with ...** 帶著⋯往前進 | **irreparable** 無法挽回的 | **go wrong** 出錯、失敗 | **transmit** 傳送 | **come along** 進展 | **make a fortune** 獲得財富、致富 | **formula** 方程式、準則、慣例 | **make a profit** 獲利 | **identity theft** 身分竊取，個資竊取 | **on the rise** 增加、上升 | **defense** 防禦 | **outweigh** 比⋯更重要 | **when it comes to ...** 當談到⋯的時候 | **frequency** 頻率 | **required** 必須的、必要的 | **detect** 偵測 | **poverty** 貧窮 | **destruction** 毀滅 | **rainforest** 雨林 | **in all likelihood** 極有可能

句型

以下來複習文章範例中出現的精選句型。☞ 後面的數字對應本書前面的句型。

開場白部分出現的句型

1 **Recent developments in ... have heightened the need for ...**
最近因為⋯的發展，對⋯有大量的需求 ☞ **請見開場白句型 100**

2 **One of the most striking features of this problem is ...**
這問題中最值得關注的是⋯ ☞ **請見開場白句型 28**

3 **A number of key issues arise from this statement ...**
由此陳述引出許多關鍵性的問題 ☞ **請見開場白句型 99**

4 **It is crucial to understand ...** 理解⋯是很重要的 ☞ **請見開場白句型 22**

5 **Sometimes** 有時候 ☞ **請見開場白句型 262**

6 **The essay has been organized in the following way:**
本文的組織架構如下： ☞ **請見開場白句型 76**

本文部分出現的句型

7 **The first part of the analysis will examine...**
第一部分的分析將探討⋯ ☞ **請見本文句型 142**

8 **It is considered that ...** 普遍認為⋯ ☞ **請見本文句型 269**

9 **mainly** 大部分／主要 ☞ **請見本文句型 206**

10 **Consider the following quotation:**
細想以下所言：／請見以下語錄： ☞ **請見本文句型 222**

11 **With this statement,** 用這段話（聲明）， ☞ **請見本文句型 183**

12 **Considered from another perspective,** 從另一個觀點思考的話， ☞ **請見本文句型 188**

13 **... is as follows: ...** ⋯如下所示⋯ ☞ **請見本文句型 311**

14 **... presents a useful concept** ⋯提出了一個有用的概念 ☞ **請見本文句型 316**

15 **And what about ...** 那麼關於⋯，你怎麼看呢？ ☞ **請見本文句型 71**

16 **So far, there has been little discussion about ...**
到目前為止，幾乎沒有對⋯的相關討論。 ☞ **請見本文句型 104**

17 **The second reason for ... is ...** ⋯的第二個原因是⋯ ☞ **請見本文句型 306**

18 **Further evidence for ... is that ...** 針對⋯更進一步的證據是⋯ ☞ **請見本文句型 274**

19 **They seem to believe that ...** 他們似乎相信⋯ ☞ **請見本文句型 35**

20 **In approaching the issue** 在處理這個議題時， ☞ **請見本文句型 42**

21 **It would also be interesting to see ...** 看到⋯也會是挺有趣的 ☞ **請見本文句型 339**

22 **Equally relevant to the issue is the question of ...**
與此議題同樣有關的是　的問題 ☞ **請見本文句型 310**

23 Today there has been little agreement on ... 至今對…仍意見紛紜 ☞ **請見本文句型 75**

24 It is precisely these differences of opinion that ...

正是因為這些意見分歧… ☞ **請見本文句型 180**

25 Little is known about ... 對…的了解不多／對…知道的不多 ☞ **請見本文句型 70**

結論部分出現的句型

26 These problems pale in comparison with ...

這些問題與…相比顯得遜色 ☞ **請見結論句型 68**

27 In view of these facts, it is quite likely that ...

有鑑於這些事實，很有可能… ☞ **請見結論句型 51**

28 In general what this indicates is that ... 整體來說，這暗示著… ☞ **請見結論句型 27**

29 Over and above, 除此之外， ☞ **請見結論句型 60**

30 If we can imagine ... 如果我們能想像… ☞ **請見結論句型 76**

範例中文翻譯

請試著練習將以下加粗的中文，翻成英文看看。

開場白

　　科學、科技、商業和國際貿易**的最新發展，已提高了**我們針對進步是如何影響我們社會此議題之仔細研究的**必要性**。這個問題中最值得關注的特點之一是：「進步」是一個正面的詞，但是進步並不總是對我們產生正面的影響。**許多關鍵性的問題都從此陳述發展。至關重要的是，要理解有時候**我們提出的一些新想法可以改善我們今日的生活，但後來才知道它們造成了無法彌補的損失。**本篇文章的組織架構如下**：我將先看看一個結果不好的進步案例，然後提出策略，防止這種情況在未來發生。

本文

　　我第一部分的分析將檢視過去三十年間個人電腦日益增加的使用率。**人們普遍認為**，個人電腦在二十世紀掀起了通訊領域的革命，它**主要是**提高我們在網際網路上記錄、儲存以及傳送訊息的能力。**細想以下**比爾蓋茲**的所言**：「個人電腦不僅僅已經成為一種強大的工具，商業的整體步調也變得更快，全球化迫使公司行號以新的方式處理事情。」比爾蓋茲**用這段話**主張個人電腦只有正面的事物。**從另一個觀點思考**，比爾蓋茲也藉由發展和改善個人電腦獲得巨大的財富。他的商業模式**如下**：創造一個需要定期更新的產品，然後販售更新的產品。做為一種商業模式，它**提出了一個有用的概念**：創建需求以滿足需求，然後獲利。

那麼那些過時的硬體和軟體、成堆的電腦教學書籍、CD 和光碟又是如何呢？到目前為止，關於電腦所產生的大量廢物及其對環境的影響的討論很少。

質疑個人電腦是否完全正面的第二個理由是，它們對我們安全的威脅。對此的進一步證據是，身分個資盜用的現象正在增加，而且駭客開始威脅到國家安全，例如核子防禦系統。談到個人電腦時，學者們對益處是否大於風險持不同意見。他們似乎相信這種科技形式蘊含著太多前景而無法被控制。

在處理這個議題時，我們首先需要找到環保的方式來更新電腦系統，例如替換小零件，而不是整套系統。就這些必要更新的頻率而言，見到產業有更好的管理也很有趣。與這個議題同樣相關的是安全問題。如今，對於如何防止駭客取得私人訊息鮮少有共識、意見紛紜，正是這些分歧的意見應讓我們感到不安。我們對於如何偵測或阻止他們的方法所知甚少。直到我們能夠做到之前，敏感資訊都應保持離線狀態。

結論

與全球貧窮、雨林破壞和人類疾病相比，這些問題顯得遜色。有鑑於這些事實，個人電腦所產生的問題很可能不會引起太多關注。整體來說，這表示我們將來極有可能會繼續擴大我們對電腦的使用。此外，電腦確實有其優勢。然而，如果我們可以想像使用它們的好處，那麼我們也應該能夠想像聰明使用它們的益處。

12

Some people believe that the Earth is being damaged by human activity. Others feel that human activity makes the Earth a better place to live. What is your opinion? Use specific reasons and examples to support your answer.

有些人相信地球正因人類的活動而遭受破壞之中。另外有些人卻覺得，人類的活動讓地球變得更適合居住。你的想法是什麼？請運用具體的理由和例子來支持你的回答。

基本架構

在寫作前先腦力激盪，來定出文章的架構。

Introduction 開場白

· 從上個世紀工業和技術的進步來看，很難否認人類在地球上的活動有所增加
介紹文章主要內容
→ 探討某些人類活動，以及該活動所帶來的效用是否勝過其對地球所造成的負擔

Body 本文

· 工業革命看似只會提升我們生活的便利性，但從 20 世紀中葉開始察覺這些進步也帶來負面影響
→ 美國政府建立了環境影響評估制度
→ 幾項政府法規開始實施
越來越多人意識到人類活動會對環境造成傷害

· 產業開發持續不斷進行
→ 但環境法規正在改變人們對待地球的方式
——比較今日的道路與 50 年前的道路
→ 人類活動也可能對環境帶來正面影響
例：搶救美州白頭鷹、淨化河水、開發替代能源等

· 人類很有可能會對地球造成有害影響，但別忘了我們有能力改變
→ 透過產業發明能讓生活變得更好
→ 以自然的方式修復過去所造成的傷害

Conclusion 結論

透過撿起路邊的垃圾等方式來一點一點做改變
→ 我們可以產生很大的影響
→ 但願大家能盡力拯救我們的地球

本書前面所學到的部分句型，會在以下文章範例中出現。

Introduction 開場白

¹**If you stop to consider** the advances in industry and technology over the last century, it is hard to deny our increased activity on Earth. ²**At the very least,** our use of fossil fuels has released more pollutants into the air than before. ³**And what about** our use of pesticides, plastics, and our expansion into wildlife habitats? ⁴**What does this have to do with** improving our lives and changing our planet? ⁵**This paper will examine** some of the human activities that are doing just that, and whether their usefulness outweighs the damage they cause to Earth.

Body 本文

⁶**At first glance, it seemed** like the industrial revolution would only bring improvements to make our lives easier, such as the vacuum cleaner, the automobile, and factory assembly. ⁷**Even if** this **is true,** by the middle of the 20th century, we started to notice some of these advances were having negative effects on our natural environment. ⁸**Subsequently,** the U.S. government established a type of system called an Environmental Impact Assessment (EIA) to determine the level of environmental risk in development and industrial processes. ⁹**This** system **was developed in response to** public outcry from an environmental movement in the 1960's. ¹⁰**Resulting from this is** that several government regulations have since been put into place. ¹¹**The most crucial point made so far is that** it is now widely recognized that human activity is causing environmental damage.

¹²**Nevertheless, one should accept that** industry and development will likely continue. ¹³**It is interesting, though, that** the environmental regulations are forcing us to think differently about how we treat our planet. ¹⁴**This point can be made by comparing** today's scenic roadways with those of 50 years ago. ¹⁵**In retrospect it is clear that** we used to freely litter our highways with rubbish. Today, they are nearly rubbish free. ¹⁶**Is it possible that** human activity can have a positive impact on our environment? ¹⁷**The answers to**

this question can be found in several examples, such as saving the American bald eagle, cleaning our waterways, and developing alternative energy sources such as wind and solar power.

[18]**In view of these facts, it is quite likely that** humans do have a damaging effect on Earth. [19]**One should, however, not forget that** we are capable of change. [20]**If we can imagine** industrial invention, we can imagine better ways of living. [21]**Or, if you prefer,** we can create change without creating damage at the same time. [22]**Better yet,** we can find natural ways to undo past damage, such as using poplar trees to filter pollutants from waterways. [23]**When all is said and done,** we have one planet. [24]**Perhaps it is time to** clean up our act. Because [25]**in the final analysis,** if we destroy our home, we destroy ourselves.

Conclusion 結論

[26]**And remember,** you don't have to be a scientist to make a difference. [27]**On that account,** all you need to do is take a bag with you on your next hike and pick up rubbish along the way. [28]**In this way,** little by little, we can each make a small difference. [29]**More important than that is** together, we can have a large impact. [30]**I ask you to** do your part to save our planet.

詞彙

fossil fuel 石化燃料 | **release** 釋放 | **pollutant** 污染源 | **pesticide** 殺蟲劑 |
wildlife 野生動物 | **vacuum cleaner** 吸塵器 | **assembly** 組裝 |
public outcry 公眾的強烈抗議 | **put into place** 開始實行 | **scenic** 風景美麗的 |
roadway 道路 | **litter** 亂丟 | **rubbish** 垃圾 | **bald eagle** 白頭鷲 | **waterway** 水道 |
alternative 替代的 | **invention** 發明 | **undo** 復原、取消 | **filter** 過濾 | **clean up** 清理 |
little by little 逐漸地 | **make a difference** 對⋯產生影響

句型

以下來複習文章範例中出現的精選句型。☞ 後面的數字對應本書前面的句型。

開場白部分出現的句型

1 **If you stop to consider...** 如果你思考一下… ☞ **請見開場白句型 46**

2 **At the very least, ...** 至少… ☞ **請見開場白句型 81**

3 **And what about ...** 那麼關於…，你怎麼看呢？ ☞ **請見開場白句型 71**

4 **What does this have to do with... ?** 這和…有什麼關聯呢？ ☞ **請見開場白句型 83**

5 **This paper will examine...** 這篇論文／報告將檢視… ☞ **請見開場白句型 9**

本文部分出現的句型

6 **At first glance, it seemed ...** 乍看之下，似乎… ☞ **請見本文句型 204**

7 **Even if ... is true,** 即使…是事實， ☞ **請見本文句型 234**

8 **Subsequently,** 而後，／隨後， ☞ **請見結論句型 49**

9 **This ... was developed in response to ...** 本…是為了…而發展的 ☞ **請見本文句型 43**

10 **Resulting from this ... is ...** …的結果顯示… ☞ **請見本文句型 47**

11 **The most crucial point made so far is that ...**
   目前為止最關鍵的一點是… ☞ **請見本文句型 258**

12 **Nevertheless, one should accept that ...** 儘管如此，應該要接受… ☞ **請見本文句型 72**

13 **It is interesting, though, that ...** 然而，有趣的是… ☞ **請見本文句型 239**

14 **This point can be made by comparing ...**
   藉由比較…可以推論出這一點 ☞ **請見本文句型 21**

15 **In retrospect it is clear that ...** 回想起來，顯然… ☞ **請見結論句型 49**

16 **Is it possible that ... ?** 有沒有可能…？ ☞ **請見結論句型 82**

17 **The answers to this question can be found in ...** 這個問題的答案可以在…找到 ☞ **請見本文句型 353**

18 **In view of these facts, it is quite likely that ...**
   有鑑於這些事實，很有可能… ☞ **請見結論句型 51**

19 **One should, however, not forget that ...** 然而，不能忘記的是… ☞ **請見本文句型 75**

20 **If we can imagine ...** 如果我們能想像… ☞ **請見結論句型 76**

21 **Or, if you prefer,** 或者如果你願意， ☞ **請見結論句型 14**

22 **Better yet,** 更理想的是，／不但如此， ☞ **請見結論句型 83**

23 **When all is said and done,** 說到最後，／畢竟， ☞ **請見結論句型 73**

24 **Perhaps it is time to ...** 或許是時候… ☞ **請見結論句型 77**

25 **In the final analysis,** 在最後的分析中， ☞ **請見結論句型 74**

範例中文翻譯

請試著練習將以下加粗的中文，翻成英文看看。

開場白

　　如果你停下來思考一下上個世紀工業和科技的進步，那麼很難否認我們在地球上的活動與日俱增。**至少**，我們所使用的石化燃料已經釋放比過去更多的污染源到空氣中。**而**我們使用的農藥、塑膠以及向野生生物棲息地的擴展**又如何呢？這與**改善我們的生活和改變我們的地球**又有什麼關係？本篇文章將檢視**部分這類型的人類活動，並且檢視它們的用途是否比它們對地球所造成的損害還嚴重。

本文

　　乍看之下，工業革命**似乎**只帶來改善，讓我們的生活更方便，例如吸塵器、汽車和工廠組裝。**即使這是事實**，在二十世紀中期，我們也開始注意到其中一些進步對我們的自然環境產生負面影響。**隨後**，美國政府建立了一套稱為環境影響評估（EIA）的系統，以評斷開發和工業流程中的環境風險等級。**這個系統是因應** 1960 年代環保運動中的公眾抗議**而開發的**。運作**的結果是**，已經有一些政府法規實施。**到目前為止最重要的一點是**，現在已經廣泛認識到人類活動正在造成環境破壞。

　　儘管如此，人們應該接受工業和發展將可能繼續的趨勢。**然而有趣的是**，環保法規迫使我們以不同的方式，思考應該如何對待我們的地球。**藉由比較**今日的風景優美的道路與五十年前的樣貌，**就可以推論出這一點。回顧過去，顯然**我們曾經隨意在高速公路上亂扔垃圾。今天，路上幾乎沒有垃圾。人類活動**是否可能**對我們的環境產生正面影響？這個問題的答案可以在幾個例子**中找到**，例如拯救美州白頭鷹、清潔我們的水道、以及開發替代能源，例如風力和太陽能。

　　有鑑於這些事實，人類很**可能**確實對地球產生破壞性影響。**然而，不應忘記**我們有改變的能力。**如果我們可以想像出**工業發明，我們就可以設想出更好的生活方式。**或者，如果你願意**，我們可以創造改變而且同時不會造成破壞。**不但如此**，我們還可以找

到復原過去破壞的自然方法，例如使用白楊樹過濾水道中的污染物。**畢竟**我們只有一個地球，**也許是時候**清理我們的行為了，因為歸根就底，如果我們破壞我們的家園，我們就是在破壞自己。

結論

　　請記住，你不必成為科學家就可以有所影響。**基於這個理由**，你所要做的就是在下次健行時隨身帶一個袋子，沿途撿拾垃圾。**如此一來**，我們可以逐漸地有所影響。**更重要的是**，我們一起做可以產生很大的影響。**我想請你**一起來盡自己的力量，拯救我們的星球。

13

Many people visit museums when they travel to new places. Why do you think people visit museums? Use specific reasons and examples to support your answer.

許多人到新的地點旅行時，會參觀博物館。你認為人們為什麼會參觀博物館？請運用具體的理由和例子來支持你的回答。

基本架構

在寫作前先腦力激盪，來定出文章的架構。

Introduction 開場白

· 每年有 850 萬人參觀巴黎的羅浮宮博物館
→ 透過博物館來學習時代、地點與文化
→ 幾乎所有人都喜歡了解我們的遺產

Body 本文

· 可參訪各種不同主題的博物館
→ 根據自己的主張來談談每類型的博物館
    例）羅浮宮博物館與首爾雞文化館

· 獨特或奇特博物館的愛好者很多
→ 芥末博物館、錘子博物館、香蕉博物館等每年都有眾多觀光客到訪

· 人們會被不尋常的事物吸引
→ 透過對這些小型博物館的興趣，來主動學習
→ 看到特別的廣告時，會忍不住繼續看下去

· 人們充滿好奇心，而博物館內處處可見珍奇異寶
→ 透過思考有哪些類型的博物館讓我們產生興趣、以及吸引我們的原因，來好好了解自己。

Conclusion 結論

· 人們基於各種理由經常參觀博物館
→ 每個人基於各自不同的理由，而對不同事物感到好奇
→ 透過博物館來認識自己

文章範例

本書前面所學到的部分句型，會在以下文章範例中出現。

Introduction 開場白

¹**You may not know** that every year 8.5 million people visit the Louvre Museum in Paris, France. ²**Some people** visit ten to twelve museums every year. ³**This situation is not unique;** ⁴**if you stop to consider** what we can learn about time, place and culture from museums, we can better understand the human race. ⁵**Almost everyone** likes to know something about our heritage.

Body 本文

⁶**Of course, you can** visit many different types of museums; there are historical museums, art museums, science museums, even eccentric museums. ⁷**We must take** each type of museum **on its own terms.** ⁸**For example,** the larger museums, like the Louvre often hold the world's most treasured paintings and sculptures. ⁹**On the other hand,** the Seoul Museum of Chicken Art holds one woman's lifetime collection. ¹⁰**Much more interesting,** ¹¹**however,** is the fact that there are visitors to both of these museums, because both have something unique to offer. ¹²**I shall argue this point at greater length in** the next paragraph.

¹³**In reality, it is found that** unusual or eccentric museums have a large following. ¹⁴**To be sure,** there is a mustard museum in Wisconsin, a hammer museum in Alaska, and a banana museum in Washington state. ¹⁵**What I didn't know was that** they get hundreds, if not thousands of visitors each year. ¹⁶**Bearing this in mind,** I have to wonder what attracts them inside. ¹⁷**This contradicts the statement that** people visit museums to learn about the human race, doesn't it? ¹⁸**Can it be that** there are that many banana and mustard fans in the world?

¹⁹**It is evident that** people are drawn to the unusual. ²⁰**This suggests that** perhaps we can learn something about ourselves by our interest in these smaller museums. ²¹**I usually** have to take a look when I see a sign

advertising, "World's Biggest Ball of Yarn!" ²²**Otherwise,** ²³if I never return to that place, I will have missed seeing something one-of-a-kind. ²⁴**That is to say,** while I have no real interest in yarn, I am interested in something truly unique.

²⁵**Look at it this way:** people are curious. ²⁶**Correspondingly,** museums are full of curiosities. ²⁷**We can see that** we have much to learn about ourselves by considering what types of museums interest us, and why.

Conclusion 結論

²⁸**To summarize,** people frequent museums for a number of reasons. ²⁹**Perhaps people cannot** see the artifacts in their own country, or they are experts or collectors of a particular type. ³⁰**In the end,** we are all just curious for our own reasons. ³¹**I am convinced that** what we each take from a museum teaches us something about humanity. ³²**Ultimately,** through museums, we learn about ourselves.

詞彙

human race 人類 | **heritage** 遺產 | **eccentric** 古怪的 | **treasured** 珍藏的 |
sculpture 雕像 | **unique** 獨特的、獨一無二的 | **unusual** 稀有的 | **following** 追隨、支持 |
mustard 芥末 | **hammer** 鐵鎚 | **be drawn to ...** 被⋯吸引 | **take a look** 看一下、參觀 |
sign 招牌 | **yarn** 紗線 | **one-of-a-kind** 獨一無二的 | **frequent** 常去，時常出入於 |
artifact 文物、工藝品 | **humanity** 人類、人性

句型

以下來複習文章範例中出現的精選句型。☞ 後面的數字對應本書前面的句型。

開場白部分出現的句型

1 **You may not know ...** 各位可能不知道… ☞ 請見開場白句型 68

2 **Some people ...** 某些人… ☞ 請見開場白句型 38

3 **This situation is not unique;** 這種情況並不特殊； ☞ 請見開場白句型 73

4 **If you stop to consider...** 如果你思考一下… ☞ 請見開場白句型 46

5 **Almost everyone...** 幾乎所有人… ☞ 請見開場白句型 37

本文部分出現的句型

6 **Of course, you can ...** 當然，你可以… ☞ 請見本文句型 98

7 **We must take ... on its own terms.**
我們必須以各自的情況（條件）來看待… ☞ 請見本文句型 79

8 **For example,** 例如，／舉例來說， ☞ 請見本文句型 193

9 **On the one hand, ... ; on the other hand, ...**
一方面…，但另一方面… ☞ 請見本文句型 283

10 **Much more interesting ...** 更有趣的是… ☞ 請見本文句型 54

11 **However,** 然而， ☞ 請見本文句型 231

12 **I shall argue this point at greater length in ...**
我將針對這點在…做更詳細的說明 ☞ 請見本文句型 53

13 **In reality, it is found that ...** 實際上發現… ☞ 請見本文句型 84

14 **To be sure,** 確定的是，／可以肯定的是， ☞ 請見本文句型 57

15 **What I didn't know was that ...** 我所不知道的是… ☞ 請見本文句型 160

16 **Bearing this in mind,** 銘記這點，／請記住，／請留意， ☞ 請見本文句型 191

17 **This contradicts the statement that ...** 這與…的說法是矛盾的 ☞ 請見本文句型 181

18 **Can it be that... ?** 會…嗎？ ☞ 請見本文句型 167

19 **It is evident that ...** 顯然… ☞ 請見本文句型 242

20 **This suggests that ...** 這意味著… ☞ 請見本文句型 260

21 **I usually ...** 我通常… ☞ 請見本文句型 354

22 **Otherwise,** 否則， ☞ 請見本文句型 327

23 **If...** 如果／假如… ☞ 請見本文句型 23

24 **That is (to say),** 也就是說， ☞ 請見本文句型 217

25 **Look at it this way:** 這麼說吧：／如此看來： ☞ 請見本文句型 330

26 **Correspondingly,** 相同地， ☞ 請見本文句型 169

27 **We can see that ...** 我們可以知道… ☞ 請見本文句型 347

範例中文翻譯

請試著練習將以下加粗的中文，翻成英文看看。

開場白

　　你可能不知道，每年有八百五十萬人參觀法國巴黎的羅浮宮博物館。**有些人**每年都會參觀十至十二個博物館。**這種狀況並非特例**，如果你停下來思索我們可以從博物館中學到的時間、地點和文化，我們就能更了解人類。**幾乎每個人**都喜歡認識我們人類的遺產。

本文

　　當然，你可以參觀許多不同類型的博物館；歷史博物館、藝術博物館、科學博物館，甚至還有怪奇博物館。**我們必須針對**每一種類型的博物館**依照其各方面來討論。例如**，羅浮宮這類較大型的博物館，經常擁有世界上最珍貴的繪畫和雕塑。**另一方面**，首爾雞文化館（Seoul Museum of Chicken Art）則擁有某位女子的畢生珍藏。**然而，更有趣的是**，這兩個博物館都有參觀者，因為兩者都有獨特之處。**我會在**下一段**針對這一點做更仔細的解說。**

　　實際上，人們發現稀有珍藏博物館或是怪奇博物館都擁有大量的支持者。**確實**，威斯康辛州有芥末博物館、阿拉斯加有鐵鎚博物館、華盛頓州有香蕉博物館。**我原本不知道的是**，這些博物館每年吸引數百甚至數千名訪客。**請記住**，我必須知道是什麼吸引了他們進入博物館。**這與**人們參觀博物館以了解人類**的說法相矛盾**，不是嗎？世界上**會有**那麼多香蕉和芥末迷嗎？

　　很明顯地，人們被稀有而奇特的事物所吸引。**這也意味著**或許我們可以藉著對這些小型博物館的興趣，認識一些關於我們的事情。當我看到一個標語廣告寫著「世界上最大的紗線球」時，我通常不得不看它一眼。**否則，如果**我永遠不會不回到那個地方，那

就會錯過目睹獨一無二事物的機會。**也就是說**，雖然我對紗線球並不是真的有興趣，但我對真正獨特的東西感興趣。

如此看來：人們是好奇的。**剛好**，博物館充滿了新奇有趣的事物。**我們可以理解**，透過思考哪些類型的博物館會讓我們產生興趣以及吸引我們的原因，就能好好地了解自己。

結論

總而言之，人們出於許多原因而頻繁參觀博物館。**也許人們無法**在自己國家看到這些文物，或者他們是特定類型的專家或收藏家。**最後**，我們都出於自己的原因感到好奇。**我深信**，我們每個人從博物館中獲得的東西，都會教給我們一些關於人類的知識。**最終**，我們透過博物館了解自己。

14

How do television or movies influence people's behavior? Use specific reasons and examples to support your answer.

電視或電影是如何影響人們的行為？請運用具體的理由和例子來支持你的回答。

基本架構

在寫作前先腦力激盪，來定出文章的架構。

Introduction 開場白

· 一般大眾認為電視與電影會對孩童的行為舉止造成影響
提及 Susan Villani 在 1999 年進行的研究結果
→ 詳細記錄了媒體暴力，對孩子的行為所造成的影響
→ 但因只觀察 25 名孩童而已，此研究結果可能有所偏差

不管是孩子或成人，或多或少都會受到媒體影響

Body 本文

· 美國家庭每戶平均擁有將近 3 台的電視
一般人每天看電視 4.5 小時
→ 電視節目看太多
→ 提出這是否會對人類行為造成影響的問題

· **觀看有暴力內容之節目的孩童，是否會做出暴力的舉動一事已被證實**
→ 但也有可能是受其它影響所致
→ 假設內含暴力內容之媒體具有種程度的影響力

· **雖然成人比孩童更常接觸任何媒體，但還是要以觀眾的年紀與成熟度的觀點來進行探究**
→ 兒童的心智因仍在發展，而更容易受到影響
→ 成人具有邏輯判斷能力

Conclusion 結論

· 媒體的播放內容會對人類行為造成影響
→ 對媒體影響力有更深一層的認識之後，便可以改變我們應對媒體的方式

文章範例

本書前面所學到的部分句型，會在以下文章範例中出現。

Introduction 開場白

¹The public in general tend to believe that television and movies influence the behavior of children. **²Today there has been little agreement on** what degree of influence this is, exactly. A study conducted in 1999 by Susan Villani documented behavioral effects on children exposed to repeated media violence. **³However, the study is limited in that** it only looked at 25 children. **⁴In my opinion,** television and movies affect the behavior of both children and adults. **⁵If you stop to consider** the number of effective advertisements that are out there, it is easy to see that we are all influenced by the media to some degree.

Body 本文

⁶According to some experts, every home in the U.S. has an average of nearly three television sets. **⁷Experts say that** the average person watches 4.5 hours of television every day. **⁸It is worth stating at this point that** this level of exposure is heavy. **⁹It follows that** heavy exposure to anything will be influential. **¹⁰But at the same time,** does this necessarily influence human behavior?

¹¹As previously demonstrated, studies have shown that children exposed to media violence will often behave violently following the exposure. **¹²The real problem, however, is that** it can be difficult to link the behavior back to the media exposure. **¹³In all actuality,** there may be other influences contributing to the child's increased violence, such as a physical confrontation with another child. **¹⁴For this purpose, ¹⁵however,** I will assume that the media exposure is at least partly influential.

¹⁶It is just as true for adults. **¹⁷By this time,** an adult aged 40 or older has been exposed to much more media than today's child. **¹⁸One should, nevertheless, consider the problem from another angle** — the age and maturity of the viewer. **¹⁹My point will be that** children's minds are still developing and more susceptible to influence. **²⁰Look at it this way:** an adult is capable of reasoning that viewing violence on television does not make it okay to be violent himself/herself. [21]**As already mentioned,** this does not mean an adult is not susceptible to media influence, however. [22]**Otherwise,** politicians, advertisers and fundraisers wouldn't rely on it so heavily.

Conclusion 結論

[23]**To sum up,** media exposure can influence human behavior. [24]**Granted that** children are more vulnerable to these influences, they do affect adults, too. [25]**Perhaps people cannot** always separate the messages and images they see on the screen from reality. [26]**Although** we are not always aware that we are being influenced, **it is not** impossible to change our thinking. [27]**From these arguments, one can conclude that** increased awareness of media influence can change the way we behave in response to it.

詞彙

conduct 行為 | **document** 用文件證明、記錄 | **behavioral** 行為的 |
to some degree 某種程度 | **influential** 具有影響力的 | **link** 連結 | **confrontation** 對抗 |
maturity 成熟度 | **susceptible to ...** 容易受…影響的 | **fundraiser** 募款人 |
rely on ... 仰賴… | **vulnerable to ...** 對…易受傷的 | **separate** 區分 |
awareness 察覺、體認 | **in response to ...** 對…回應

句型

以下來複習文章範例中出現的精選句型。☞ 後面的數字對應本書前面的句型。

開場白部分出現的句型

1 The public in general tend to believe that ...
一般大眾傾向於相信（大部分人都相信）… ☞ **請見開場白句型 64**

2 Today there has been little agreement on ...
至今對…仍意見紛紜 ☞ **請見開場白句型 75**

3 However, the study is limited in that ...
然而，這份研究受限於… ☞ **請見開場白句型 80**

4 In my opinion, 就我的觀點而言，／個人認為， ☞ **請見開場白句型 78**

5 If you stop to consider... 如果你思考一下… ☞ **請見開場白句型 46**

本文部分出現的句型

6 According to some experts, 根據一些專家的說法， ☞ **請見本文句型 290**

7 Experts say that ... 專家表示… ☞ **請見本文句型 285**

8 It is worth stating at this point that ...
在這個論點上值得一提的是… ☞ **請見本文句型 281**

9 It follows that ... 由此可見… ☞ **請見本文句型 261**

10 But at the same time, 但同時， ☞ **請見本文句型 326**

11 As previously demonstrated, 如前所述， ☞ **請見本文句型 248**

12 The real problem, however, is that ... 然而，真正的問題是… ☞ **請見本文句型 335**

13 In all actuality, 事實上， ☞ **請見本文句型 350**

14 For this purpose, 為此， ☞ **請見本文句型 34**

15 However, 然而， ☞ **請見本文句型 231**

16 It is just as ... 這正是…／這就跟…一樣 ☞ **請見本文句型 99**

17 By this time, 到這個時候，／此時，… ☞ **請見本文句型 299**

18 One should, nevertheless, consider the problem from another angle — ...
然而，人們應該從其他角度思考這個問題－… ☞ **請見本文句型 331**

19 My point will be that ... 我的重點是… ☞ **請見本文句型 256**

20 Look at it this way: 這麼說吧：／如此看來： ☞ **請見本文句型 330**

21 As already mentioned, 如先前所提到的， ☞ **請見本文句型 318**

22 Otherwise, 否則， ☞ **請見本文句型 327**

23 **To sum up,** 總結來說， ☞ 請見結論句型 16

24 **Granted that ...** 即使… ☞ 請見結論句型 36

25 **Perhaps people cannot ...** 或許人們不能… ☞ 請見結論句型 37

26 **Although ..., it is not ...** 雖然…，但不… ☞ 請見結論句型 30

27 **From these arguments one can conclude that ...**
從這些論點可以得出…的結論 ☞ 請見結論句型 19

範例中文翻譯

請試著練習將以下加粗的中文，翻成英文看看。

開場白

　　一般大眾通常傾向相信電視和電影會影響兒童的行為。**在今日，關於**這類影響的確切程度**尚無共識，仍意見紛紜**。蘇珊‧薇拉妮於 1999 年進行的一項研究中，記錄了孩童暴露在不斷出現的媒體暴力中所受到的行為影響。**然而，這項研究卻局限在**只觀察二十五名兒童。**我的看法是**，電視和電影會影響兒童和成人的行為。**如果你停下來思考**外界那些具有影響力的廣告數量，很容易看出我們在一定程度上都受到媒體的影響。

本文

　　根據一些專家所言，美國每個家庭平均擁有近三台電視機。**專家表示**，每個人平均每天看電視 4.5 小時。**值得一提的是**，這樣的閱聽量很大。**由此可見**，如此大量接觸任何事物都會產生影響。**但同時**，這是否一定會影響人類的行為？

　　如前所述，研究顯示暴露於媒體暴力的兒童通常會在此之後表現出暴力行為。**然而，真正的問題在於**很難將行為與媒體暴露聯繫起來。**實際上**，可能還有其他因素導致孩子的暴力行為增加，例如與另一個孩子的肢體衝突。**然而，為此**，我假設媒體暴露至少造成部分影響。

　　這對於成人也是**如此**。**現在**，40 歲以上的成年人暴露於媒體的量比今天的孩童多得多。**不過**，人們應該從另一個角度考慮這個問題—觀眾的年齡和成熟度。**我的重點是**，兒童的心智仍在發展，而且更容易受到影響。**如此看來**：一個成年人能夠判斷，在電視上觀看暴力並不代表他／她自己會變得暴力。**如先前所提到的**，這並不意味著成年人不容易受到媒體的影響。**否則**，政客、廣告商和募款人不會如此依賴它。

結論

　　總而言之，接觸各類媒體會影響人類行為。**即使**兒童比較容易受到這些媒體的影響，但它們的確也影響了成年人。**或許人們無法**一直區分出他們在螢幕上所看到的消息和影像，與現實之間的差別。**雖然**我們並不總是意識到自己正在受到影響，**但**改變我們的想法**並非**不可能。**從這些論點可以得出這個結論**，只要提高對媒體影響的警覺性，便可以改變我們應對媒體的方式。

15

People have different ways of escaping the stress and difficulties of modern life. Some read; some exercise; others work in their gardens. What do you think are the best ways of reducing stress? Use specific details and examples to support your answer.

人們有許多方法逃離現代生活中的壓力和困難。有些人閱讀、有些人運動，另外有些人會在自己的花園裡忙東忙西。你認為減輕壓力最佳的方法有哪些？請運用具體的理由和例子來支持你的回答。

基本架構

在寫作前先腦力激盪，來定出文章的架構。

Introduction 開場白

· 提到壓力的定義
壓力造成的健康問題正在增加
介紹文章主要內容
→ 針對有助於降低壓力及相關健康問題的方法來做探討

Body 本文

· 提及壓力對人體造成的影響
→ 可能會引發高血壓、疲勞、胃病等各類健康方面的問題
→ 壓力持續過長可能會造成永久性傷害

· 紓解壓力的方法很多
→ 寫出最容易達到紓壓的方法

· 冥想與瑜珈
冥想－透過練習可達到舒壓效果
瑜珈－放鬆僵硬的肌肉，促進血液循環

· 規律的運動
→ 能讓你耳目一新，頭腦保持清醒，身體充滿活力
→ 對心臟、血壓與神經系統有益

· 大笑
→ 研究報告指出，大笑可增加體內腦內啡的分泌，讓人產生幸福感

Conclusion 結論

· 前述內容只是緩解日常生活壓力的其中幾種方法而已
→ 應找出對自己有效的紓壓方法
→ 最好找到兩種以上的方法

本書前面所學到的部分句型，會在以下文章範例中出現。

Introduction 開場白

Stress ¹**is commonly defined as** "physical, mental, or emotional strain or tension." ²**We live in a world in which** stress is a part of everyday life. ³**One of the most striking features of this problem is** the increasing number of health problems resulting from stress. ⁴**It is a well-known fact that** people can lower their risks for stress-related health problems using a variety of methods. ⁵**This essay will discuss** some of those methods.

Body 本文

⁶**Let us start by considering the facts about** stress on the human body. ⁷**The fact is that** stress can cause high blood pressure, fatigue, stomach problems, headaches, chest pain, insomnia, and depression. ⁸**Moreover,** ⁹**if** the stress continues for too long without relief, it can ¹⁰**sometimes** cause permanent damage.

¹¹**There are many different kinds of** stress relief. ¹²**Assuredly, there are certain** methods that work well for some people but not others. ¹³**With this in mind,** I will try to cover the methods that are most easily accessible.

¹⁴**First,** there's meditation. ¹⁵**Although I sometimes** have trouble clearing my mind, with practice, meditation can be quite effective. ¹⁶**In reality, it is found that** people who practice meditative thought on a daily basis live healthier lives than most. ¹⁷**Similarly,** yoga is effective for loosening tight muscles and increasing blood flow. ¹⁸**Indeed,** yoga and meditation often go hand in hand as stress relievers.

¹⁹**Second,** regular exercise is a well-known stress reliever. ²⁰**One must admit that** a brisk walk is refreshing and leaves your head clear and your body energized. ²¹**In the second place,** exercise is good for your heart, your blood pressure, and your nervous system.

²²**Finally,** laughter really is the best medicine at times. ²³**Can it be that**

stress relief is that simple? ²⁴There is a great deal of research that confirms this. ²⁵Notably laughter produces endorphins in the body. ²⁶It has been found that endorphins generate feelings of well being. ²⁷It could be said that a good joke is good for your health!

Conclusion 結論

²⁸To summarize, these are just a few methods of relieving the stress of everyday living. ²⁹Sooner or later, we are all faced with stressful situations. ³⁰Accordingly, we must each find ways to reduce stress which are effective for ourselves. ³¹I definitely prefer to laugh, but this is not always easy when I am stressed out. ³²That is why, in my opinion, it is good to have more than one method to rely upon.

詞彙

mental 心智上的 | strain 緊繃 | a variety of 各式各樣的 | high blood pressure 高血壓 |
fatigue 疲勞 | chest 胸部 | insomnia 失眠 | depression 沮喪 | relief 抒發 |
permanent 永久的 | cover 報導 | meditation 冥想、靜坐 | meditative 冥想的 |
on a daily basis 每天 | loosen 放鬆 | blood flow 血液流動 |
go hand in hand 相伴一起地 | reliever 紓壓方法 | brisk 輕快的 | refreshing 提神的 |
energize 精力充沛地做事 | nervous system 神經系統 | at times 有時、偶而 |
endorphin 腦內啡 | stressful 有壓力的 | be stressed out 壓力太大

句型

以下來複習文章範例中出現的精選句型。☞ 後面的數字對應本書前面的句型。

開場白部分出現的句型

1 **...is commonly defined as ...** …普遍被定義為（被視為）… ☞ 請見開場白句型 17

2 **We live in a world in which ...** 我們活在一個…的世界 ☞ 請見開場白句型 26

3 **One of the most striking features of this problem is ...**
這問題中最值得關注的是… ☞ 請見開場白句型 28

4 **It is a well-known fact that ...** …是眾所皆知的事實 ☞ 請見開場白句型 25

5 **This essay will discuss ...** 這篇文章將討論… ☞ 請見開場白句型 11

本文部分出現的句型

6 **Let us start by considering the facts about ...**
讓我們從思考...的真相開始 ☞ 請見本文句型 4

7 **The fact is that ...** 事實是… ☞ 請見本文句型 85

8 **Moreover,** 此外，／更甚者 ☞ 請見本文句型 99

9 **If...** 如果／假如… ☞ 請見本文句型 23

10 **Sometimes** 有時候 ☞ 請見本文句型 262

11 **There are many different kinds of...** …有很多不同的種類 ☞ 請見本文句型 165

12 **Assuredly, there are certain ...** 當然，有特定… ☞ 請見本文句型 166

13 **With this in mind,** 有鑒於此，／請記住， ☞ 請見本文句型 190

14 **First(ly),** 首先， ☞ 請見本文句型 122

15 **Although I sometimes ...,** 儘管有時候我…， ☞ 請見本文句型 94

16 **In reality, it is found that ...** 實際上發現… ☞ 請見本文句型 84

17 **Similarly,** 同樣地， ☞ 請見本文句型 168

18 **Indeed,** 的確， ☞ 請見本文句型 81

19 **Second(ly),** 其次， ☞ 請見本文句型 123

20 **One must admit that ...** 必須要承認的（一點）是… ☞ 請見本文句型 73

21 **In the second place,** 其次， ☞ 請見本文句型 124

22 **Finally,** 終於，／最後， ☞ 請見本文句型 127

23 **Can it be that... ?** 會…嗎？ ☞ 請見本文句型 167

24 **There is a great deal of research ...** …的研究很多 ☞ 請見本文句型 211

25 **notably** 特別地／明顯地 ☞ 請見本文句型 200

26 **It has been found that ...** 研究發現…／人們發現 ☞ 請見本文句型 271

27 **It could be said that ...** 可以（這麼）說… ☞ 請見本文句型 263

範例中文翻譯

請試著練習將以下加粗的中文，翻成英文看看。

開場白

　　壓力**通常被定義為**「身體、精神或情緒上的緊張或緊繃狀態」。**我們生活在一個**壓力為日常生活一部分**的世界中**。這個問題最令人關注的特點之一是：由於壓力導致的健康問題數量不斷增加。**眾所周知的事實是**，人們可以使用多種方法來降低與壓力有關的健康問題風險。**本篇文章將討論**其中一些方法。

本文

　　讓我們從思考人體承受壓力**的真相開始**。**真相是**壓力會導致高血壓、疲勞、胃部疾病、頭痛、胸痛、失眠和抑鬱。**此外，如果**壓力持續太長時間而無法緩解，**有時**會造成永久的傷害。

　　有許多種緩解壓力**的不同方法**。**當然，一定會有些**方法對某些人有效、但對另一些人無效。**有鑒於此**，我將嘗試介紹最容易理解的方法。

　　首先是冥想。**雖然有時候**清空頭腦對我來說很困難，但透過練習，冥想會非常有效。**實際上，人們發現**每天練習冥想的人，比大多數人活得更健康。**同樣地**，瑜伽可有效放鬆緊繃的肌肉並增加血液循環。**確實**，瑜伽和冥想時常是齊頭並進用於緩解壓力的方法。

　　第二，定期運動是一種眾所周知緩解壓力的方法。**人們必須承認**，快走可以提神，而且讓你的頭腦保持清醒、讓身體充滿活力。**其次**，運動對心臟、血壓和神經系統都有好處。

　　最後，笑有時確實是最佳良藥。紓解壓力**有可能**就這麼簡單**嗎？有大量研究**已經證實了這一點。**尤其是**笑會在體內產生腦內啡。**人們已發現**腦內啡會產生幸福感。**可以這麼說**，開個好玩笑對你的健康有益！

結論

　　總而言之，這些只是緩解日常生活壓力的幾種方法。我們所有人**遲早**都會面臨有壓力的狀況。**因此**，我們每個人都必須找到對自己有效的減壓方法。**我當然偏好選擇**大笑，但是當我感到壓力很大時，這並不是那麼容易做到。**依據我的觀點，這就是為什麼**有多種方法可以依靠會是很好的事。

16

Do you agree or disagree with the following statement? The best way to travel is in a group led by a tour guide. Use specific reasons and examples to support your answer.

你贊不贊同以下敘述？最好的旅遊方式，是參加一個由導遊帶領的旅遊團。請運用具體的理由和例子來支持你的回答。

基本架構

在寫作前先腦力激盪，來定出文章的架構。

Introduction 開場白

· 旅遊度假的品質取決於旅客希望實現的目標
→ 到當地旅遊是認識當居民的好機會

有人認為跟團旅遊是探索世界的最佳方法
→ 旅行的目的是為了要了解當地史實，並結識其他旅客

應自行決定自己偏好哪一種形式的旅行

Body 本文

· **獨自到陌生的地方探索，確實會有益處**
→ 在陌生的街道上閒逛、體驗當地人事物，或是偶爾迷路也都是很棒的事
→ 認識城市的日常生活，旅行中發生的任何小事都很有魅力

· **想要完全認識當地的文化背景，跟團旅遊是最佳方式**
→ 導遊會詳細介紹歷史文化知識，並導覽各種有趣的建築或景點。

· **導遊也扮演著其它角色**
→ 不懂當地語言的情況下，能為旅客說明各種事物，並解答所有疑難雜症
→ 能提供關於餐廳、購物、飯店等各方面的建議

· **跟團旅行的其它好處**
→ 從飯店接送，直接前往有趣的地點
→ 毋須浪費時間或冒任何險，能快速地返回飯店

· **跟團旅行是結識新朋友的好方法**
→ 能結識同國籍以及來自世界各國的新朋友

Conclusion 結論

· **推薦跟團旅行**
→ 能完整參觀自己選擇的地點 → 最好找到兩種以上的方法

本書前面所學到的部分句型，會在以下文章範例中出現。

Introduction 開場白

¹**The quality of** a vacation to a new place depends on what the visitor hopes to accomplish. ²**For the great majority of people,** it is an opportunity to learn about the location and its people. ³**We often hear that** organized tours are the best way to see the world. ⁴**It seems to me that** ⁵if your goal is to learn facts and meet other tourists, this is true. ⁶**Everyone has to** decide for themselves how they prefer to sightsee. ⁷**In my decision-making,** I prefer the organized tour led by a guide.

Body 本文

⁸**The first thing that needs to be said is that** there are definite benefits to exploring a new place on your own. ⁹**From my experience, I think it is** great to wander the streets of an unfamiliar city, watch the people who live there, and even get lost now and then. ¹⁰**This, in turn,** gives you an appreciation for the city's daily life and subtle charms that may not be part of a tour.

¹¹**In order to properly understand** a location, ¹²**however,** the organized tour is the best way to go. ¹³**Generally speaking,** the tour guide can share historical facts and show you specific buildings or sites of interest. ¹⁴**To this end,** there are many sites of interest that may not be marked as such. ¹⁵**Thus,** wandering on your own, you might walk right past an historic battlefield without ever knowing it!

If you don't speak the native language, the tour guide can also interpret much of what you see and answer your questions, too. ¹⁶**To be sure,** most tour guides are locals. ¹⁷**For this reason,** they are usually very knowledgeable about the location. ¹⁸**One should note here that** the tour guide can also make recommendations, ¹⁹**including** restaurants, shopping, and hotels.

²⁰**Another** benefit is that the organized tour will often pick you up at your hotel and deliver you right to the site of interest. ²¹**Conversely,** much time can

be lost to exploration activities, **²²such as** hailing cabs and figuring out maps and bus schedules. **²³Another possibility is** you could become lost in a dangerous part of town. **²⁴Rather than** waste precious vacation time or take chances, an organized tour will deliver you safely back to your hotel.

²⁵To return to an earlier point, the organized tour is also a good way to meet people. **²⁶Not only** will there be others sharing the tour, **but** they may **also** be from your home country. **²⁷What is more,** you will often meet people from a variety of countries.

Conclusion 結論

²⁸In conclusion, I recommend taking an organized tour. **²⁹All things considered,** you are guaranteed to see the sites you've chosen. **³⁰Accordingly,** you will not waste time trying to find them on a map or figuring out how to get there. **³¹While I can** enjoy a bit of exploration myself from time to time, **I prefer** to let someone else do the driving most of the time. **³²I ask you to** give the organized tour a try; if it is not for you, then you can always explore on your own.

詞彙

accomplish 達成 | **organized** 有組織的、事先安排的 | **sightsee** 遊覽、觀光 |
definite 肯定的 | **wander** 閒晃 | **unfamiliar** 不熟悉的 | **get lost** 迷路 |
appreciation 欣賞 | **subtle** 微妙的 | **charm** 魅力 | **site** 地點 | **mark** 標示 |
as such 本身 | **on one's own** 自己、自助 | **battlefield** 戰場 | **interpret** 解說 |
knowledgeable 博學多聞的 | **exploration** 探索 | **hail** 招呼、呼叫 | **figure out** 搞清楚 |
precious 寶貴的 | **take chances** 冒險 | **guarantee** 保證 | **a bit of** 一點

句型

以下來複習文章範例中出現的精選句型。☞ 後面的數字對應本書前面的句型。

開場白部分出現的句型

1 **The quality of ...** …的品質（本質）… ☞ 請見開場白句型 18

2 **For the great majority of people,** 對大部分的人來說， ☞ 請見開場白句型 32

3 **We often hear that ...** 我們常聽說… ☞ 請見開場白句型 20

4 **It seems to me that ...** 對我來說，…似乎… ☞ 請見開場白句型 41

5 **If...** 如果／假如… ☞ 請見開場白句型 23

6 **Everyone has to ...** 每個人都應該要… ☞ 請見開場白句型 43

7 **In my decision-making,** 為了做出決定， ☞ 請見開場白句型 33

本文部分出現的句型

8 **The first thing that needs to be said is that ...**
   必須說明的第一點是…／首先要說的是… ☞ 請見本文句型 5

9 **From my experience, I think (it is) ...** 根據我的經驗，我認為… ☞ 請見本文句型 16

10 **This, in turn,** 這反而… ☞ 請見本文句型 12

11 **In order to properly understand ...,** 為了正確理解…， ☞ 請見本文句型 30

12 **However,** 然而， ☞ 請見本文句型 231

13 **Generally speaking,** 一般而言， ☞ 請見本文句型 28

14 **To this end,** 為此， ☞ 請見本文句型 44

15 **Thus,** 因此， ☞ 請見本文句型 50

16 **To be sure,** 確定的是，／可以肯定的是， ☞ 請見本文句型 57

17 **For this reason,** 因為這個原因， ☞ 請見本文句型 52

18 **One should note here that ...** 在此應該注意的是 ☞ 請見本文句型 76

19 **including...** 包括…／包含… ☞ 請見本文句型 196

20 **Another ...** 其他…／另一個... ☞ 請見本文句型 135

21 **Conversely,** 相反地，／反過來， ☞ 請見本文句型 177

22 **such as...** 像是… ☞ 請見本文句型 197

23 **Another possibility is...** 另一個可能性是… ☞ 請見本文句型 184

24 **Rather than ...,** 不是…，而是… ☞ 請見本文句型 173

25 **To return to an earlier point,** 回到先前的重點， ☞ 請見本文句型 86

26 **Not only ..., but (also)...** 不只…，而且… ☞ 請見本文句型 104

27 **What is more,** 而且， ☞ 請見本文句型 102

範例中文翻譯

請試著練習將以下加粗的中文，翻成英文看看。

開場白

　　到一個新地點度假的**品質**取決於遊客希望實現的目標。**對絕大多數人來說**，這是一個了解地區和人民的機會。**我們經常聽到**安排旅遊是見識這個世界最好的方法。**似乎對我而言**，如果你的目的是了解狀況並認識其他遊客，那麼這個說法就是正確的。**每個人都必須**為自己決定喜歡的觀光方式。**要做出一個決定的話**，我更喜歡由導遊帶領的團體旅行。

本文

　　必須說明的第一點是，獨自探索一個新地方絕對有好處。**從我的經驗來看，我認為**在一個陌生城市的街道上閒逛、看著住在那兒的人、甚至偶爾迷路，是很棒的。**這樣反而**能讓你可以欣賞這座城市的日常生活以及一些微妙的魅力，這可能並不是旅行的一部分。

　　然而，為了更適當地了解一個地方，團體旅行是最好的方式。**一般而言**，導遊可以分享歷史故事，並帶你遊覽特定的建築物或名勝古蹟。**為此**，有很多名勝古蹟可能沒有被標示。**因此**，你自己閒逛的話可能會不知不覺地走過歷史悠久的戰場而不自知。

　　如果你不會說當地的語言，導遊也可以解釋你所看到的大部分內容，並回答你的問題。**確實**大多數的導遊都是當地人，**因為這個原因**，他們通常對那個地點非常了解。**在這裡應該注意的是**，導遊也可以提供建議，**包括**餐館、購物和旅館。

　　另一個好處是，團體旅行通常會到你住的飯店接你，然後將你帶到感興趣的地點。**相反地**，自助旅行可能會浪費很多時間在探索，**像是**招計程車、弄清楚地圖和公車時刻表等。**另一種可能性是**，你可能會在城鎮的危險區域迷路。團體旅行**不會**浪費你寶貴的假期或機會，**而**可以安全地將你送回你的飯店。

回到**先前的論點**，團體旅行也是結識新朋友的好方法。**不僅**會有其他人分享這次旅程，他們可能**也**來自你的家鄉，**而且**你經常會遇到來自不同國家的人。

結論

最後，我建議參加團體旅行。**考慮一切之後**，你保證可以參觀到你選擇的地點。**因此**，你將不會浪費時間嘗試在地圖上找到它們、或弄清楚如何到達那個地方。**儘管我自己會**時不時享受一下探索的樂趣，但**我偏好**在大多數時間讓別人開車。**我想請你**試試看團體旅行；如果不適合你，那麼你永遠可以自行探索。

17

Do you agree or disagree with the following statement? Only people who earn a lot of money are successful. Use specific reasons and examples to support your answer.

你贊不贊同以下敘述？只有賺很多錢的人才是成功的。請運用具體的理由和例子來支持你的回答。

基本架構

在寫作前先腦力激盪，來定出文章的架構。

Introduction 開場白

· 過著成功光環人生的例子很多
→ 這些人中有些是富裕的人，有些是不富裕的人

提及文章的主旨
→ 真正的成功，並非完全取決於財富多寡，而是能否對自己的人生感到滿足且值得回憶

Body 本文

· 現今絕大多數人都是藉由金錢和物質財富的積累，來衡量人生的成功
→ 得建立在是否一步一腳印地努力累積財富的基礎上
→ 毫不吝嗇地投入公益，也是一種成功

最傑出的成功型態，是為周遭的人服務與奉獻
· 德蕾莎修女
→ 終生奉獻於照顧他人，也因此豐富了人生

· 梵谷
→ 雖然創作出世上最有名的畫作，但死的時候卻身無分文
→ 但因為遺留了世上最出色的美術作品在人間，也算是一種成功

· 奧地利事業家卡爾‧拉貝德
→ 變賣財產並捐給慈善團體

· 同意財富累積是成功的一種標準
→ 但不認為這是最好的標準，且不是所有人都認為是這樣

Conclusion 結論

· 分別以自己的標準來衡量成功
→ 擁有金錢的富裕並非一定滿足
→ 試想一下我們一生中真正有價值的東西是什麼，並為此全力以赴

 **文章範例**

本書前面所學到的部分句型，會在以下文章範例中出現。

Introduction 開場白

[1]**The world offers us numerous examples of** people who have lived successful lives. [2]**It is generally agreed today that** [3]if a person is wealthy, he/she is successful. [4]**However,** [5]**there are some people who** are considered successful yet lived their lives without much money at all. [6]**It is undeniable that** there are different viewpoints as to what makes a person successful. [7]**In this paper I argue that** real success isn't measured by money alone, but in living a satisfying and memorable life.

Body 本文

[8]**It is true that** the great majority of people today measure a successful life by the accumulation of money and material possessions. [9]**Assuming that** a person has accumulated them honestly and through hard work, I believe this to be true. [10]**What is more,** if that person gives freely money to charity, I consider him/her to be especially successful. [11]**I personally believe that** the purest form of success is in serving our fellow man.

[12]**To this end,** Mother Theresa lived to serve the poor and sick. [13]**In short,** she gave her lifetime to serving others, rather than trying to become rich. [14]**Despite that,** she lived a rich life full of human interaction and giving to her fellow man. [15]**Many people believe that** her life was remarkable enough to consider her for sainthood.

[16]**Even though** Vincent Van Gogh created some of the world's most famous paintings, he died penniless. [17]**Chiefly** this was due to the mental illness he suffered all his life. Despite that, however, his life could be considered successful because he left the world his magnificent art. [18]**Truly,** his life was a difficult one. [19]**Nonetheless,** he was a highly creative and productive artist who left a legacy recognized around the world.

[20]**And then** there are the millionaires who decided to give all their money to

charity. **²¹Take, for example,** Austrian businessman Karl Rabeder. He explained that his life had become "soulless," and he had become "a slave for things (he) did not wish for or need." **²²In brief,** he sold his possessions and donated the money to a charitable organization. **²³By this time,** he has likely moved to a modest hut in the mountains of Austria.

²⁴I totally agree that accumulating wealth is a measure of success. However **²⁵I don't agree with the statement that** it is the best measure or the desire of every person. **²⁶Make no mistake about it,** I would not complain if I suddenly became wealthy. **²⁷At the same time,** I would make an effort to give back to those less fortunate than myself.

Conclusion 結論

²⁸All things considered, we each measure success by our own standards. **²⁹After all,** when you don't have monetary wealth, you aspire to have it. **³⁰The consequence is that** having it is not always as satisfying as one might think. **³¹It might be useful to** think about what we truly value in this life, and devote ourselves to it. **³²When all is said and done,** which would you rather have at the end of your life — family, memories, and pure heart, or a pile of money? **³³It is often said that** you can't take it with you.

詞彙

wealthy 富有的 | **viewpoint** 觀點 | **measure** 衡量 | **memorable** 難忘的 |
accumulation 累積 | **possessions** 財產 | **freely** 大量地 | **charity** 慈善機構 |
pure 純粹的 | **fellow man** 同胞 | **remarkable** 非凡的、卓越的 | **sainthood** 神聖的行為 |
penniless 身無分文的 | **magnificent** 偉大的 | **legacy** 遺產 | **millionaire** 百萬富翁 |
soulless 沒有靈魂的 | **slave** 奴隸 | **donate** 捐獻 | **charitable** 慈善的、慈悲為懷的 |
modest 低調的、有節制的 | **hut** 小屋 | **make an effort** 盡力、努力 |
monetary 貨幣的、金融的 | **aspire** 渴望的 | **devote** 奉獻給

句型

以下來複習文章範例中出現的精選句型。☞ 後面的數字對應本書前面的句型。

開場白部分出現的句型

1 **The world offers us numerous examples of ...**
這世界上有許多…的例子 ☞ **請見開場白句型 27**

2 **It is generally agreed today that ...** 當前普遍認為（同意）… ☞ **請見開場白句型 31**

3 **If...** 如果／假如… ☞ **請見開場白句型 23**

4 **However,** 然而， ☞ **請見開場白句型 231**

5 **There are some people who ...** 有些人… ☞ **請見開場白句型 39**

6 **It is undeniable that ...** 不可否認（無庸置疑地），… ☞ **請見開場白句型 40**

7 **In this paper I argue that ...** 在這份報告中，我主張（認為）… ☞ **請見開場白句型 19**

本文部分出現的句型

8 **It is true that ...** …是真的 ☞ **請見本文句型 15**

9 **Assuming that ...,** 假設…，… ☞ **請見本文句型 24**

10 **What is more,** 而且， ☞ **請見本文句型 102**

11 **I personally believe that ...** 我個人相信… ☞ **請見本文句型 17**

12 **To this end,** 為此， ☞ **請見本文句型 44**

13 **In short,** 簡而言之， ☞ **請見本文句型 215**

14 **Despite that,** 儘管如此， ☞ **請見本文句型 225**

15 **Many people believe that ...** 許多人相信… ☞ **請見本文句型 270**

16 **Even though ...,** 即使…， ☞ **請見本文句型 228**

17 **chiefly** 主要 ☞ **請見本文句型 205**

18 **Truly,** 確實，／真的， ☞ **請見本文句型 220**

19 **Nonetheless,** 儘管如此， ☞ **請見本文句型 223**

20 **And then...** 然後… ☞ **請見本文句型 153**

21 **Take, for example, ...** 以…為例，／舉例來說， ☞ **請見本文句型 291**

22 **In brief,** 簡而言之， ☞ **請見本文句型 304**

23 **By this time,** 到這個時候，／此時，… ☞ **請見本文句型 299**

24 **I totally agree that ...** 我完全同意… ☞ **請見本文句型 321**

25 **I don't agree with the statement that ...** 我不同意…的說法 ☞ **請見本文句型 323**

26 **Make no mistake about it,** 毫無疑問地，／的確， ☞ **請見本文句型 328**

27 **At the same time,** 同時， ☞ **請見本文句型 325**

28 **All things considered,** 考量一切根據， ☞ 請見結論句型 11

29 **After all,** 結果，／畢竟， ☞ 請見結論句型 3

30 **The consequence is that ...** 結果是… ☞ 請見結論句型 8

31 **It might be useful to ...** …可能會有用 ☞ 請見結論句型 79

32 **When all is said and done,** 說到最後，／畢竟， ☞ 請見結論句型 73

33 **It is often said that ...** 人們常說…／常言道… ☞ 請見開場白句型 21

範例中文翻譯

請試著練習將以下加粗的中文，翻成英文看看。

開場白

　　這個世界為我們提供了許多榜樣人物，他們過著成功的生活。**在今天，**普遍認為如果一個人有錢，他／她就成功了。**但是，有些**被認為是成功人士**的人**卻並非過著富有的生活。**不可否認的是，**對於一個人是否成功有不同的看法。**在本篇文章中，我認為**真正的成功不單靠金錢來衡量，而在於擁有令人滿意和值得回憶的人生。

本文

　　的確，當今絕大多數人是以金錢和物質財富的積累來衡量成功的人生。**假設一個人**誠實並透過努力積累這些金錢，我相信這是真的。**而且，**如果這個人將大量的錢捐給慈善機構，我認為他／她特別成功。**我個人認為，**成功的最純粹形式就是為我們的同胞服務。

　　為此，德蕾莎修女活著就是為窮人和病人服務。**簡而言之，**她一生致力於服務他人，而不是試圖致富。**儘管如此，**她過著充滿人際互動並奉獻給同伴的豐富生活。**許多人相信，**她神聖的行為足以使她的人生堪稱卓越。

　　即使文森·梵谷創作了許多世界上最著名的畫作，他過世時身無分文，**主要是**因為他一生都苦於精神疾病。然而儘管如此，他的一生仍然可以被認為是成功的，因為他留給世界偉大的藝術。**誠然，**他的人生很困苦，**但儘管如此**他還是一位極富創造力和生產力的藝術家，留下了享譽全球的遺產。

　　還有那些決定將所有財產拿去做慈善的百萬富翁。**以**奧地利商人豪拉伯德**為例。**他解釋自己的人生已經變得「沒有靈魂」，而且他已經變成「他不想要、也不需要的事物的奴隸」。**簡而言之，**他賣掉了自己的財產，並將這筆錢捐給了慈善機構。**此時，**他可能已經搬到奧地利山區的一個低調小屋裡。

我完全同意積累財富是成功的方法之一，然而，**我不同意這種說法**是最好的方法或者是每個人的願望。**毫無疑問地**，如果我突然變得富有，我不會抱怨。然而，我**同時**會努力回饋那些比我自己不幸的人。

結論

　　考量一切後，我們每個人都以自己的標準衡量成功。**畢竟**，當你沒有經濟上的財富時，就會渴望擁有它。**結果**，擁有它並不總是像人們想像的那樣令人滿意。思考一下我們這一生的真正價值並全心投入其中，**或許會很有用**。**畢竟**，在你生命的盡頭，你寧願擁有的是─家庭、記憶以及純潔的心，還是一堆錢？**有句話是這麼說的**，錢生不帶來、死不帶走。

18

A gift (such as a camera, a soccer ball, or an animal) can contribute to a child's development. What gift would you give to help a child develop? Why? Use specific reasons and examples to support your choice.

禮物（例如相機、足球、或動物）有助於兒童的發展。你會送什麼禮物，來幫助孩子成長？請運用具體的理由和例子來支持你的選擇。

基本架構

在寫作前先腦力激盪，來定出文章的架構。

Introduction 開場白

· 近來孩子們沉迷於電玩、手機、電子音樂
→ 電子產品對孩子來說並非一直是最棒的禮物
→ 書籍是可以送給孩子的最佳禮物之一
→ 從書中找到獨特的樂趣

Body 本文

· 書籍是孩子智能發展最重要的一部分
→ 雖然大部分資訊都能從網路上搜尋到，但我們仍重視書籍
→ 停止出版紙本書籍雖可拯救樹木，但會失去手持紙本書籍的體驗

· 閱讀的本質不僅僅只是單純地吸收文字和其語意
→ 書籍有其美妙之處

· 一般大眾傾向認為書籍是我們最佳的學習工具
→ 但基於某些理由，有些人可能會對某些書籍的內容持反對態度
　例：哈利波特系列：被認為有巫術與惡魔思想的崇拜
→ 禁書的問題：書籍是為了帶給我們資訊與趣味
→ 書籍是言論自由的基礎，也是孩子一生中最重要的發展工具

· 關於紙本書籍與電子書兩者哪個比較好，仍意見紛紜
→ 重要的是要體認到當孩子手中拿著書時，他／她能吸收到知識

Conclusion 結論

· 書籍是鼓勵孩子學習的最佳禮物
→ 刺激創意與理解力，鼓勵終生學習
→ 讓孩子們一輩子都熱愛閱讀書籍

文章範例

本書前面所學到的部分句型，會在以下文章範例中出現。

Introduction 開場白

[1]**These days,** children are drawn to electronic toys and games, cell phones and digital music. [2]**At the very least,** most children have access to a home computer. [3]**In my opinion,** electronics are not always the best gift for a child. [4]**It seems to me that** one of the best gifts you can give a child is a book. [5]**I'd like to suggest that** [6]**while** electronics can contribute to a child's development, there is still unique joy to be found in books.

Body 本文

[7]**First of all,** books are still an important part of a child's intellectual development. [8]**Even though** we can now find most information on the Internet, we still value books. [9]**There has been much debate about** whether electronic reading will replace books soon. [10]**On the one hand,** we could save trees if we stopped printing books. [11]**On the other hand,** we would lose the experience of the hand-held book.

[12]**The quality of** a reading experience is more than simply taking in words and meaning. [13]**Some people** enjoy sitting in a comfortable chair with a book in their lap by the fireplace. [14]**It is undeniable that** a book is a beautiful thing. [15]**If we think about** how it is put together, the leather and binding, the illustrations, it's quite remarkable. [16]**There are some people who** collect books, build their own libraries and read their favorites over and again.

[17]**The public in general tend to believe that** books are our finest learning instruments. [18]**In the past,** some people have tried to ban books that they felt were a threat to society. [19]**There are many reasons why** a person might object to a book's content. [20]**In the case of** the Harry Potter series, some parents felt it promoted witchcraft and devil worship. [21]**There's just one problem** with book banning: books are meant to inform and entertain us. In my opinion, they are fundamental to freedom of expression, and perhaps the single most important development tool in a child's life.

²²And what about paper books vs. reading on the computer? **²³It is a complicated question** involving ecology and expense. **²⁴There is still no general agreement about** which is best. **²⁵It is important to recognize,** though, that when a child possesses a book in his/her hand, he/she possesses knowledge. It seems to me that this is a powerful gift to the developing child.

Conclusion 結論

²⁶Therefore, I suggest that books will always be excellent gifts to encourage a child's development. **²⁷All things considered,** they are both entertaining and informative. **²⁸Accordingly,** they stimulate creativity and understanding and encourage lifelong learning. **²⁹One thing's for sure:** a book will enrich a child's mind in ways an electronic game cannot. **³⁰Ultimately,** it can instill in him/her a love for reading that he/she will enjoy throughout his/her life.

詞彙

be drawn to ... 受⋯吸引 | **hand-held** 手持的 | **take in** 讀取、取得 |
comfortable chair 舒適的椅子 | **fireplace** 壁爐 | **put together** 組成 |
leather 皮革、皮質的書皮 | **binding** 裝訂邊 | **finest** 優良的 | **ban** 禁止 | **promote** 宣傳 |
witchcraft 巫術 | **devil** 惡魔 | **worship** 崇拜 | **entertain** 娛樂 | **ecology** 生態 |
expense 費用、成本 | **informative** 教育性的 | **stimulate** 激勵 | **creativity** 創造力 |
lifelong 一生的 | **enrich** 豐富 | **instill** 逐漸教導 | **throughout** 從頭到尾

句型

以下來複習文章範例中出現的精選句型。☞ 後面的數字對應本書前面的句型。

開場白部分出現的句型

1 **These days,** 最近， ☞ **請見開場白句型 88**

2 **At the very least, ...** 至少 ☞ **請見開場白句型 81**

3 **In my opinion,** 就我的觀點而言，／個人認為， ☞ **請見開場白句型 78**

4 **It seems to me that ...** 對我來說，…似乎… ☞ **請見開場白句型 41**

5 **I'd like to suggest that ...** 我想建議…／我想提議… ☞ **請見開場白句型 79**

6 **While..., ...** 儘管…，但… ☞ **請見開場白句型 49**

本文部分出現的句型

7 **First of all,** 首先， ☞ **請見開場白句型 9**

8 **Even though ...,** 即使…， ☞ **請見開場白句型 228**

9 **There has been much debate about ...** 關於…曾有過許多爭論 ☞ **請見開場白句型 31**

10 **On the one hand,** 一方面， ☞ **請見開場白句型 61**

11 **On the other hand,** 另一方面， ☞ **請見開場白句型 62**

12 **The quality of ...** …的品質（本質）… ☞ **請見開場白句型 18**

13 **Some people ...** 某些人… ☞ **請見開場白句型 38**

14 **It is undeniable that ...** 不可否認（無庸置疑地），… ☞ **請見開場白句型 40**

15 **If we think about ...** 如果我們想想（思考）… ☞ **請見開場白句型 45**

16 **There are some people who ...** 有些人… ☞ **請見開場白句型 39**

17 **The public in general tend to believe that ...**
一般大眾傾向於相信（大部分人都相信）… ☞ **請見開場白句型 64**

18 **In the past,** 在過去， ☞ **請見開場白句型 52**

19 **There are many reasons why ...** 基於許多原因，… ☞ **請見開場白句型 65**

20 **In the case of ...,** 關於…， ☞ **請見開場白句型 86**

21 **There's just one problem:** 只有一個問題： ☞ **請見開場白句型 92**

22 **And what about ...** 那麼關於…，你怎麼看呢？ ☞ **請見開場白句型 71**

23 **It is a complicated question** （對…來說，）這是個複雜的問題 ☞ **請見開場白句型 72**

24 **There is still no general agreement about ...**
目前對於…仍未有共識 ☞ **請見開場白句型 74**

25 **It is important to recognize...** 認識…非常重要 ☞ **請見開場白句型 94**

26 **Therefore,** 因此， ☞ 請見結論句型 1
27 **All things considered,** 考量一切根據， ☞ 請見結論句型 11
28 **Accordingly,** 因此， ☞ 請見結論句型 20
29 **One thing's for sure:** 有一點可以肯定的是： ☞ 請見結論句型 66
30 **Ultimately,** 終究，／最終， ☞ 請見結論句型 71

範例中文翻譯

請試著練習將以下加粗的中文，翻成英文看看。

開場白

　　最近，孩童受電玩和遊戲、手機和數位音樂所吸引。**最起碼，**大多數孩子都會使用家庭電腦。**個人認為，**電子產品並非總是給孩子最好的禮物。**似乎對我來說，**你可以送給孩子最好的禮物之一是書。**我想建議，儘管**電子產品可以幫助孩子的成長發展，但在書中仍然可以找到獨特的樂趣。

本文

　　首先，在兒童智力發展階段，書本仍扮演的重要角色。**即使**我們現在可以在網際網路上找到大部份的資訊，我們仍然重視書籍。**關於**電子閱讀是否會很快取代紙本書籍**一直存在很多爭論。一方面來說，**如果我們停止印刷書籍，我們可以拯救樹木。**另一方面，**我們可能會失去手拿著書本的體驗。

　　閱讀**的本質**不僅僅是單純吸收文字和其意義。**有些人**喜歡坐在壁爐旁舒適的椅子上，膝蓋上放著一本書。**不可否認的，**書是美麗的事物。**如果我們思考**一本書是如何組成的，書封和裝訂邊、插圖，這非常了不起。**有些人**會收集書籍，建立自己的圖書館，並一遍又一遍地閱讀他們最喜歡的書。

　　一般大眾通常傾向於相信書籍是我們最好的學習工具。**過去，**有些人曾試著禁止他們覺得對社會構成威脅的書籍。一個人可能會**基於許多原因**反對書的內容。**以**《哈利波特》系列**為例，**有些父母認為它宣傳巫術和魔鬼崇拜。**關於禁書只有一個問題：**書本是用來給予知識和娛樂我們。就我的觀點來看，它們是言論自由的基礎，也許是兒童生命中最重要的發展工具。

　　關於紙本書籍與在電腦上閱讀**又如何呢？這是一個**涉及生態和花費**的複雜問題。**目前對於哪種最佳**尚無普遍共識。**然而，**認清**這點是**很重要的：**當孩子手裡擁有一本書時，他／她便擁有知識。似乎對我來說，這對成長中的孩子來說是個強而有力的禮物。

因此，我建議書本永遠是激勵孩子成長的最佳禮物。**考量過一切後**，書本既有娛樂性也有教育性。**因此**，它們可以激發創造力和理解力，並鼓勵終身學習。**可以肯定的一件事是**：書將以電子遊戲無法提供的方式豐富孩子的心智。**最終**，它可以向他／她灌輸對他／她將受用一生的閱讀之愛。

19

In some countries, people are no longer allowed to smoke in many public places and office buildings. Do you think this is a good rule or a bad rule? Use specific reasons and details to support your position.

在某些國家，人們不再被允許於許多公共場所或辦公大樓吸菸。你認為這是好的規定還是不好的規定？請運用具體的理由和例子來支持你的立場。

基本架構

在寫作前先腦力激盪，來定出文章的架構。

Introduction 開場白

· 抽菸會致癌這件事是廣為人知的事實
→ 吸二手菸也有可能讓非吸菸者罹患癌症

提及文章的目的
→ 為了要說明公共場所禁菸為何是很好的規定

Body 本文

· 有必要針對二手菸相關事實進行探討
→ 談到誘發癌症、導致成人和孩童的氣喘發作，以及引發肺部感染、耳朵感染等問題的原因
→ 可能導致孕婦早產

· 香菸中含有 4000 種以上的化學物質
→ 其中有 60 多種會致癌

· 非吸菸者在煙霧瀰漫的環境下會覺得不舒服
→ 除了會影響呼吸之外，菸味還會殘留在頭髮跟衣物上
→ 破壞用餐氣氛，搭電梯時，電梯裡的菸味讓人難聞

吸菸者看不到自己所造成的這些麻煩
· 孩童與嬰兒受二手菸的影響最為嚴重
→ 因為在家裡沒有保護他們免於吸二手菸的法規，因此公共場合的保護法規很重要

· 公共場所禁菸是維護非吸菸者的公民權利
→ 公民權利在不對他人造成危害的條件下，應得加以被維護

Conclusion 結論

· 上述所有一切都顯示，公共場所禁菸是很好的規定
→ 規定剛開始施行時對吸菸者來說應該會深感不便，但隨著時間過去，就會適應
→ 應該要在公共場所的某處設置吸菸區

 **文章範例**

本書前面所學到的部分句型，會在以下文章範例中出現。

Introduction 開場白

¹**It is a well-known fact that** smoking can cause cancer. ²**One of the most striking features of this problem is** that we now know that second-hand smoke (SHS) can cause cancer in the non-smoker. ³**This issue is one that** is argued by smokers who feel they are being pushed out of public places where smoking is no longer allowed. ⁴**They may** look at smoking as a civil right, rather than as a health hazard to others. ⁵**The aim of this essay is to** show why a ban on smoking in public places is a good rule.

Body 本文

⁶**We must first examine** the facts about second-hand smoke. The American Cancer Society ⁷**makes a good point that** ⁸**not only** can SHS cause cancer in the non-smoker**, but** it contributes to the development of asthma attacks, lung infections and ear infections in exposed children and adults. ⁹**In fact,** exposed pregnant women are at risk to have a child with low birth weight. ¹⁰**As for** cancer, tobacco contains over 4,000 different chemicals, 60 of which are known to cause cancer. ¹¹**Thus, although it is true that** non-smokers are better off than smokers, they are still at risk when breathing in SHS.

¹²**In addition to that,** non-smokers are made uncomfortable by smoky environments. Not only does it irritate their breathing, but their clothes and hair smell like smoke. ¹³**What is more,** these irritations can ruin a nice meal at a restaurant, or make an elevator ride unbearably long. ¹⁴**It is difficult to believe that** the smoker cannot see these impositions. ¹⁵**And yet,** his addiction is powerful enough to cause him to justify exposing others to his habit.

¹⁶**Perhaps it is worth acknowledging here that** children and babies are the most vulnerable to SHS. ¹⁷**In effect,** they are more likely to develop breathing problems early in life, and more prone to ear infections. ¹⁸**What's

worse is that there are few laws to protect children and babies from SHS in the home. **¹⁹That is why, in my opinion,** it is especially important to protect them from SHS in public. **²⁰If** we can protect them at least part of the time, their risks for developing health problems will be lowered.

²¹Bearing this in mind, does a public ban on smoking violate the civil rights of smokers? **²²On the contrary,** it upholds the civil rights of the non-smokers. **²³This is consistent with** the idea that the civil rights of a person are upheld only when they do not cause harm to others. **²⁴There is a great deal of research** that proves SHS does indeed cause harm to others. **²⁵In short,** the non-smoker's civil rights win over the smoker's because his demand to enjoy a smoke-free environment causes harm to no one.

Conclusion 結論

²⁶All of this would indicate that a ban on smoking in public places is a good thing. **²⁷Though** it is at first difficult for the smokers, I think over time they adjust to the rule. **²⁸If this is to happen,** though, designated smoking areas need to be established outside the public space. **²⁹I'm sure that** the smokers want their needs to be recognized, too. **³⁰But, as for me, it's** simple. **³¹I definitely prefer to** dine in a smoke-free restaurant.

詞彙

second-hand 二手的 | **push out of ...** 強迫離開 | **civil right** 公民權 | **hazard** 危機 | **asthma attack** 氣喘發作 | **infection** 感染 | **tobacco** 菸草製品 | **chemical** 化學物質 | **better off** 情況較佳 | **breathe** 呼吸 | **smoky** 煙霧瀰漫的 | **irritate** 刺激 | **ruin** 破壞 | **unbearably** 難以忍受地 | **imposition** 強迫接受 | **addiction** 上癮 | **justify** 認為…是正當的 | **prone to ...** 易於 | **lower** 降低 | **violate** 違反 | **uphold** 支持 | **win over** 獲得贊同 | **smoke-free** 無菸的 | **adjust to ...** 適應於… | **designate** 指定 | **dine** 用餐

句型

以下來複習文章範例中出現的精選句型。☞ 後面的數字對應本書前面的句型。

開場白部分出現的句型

1　**It is a well-known fact that ...** …是眾所皆知的事實 ☞ **請見開場白句型 25**

2　**One of the most striking features of this problem is ...**
   這問題中最值得關注的是… ☞ **請見開場白句型 28**

3　**This issue is one that ...** 這個議題（是）… ☞ **請見開場白句型 29**

4　**They may...** 他們可能… ☞ **請見開場白句型 36**

5　**The aim of this essay is to...** 這文章的目的是為了… ☞ **請見開場白句型 1**

本文部分出現的句型

6　**We must first examine ...** 我們必須要先檢視… ☞ **請見本文句型 3**

7　**... makes a good point that ...**
   …說…是很有道理的／提出了一個很好的觀點： ☞ **請見本文句型 56**

8　**Not only ..., but (also)...** 不只…，而且… ☞ **請見本文句型 104**

9　**In fact,** 事實上， ☞ **請見本文句型 82**

10　**As for ...,** 至於…， ☞ **請見本文句型 87**

11　**Thus, although it is true that ...** 因此，雖然…是事實，但… ☞ **請見本文句型 96**

12　**In addition to that,** 除此之外， ☞ **請見本文句型 110**

13　**What is more,** 而且， ☞ **請見本文句型 102**

14　**It is difficult to believe that ...** 很難相信… ☞ **請見本文句型 134**

15　**And yet,** 然而， ☞ **請見本文句型 93**

16　**Perhaps it is worth acknowledging here that ...**
   或許在這裡值得被承認的是…／或許在這裡值得被注意的是… ☞ **請見本文句型 351**

17　**In effect,** 事實上， ☞ **請見本文句型 349**

18　**What's worse is that ...** 更糟的是… ☞ **請見本文句型 334**

19　**That is why, in my opinion,** 這也是為什麼我認為… ☞ **請見本文句型 33**

20　**If...** 如果／假如… ☞ **請見本文句型 23**

21　**Bearing this in mind,** 銘記這點，／請記住，／請留意， ☞ **請見本文句型 191**

22　**On the contrary,** 反而， ☞ **請見本文句型 176**

23　**This is consistent with ...** 這與…一致 ☞ **請見本文句型 179**

24　**There is a great deal of research ...** …的研究很多 ☞ **請見本文句型 211**

25　**In short,** 簡而言之， ☞ **請見本文句型 215**

26 **All of this would indicate that ...** 這一切顯示… ☞ 請見結尾句型 21

27 **Though ...,** 雖然…， ☞ 請見本文句型 232

28 **If this is to happen,** 如果發生這種情況， ☞ 請見結尾句型 34

29 **I'm sure that ...** 我確信… ☞ 請見結尾句型 42

30 **But, as for me, it's ...** 但這對我來說… ☞ 請見結尾句型 32

31 **I definitely prefer to ...** 我當然偏好選擇… ☞ 請見結尾句型 41

範例中文翻譯

請試著練習將以下加粗的中文，翻成英文看看。

開場白

　　吸菸會導致癌症**是眾所周知的事實**。這個問題最引人關注的其中一點是，我們現在知道二手菸（SHS）會導致非吸菸者罹患癌症。**這是**吸菸者爭論**的一個議題**，他們認為他們被迫離開不再允許吸菸的公共場所。**他們可能**將吸菸視為一項公民權利，而不是對他人的健康危害。**本篇文的目的是**說明為什麼在公共場所禁止吸菸是一個好規定。

本文

　　我們必須首先檢視有關二手菸的真相。美國癌症協會**提出了一個很好的觀點**：二手菸**不僅**會導致非吸菸者罹患癌症，而且**還會**導致暴露在二手菸下的兒童和成人氣喘發作、肺部感染和耳部感染。**實際上**，暴露在二手菸中的孕婦會有風險分娩出體重不足的嬰兒。**至於**癌症，菸草包含超過四千種不同的化學物質，其中六十種已知會引起癌症。**因此**，**儘管**不吸菸者的身體**確實**比吸菸者健康，**但**他們在吸二手菸時仍處於危險之中。

　　除此之外，非吸菸的人在煙霧瀰漫的環境中會感到不舒服，這不僅刺激他們而造成呼吸難受，也讓他們的衣服和頭髮聞起來有菸味。**再者**，這些惱人的刺激物還會破壞餐廳的美味佳餚，或者讓搭電梯的過程變得難以忍受地久。**很難相信**吸菸者沒有意識到自己加諸在他人身上的種種，**然而**，他的菸癮強大到足以使他有理由將他人暴露在自身習慣中合理化。

　　在這裡，也許值得承認的是，孩童和嬰兒最容易受到二手菸的傷害。**實際上**，他們可能在生命早期出現呼吸問題，並且更容易耳部感染。**更糟糕的是**，很少有法律可以保護家庭中的兒童和嬰兒免受二手菸的侵害。**就我的觀點來看**，這就是為什麼保護他們免於公共場所的二手菸尤其重要。**如果**我們能夠至少在部分時間保護他們，那麼他們出現健康問題的風險將會降低。

請注意，禁止吸菸的政府規定是否違反了吸菸者的公民權利？**相反地**，它維護了非吸菸者的公民權利。**這與**「個人的公民權利只有在不對他人造成傷害的情況下才得到維護」的觀念**相符**。**有許多研究**證明，二手菸確實會對他人造成傷害。**總之**，非吸菸者的公民權利凌駕於吸菸者的公民權之上，因為非吸菸者要求享受無菸環境一事不會對任何人造成傷害。

結論

這一切都顯示，在公共場所禁止吸菸是一件好事。**雖然**一開始對吸菸者來說很困難，但我認為隨著時間流逝，他們會依照規定自我調適。**然而**，**如果這將發生**，在公共場所外有必要建立指定的吸菸區。**我確信**吸菸者也希望他們的需求得到認可。**但是**，**對我來說這**很簡單。**我絕對偏好**在無菸餐廳用餐。

20

Plants can provide food, shelter, clothing, or medicine. What is one kind of plant that is important to you or the people in your country? Use specific reasons and details to explain your choice.

植物被用作食物、避難所、衣服和藥物。哪一種植物對你或你們國家的人是很重要的？請運用具體的理由和例子來支持你的選擇。

基本架構

在寫作前先腦力激盪，來定出文章的架構。

Introduction 開場白

· 我們所使用的物品中，很多都是由植物製成的
→ 植物的壽命及其經濟價值，在各國都不太一樣
  例：觀察巴西、中國、美國的情況

· 提及文章的目的
→ 玉米在美國是具高價值的經濟作物，並被廣泛使用

Body 本文

· 玉米基於許多理由成為了美國的重要作物
→ 玉米對美國原住民來說很重要

· 提及玉米的起源
→ 大部分人都認為玉米源自於墨西哥或南美洲
→ 玉米在美國歷史上佔有重要地位，至今仍是如此

· 玉米是極佳的食物來源
→ 是人類愛吃的食物，也作為農場動物的飼料，還被做成玉米糖漿

· 玉米也被用來生產乙醇
→ 在生產的過程中雖然不節能，仍是美國經濟的重要一部分

· 提及玉米的其它用途
→ 玉米在美國經濟上至少有 3500 種用途

Conclusion 結論

· 玉米是美國唯一最重要的作物
→ 玉米是傳統的作物
→ 建立美國過去輝煌的歷史，亦持續塑造美國的未來

本書前面所學到的部分句型，會在以下文章範例中出現。

Introduction 開場白

[1]**If you stop to consider** all the things we use that are made from plants, there are many. [2]**We live in a world in which** the plant life and its economic value varies from country to country. [3]**While** Brazil's climate and terrain are good for growing the rubber tree plant, China's are better suited for growing rice and tea. [4]**If we think about** plants that are important to the U.S. economy, I would have to place corn at the top of the list. I'm going to prove that corn has a variety of uses highly valued in the U.S.

Body 本文

[5]**There are many reasons why** corn is important to the U.S. [6]**Most people don't know** that it was as important to the Native Americans as rice is for the peoples of Southeast Asia. [7]**In reality, it is found that** there are hundreds of varieties of corn. [8]**Scholars disagree on** corn's origins, but most believe it came from either Mexico or South America. [9]**By many accounts,** for more than 250 years after Jamestown, Virginia was settled, corn remained the primary crop of 90% of farmers. [10]**So,** corn has always been a vital part of America's history, and remains a vital part today.

[11]**To start with,** corn is an excellent food source. [12]**First of all,** people enjoy corn, both on and off the cob, as popcorn, corn chips, and corn cereals, for example. [13]**Next,** many of our farm animals are fed corn, [14]**including** chickens and cattle. [15]**In addition,** corn syrup is used to sweeten many products, like ice cream, candies, and baked goods.

[16]**Another reason why** corn is important in the U.S. **is** its use in producing ethanol. [17]**However, the problem is that** while this alternative fuel can be made from corn, the process for making it is not energy efficient. [18]**As a result,** corn grown to produce ethanol may lose its importance unless a more efficient process can be identified. [19]**For now,** [20]**however,** it continues to be a vital part of the U.S. economy.

²¹**And what about** other uses of corn? ²²**You may not know** that corn is used to make a kind of packing peanuts, fiberboard panels, cleaning fluids, ink and absorbent materials, ²³**such as** diapers. ²⁴**The point is,** corn is not just a food source. ²⁵**Truly,** it has at least 3,500 uses in the U.S. economy today.

Conclusion 結論

²⁶**Thus we can see that** corn may very well be the single most important plant in the U.S. ²⁷**I'm sure that** arguments could be made for cotton, tobacco or peanuts, as well as many other plants. ²⁸**I definitely prefer to** think of corn as our country's heritage plant. ²⁹**Ultimately,** it shaped our past and continues to shape our future. And, ³⁰**while I can** appreciate a fine cotton shirt, **I prefer** to enjoy a plate full of steaming corn on the cob.

詞彙

vary 變化 | **terrain** 地域 | **rubber** 橡膠 | **suited for ...** 適合… | **crop** 作物 | **vital** 主要的 | **cob** 玉米 | **baked goods** 烘焙食品 | **ethanol** 乙醇 | **energy efficient** 節能高效的 | **identify** 發現 | **packing peanut** 包裝豆（花生形狀，放在箱子裡防止物品間的碰撞）| **fiberboard panel** 纖維板 | **cleaning fluid** 清潔劑 | **absorbent material** 吸水材質 | **diaper** 尿布 | **heritage** 世代遺留下的 | **plate** 盤子

句型

以下來複習文章範例中出現的精選句型。☞ 後面的數字對應本書前面的句型。

開場白部分出現的句型

1 **If you stop to consider...** 如果你思考一下… ☞ 請見開場白句型 46

2 **We live in a world in which ...** 我們活在一個…的世界 ☞ 請見開場白句型 26

3 **While..., ...** 儘管…，但… ☞ 請見開場白句型 49

4 **If we think about ...** 如果我們想想（思考）… ☞ 請見開場白句型 45

本文部分出現的句型

5 **There are many reasons why ...** 基於許多原因，… ☞ 請見開場白句型 65

6 **Most people don't know ...** 大部分的人不知道… ☞ 請見開場白句型 67

7 **In reality, it is found that ...** 實際上發現… ☞ 請見本文句型 84

8 **Scholars disagree on ...** 學者對…持不同意見 ☞ 請見本文句型 355

9 **By many accounts,** 許多依據顯示，／由於許多原因 ☞ 請見開場白句型 58

10 **So,** 所以， ☞ 請見結論句型 2

11 **To start with,** 首先， ☞ 請見本文句型 8

12 **First of all,** 首先， ☞ 請見本文句型 9

13 **Next,** 接下來， ☞ 請見本文句型 131

14 **including...** 包括…／包含… ☞ 請見本文句型 196

15 **In addition,** 另外， ☞ 請見本文句型 108

16 **Another reason why ... is that ...** 為什麼…的另一個原因是因為… ☞ 請見本文句型 305

17 **However, the problem is that ...** 然而，問題是… ☞ 請見本文句型 336

18 **As a result,** 因此， ☞ 請見本文句型 342

19 **For now,** 現在，／目前， ☞ 請見結論句型 33

20 **However,** 然而， ☞ 請見本文句型 231

21 **And what about ...** 那麼關於…，你怎麼看呢？ ☞ 請見開場白句型 71

22 **You may not know ...** 各位可能不知道… ☞ 請見開場白句型 68

23 **such as...** 像是… ☞ 請見本文句型 197

24 **The point is,** 重點是… ☞ 請見本文句型 216

25 **Truly,** 確實，／真的， ☞ 請見本文句型 220

結論部分出現的句型

26 **Thus we can see that ...** 因此我們可以知道… ☞ 請見結論句型 23

27 **I'm sure that ...** 我確信… ☞ 請見結論句型 42

範例中文翻譯

請試著練習將以下加粗的中文，翻成英文看看。

開場白

　　如果你停下來思考，我們使用很多以植物製成的東西。**我們生活在一個**植物生機及其經濟價值因國家而異**的世界。儘管**巴西的氣候和地形有利於橡膠樹的種植，**但**中國則更適合種植水稻和茶。**如果我們思考**對美國經濟重要的植物，我必須把玉米放在第一位。我將證明玉米在美國具有各種高價值的用處。

本文

　　玉米對美國很重要**的原因有很多，大多數人都不知道**玉米對美國原住民的重要性就像水稻對東南亞人民一樣。**實際上，人們發現**有數百種玉米。**學者對**玉米的起源**沒有共識**，但大多數人認為玉米來自墨西哥或南美洲。**許多依據顯示，**在定居於維吉尼亞州詹姆斯鎮超過兩百二十五年間，玉米仍佔農民主要農作物中的百分之九十。**所以，**玉米始終是美國歷史上至關重要的部分，而且直到今日仍然擁有至關重要的地位。

　　首先，玉米是一種絕佳的食物來源。**第一，**人們喜歡玉米，玉米棒或玉米粒都一樣，例如爆米花、玉米脆片和玉米穀物。**其次，**我們的許多農場動物都餵養玉米，**包括**雞和牛。**另外，**玉米糖漿用來使許多產品變甜，例如冰淇淋、糖果和烘焙食品。

　　玉米在美國**之所以如此重要的另一個原因是**，它用來生產乙醇。**然而，問題在於**儘管這種替代燃料可以由玉米製成，但製造過程並不節能。**因此，**除非可以發現更有效的製造方法，否則種植用來生產乙醇的玉米可能會失去其重要性。**然而，目前**它仍然是美國經濟極重要的一部分。

　　那玉米的其他用途**呢？你可能不知道**玉米可以用來製造包裝豆、纖維板、清潔劑、墨水和吸收性材質的材料，**像是**尿布。**重點是，**玉米不僅僅是食物來源。**確實，**到今天為止，它在美國經濟中至少有三千五百種用途。

結論

　　因此，我們可以發現，玉米很可能是美國最重要的植物。**我確信，**相同的論點可以延伸到棉花、菸草或花生等許多其他植物。**我當然偏好選擇**將玉米視為我國世代傳承的

植物。它**終究**塑造了我們的過去，並繼續成就我們的未來。而且，**雖然我可以**欣賞一件精美的棉襯衫，但**我更喜歡**享用一盤滿滿的煮玉米。

台灣廣廈 國際出版集團
Taiwan Mansion International Group

國家圖書館出版品預行編目（CIP）資料

英文寫作公式 / 白善燁著. -- 初版. -- 新北市：國際學村，2021.07
面； 公分
ISBN 978-986-454-156-0
1.英語 2.作文 3.寫作法

805.17 110004660

 國際學村

英文寫作公式

作 者／白善燁　　　　　編輯中心編輯長／伍峻宏・編輯／古竣元
翻 譯／梵妮莎・許竹瑩　　封面設計／曾詩涵・內頁排版／菩薩蠻數位文化有限公司
　　　　　　　　　　　　製版・印刷・裝訂／東豪・弼聖・紘億・秉成

行企研發中心總監／陳冠蒨　　媒體公關組／陳柔彣
　　　　　　　　　　　　　　　綜合業務組／何欣穎

發 行 人／江媛珍
法 律 顧 問／第一國際法律事務所 余淑杏律師・北辰著作權事務所 蕭雄淋律師
出 版／國際學村
發 行／台灣廣廈有聲圖書有限公司
　　　　地址：新北市235中和區中山路二段359巷7號2樓
　　　　電話：（886）2-2225-5777・傳真：（886）2-2225-8052
讀者服務信箱／cs@booknews.com.tw

代理印務・全球總經銷／知遠文化事業有限公司
　　　　地址：新北市222深坑區北深路三段155巷25號5樓
　　　　電話：（886）2-2664-8800・傳真：（886）2-2664-8801
郵 政 劃 撥／劃撥帳號：18836722
　　　　劃撥戶名：知遠文化事業有限公司（※單次購書金額未滿1000元需另付郵資70元。）

■出版日期：2021年7月　　ISBN：978-986-454-156-0
　　　　　2024年6月9刷　版權所有，未經同意不得重製、轉載、翻印。